CAERPHILLY COUNTY BOROUGH COUNCIL

3 8030 08161 6487

SLOW
TWITCH

D1390824

www.totallyrandombooks.co.uk

Other titles in the Brenna Blixen series:

Double Clutch
Junk Miles

Also by Liz Reinhardt

Fall Guy

CASSELL & COUNTY BOROUGH COUNCIL

WITHDRAWN FROM STOCK

COMMUNITY EDUCATION, LEISURE & LIBRARIES

SLOW TWITCH

LIZ REINHARDT

Definitions

SLOW TWITCH
A DEFINITIONS BOOK 978 1 782 95138 4

First published in Great Britain by RHCP Digital,
an imprint of Random House Children's Publishers UK
A Random House Group Company

RHCP Digital edition published 2013
Definitions edition published 2014

1 3 5 7 9 10 8 6 4 2

Copyright © Elizabeth Reinhardt, 2013
Front cover artwork © Getty Images, 2013

The right of Elizabeth Reinhardt to be identified as the author of this work has
been asserted in accordance with the Copyright, Designs and Patents Act 1988.

All rights reserved. No part of this publication may be reproduced, stored in a
retrieval system, or transmitted in any form or by any means, electronic,
mechanical, photocopying, recording or otherwise, without the prior
permission of the publishers.

The Random House Group Limited supports the Forest Stewardship
Council® (FSC®), the leading international forest-certification organisation.
Our books carrying the FSC label are printed on FSC®-certified paper. FSC is
the only forest-certification scheme supported by the leading environmental
organisations, including Greenpeace. Our paper procurement policy can
be found at www.randomhouse.co.uk/environment

MIX
Paper from
responsible sources
FSC® C016897

Set in Palatino

Definitions are published by Random House Children's Publishers UK
61–63 Uxbridge Road, London W5 5SA

www.**randomhousechildrens**.co.uk
www.**totallyrandombooks**.co.uk
www.**randomhouse**.co.uk

Addresses for companies within The Random House Group Limited
can be found at: www.randomhouse.co.uk/offices.htm

THE RANDOM HOUSE GROUP Limited Reg. No. 954009

A CIP catalogue record for this book is available from the British Library.

Printed and bound in Great Britain by Clays Ltd, St Ives plc

To my baby sister Katie, who will forever be my closest confidante. I've always felt lucky to have you to share my memories and dreams with. You've been my best friend and my biggest cheerleader. And you totally deserve Saxon. All my love.

Slow Twitch: *muscle fibres that determine if a runner is suited to distance running.*

Brenna 1

The day I met Jake Kelly and Saxon Maclean, my heart thumped, strummed, sang and dived through every single exhilarating hour of that day right up until I fell asleep that night. The moment I laid eyes on them, it was like I'd been waiting for the day I was supposed to meet them, and the chemistry was like an electrical storm. I thought that it had to do with like. Or lust. Or chemistry. And I thought it happened because I was a girl and they were very attractive guys.

Then, nearly a year later, my plane landed in Dublin, Ireland, thousands of miles away from either of them. I stared at the gray, sterile dormitories that would be my home for the next few weeks while I was on a summer study abroad program in Irish literature, and shivered with a cold sweat brought on by worry and alien loneliness. I was sure I'd made a huge, stupid mistake in coming across the entire Atlantic for weeks on end. The little part of me that had wanted to just stay in New Jersey and keep things easy and fun wrestled energetically with the part of me that was ready to cliff-jump into whatever changes were coming. To grow or not to grow? To accept change or claw at its eyeballs, kicking and screaming all the way?

I was desperate for a sign, any sign to give me some reassurance that I wasn't going to rot in dejected unhappiness without the boy I loved and the one I sort-of-loved-in-a-whole-different-way.

Then I saw a face that felt like tasting my mother's homemade flaky-pastry, whipped-cream-topped apple pie after Thanksgiving dinner.

My entire focus pinpointed on a smile so bright and sweet, I felt wobbly in my particularly gorgeous buttercup-yellow espadrilles, like the muscles in my ankles spontaneously lost their strength. That smile was familiarly comforting the moment I saw it and I felt like I was peeking at something special and real. I knew I should be normal and introduce myself, but I was uncharacteristically tongue-tied.

But the object of my attention didn't wait for me to come over and make social niceties.

Before I knew it, a hand with delicate fishnet-embellished nails reached out and shook mine.

'I just came over to introduce myself and say those are the goddamn darlingest fucking shoes I've ever laid eyes on, and I might steal them like a thief in the night if you don't sleep in them.' She pumped my arm up and down and these Arctic-blue eyes stared right at me, with a weird combination of frigid interest and melting friendliness that matched the cool-worded, honey-sweet-drawl of her voice. 'Evan Lennox. Don't look at me like that. I swear on all that's holy, if I do bite you, it will barely hurt.'

'Brenna Blixen.' I gasped my name out while my eyes slid down her long, curvy legs, drank in the most decadently sexy peep-toe kitten heels I'd ever seen, and felt an instant kinship. 'What's your shoe size?'

When her smile cracked wide, it was apparent that her bee-stung lips looked even plumper because of the slightest overbite. 'If I'm gonna run a mile? A straight eight. If a pair of shoes starts flirting with me and then gets frisky, a seven won't even pinch.' She turned her heel to the side and showed off a perfectly arched foot. 'You?'

'Nine. Always. I can't deal with pinched toes.' I smoothed my hand over my skirt, and felt a strange, shy blush when she looked at me with frank approval.

'That's good news for me, and I have some for you.' She locked her arm through mine and leaned her head so close her long, glossy brown hair tickled the inside of my elbow. 'I'll put up with a pinch that will deform my feet, but I will never, ever wear a shoe that slides around. It ruins the entire silhouette. You know what?

I don't think I would have stolen those shoes, no matter what size. I like you too much already.'

She moved her icy eyes left and right, watching the other students claim their rooms and settle their luggage, squeal, hug and commiserate, and she slapped that gorgeous smile right at me. It was so neon bright I almost missed catching the nervous flutter of her lashes. 'So, let's room next to each other. You want to?'

I did.

'That sounds perfect.' We exchanged tentative smiles for a split second before we nodded and got to work.

Evan and I gathered our suitcases with a flurry of giggles and uncoordinated maneuvering and crammed the contents of them into our tiny dorm rooms. She claimed that she was happy enough to let all of her worldly possessions topple onto the scratchy cream blanket on her bed and call her room done, then followed me to mine and watched while I hung up all the clothes and put all my underwear and accessories in the appropriate drawers.

'Brenna, I just want to tell you that you are so neat it's exhausting.' She pulled a nail file out of a tiny clutch bag studded with pink leather rosebuds and leaned back in the old wooden desk chair, legs crossed like a lady, while I made hospital corners on the bed.

'Doesn't it just feel better when you come into a room and everything's put away? More like home?' I blew my fringe out of my eyes and stretched across the mattress to more firmly tuck in the sheet while Evan made minuscule adjustments to the length of her nails with quick swishes of the file.

'I guess. But it doesn't matter how it *feels*. It's never really home anyway, is it?' She stopped swaying her foot back and forth, and scowled at her innocent, lovely shoe.

'Are you homesick?' My voice came out just a fraction louder than a whisper, and my gut clenched with organ-deep sympathy. I turned down the bed and smoothed a hand over the pillow, then looked around. I would have sat on the desk chair to avoid mussing the bed I had just perfected if Evan wasn't already sitting there, and I wondered, briefly, if it would be totally strange if I sat on the floor instead. But Evan's stricken face and far-off stare made me forget my neat-nick habits, and I sat on the edge of the mattress, barely noticing the sheet that came half-untucked, and reached out to put a comforting hand on her shoulder. 'Because I get being homesick. I really do. This trip? It's the first time I've been away from my parents in my life. And my boyfriend and I wanted to spend the summer together, but I'd signed up for this. So, if you're homesick, I don't think that's weird.'

Her chin jerked up and she looked up at me, wild-eyed, nostrils flared, mouth pinched tight. 'You can't be homesick if you haven't got a home to go back to.' Her voice grated harshly. Shock knotted any words of comfort I knew I should try to say, and her mouth softened. 'Oh, Lord, ignore me! I'm dead serious, ignore ninety per cent of what comes out of my mouth. I'm just being a drama queen.' She sneaked me a side-long glance. 'But my daddy *did* fuck up big time, and the house *is* officially gone.'

'You lost your house?' I pressed my lips together and held my breath, trying to imagine what it would be like to lose your *house*. Where would she go? What would her family do? I'd just met her, but she already made my worry radar buzz out of control. I grabbed her hand, almost by instinct, eager to offer her some kind of comfort. She squeezed my fingers tight.

Evan blinked hard a few times and scratched at her eyebrow, which was bold and dark and wouldn't have worked on a face any less gorgeous than hers. 'I can't believe I'm just spouting this all out. I mean, I know we only just met, and you don't really know anything about me, and here I am just blabbing all these things I haven't told a single soul back home.'

'You don't have to tell me anything you don't want to.' I felt awkward holding her hand now, and our palms were both a little sweaty, but it also seemed unfriendly to break the connection. Just as the thought ran through my head, she squeezed my fingers tight again.

Her lips wobbled a little, and she had to snatch her hand away because she was on the precipice of crying. 'I use eighteen coats of mascara.' She laughed a watery laugh, and waved a hand in front of her eyes. 'It's my lucky number, eighteen. But it's going to leave a sludge pit on my face if I don't mop it up this second.'

I grabbed my purse and handed her a little crinkly packet of tissues. She blotted the tears and pressed her lips together. 'Brenna Blixen? My name is Evan Lennox and, even though I am a self-proclaimed drama queen, I mean it when I tell you that my life is about to fall apart.'

I crooked a tiny smile in her direction. 'Hi, Evan.'

She chuckled, blotted a little more, until the whole tissue was dotted with sooty black patches, and blew out a long, shaky breath. 'Ever feel like you're just wearing this mask for everyone's benefit, and if you have to keep it up for one more second, you're going to have a nervous fucking breakdown?'

I realized that it was my good luck that I actually never felt that way. And my thoughts immediately pounced on Saxon and the mask he never seemed to be able to get rid of, no matter how exhausted it made him. 'Don't keep it on, then,' I suggested gently. 'Take the mask off, Evan. Because honestly, I hardly know anything about you, but I like you already. I don't think you should fake anything about yourself.'

She licked her lips, then reached into her little pink clutch bag and took out a lipgloss. She smoothed some on with two neat strokes and passed it to me. I coated my lips, and they smelled like raspberries. *Our* lips smelled like raspberries, and that made me feel weirdly, wonderfully linked to her. She looked at the tube and smiled. 'I thought this trip was going to be total shit. Now I'm really glad I came.'

I got to my feet and held out my hand to pull her up.

'Where are we going, dollface?' She ran a quick hand over her hair and gave me a falsely bright smile.

'We're going to your room. You sit and talk about whatever you want. I'll make hospital corners on your bed and hang all your clothes up. It will make you feel better. I promise.' I opened and closed my hand and tilted my head. 'C'mon.'

She blew her nose and wadded up the tissue, then took my hand and stood up. 'You know what? I think I might love you already.'

Listening to her voice was like listening to my mother's Celtic music, minus the Irish accent, of course. It was so gorgeous and sad – lilting with its waves and twists – that I was fairly sure she could read me a trigonometry textbook or a Joseph Conrad short story and it would sound like pure music. I made her sit on the chair while I fixed her bed, but when it was done I patted the neatly made surface, inviting her to sit.

'Thank you for doing this, by the way. You seriously don't have to. And I'm not sitting there. You actually have sweat on your forehead from tucking all that in so perfectly. I'm not messing it up.' She shook her head and all that glossy hair swished from side to side like long, dark grass in the wind.

'I like doing this. It's very soothing for me. Come on. Sit. I'm not that anally retentive, I promise. Sit.' I coaxed her over and she did sit while I went through her clothes.

My parents had never had money problems, and they were always very generous when it came to an allowance for my clothes. I also made a nice chunk of my own money designing T-shirts back home, so I was able to shop in some fairly upscale stores. Or so I thought.

Evan's clothes had labels from stores and designers I'd only ever read about in celebrity magazines. Every piece was more beautiful than the last. If I didn't like her so much already, my blood would have been poisoned with pure, hateful clothing envy.

'I see you eyeing that pink suede skirt,' she accused

happily from her spot on the bed. 'We can't switch shoes, but I bet we'd be able to share clothes if you want.'

'I have to admit, I'm having a hard time not hating your guts right now.' I held up a canary-yellow dress with wild black floral patterns all over it and a designer label that I couldn't help but run my greedy fingers over. 'This is a dress that could make a girl do bad, desperate things.'

'Don't hate me.' She sighed and fell back on the bed, flopping her long arms out on either side of her body, wrinkling the covers. 'That dress was an apology from my daddy for missing my end-of-year dance recital. Also, he had to cancel my private dance classes for a few months because we were so behind on the bill. And, of course, we were losing the house.'

I edged my fingers over the delicately embroidered fabric and tried to follow the swirling floral designs, but it made my eyes pop. And the story behind the dress made my heart squeeze. This dress was seductively gorgeous, like electric sunshine and deep, velvet midnight, but with that back story, I couldn't imagine there was any way Evan could wear it and taste anything but the hard swallow of bitter misery.

'That sucks.' It was all I could think to say as I slid the dress on the hanger and slipped it into the tiny, dark closet.

Evan's voice twined in my ears. 'Money means everything to my parents. Daddy especially, because his family seems to have this knack for losing it all every generation or so. Mama comes from money, too, but my daddy can waste a whole lotta money. Two family-fortune's worth. Piles and piles and piles of money.' Her voice sing-songed a little, and she turned her face toward me, her forehead wrinkled and her eyebrows squished low over her eyes. 'You know, I've never told my best friend any of this. I never even told my boyfriend.' She pulled her hands in and folded them over her stomach. 'I just feel like I can trust you.'

I finished hanging the last of her dresses and surveyed the now-neat room, feeling totally content. I fell onto the bed next to her, only caring a tiny bit that all the tight corners had loosened up. 'You can trust me. I won't tell anyone.' She was chewing her lips with such quick, desperate nips, I was sure her teeth would bite right through the skin. 'So, you have a boyfriend back home?' I asked to take her mind off of everything in her world that was buckling and folding like cheap luggage.

She rolled her eyes in a circle so wide it had to be nerve-damaging and popped up onto her elbow. 'It's very, very, very complicated. Very crazy and tempestuous and all this make-up and break-up drama. Ugh. And complicated.' She covered her eyes with her hands and laughed. 'Did I mention complicated already?'

'So, was he upset about you coming here?'

My boyfriend Jake was so good. Deliciously good. Amazingly good. He was the one wiping my tears before we left for the airport. He was the one who bought me a guide to Dublin and spent nights going over how awesome this whole experience would be until I calmed down and slept with peaceful Irish dreams dancing in my brain. He was my rock, and I missed him so much at that moment, the ache of it cut me to the quick.

'Rabin doesn't get upset.' She raised her dark eyebrows. 'He gets wild. Like Heathcliff and Cathy wailing on the fucking wild moors.' She shrugged. 'But he's beyond hot. I swear to God, I've never been with a guy who does the kinds of things he does to me. He has, like, no boundaries.' She laughed and clapped a hand over her mouth. 'I just shocked the hell out of you, didn't I?' she said from behind her slightly splayed fingers. 'I can see it in your face. I'm sorry. It's weird right? I talk too much. Just tell me to shut my big mouth.'

'No, it's not weird. That he's . . . hot. That hot. I'm glad.' I stumbled all over the words and tried to kick back the images that suddenly flooded my brain of my imagined version of hot Rabin doing things that were sexy and forbidden with Evan. I noticed her watching my hand smoothing the blanket frantically, but by the time I stopped myself, it was too late to take my nervous twitch back.

'I know why you're so shocked. You look more like a logical love girl. Like a Lizzie Bennett. You like to think it all out, right? You're not going to go wild and throw yourself off the turret over some chump with a big dick.' Her laugh ribboned around me, pulling me in.

'Jake . . .' I cleared my throat before I continued. 'Jake is amazing. And I love him, so much. He's like my best friend and the guy I love. And, I mean, I try to be logical, but I don't know if I really am with him. See, he has this brother and he and I got together for a while. It was a big mistake, really big, and I knew it was—'

'No! You did not!' Evan jumped off of the bed so fast the springs didn't have time to squeak. She pointed at me, the look on her face pure, undisguised glee. 'But you have that sweet look. My gramma would say that butter wouldn't melt in your mouth if she saw you!'

I was collecting the words to explain, but the door swung open and a girl with a strawberry-blonde pixie cut said, 'Hiya! A whole bunch of us are going out to find something edible in the city. You girls wanna come with?'

Evan nodded and clapped, then turned to me. 'Food? Yes?'

'Sure.' I slid off the bed, and we headed out with a big gaggle of girls, Evan bumping my shoulder now and then to let me know that she hadn't forgotten my partial confession and *would* grill me later.

We crossed the hallway, and the girl with the pixie cut ducked into an open room where a whole group of guys were playing video games. Several of them got up to join our crew. One looked so familiar for a reason I couldn't put my finger on. He had his back to us and was tall with tousled brown hair and a lanky, loose frame, but what I really homed in on was his vest. It was blue and brown paisley, not easy for anyone to wear, but this guy was pulling it off like nobody's business, and the fashionista in me was turning multiple one-armed cartwheels.

'Mmm, he's gorgeous. Too bad he's gay,' Evan said, following my gaze. 'Anyway, aren't two brothers enough for you?'

I jabbed her with my elbow and we doubled over in a fit of giggles. 'It wasn't the guy, for your information,' I said with a determined glare in her direction. I did not want her to know how easily she charmed me, especially since I had the feeling any encouragement would bring out even worse behavior. 'I mean, he's cute, but it's his vest I'm falling hard for.

I love it. I wish my boyfriend would try to pull something like that off. Jake's got pretty simple tastes when it comes to clothes.'

'Ooh, wait! I'm so good at this. Let me guess your boyfriend, OK, and you tell me how close I am. Ready? Jake ... hmm, Jake is ... the captain of the football team, jockish but smart, and he never leaves home without his Peyton Manning jersey?' Evan batted her lashes in assumed triumph.

'Wow that is ...' I enjoyed watching her preen turn to a pout as I finished, 'so dead wrong. Not even remotely Jake.' I screwed my eyes shut and let the image of Jake tease through my mind for one quick, breathless minute.

We followed the crowd of our rowdy, yelling classmates down the uneven cobblestones and past gray buildings that had old architectural charm. Evan and I clung to each other's arms to stabilize ourselves on roads that were definitely not made with glamorous shoes in mind.

She held a finger up. 'OK, I'm going to guess again. I got it this time. I got it. He's the class president, smart but humble. He's neat and sweet and has a shirt and coordinating tie in every color of the rainbow,' she tried, narrowing one eye and giving me a hopeful half-smile.

I shook my head and she was about to guess again

when she teetered on the edge of her too-narrow heel and almost crashed over. I tried to grab her arm, but I wasn't very steady on my own admittedly-lovely-but-treacherous shoes. Thankfully, Paisley Vest happened to be right behind her, and he caught her before she went down like a sack of cutely attired potatoes.

'Good Lord, I'm the queen of klutzes today!' Evan said between gasping laughs as she steadied herself. 'You must be a true Southern boy to come to my rescue like some gentleman hero.' Her drawl was twice as sticky sweet when it was directed at him.

'Sorry. You can't get more Yankee than New Jersey,' he said with a shy duck of his head, and it was that shy head duck that made me look closer and finally see what had been screaming in my face since I noticed his vest.

'Devon!'

His face drained of all blood and his eyes snapped wide with panic, but he seemed to shake it off in a second. 'Brenna.' He didn't sound nearly as surprised to see me as I was to see him.

'You know my knight in shining armor?' Evan squeezed my arm and relished the drama that she seemed to feed off through her pores.

'Yes,' I said dumbly, but my mind was yelling 'No!' Because I recognized Devon after I saw him up close and heard his voice and it all registered and clicked in the rational portion of my brain, but who the hell was this well-dressed, handsome, confident guy standing in front of me in an Irish literature honors program? It sure as hell couldn't be dorky, disorganized, partial social pariah Devon Conner. 'Evan, this is Devon. Devon, Evan.'

She grabbed just his fingers and shook with gentle pressure. It was a much more delicate shake than the enthusiastic one she'd given me a few hours before. 'A pleasure.' Her smile was like a big, welcoming spider web. 'I hope it's not going to be weird that we have that rhyming name thing going on. I have a friend named Nate and when he started dating this girl Kate, I didn't give one goddamn that she was Miss Teen Georgia. I was shooting daggers at their whole goopy love scenario just because it was too irritatingly matchy-matchy.'

Devon tilted his head to the side and gave her a long look. 'We should just never date. That would solve it, I guess.' Evan rewarded him with a megawatt, toothpaste commercial, politician smile.

Devon motioned with his hand that we should try to catch up with the rest of the group, which had left us behind after it was clear that Evan was going to be all right. We walked, and Devon studiously avoided my gaze.

'So, Evan, huh? I've never heard that as a girl's

name before.' He stuck both hands in his pockets, but didn't seem to mind at all when Evan took his arm with easy confidence and leaned close to tell him her secrets.

'It's an old family name. My great-gramma was an Evan, and some other poor Lennox will probably get it someday. And I know it's not all that common, but I'm one of three Evans in my school, believe it or not.' She stared at his incredulous frown and shook his arm. 'Cross my heart and hope to die.'

'Evan Lennox?' Devon let her name roll on his tongue with an easy confidence that left me shocked into silence. 'Of Lennox Lace and Textiles?'

'Lace and textiles?' I repeated.

Evan's teeth crept out and chewed on her lips nervously. 'One and the same.'

'Your family's mills pretty much propelled Georgia into the Industrial Revolution.' Devon's eyes gleamed as he rattled off names and dates and factory locations, and Evan dropped his arm and nodded along as her shoulders went limp and her eyes glazed.

'Devon?' I had to say his name twice before he allowed me to interrupt his catalogue of Lennox offshoots.

He snapped out of his monologue and gave me a questioning look, then followed my nod to Evan, who had her eyes cast down and her mouth set in a tight, thin line. I honestly had no clue if Devon would even pick up on a social cue that subtle, but he nodded back and shut up.

Which wound up being just as strange, because now there was all this bizarre quiet. I broke it by asking the one question that had been screaming in my brain since I recognized my school friend. 'Devon, what the hell are you doing here?'

For a moment, the cool, lanky-limbed, confident guy balled up and retreated, leaving twitchy, bug-eyed, over-anxious Devon in his wake. 'I, uh, applied.' He lifted and lowered his hands like he didn't know what to do with them or where to put them.

Evan clicked out of her quiet melancholy and hooked one arm through Devon's again and one through mine, making us a tiny human chain. 'OK, new, awesome friend and knight in shining armor, how do you two know each other exactly?'

'We're, like, friends. We, uh, go to school. The same one.' Devon ran his free hand through his carefully styled bed-head hair. Since when did he use *product*?

'You two go to the same school, but had no clue that you were both going to be in Ireland in this highly selective nerd program this summer?' Her eyes roved from my face to Devon's, then she pulled us close and tight, so we made a little three-person knot. 'Curiouser and curiouser.'

'I knew Bren would be here,' Devon offered.

'Well, yeah. I told you! Why didn't you tell me?' I demanded. *And when did you get a makeover? And why didn't you tell me that?* Maybe it was weird to feel so betrayed. Devon and I weren't exactly best friends. But he knew I was coming here. And we were friends. I accepted him. Listened to his problems with a pretty sympathetic ear. Tried to help him navigate high school. He must have seen me at the dorms. Why all the secrecy?

'I didn't think it would happen.' Devon held his hand out and shook it with frustration. 'My grades were too low but, based on my essay, I got waitlisted. When they didn't call by the time school was over, I figured there was no point, so I went to Chicago with my aunt. I got the call there, telling me some kid who was supposed to go got appendicitis or something. So I came, but it was, like, two days' notice.'

'You better kiss your aunt's ass if she's the one who inspired this whole . . .' I screwed up my mouth and raised my eyebrows, at a loss for words.

'Metamorphosis?' he suggested with a glance down at his vest, dress shirt with the cuffed sleeves, his dark-wash jeans, and brown leather and suede shoes.

'Were you a caterpillar before?' Evan asked as we followed the jostling group into a small, dark pub.

'If by "caterpillar" you mean "seriously shitty

dresser with bushy eyebrows and a crap haircut", then yes.' Devon took Evan under the elbow and led both of us to a table over in the corner, private and away from the others. 'And I may be a better-looking butterfly, but I'm only nominally better at the big-social-gathering thing.'

'You're adorable,' Evan gushed, her eyes cutting to me and sparkling, like he was a cute secret we both shared. 'Who uses words like "nominally" in real life?'

'Guys who get waitlisted for study-abroad nerd programs,' I groused.

'Are you pissed off?' he asked as the waitress came over.

Evan sat up straight, cleared her throat, cocked a brazen eyebrow and said, 'I'll have a shot of whiskey and a glass of the dark stuff.'

The waitress rolled her eyes and barely stifled a sigh. 'I take it you're needin' a pint of Guinness and a whiskey chaser?'

Evan shook her finger in the waitress's direction and broke open a wide, sweet smile that was so catchy it was practically viral. 'That's it! I guess the slang is different in America.'

The waitress didn't attempt to cover-up her full-on sigh and wrote the order down without fanfare. Evan's success made us brave, so Devon shiftily asked for a pint of Guinness, and I seconded his order. When the waitress left, Devon repeated his question. 'Are you pissed off with me?'

'No,' I ground out. He narrowed his eyes at me. 'Maybe! Jesus, Devon! I was scared to come here. And I felt like I was by myself until I met Evan. It would have made it a little easier to have stuck by you from the beginning.'

He nodded. 'Fair enough. But, uh, Bren? I don't want to offend you, so don't jump down my throat, OK? I wanted to come here and, you know, make some new connections. I wanted to try being . . . the way I am now. Not chickenshit Devon who's Frankford's resident freak. It was sort of my summer resolution. Make sense?'

Evan pulled her hair into a perfectly messy bun and secured it with a few bobby pins she pulled out of her pocket, then spoke in her sweet, melting voice. 'So, wait? Let me get this whole mess straight. You,' she said, pointing at Devon with a bobby pin, 'are some kind of outcast freak back home?'

He gave a curt nod. 'That would be correct, basically. But also a massive understatement.'

She stuck another pin into her glossy hair and clicked her tongue. 'Fuck that. You aren't a freak now. I know you're gay and all, so don't take this the wrong way, but I think you're seriously hot. Like aesthetically, not like I'm looking to be your fag hag or anything.'

'Evan!' A jolt of shock propelled my voice.

'What?' Her mouth quirked into a cute, pleased-with-herself smile. 'Sorry if I've offended you, Devon. But, back to my point here . . . you guys are pretty shitty friends if you never said all this! Devon is sweet and gorgeous, natch. And, Brenna, he's right. He needs to get over whatever crazy shit he's going through back home, and he can do that here. So let him. Plus, I'm really happy you weren't attached to his ass when we got here.' She swallowed hard and blinked rapidly, a few times in a row. "Cos I can't compete with that fucking paisley vest! He owns it. You never would have been able to take your eyes off of it to notice my kitten heels, cute as they are.'

'You're from one of the most conservative states in the country, right?' Devon demanded.

'Georgia is known for hanging on to every bygone tradition with white knuckles,' Evan conceded.

'And you're not freaked out? That I'm gay?' His eyes dart in my direction. 'It's not – it hasn't been, like, an *intentional* secret. But I haven't exactly taken out advertisements. You know?'

'You don't think the paisley vest is an advertisement?' Evan raised her dark eyebrows high.

'That's a new development,' I cut in, darting a look at Devon, who was meticulously chewing his bottom lip into raw slivers.

'Well, sweetie, I'm not saying all Georgians would be tolerant. I'm unique, in case you hadn't noticed. But I'm fine with it, and I think most people with a solid mass of brain between their ears are, nowadays. Especially if you keep wearing that vest. I'm overwhelmed. And I rarely am by anyone else's style. Especially a man's. Even if he's as gay as the day is long.'

'Evan!' I cry a second time, but Devon brushes off my panic.

'It's fine. It is. She just made me feel so much better in a weird way. I know you –' He points at Evan and gives her a twisted smile. 'You might annoy the crap out of me, but you shoot from the hip. So if you're cool with me being gay, especially coming from an, um, less open-minded part of the country, I think I may be able to open up a little in Sussex County.'

'Amen, sugar,' Evan said, straight-faced.

The waitress brought over our drinks and took our order for food before I could say a word to Evan. And once all that dark, frothy alcohol was on the table, there was no going back to the sweet words she said before that made all the fine hairs on my neck stand on end.

'Toast!' Evan cried and plopped her whiskey into her pint. The three of us watched, eyes soldered to the glass as the shot sank and the Guinness sloshed over the rim and onto the table. She picked it up carefully and held it up to us. 'To getting rid of all the fucking bullshit in our lives. And to new friends who rock the perfect shoes and vests. As they say in Ireland, Sláinte.'

'Sláinte!'

We clanked our glasses together and took deep, long draughts. Devon and I slammed them onto the table when we were choked with alcohol. But Evan just kept drinking, her throat tightening and relaxing, two rivulets of beer dribbling out the sides of her mouth.

Watching her made me feel like I was drowning, like I needed to take a breath for her, but she finally hammered the glass down in triumph and wiped a victorious wrist across her lips.

'Holy shit, loves. Y'all are gonna need to carry me back to the dorm. Whew!' She shuddered and hiccupped. 'So, wait, I wanna win the game we started before.' She put an unsteady finger out and bopped me gently on the tip of my nose. 'Jake. Jake, Jake, Jake. He is ... artsy? Kind of quiet, but cool. Always wearing his paint-speckled shirt and ripped-up jeans. Ironic and sensitive.' She held her hands, prayer-style in front of her and raised her eyebrows high.

Devon's laugh sputtered beer across the table. 'What? That's so not Jake. Like, the polar opposite.'

'He's artsy,' I argued, thinking of his amazing projects and sketches. I took another long drink of bitter beer without even wincing. 'But, no, you're wrong.'

Evan slammed both hands palms down on the shiny wood table. 'This is so embarrassing, OK? I'm usually, like, an oracle when it comes to guys. I can just . . .' She paused and waved her hands in front of her face before she continued, 'I can visualize the guy just by looking at the girl. I can't believe this is, what, my third or fourth guess? It's the ocean between you two. That's it, that's what I'm blaming it on.' She turned her pale eyes on Devon. 'Give me a hint.'

'A hint?' Devon frowned. 'What kind of hint?'

'About Jake!' Evan drummed on the edge of the table fast and hard. 'Here is gorgeous, smart, amazing Brenna. And she dates this mystery guy. Well, a mystery to *me*, anyways. But he's not captain of the football team. And he's not president of the student council. And he's not sensitive and artsy. I've used every last ounce of pixie dust, Devon. Help a sister out.' She popped her shiny bottom lip in a pout. 'C'mon, don't leave me all embarrassed.'

'A hint?' Devon tapped his fingers on the condensation-fogged side of his glass. 'About Jake? OK. Um, I guess "truck"?'

'Truck?' Evan repeated and leaned across the table

until she was only a few inches away from me. 'Truck. Big backseat? Oooh, I know I'm right because you have the prettiest blush, Miss Brenna. OK, truck?' She took a deep breath. 'All right, where I come from, a big ol' pick-up means "hick". But isn't New Jersey a whole lotta city? So there can't be hicks, right?'

She gave us a half-smile that let us know she was fully aware of how far she'd pushed her luck. 'Now you're just taking potshots at our lovely state,' Devon murmured wryly. 'And, can I remind you, it's the *Garden State*? OK? So stop being a terrible stereotyper.'

Evan laughed maniacally. 'So many apologies. And, before we get into a battle of wits about states, I swear on baby Jesus if either one of you talk about peaches or sing that "Georgia on my mind" song, I will kill you both. Not very Southern lady-like of me, but I will.' She stretched her neck to one side, then the other, bringing out a series of little pops that made her sigh. 'Truck, truck, truck. Jake, Jake, Jake. Hmmm.' She pressed her lips together, squinted and burst out, 'Hot older guy who owns a landscaping business?'

I felt so much relief when the waitress came back at that second, I considered kissing our frazzled server. Evan ordered a second round for herself, but Devon and I were still nursing our beers, and I was wishing I'd ordered a water or soda. Evan picked up her sandwich, took a huge bite and moaned with unbridled happiness.

'This sandwich is making me mouth-gasm.' She moaned a second time, a piece of sandwich in each hand. The deliciousness of her meal kept her busy for about three minutes before she zeroed in on Devon. 'Spill. Right now. Tell me all about the mysterious Jake and his brother. My sixth sense is obviously broken in Europe.'

Devon took a huge bite of his burger and caught my eye. I shrugged and poked at my food with my fork, suddenly nervous to have Jake dissected in front of Evan.

Devon chewed, swallowed, and said, 'Jake is a really great guy. He's smart, but not a big-time academic. He works hard. Seriously, this guy could put grown men to shame with the hours he pulls. He goes to the technical school, and he's definitely brilliant in the trade he's doing. He's got one of those bad boy pasts everyone talks about, but he's put it all behind him now. And he loves Brenna. I'm not gonna lie . . . it's slightly nauseating. But, since I'm being all honest and wearing a paisley vest, I guess I'll admit that it's also incredibly, vomitously sweet.'

My heart overheated like a little old lady who needed someone to wave a fan in her face to revive her.

Evan chomped on a pickle and assessed me with steady, icy-hot eyes. 'A hard-working, blue-collar,

truck-driving boy from the wrong side of the tracks?'
The waitress came back with her drink. Evan thanked
her, then caught the whiskey by the edge of the glass
and let it dive into her beer. 'He sounds like perfection
worthy of a toast.' She lifted her glass gingerly and
announced, 'To Jake, Brenna's dream guy.'

Devon and I took our still half full glasses and were
about to clink, when she pulled back.

'Wait. Wait a minute!' Evan's black eyebrows
pressed so low over her eyes, her eyelashes mingled
with them. 'All facts point to Jake being amazing. So
what's so tempting about the brother?'

'Saxon?' Devon's voice dripped with sarcasm,
grudging respect, and the fascination that that particular name always seemed to dredge up in everyone.

'Saxon?' Evan tasted the name on her lips and her
smile stretched until I could see past the sharp points
of her eyeteeth and back to her molars. 'Saxon is the
brother.' She half-closed her eyes so they fluttered
slightly. 'Mmm. My psychic powers are absolutely
constipated. Devon, my love, hit me with another
hint.'

Devon put his palms on the edge of the table and
pushed back, shaking his head and blowing out a long
breath. He sat back and brought his glass to his lips to
drink before he answered. 'No words. Just, sorry.
Nothing comes to mind.'

My throat felt tight and dry, and I couldn't make eye-contact with Evan.

'Brenna, can you give a hint?' Her fantastic kitten heel bumped my calf under the table. 'Or the whole story? Or just stare into your beer like some sad old drunk. Brenna? Hellooo?'

My eyes were inexplicably pricked with tears. I stood up and looked for the bathroom. 'I . . . uh, I have to go pee.' My hip bumped the table and everyone's drink spilled a little. I rushed away, leaving an open-mouthed Evan and Devon staring at my back.

In the cold, tiled bathroom, I put my back against the door of one of the stalls and shoved the heels of my hands into my eyes. 'Why are you crying?' I whispered to myself. 'Stop it. Stop!'

Maybe it was the weight of all that jet lag I hadn't slept off. Or the strong beer I wasn't remotely used to drinking. Or the excitement of meeting Evan coupled with the shock of seeing Devon. Or the memory of Jake's lips on mine, urgent and a tiny bit desperate at the airport.

'You have a great time, OK?' His fingers had bitten into my arms and he wouldn't let go.

'It will be fine,' I promised. I didn't say what we were both thinking. *Not like last time*.

'No doubt. Bring me back a shamrock or a pot of

gold.' His attempt to smile at his own sad joke made his mouth quake in a way that drew-and-quartered my heart.

'Maybe just a fairy or a rainbow?' I traced my fingers over his face when he closed his gray eyes and, I knew, told himself not to worry.

He buried his face in my hair and his voice was all choked when he said, 'I love you so damn much.'

'I love you, too.' I held on twice as tight.

The memory dropped away when I heard the bathroom door creak open too slowly for it to be a regular patron. I grabbed some toilet paper and blotted my eyes and nose.

'Brenna?' Evan's voice called out, smoky and quiet.

'I'm . . . I'm, uh, sorry. I have no idea what's up with me. I just . . . you know, I think I'm just tired, I guess.' I peeked through the crack in the stall door, not ready to face anyone just yet.

She slid up on a sink and fished in her rosebud purse until she found a silver case. She flicked it open and took out a short, dark cigarette that she pursed between her lips and lit up with a tiny vintage gold lighter. The smell it gave off wasn't the acrid burn of a regular cigarette. It was a smoky-sweet mix that made me think of Halloween and pumpkin spiced coffee that my mother always got in October.

'I was being a monster, sweetie.' She closed her eyes

and let her head fall back on the mirror. 'Devon gave me a few hints about Saxon, so I understand a little bit, I think. You're not gonna mess it up with Jake here.'

'I know.' The words flopped out too fast. 'I mean, I don't think that's going to happen or anything.'

'Of course you do.' She flicked the dull gray ash into the pristine white sink. I wondered if it was OK to smoke here. I doubted it, but it was clear that Evan operated above the rules. 'I know you think I was joking back there about being psychic, but I have this teeny-tiny sixth sense. My daddy used to take me to the track because I could always pick the winning horse. Every single time, I'm telling you. He stopped after this one time when I was twelve and he forced me to go with him instead of letting me hang out with my new boyfriend at the mall. I picked all the wrong ones just to piss him off.' When she chuckled, rings of bluish smoke coiled out of her mouth. 'I knew you were a winner the minute I saw you. I really do have a harder time with guys. It's girls and horses with me, I swear to God. Guys? I just don't see them clearly. Hence . . . well, Rabin most recently.'

'What did you see when you saw me?' I had my fingers on the deadbolt, almost ready to slide it open and sit next to her on the sink, maybe take a drag of her sweet cigarette.

She took a long, slow drag and opened her eyes,

but just stared at the ceiling for a few seconds before she answered, 'I saw what I wanted.' She gestured with her cigarette like a kid writing a flash of a message with a sparkler. 'I wanted to know you. To be your friend. And I wanted to have what you have. Not your stuff, though I do love those fucking gorgeous shoes. I saw this, I can't really explain . . . like this love in you. And I saw the guilt, too, so I knew you weren't just this bambino in the woods. I knew it was real.'

I knocked my forehead against the bathroom door. 'Oh, it's real. It's so real, it's scary. I feel so much about them both, but it's so incredibly different, and I just have to shut up about it, you know?'

'You don't.'

I'd never heard a person say things and make them sound like a question and a non-negotiable fact at the same time, but Evan managed that.

I slid the bolt with shaky fingers and flew to the sink. Evan was already holding the cigarette out to me. I took a quick drag and was disappointed to find that it was still acrid and burning, just like a regular cigarette.

'What do you mean?'

She patted my hair back from my face and tucked it with smooth, quick fingers behind my ears. 'I just mean that you shouldn't shut up about anything that's important to you. If it matters, say it. And if you really love Jake and are worried, don't hide things from him. Try to explain, and maybe some of this nervousness will go away, you know?'

I watched the cigarette smolder. 'If I say it, I'll just hurt people. It never comes out right. No matter how hard I try, it's just all wrong, and I sound like a jerk. That sounds lame, but I don't know how else to explain it.'

She plucked the cigarette from my fingers and stubbed it out in the sink. 'People always want girls to be nice. Fuck nice, Brenna. Be honest. Say what you need to say, and don't shut up. You're a good person, and you love him, so it will work out.' She slid the pins out of her hair and it swooped down, piece by piece, around her shoulders.

'It's not that easy.' I ran the tap so the black, smeared ashes funneled down the drain, and tossed the butt into the garbage.

'Nothing that's really important ever is, sweetie.' Evan kissed my cheek and took my hand. 'It's never easy, and it's never neat. Ever. You don't have to listen to me, but I'm saying it because I like you so much, and I know what happens when you try to lock secrets away and cover them with lies, no matter how good your intentions might be.' Her eyes went dark, like lake water, crystal clear until its murky bottom gets agitated.

All the hair on my arms stood on end at her words, and a cold chill twisted up and down my spine.

I thought about what she said as we headed back to Devon. Evan gulped down one more drink, and Devon did wind up carrying her more than halfway back to the dorms, just like she'd predicted. We managed to get her tucked in, and I took a minute to pull the covers up to her chin, the way I liked them.

'She's a little crazy,' Devon whispered, rubbing the kinks out of the shoulder he'd carried her over during the long walk home.

I looked down at her long hair spilled over the pillow, her mascara-coated lashes flecking bits of black under her eyes, and her puffy red lips, half-parted in sleep. 'Crazy beautiful.'

Devon shook his head as he left the room. 'Geez, you fall in love fast, Bren.'

'Yup,' I said as I pulled the door shut. 'I'm full of it.'

Saxon 1

I was always fairly hard to shock. In fact, I was good at being the shocking one, and I liked that. It kept everyone guessing, and that was always the best way with me. Once in a while, I'd get soft and let my heart leak out on my sleeve, but I've always regretted it. Every single time, it's bitten me in the ass. Once in a while, once in a really rare while, I manage to shock myself.

That's where I was just after the end of my un-impressive junior year at Frankford High. I had missed almost as much school as I had attended. I'd hit on my brother's foxy girlfriend and practically convinced her not to completely hate me, then fucked it all up and lost my one chance to be with a girl whose brain interested me more than her tits. I boozed a little more than I should have and blacked out one too many Saturday nights . . . and Wednesday afternoons . . . and Monday mid-mornings.

Then I was doing enough recreational drugging

and drinking that I needed the kind of money that would arouse suspicion if I asked Mommy Dearest for it, so I started dealing. I'm not remotely interested in sad-sack stories about innocent fucking school kids buying bags of crack and hurling themselves off of tall buildings. I was a dealer; I knew exactly who bought. It was other assholes like me. Losers who needed to forget just how shitty life was.

'Cos mine was. I lived in a big piece-of-shit house that had been featured in twelve different architectural magazines, but still managed to creep my ass out and made me feel like I lived in a really shitty modern-art museum. I'd slept with every delicious piece of ass in a hundred-mile radius, but the only chick I really dug was with my brother, Jake, and they were so in love it even made my icy heart thaw a little. I had a hot car, a bitching Charger, but it was pretty hard to drive it when it was locked in my piece-of-shit father's garage. I was captain of the soccer team, an honors student, a badass, and a bit of a rebel. So how the fuck did I end up in the back of my aunt Jackie's shitty Mazda, zipping down the highway towards a tiny piece of urban Jersey hell? Why was my life so shitty?

Did I do drugs because my life was such a steaming pile of shit, or was my life such a steaming pile of shit because I did drugs?

My theory was that it was a nice bundle of both

theories. I just chose the wrong drug. Coke made me see things more clearly, have more energy. For what? I had no one to do anything with, considering I'd screwed the love interest of every guy friend I'd ever had, and I never hung out with girls unless they had the only thing I'm interested in on their minds. I already had a genius IQ, like it or not. And, despite smoking a pack a day, I was a star athlete without the drugs. So the coke just made everything more clearly, draggingly miserable. That's why I wasn't good at hiding it. That's why my mom found it.

A lot of it.

Trust me, the amount matters. Lylee didn't wig out because she feared for my life and health. She would have been cool with a little line here and there. It was the fear of being caught with so much of the shit in her house that made her squawk to my father, the shithead who left when I was young enough to still feel like a dad might be a good idea. Lylee wasn't about to give up her bourgeois whoring and partying and her cushy professor job because I was being fruitful and selling enough of the shit to get attention from the bigger city dealers (another bad thing that was about to get a whole lot worse). So dear old Daddy came down and slapped me around a little and threatened to take away the only thing that can still make my granite heart skip a beat: my inheritance.

Hey, it was blood money, but it was fair and square blood money. Jake would get his, I'd get mine, and so would the two dozen or so other Maclean cousins and grandkids and whoever else is a direct descendant. It was old money, it was my due, and I'd take it happily.

But Daddy told me no money unless I cleaned up my act, and he wasn't about to take my word for it. I was put in the back of Jackie's hideous purple Mazda with a duffel bag of necessities and sent somewhere that was pretty much going to be tailor-made hell for me.

I was being sent to work in a diner.

I had been to rehab. Twice, actually. It was all idiotically kind, dumb therapists who always acted like there might be secret VH1 reality show cameras documenting every deep, heart-string-pulling conversation. There was usually a lot of nature (ocean, mountains, trees, whatever) and a lot of meetings with other losers. It was like a very lame vacation.

And I had been out of the country. Lylee spirited me to Paris, which was only made bearable by the company of Brenna Blixen, Jake's hot girlfriend. We spent a lot of time kissing and twice as much time pissing each other off. It was clear to me from the beginning that I was a reluctant experiment at best. She'd been in love with Jake since the first second she met him. He was always a good-looking guy, and I could admit that honestly because our spectacular genetics couldn't be denied.

Jail would have sucked. That was probably next, or maybe juvenile hall. But eighteen was coming up quick, and any sane judge would have wanted to teach me a real lesson about the harsh realities of drug use and dealing.

But I escaped the slammer.

I got indentured service, family style.

Daddy's family owned all kinds of random shitty businesses, and one of them was this weird diner that played oldies and had girls skate out to your car with food like some shitty *Happy Days* episode. I got to be a dishwasher, lowest of the low men on the totem pole. And I would have to shack up with some geezer great-aunt of mine who used to babysit me and Jake, and was living off her paltry Maclean stipend in her piss-stinking, shag-carpeted, doily-decorated house.

As if this shit storm wasn't bad enough, Aunt Jackie was blaring Celine Dion. Who the hell listens to Celine Dion willingly?

'Can you turn this crap down?' I asked as nicely as I could manage.

Aunt Jackie glared at me and turned the knob on the stereo up a little. Celine's ferociously annoying voice filled the inside of the car and battered against my eardrums.

'You are not here on vacation, Saxon,' she lectured. 'This is not about you enjoying yourself. You have been stripped of all privilege and comfort for a reason. I am certainly not playing one of the greatest singers and divas of all time to punish you, but knowing that it irritates you is a bonus.' She narrowed her eyes at me. 'You are supposed to be thinking about why you are where you are instead of enjoying your summer with the family in New York like your brother Jake.'

I groaned at his name. 'If I hear about your damn golden boy one more time, I'm going to hurl.' I reached instinctively for my cigarettes. Damn! Those were gone, too.

'Jake is someone you should look up to,' Aunt Jackie droned. 'He's making a real effort to fit in and he knows the value of hard work. That's a Maclean gene he seems to have in abundance, even if it did manage to skip right over you.'

'I work hard,' I drawled, keeping my voice irritatingly lazy. 'Do you know how much effort it took to turn potheads into cokeheads? No easy feat.'

Aunt Jackie blew a long breath through her flared nostrils and cranked Celine even louder. When I closed my eyes and moaned at 'My Heart Will Go On', Aunt Jackie punched the repeat button. I had to smile a little. Sly bitch.

Finally we were at the diner. Aunt Jackie pulled in

and turned to me. 'I'm not letting you get dumped on poor Aunt Helene so you can sit on your laurels while she gives you coffee and cookies. I'll drop your bag at her house. You work here, and you can walk to her place. Tony has directions for you, and there are a few other kids who live in that area, so you won't be walking alone. Go ahead. It's time to get to work.'

She looked as prim and sour as some old English governess. 'Thanks for the ride,' I said and got out of the car.

I hated feeling trapped. I hated not knowing what the hell I was doing. I hated working for anyone, especially someone who knew that I was in a shitload of trouble and couldn't leave or cause any shit. I stood looking at the double back doors, the ones for employees. I was that. An employee.

Even if the word made me want to choke myself with my own tongue.

It wasn't that I needed to gather the courage to go in. It was more like I needed to suppress the need to break something or swear up a storm or just generally bring more bad shit down on my head.

Then I heard a weird sound, a clack and roll, clack and roll. I looked behind me and saw a girl. A damn pretty girl.

She was long and curvy in every place that it's perfect for a girl to be curvy in. Then I realized that she might have just seemed long because she was on skates. Roller skates. Her face was wide-eyed and fine as a Russian model's. She had green eyes, real green like a Halloween cat's and jet black hair, pulled back off of her face in a high ponytail. And the outfit. Mmm. A short red skirt, something like a cheerleader would wear and a white shirt, nice and tight against the generous swell of her tits.

'The entrance is around the front, sir,' she said, her voice sweet and polite.

I smiled, a smile I know for a fact melted girls into puddles. 'I'm not here to eat, baby. I work here. I'm Saxon Maclean.'

'The cokehead?' Her voice changed instantly, suddenly snappy like the crack of a lion tamer's whip. I realized that the honeyed-up voice must have been solely for the customers. 'Well, what are you doing out here? This isn't a drug den, dumb-ass. In through the double doors and to the back. I assume you're too stupid to do anything but wash dishes? You'll find the sinks. They're big and metal and lots of water goes in them.' She made her voice high and unnaturally sweet, thick with sarcasm. 'I have my eye on you, asshole.'

'Nice to meet you, too.' Something electric tingled through me. 'I didn't catch your name.'

The girl was already skating away, and I had a nice view of her curvy rear end.

'Cadence,' she called over her shoulder. 'Cadence Erikson.'

Erikson. The owners of the diner. Had I just met the owner's daughter?

I shrugged and went in through the double doors, intrigued by pretty, mouthy Cadence and ready to see her again soon.

I walked into a hot, chaotic clusterfuck unlike anything I had ever seen. People in white aprons were running baskets of sizzling fries and spatulas with hamburgers and hotdogs covered in sauerkraut back and forth, setting them on red trays and beating on a silver bell until it looked like it was going to explode.

A balding man with bulgy eyes noticed me.

'Who are you?' he asked brusquely.

'Saxon Maclean.' I offered my hand.

He eyed my outstretched hand uncertainly, then shook – a limp, wet-fish shake. 'The cokehead? Tony doesn't tolerate drugs.'

'I know.' I felt my back go up a little. Did everyone know why I was here? Jesus Christ.

'Aprons over there. Get one on. Hurry up. I've got three minutes to teach you before the next batch of fries comes out. I'm Dan. Jesus, Brian, flip those burgers before they're charred, for God's sake! Please tell me they were supposed to be well done?' He pushed past a spacey-looking guy flipping burgers and led me to a long stainless-steel table with a huge box at the end. He grabbed a handle and pulled up, lifting the box, which was, in fact, an industrial dishwasher.

'Put the cups and silverware and plates in the trays, slide them in here, close it all the way and they get washed. It's magic!' He shook his hands and rolled his eyes. 'Anything you can't wash in there, throw it in the sink and we do it later. When the trays come out of the dishwasher, put them there.' He pointed to another low stainless shelf where girls in outfits like Cadence's and guys in black pants and white T-shirts with the sleeves rolled were picking up food. 'When it's slow, take the trays out front and fill up the glasses and silverware under the counters. Questions?'

I shook my head. This was going to be fucking great. Magic!

A busboy in a white apron came over and slammed a full bucket down on the stainless tray.

'Hey, I'm Will,' the guy said. He was skinny and blond. 'You must be the crackhead.'

'Saxon,' I said through gritted teeth.

'Well, we're on shift together, so hey.' He checked out the ass of one of the waitresses who leaned over to get her pen. 'I'll help bring the dishes out when I can, man. Gotta go. Oh, and load quick. One of the dumb-ass new girls dropped a tray of glasses so we're low on them.' He grabbed a clean bucket, and I looked dubiously at what was left in the dirty bucket he had dropped.

Maybe I've lived a little bit of a privileged life, but I never gave much thought to what happened once I ate my hamburger at some shitty little diner. It never occurred to me that some poor jerk-off in some shitty back corner was going to have to paw through my ketchup-soaked napkins, scrape my half-eaten food into the garbage, and pick through partially-melted sundae remains for lost silverware. I never thought about how a job can be fairly easy, but so freaking boring you could poke your own eyes out with said lost silverware. And I never thought I could work around a good fifty people and feel like I was stranded in the middle of goddamn nowhere without a soul to talk to. At least there was angry death metal playing in the back. It suited my mood to a tee.

But I was mostly just feeling sorry for myself. My life had started a pretty steady downward spiral a few months back, and it didn't seem like working at this shithole diner was going to make anything look up in a hurry. In fact I would have thought that I might have hit a kind of rock bottom, except I didn't want to jinx myself.

By the end of my shift (which was ten hours long;

in at two, out at midnight), my arms ached from carry-ing trays of hot glasses, I was covered up to my elbows in chocolate syrup embedded with tiny pieces of candy that typically gets sprinkled on ice cream, bits of relish and mustard, splatters of soda and milkshake, and a million other unidentifiable things. I kept my section fairly clean, and was feeling dead on my feet when Brian, the space-cadet with the burgers, came over with a crapload of greasy, hot, dripping stainless steel stuff and dumped it in the soapy water in one of the sinks.

'What the hell is that?' I asked.

'Kitchen shit.' He looked over at me with half-glazed eyes. 'Dan will bring over the grill guards and baskets in a minute.'

Will appeared next to me. 'I told you I'd help. This is the shittiest part of the dishwashing thing.' He grabbed a scrub brush and handed me one. 'Tony comes and looks everything over himself, so make sure you get all the shit off of it. He'll keep you all night if he doesn't like how you cleaned up.'

Exhaustion ripped through me. I'd been hopped on coke for the last few weeks. I wasn't used to relying on my own energy sources, and I was dropping. My days were typically a lot more work shy, and I liked it just fine that way. Plus, I'd been operating on a coke high for a few months, so the cold turkey approach left

47

me pretty sapped. For one second I considered throwing my scrub brush down and telling them all to fuck off. Two things stopped me.

The first and most important was that I would have enough money waiting at the end of this shitty summer work deal to get my ass anywhere I needed it to be. The second was that once I walked out of those double doors, I didn't have one person to call and pick me up. Lylee's house was more than two hours away. Short of taking my chances hitchhiking, I didn't have a way to get back home. And this wasn't exactly an area where a good-looking guy could feel comfortable sticking his thumb out on a dark road. So I picked up the scrub brush and went to work with Will until Tony himself came in.

He was as big as a damn grizzly bear. He had Cadence's green eyes, but, other than that, he was all bushy red-blond hair, like a gigantic Viking. He stood with his arms crossed and watched us work for a while. Then he said, 'Good job, guys. Will, when this batch is done, you're free to go. Brian, come and help Will finish. Saxon, you come with me.'

He didn't look back to see if I followed him, but I did. 'Cos he scared the shit out of me, though I didn't like admitting it.

I followed him all the way to a little back room, and I was hoping he didn't plan on beating my ass in, because there was no escaping. At all.

He sat behind a neat desk in a big leather chair and nodded for me to sit across from him.

'Did your father explain what you're going to do here?'

I shrugged. 'Work, I guess.'

He narrowed his eyes. 'Call me old-fashioned, but I expect younger people to call me "sir" when they address me.' His voice was like the voices of the guys they always use as the scary military ops leaders in movies.

'Work, I guess – sir,' I ground out, keeping my mind focused on the small fortune that saying 'sir' was going to get me.

'Yes.' He steepled his fingers like some kingpin and nodded. 'We're open six days a week, Tuesday to Sunday. You'll have Mondays off, but those will be spent running Great-Aunt Helene's errands with her. You'll have access to her car to drive her. You will take her wherever she needs or wants to go, and that will last all day Monday. Clear?'

'Yes.' He glared at me. 'Sir.'

'Here, at Tony's, you'll start as a dishwasher. But there's room for you to move up. There are better jobs here, but every single person starts as a dishwasher, at least for one shift. I think it's important to know what the most menial laborer is doing. It helps foster respect among the workers. Your shift will be closing, so you won't have to come in until five, and you'll stay until around midnight. My daughter Pamela will drive you home with some other workers every night. Do you have any questions?'

'Do I get paid? Sir.'

'You do.' Tony's mouth finally curved into a smile. His eyes were all sparkly, like a wolf that just saw a fat deer wander into its path. 'But that money goes directly into Aunt Helene's bank account. Room and board, of course. You'll get your lump if you last the summer, won't you?'

I stood then. 'Yes.' I grinned. 'Sir.'

He stood too, stuck his hand out and we shook. He was trying as hard as he could to break my hand. I had to blink hard to keep my goddamn eyes from tearing up.

'Good night son. Good job today.' That was out of fucking left field.

'Thanks. Sir.'

I walked out to the kitchen, and Will showed me a bin where I could throw my apron. I washed my arms and asked for Pamela.

I was pointed in the direction of a fairly beat-up black Jetta. A tall girl with reddish hair and eyes like Cadence's was leaned against the driver's door, talking on a cell phone. There was a boy, maybe fifteen, playing with the dials on the stereo, which was pulsing with some kind of rap. He had Tony's coloring and looked about as tall as his dad, but a good two hundred pounds lighter, and Tony was no fat ass. And there was Cadence herself, counting a thick stack of what looked like twenties. Holy motherload.

I walked up to the car. Cadence looked at me, her eyes narrowed, and she turned to Pamela.

'Crackhead's here!' she called. Pamela slid her phone into her pocket and climbed in the driver's seat.

'Get in!' Pamela leaned out the driver's window and waved for me to get in. I slid in the back seat, next to Cadence. She didn't even look over at me.

'I thought you lived a few blocks away.' My voice sounded overloud in the ridiculously small car.

Pamela looked at me in the rearview mirror and smiled. It might have been the first real smile I'd seen all day, and I'd be lying if I said it didn't make my heart jump a little. This job was turning me into a fucking pussy.

'We do. Live close. But it's late, and I don't get to drive much, so Dad humors me. How was your day?'

I was a little shocked by her friendliness. Cadence rolled her eyes and leaned forward. 'Don't engage the druggie,' she said to her sister. 'He's a lowlife.'

Pamela smiled at Cadence indulgently. 'She's mean, right? So, how was your day?' She started the engine and pulled out of the parking lot.

'OK,' I lied. 'Dishwashing sucks.'

'Seriously.' The boy twisted around in the front seat to look at me and laughed. A full mouth of metal glinted. 'I'm Jimmy.'

'Hey, man,' I said, and we shook hands. 'Nice to meet you. You dishwash, too?'

He laughed like a donkey braying. 'I'm a slave. I do whatever my mom tells me to.'

'Your mom?' Obviously there was a mom. I just hadn't met her yet.

The car got quiet. Pamela looked at me in the rearview mirror. 'Our dad, it seems like he runs the show. But our mother is the real muscle. Don't mess with her. Do what she says. Always. I'm not kidding. And don't ever talk back to her. Ever.' The car stayed ominously quiet.

'Um, OK.' Weird! 'So she's really scarier than your dad?' I asked.

'My dad is Mary Fucking Poppins next to her,' Cadence quipped. 'She had a day off today, so she'll be in tomorrow. And she'll be ready to meet you.'

That made every one of them laugh like a bunch of lunatic hyenas. I felt a little chill on the back of my neck. Good God, what the hell was I in for? Suddenly the car lurched to a stop in front of a narrow, dingy terraced house, depressing and dilapidated.

'This is your place, Saxon.' Pamela tossed me

another sugar-sweet smile, and, I'll admit, I melted. 'Do you need a ride in tomorrow?'

'Do you mind?'

'No problem. Be ready by four thirty. I'll swing by.' One more time, that awesome smile. 'Have a good night.'

I paused and smiled back at her. 'Thanks, Pamela. You guys, too. Good night.' My manners may have been a little rusty, but I had them.

I got out, stood on the sidewalk, and took a long look at the house. It was faintly familiar. My mom and Jake's mom used to drag our asses here when we were just kids. They liked to party too long and hard for any normal babysitter's hours. Aunt Helene was sweet and old and always had lots of cookies, like a grandmother, but a hell of a lot better. Well, a hell of a lot better if the only grandma you had to compare her to was Mama D. The place had definitely gotten more run down since the last time I saw it, and that was saying something, since it was always a shithole.

I hadn't seen Aunt Helene in years, and I wondered why she was putting me up. Money, probably. Everything in my family went back to money. I bet she was getting most of my wages for bed and board in addition to her stipend. Plus my ass was responsible to drive her around, so there was that. Well, maybe she still made fucking cookies. I wasn't a total asshole. Even I liked cookies.

I walked up to the door quietly and let myself in. It wasn't locked or anything. The kitchen was dirty yellow. The light fixture flickered and there was a note on the old avocado-colored fridge in chicken scratch.

Dear Saxon,
There is a plate for you in the stove.
Love, Aunt Helene

I felt a weird twinge when I read that note. I opened the stove, which was on warm, and saw a plate with meatloaf, carrots and mashed potatoes. Jackpot.

It occurred to me then that I hadn't eaten a thing all day, though I'd been at a restaurant. I figured I was probably entitled to things like meals and breaks, but that was all something I could find out another day. I took the plate to a small table covered in a dingy plastic tablecloth that looked like it was for Christmas or something. I opened the fridge and found a twelve pack of Dr Pepper, unopened. I wondered if Aunt Helene had picked it up because I was coming. It was weird to think about someone looking out for me like that. I grabbed a soda and sat down in the flickering light to eat. When I was done, I put the plate in the sink, but that felt kind of dick, so I washed it and my fork and left them on the counter. Aunt Helene had been cool enough to leave me dinner; I wasn't going to make her clean up after me.

I walked down the hall and saw Aunt Helene's room. She was snuggled in her bed like a wrinkly little doll. There was a tiny bathroom next to her room, where I noticed she had put my toothbrush out, and, next to that, what I guessed was my room. It was dark and small, but the old single bed was made with scratchy polycotton sheets in baby blue. It's not like I had to have silk sheets or anything. It's just that I'd always had silk sheets. And they were damn comfortable.

I sat on the creaky little bed, then looked around the room. There was a tall dresser. When I opened the drawers, I saw that all of my clothes had been put away. There really wasn't much besides the bed and the dresser and a closet, one little window with aluminium Venetian blinds over it, and a mirror on the tiny closet door. A shithole, but a clean, neat shithole. It could be a lot worse.

I should have been dead on my feet, but for some reason, I felt buzzed. I wanted to talk to someone, but it was almost two in the morning. Like it made a fucking difference. If it had been six at night I still would have had no one to talk to.

Then, suddenly, I remembered Brenna Blixen. Lovely, smart Blix across the Atlantic and a good five hours ahead of me. That put her right around seven in the morning, and I knew she would be up, out for a morning run. I punched in her number. She picked up on the third ring.

'Hello?' I could hear her breathing hard.

'Run, Forrest, run.'

'Saxon!'

I felt a good, calm glow at her excitement. In a world of haters, here was one person who loved me, even if she knew what a rotten apple I was.

'How's Ireland? Let me guess. Green and wet?'

She laughed, a happy sound that made me smile. She had a great laugh. 'You got it. And I'll tell you what. I know why Ireland doesn't have any kickass runners. Who could run on slimy, mossy cobblestones? I almost busted my ass three times.'

'Don't do that.' I lay back on my bed and let the image of her lovely backside take away some of the day's pain. 'That ass is too fine to get busted. How's your nerd class going?'

'Lots of Joyce,' she griped. 'But I'm writing my *bildungsroman.*'

'Really?' I drawled, grinning. 'You're not even seventeen. Don't you think you have a few more formative years ahead of you?'

She laughed again. 'Seriously. But that's the assignment, so I have to give it a try,' she said. 'So how's work? God, that's a question I never imagined I'd be asking you.'

Now I laughed. 'Well, it's shitty. The people all know about my drug-dealing past, so I'm referred to as "Crackhead", officially. My bosses are Scary and Crazy Bitch Scarier, apparently, and their daughter is hot, but probably wants to stick a kitchen knife through my heart.'

'Maybe you should write a novel about it when you're done,' Brenna mused. I thought about it for a minute, but she obviously interpreted my silence as evidence that she had hurt my feelings or something. Good lord, I know I've been a fucking cry-ass lately, but I'm not that soft. 'I'm just kidding, Saxon,' she said all gently.

'Blix, come on. You're not going to hurt my feelings.' I remembered how it felt to lay my head in her lap and let her brush her fingers over my hair. I imagined what it would be like to do that again. Then I shook myself out of that train of thought. She wasn't mine. She really wasn't mine. She was Jake's, and even this call was just me bullshitting myself.

'I worry about you,' she said, her voice wavery with emotion. 'I think working might be good for you. And don't worry about the other people there. You'll grow on them.' Again that laugh. 'You're obnoxious, but you have an undeniable charm.'

'Thanks.' I closed my eyes and exhaled slowly. 'Look, I know you have to finish your run before your depressing nerd class, so I'll let you go. I just needed a sympathetic ear to bitch into.'

'Well, I'm here. Anytime,' she said earnestly. 'Take care of yourself, Saxon.'

'Will do. You do the same.' And we clicked off. It was like severing the last connection to any person who gave a shit about me. I looked at my hand, holding my cell, and the silvery scar where I had sliced myself open to become Jake's blood brother. Which was pretty unnecessary, since we've been blood brothers since he was born. Not that I'd been a very good one.

I lay down on my hard mattress and started counting off things in my life that I had fucked up. It was better than sheep, and there wound up being so many things that I was asleep before I knew it, a deep, mercifully dreamless sleep.

Next morning I woke up to the clatter of pans and the smell of bacon. It was eight o'clock. Aunt Helene must have been making breakfast. I got in the shower and washed with her Dove soap and Suave berry-smelling shampoo and conditioner. I brushed my teeth with her gritty baking soda toothpaste and got dressed in my little closet of a room. I did make my bed and left my dirty laundry in the basket. She didn't need to pick up after me like I was some little kid.

I hadn't seen my Aunt Helene since before I learned to ride a bike, but my memories of her were all good. I ducked into the kitchen, and she cried out like her lost kid had just come back from the dead.

'Saxon! Oh, Saxon.' She came at me with her old, flubbery arms open. She crushed me in a tight hug. Granted it was a strange little hug, since she came up to just over my bellybutton. 'Look at you!' she cried. 'So handsome! So handsome. And strong. Come and sit. You must be hungry, and I made you a big breakfast.'

She wasn't kidding. Little, tanned, wrinkled Aunt Helene scooped so much food onto my plate I could have eaten for three days. She sat with me, but she only drank a cup of creamy coffee with lots of sugar, like a kid.

'So, what is your work like?' She watched me with her bright eyes.

'Shitty,' I said around a mouthful of perfectly cooked eggs over easy. I washed it down with what had to be fresh-squeezed orange juice. 'Sorry. I mean it's hard work. But I'll be here 'till four thirty every day, so I'll mostly only waste my nights there.'

She patted my hand. 'Erikson is a fair man. And his wife? She's firm, but fair also. You will do well working for them.' She beamed at me, so I made my mouth smile back at her. She was a nice woman, and nice was becoming a hot commodity in my life as it currently stood.

'So, what do you do all day, Aunt Helene?' I asked while she cleared away my plate.

'Oh, it's too boring for a man!' she cried. 'Just cleaning up, gardening, cooking. You should go out, find some fun! A handsome devil like you should have a few girls around. Am I right?'

I grinned. 'Give me a little time. Let me help though. I like to keep busy.' Wow, how full of shit was I? But this place was a dump. She needed help.

'Well,' she said carefully. 'The Erikson boy was going to help do my gutters, but they had to fire a few kids, so he's been really busy at the diner. Maybe . . .'

I didn't have a damn clue how the hell to clean a gutter. But I had an iPhone and access to Google.

'I'm on it.' I went outside with my phone in hand.

One ladder with rotten rungs, two near slips off the roof, three tons of fermenting leaves, and four hours later I was covered in scum, panting for breath, and smelled like I had just climbed out of a toilet bowl in McDonald's.

'Why do leaves smell like ass?' I griped, shaking my arms. And it would have seriously screwed up my mood for the day, except that Aunt Helene was clucking around me, worried about my filthy self and telling me how she'd fried some kind of crazy Polish cookie and that I should get right in the shower.

And it felt good to have someone give a shit about me.

I took a shower and ate some knock-you-off-your-ass fantastic cookies and took a nap, and then it was time to go. Pamela was in the driveway, waving at Aunt Helene and accepting a plastic baggie full of cookies. Jimmy yelled thank you, Cadence waved, and then we were off. The car stayed weirdly quiet with all three of them eating cookies.

'You're so lucky!' Jimmy wiped crumbs off of his chin. 'Your aunt is so nice and she makes the best food.'

Pamela's smile showed her perfect white teeth. 'Seriously, dude. You have it made.'

Cadence glared, nibbled on a cookie, then rolled her eyes at me. 'It's not like he deserves it.'

And I might have agreed. If I didn't have remnants of gutter sludge under my fingernails. And a mental list of shit I had to pick up from a hardware store. Because Aunt Helene needed my help, so I'd give it to her.

And it hit me then, that maybe I was pretty fucking lucky.

Jake 1

When I first saw my dad in the flesh, it was like looking at myself, but in the future. Gerald Maclean looked just like me, and it occurred to me that fate had kind of screwed up in that respect. Saxon was his legitimate son, the son of the rich, perfect wife his family had pretty much expected him to marry. But Saxon is as dark as his mother, with that straight, shiny black hair and eyes that are brown-black too. Then there's me, the result of a fling with a girl from the wrong side of the tracks, and I wound up looking so much like my dad there's no denying that I'm his.

Even if I wanted to.

Which I did, pretty quickly.

My girlfriend, Brenna, who was incredibly smart and amazing, didn't know her birth father, and I knew it was irritating her that I wanted her to know more about him. But she was totally misunderstanding why. It really opened your eyes to see where you came from, and how little it really mattered.

I wanted her to see that because I thought she was still a little shallow about things like how you were raised and how much school you went to and what other people thought about you. Her mom had a lot to do with that. Her mom got herself an education and social status and all that late in life, so she hated any reminder of a time when she didn't have all of it. And she wanted Brenna to have a totally different experience. Like, specifically, she wanted her to marry the right kind of person.

Just like my dad's family had wanted for him. And look how that all turned out.

My dad showed up at my stepdad's house in an early 70s cherry red Mustang with an engine that roared so loud the vibrations alone could give you chills. My stepdad was out bowling, and I was glad. Because he drove a beat-up old Ford. Maybe he would have had money for a better car, but he was busy spending what he earned in raising a kid. A kid who wasn't even his.

'Hey.' I threw my stuff in the back seat. My dad stared at me. He had that kind of teary look like he wanted to hug me. Oh God.

'Jake.' His voice came out a little scratchy. 'I've been waiting a long time to meet you.'

It was a lame thing to say. It wouldn't be the last lame thing my dad said to me.

63

'Well, I've been right here for the last seventeen years.' I flicked my thumb at the beat-up house I'd lived in all my life. 'And Saxon's been ten minutes away.'

I had a love/hate thing going with Saxon, but he was still technically my brother, and I had a feeling a lot of his fucked-up bullshit could have been avoided if our dad bothered to stick around.

'I made a lot of mistakes.' He shook his head in what I knew was supposed to be a regretful way, but it felt like watching a crappy made-for-TV movie.

I knew what my next line was supposed to be. I was supposed to say something reassuring. Like, *Well, you're here now*. Or, *We all make mistakes, Dad*. But all I could think was, *Why would my mom have had her heart wrapped around such an obvious asshole?*

'Yeah,' I finally said. 'You did. Ready to go?'

We climbed into the car and he chuckled. 'You're a straight shooter, son. Just like your mother.'

I think that was supposed to make me feel better, but it made me clench my fists to keep from beating the crap out of my own flesh-and-blood father. I just nodded. He pulled out and we drove silently for a while. I sneaked a look at him, and it was just strange how much he looked like me. Or rather how much I looked like him. Same weird gray eyes, same brown hair. Hell, we even had the same turned eyetooth.

'Why didn't you get braces?' I asked suddenly.

'Why do you ask?' He glanced over from behind expensive douchey Ray-Bans.

'You come from big-time money. And we have the same twisted-out tooth. I would have had that fixed if I were you.'

He smiled. 'Why didn't you get braces?'

'Because my stepfather works in a damn pharmaceutical factory.' The words hammered out like a blunt punch. 'And his medical package is a big piece of shit.' I knew it was weird that I would even know about medical packages, but my stepdad had always been honest about why he couldn't do more for me, why we had only the basics at best.

'That's all going to change now, son.' Gerald's voice came out pretty self-righteous for a guy who skipped seventeen years of his son's life and drove a car that cost about twice what my stepfather earned in one year at work.

I just kept my mouth shut and thought about Brenna. She would be gone for a few weeks at her Irish camp, and it sucked to be away from her, in the summer, when we should have been having a good time together. Specifically, having a good time on my truck's big bench seat.

Bren was so damn pretty it still freaked me out a little. She was also really smart, like she devoured books in a few hours. She was a great artist. And she was sexy as hell. I'd been with a lot of girls over the years, and no one had ever managed to turn me on the way Brenna could. Just thinking about her was threatening to give me a boner, so I turned my attention to the radio.

My dad had all of the 'cool' stations pre-programmed into his radio. I had to flip through to find a classic rock station.

'Good choice, Jake.' Like I was a dog who caught a ball he tossed.

I sank into my seat and closed my eyes, doing that pretend sleeping thing that I always thought was such a classic dickhead teenager move. But I was feeling a lot like a dickhead teenager, and I didn't mind playing the part. Eventually my fake sleep turned real, and before I knew it, my dad was shaking my arm.

'Wake up, Jake.' His smile was so disgustingly cheesy, it could have come in a can. 'You're home.'

I knew he wanted those words to mean something. Like, *This is your real home, and you're finally able to be here and enjoy it.* But I didn't acknowledge that bullshit. This was no more my home than my stepdad's run-down place.

I didn't really have one. Yet.

My plan, long term, was to make my own home. One filled with people I chose. I had spent my entire childhood waiting for someone to give a crap and make me a nice place, but it never happened. So here I was.

The house stood fortress-colossal. My guest room had its own porch that overlooked a lake. The furniture was old and expensive, and there were vases of fresh flowers everywhere and all kinds of valuable little pieces of crap set out to make it look nice.

I wasn't so much of a bumpkin that I didn't know what nice stuff was like. But it was one thing to see it in movies and pictures. It was a totally different thing to bump into antiques every time you tried to turn around. Dad showed me my room and told me we'd be eating dinner in forty minutes. I opened my bag and put my stuff away, glad that Brenna helped me dress up my sad-ass wardrobe.

Brenna always looked like she just jumped out of the pages of some high-class fashion magazine. Which was so intimidating until you got to know her. Because she was funny and sweet, and even though she loved clothes, she had no clue what a complete knockout she was. Anyway, with her help, my clothes were nice enough that I didn't have to feel embarrassed.

Even as that thought crossed my mind, I was pissed-off. Brenna was worried I would change, and I told her there was no way. But here I was, one hour in this fancy, wallpapered, decked-out room, and I was already glad that the tag inside my shirt said Banana Republic. It was pathetic.

I wanted to call Brenna, but the time difference meant it was almost eleven at night in Ireland, and I didn't want to bug her. She'd only just got there, and I knew she had lots of work to do with her writing. So I lay back on my bed and thought.

Which is not something I'd ever had a lot of time to do. I'd always been busy. When I was young, I was busy taking care of things that a normal mom and dad would have done, since I didn't have that kind of normal. When I got older, I was busy partying and making chaos with Saxon. When I outgrew that, I got busy working hard, then busier getting Brenna to say yes to dating me. I'd never had a lot of downtime.

And I'd never had a vacation. This was all kind of new and weird. After a while I got up and washed my face in the little boat-decorated bathroom that linked to my room. That seemed to be another thing if you had a lot of money. No one wanted to use the same bathroom. Every room had its own, and there were three more for guests. It was like they were petrified to admit that there was shit in the world or that they made any of it.

I was laughing at my own thoughts when I heard a knock on my door. I expected my dad, but was surprised to see a girl. Right around my age, cute and red-haired.

'Hey.' She smiled, her teeth perfect and white. She had dark eyes that looked strange since she was so light; light hair, light skin, even blonde eyebrows. Her lashes probably would have been light too, but she had make-up on, so they looked black.

'Hey.' I walked over to her and stuck my hand out. 'Jake Kelly.'

She stuck hers out and shook. 'I know. Everyone does. I'm Caroline Morgenstern.' She looked around my room, then walked in and peered out the window, acting like she owned the place. 'They must like you. This is the best guest room by far.'

'Why would you say that?' Really, they all looked the same to me; kind of like they came from a magazine, and all with the same lame boat theme.

'The view.' She cocked one hip on the windowsill and gazed out. 'You get a view of the lake and trees. And a good one. See that house?' She pointed to a gigantic white mansion.

'Yeah.'

'That's my family's. We're neighbors.' When she smiled at me, it was the slow, sexy smile I'd seen on girls' faces way too many times, and it freaked me out.

'That's nice. I have to go eat dinner soon, so, I'd love to talk, but—'

'We're eating together.' Her voice was light and confident. 'The families.'

Only I'm pretty sure she meant 'The Families'.

'What does that mean? The Families? Are you my cousin or something?'

She wrinkled her nose. 'No. Thank God. I'm not really a kissing cousins type, you know. The families are the Macleans, the Morgensterns, the Kicklighters and the Coopersmiths. Our families are some of the oldest on the East Coast. Haven't they drilled this into your head?' Before I could explain, she popped her hand over her mouth like she was really worried about offending me. 'Oh, I forgot. You're the—'

'Bastard.' A tiny blaze of anger lit me up. If there was one thing I couldn't stand it was an innocent act. Just say what you wanted to say if you were going to open your big mouth at all. But I knew how to play it cool. 'I'm starved. So, let's eat.'

I had tried to give Caroline a pretty clear brush off, but I realized too late that was probably the worst thing I could have done. I'd met a few girls like her. *Slumbunnies* was what Saxon and I called them. They were rich, bored girls usually visiting some relative in Sussex County who decided to slum it with some badass country kids. They were always the most wild, the most willing to get in bed with you and get freaky, the ones who'd drink or snort or shoot whatever there was. Definitely not my bag, but Saxon had been with a few. Of course, technically, Saxon was whatever the male version of a *slumbunny* was.

Caroline smiled at me with that glint of a challenge I'd seen so many times in Saxon's eyes, and I knew I was in deep whether I liked it or not. She curled her fingers around my arm when we walked down to dinner, and everyone at the table looked up and glowed like we were the sweetest couple they'd ever seen. They all shouted out their welcome to me. It was pretty overwhelming. Every single person got introduced to me, but I couldn't remember one of their names.

There were about seven courses and it was pretty fancy, but I didn't worry about what fork to use or what to do or any of that crap. Brenna and I had eaten at some swanky places, and she'd always just rolled her eyes and told me to relax when I got nervous, so I figured I'd take her advice. I ate with whatever fork or spoon was nearest my hand, and I didn't talk with my mouth full or put my elbows on the table, but other than that, I wasn't minding my 'p's or 'q's.

'So, Jake, dear, what colleges are you looking at?' asked the silver-haired woman sitting across from me. My grandmother. She had dark red fingernails and a pretty, too-young face. I figured she'd probably had plastic surgery, but not the kind that made women look like crazy lion-women hybrids. I couldn't imagine her kissing my cuts and scrapes or passing out cookies, but she looked fairly nice.

'To tell you the truth, I hadn't thought about it much.' I put down my fork and tried not to bug out when every person at the table stopped talking and looked my way. 'My finances aren't the best, and I figured I would do two years at the community college and move on to Rutgers maybe. If my grades are good enough.' Brenna promised to help me with my academic work if I went.

The table went quiet.

'Rutgers?' My grandma's voice questioned what I said, not too snotty, but not nice, either. 'The state university?'

'Yes, ma'am.' My ears burned, so I knew they were bright pink, and I hated feeling like everyone looked my way and thought, *Stupid*. 'It's been around since the late 1700s. I'm sure you know it.' I was aware I might come off as a simpleton, but I wasn't, and I knew a barb when one hit.

'Well, like you said, that was when finances were a question. That's not really an issue any more,' she sing-songed. Everyone laughed like that was the best joke they'd heard in a while.

Caroline winked at me from across the table. I noticed she was drinking wine. So were the couple of other teenagers. I guessed it just wasn't a big deal.

'So, do you have a girlfriend, Jake?' asked a woman who looked like Caroline, just older. Her mother? She looked much more like a sister, but this was a world where people obviously hated aging, so it was a little hard to tell.

'Yes, ma'am.' I cleared my throat, happy to be able to announce it in front of Caroline. 'Her name is Brenna Blixen. She's in Ireland right now taking a writing course,' I bragged. Man, I wished I had Brenna there next to me. She could have handled this whole snooty gang, no problems.

'Blixen?' My grandmother wrinkled her brow. 'Where do I know that name from?'

'Lylee's friend,' Caroline's mother drawled. 'Don't you remember, Mama D? She went on and on about her in Bermuda this spring.'

'Oh, that's it. The art history professor who's shaking it up in little old Sussex County.' She sighed. 'Why do these women insist on wasting their talents in community colleges when universities would scoop them up?'

I clenched my jaw tight. Brenna's mom didn't have many warm feelings towards me, but she was a damn good teacher and a smart woman. 'Mrs Blixen likes to help students who don't think of themselves as college material.' Everyone stopped talking again and looked down the table at me. 'She knows how much it means for people to get equitable treatment, even if they are just community college students.'

'Bravo, Jake,' my dad slurred, obviously a few drinks in.

'Well.' My grandmother pasted on a smile. 'He's certainly a Maclean, isn't he? All piss and vinegar!'

Then the whole dinner party laughed, and I felt like a champion ass. My grandmother (everyone called her Mama D; I wasn't even sure what her name was) dominated the conversation until dessert, and I spent a lot of time looking at people who had my features, used my gestures, had my DNA running strong through them, but were nothing at all like me. Once we'd eaten our fresh cherry pie, the adults went to the drawing room for after-dinner drinks, the little kids were ushered off to bed, and the teenagers were set loose on the lake to have a bonfire.

Caroline attached herself to my side. 'Brenna Blixen? In Paris she and Saxon were joined at the hip. Or the mouth. Or whatever.' She giggled behind her perfectly manicured little hand.

I stopped in my tracks. 'Look, Caroline? That's my girlfriend you're talking about. I don't listen to rumors about her, and anyone who wants to spread them should keep the hell away from me.' I kept walking and she ran to catch up.

'Wait! Jake!' She tried to link arms with me again. I shook her off. 'C'mon, I was just kidding around,' she sulked.

'Then I must have a really shitty sense of humor.' I stalked forward, hands deep in my pockets. 'Maybe it's best if you and I keep our distance.'

'I don't think we need to do that.' Her voice came out like a purr. 'I'm just sort of outspoken, OK? The thing is, I always know what I want, and I tend to get it. So, why not just come along for the ride?' She smiled like she'd practiced her seductive look in the mirror every night.

She was pretty. Really pretty, and probably smart and possibly great in bed. But just because I could acknowledge those things didn't mean that I wanted her. I knew her type, and I wasn't about to be the object of her slumbunny attention.

'I get that you're probably used to getting what you want.' I took two steps away from her. 'But get ready for a shock, Caroline. I have no interest in you. And I'm not going to be your summer entertainment. So find someone else to screw.'

'I've screwed them all.' She spit the words out, then relaxed and took a breath. Her face was calm, like she wasn't remotely offended by what I said. 'It's practically incestuous here. You're new, that's all.' She shrugged. 'If you're so committed to your little girlfriend, then forget I said anything. We can just hang out, if that's cool.'

I knew there was no trusting a girl like her, but I wasn't about to get on her bad side. 'Sounds cool.'

She caught up with me and we walked the narrow path to the beach. 'Do you want a beer?' She pointed to a big aluminium bucket packed with ice and gleaming bottles.

We were down by the beach, and there was a huge pine branch fire crackling on the sand. It smelled like hot sap and dusky smoke. 'No.' I shook my head. 'Thanks, but I don't drink any more.'

'Ooh, so you used to be a bad boy.' Caroline ran her hand lightly down my arm. 'Do you go to the gym?'

'Is that your best pick-up line?' I couldn't help smiling at her. She might be a pain in the ass, but her persistence was admirable.

'I have better. Should I try them out on you?' She made a kissy face at me and laughed a little. It seemed like a decently real laugh, so I joined in.

'Who's your buddy, Caro?' Suddenly there was a guy who looked like an Abercrombie model jonesing for a fight.

'Back off, Bryce.' Caroline put a palm on his chest and pushed with all her meager strength. 'We're just talking. Can't you go bother someone else?'

He looked at me for a long, drawn-out minute, then turned on his heel and stalked away.

'Friend of yours?' I watched his flip-flops nearly fall off his feet as he stormed through the sand.

'That's Bryce Kicklighter. He and I've fooled around practically every summer since we were in grade school, and he has this crazy idea that we should be monogamous this summer.' She rolled her eyes. 'He's so fucking boring I could fall asleep under him.'

'OK.' Her bored, edgy way of seeing the world threw me, and I sat down on the sand next to her with the feeling I should get up and leave nagging at the back of my mind. I took inventory of the kids who sat by the fire, some of them my blood cousins.

Money sure as hell didn't buy automatic good looks, but it bought straight white teeth, professionally cut and colored hair, skin treated by dermatologists, and expensive clothes. There was a lot of noise coming from all of their little groups, but it wasn't really happy. Just loud.

'What's wrong?' Caroline brushed her fingers over my forearm to get my attention. 'You should really have a beer.'

'Wow, you're persistent. I said no.' I turned my arm so her fingers would slide off without me having to tell her to stop touching me.

'It might help you relax. You're among friends now.' She flipped a strand of reddish-blonde hair behind her shoulder and stretched like a cat in heat.

'I've done the whole drinking thing.' My eyes followed the volleyball that bounced back and forth over a net in the most half-hearted game I'd ever seen. 'I'm over it.'

'I didn't say you should get blitzed.' She slid her foot out of her sandal and pulled it along my leg. 'One beer? Maybe two? What's the big deal?'

Her tone aggravated me, and that was pretty out of character. I was usually a laid-back guy. And I guessed I was feeling pretty coiled up, and it was just one beer and getting one would get her off my back, so I went over and cracked one open. Once I chugged it down, the whole gathering-on-the-beach thing did look more fun. After three beers the fire started to look really beautiful, and I had a fifth in me when someone suggested skinny-dipping.

Five isn't usually a lot for me, but it had been a long time since I'd drunk anything. I joined the cavorting crowd running down to the lake just like I suddenly belonged, and in my bleary head I wondered about the old saying 'blood is thicker than water'. What about beer and blood? My brain sloshed through my thoughts dizzily.

Caroline led me off to the side. She was definitely drunk. She could hardly stand up straight.

'I was hoping you'd do this.' She peeled her tank top over her head and shimmied out of her little skirt.

'Why's that?' My voice sounded fuzzy in my own ears. I pulled my shirt off and let my pants fall.

'Because I wanted to see you ... naked,' she whispered. She unsnapped her bra and her breasts were out in the moonlight, her nipples hard in the cold night air. She slid her panties down her legs, and I saw that she was totally shaved.

I kicked off my boxers, and she drew a finger along my chest. 'Just as good as I imagined.' Her smile twisted on her lips.

I was on my way to being good and drunk, but I wasn't there yet. I was mostly just without any worries or very sound decision-making skills. The moon was big and bright and the water wasn't completely freezing. We jumped off the dock. I dived under, and the shock of the cold water was absolute. For a minute, I swam just under the surface, and the realization of what I was doing rushed over me.

I was drinking. With Caroline. It was innocent right at that minute, but it could turn into something else so fast I wouldn't realize the full extent of what was happening until the deed was done.

That wasn't what I wanted.

I popped back up away from the others and scanned the water for Caroline, but I didn't see her. I figured she was just in the crowd, and swam for shore. I had my boxers back on when I heard someone scream.

I jumped back in and swam, because I knew without having to ask that it was her.

I swam hard and fast to where she was floating, face down. I grabbed her under the arms and dragged her in. By then everyone was screaming, the girls were crying, and without really thinking, I pulled her onto shore and gave her the best version of CPR I knew. It was mandatory training at Zinga's, but it had been a while since I got my certificate. I had a general idea of what to do. I did a few chest compressions, tilted her head, opened her mouth, pinched her nose and , filled her lungs with my breath, pumped at her chest, and did that jerky rotation a few more times until she coughed and choked. I turned her on her side so the water could come out.

'Someone bring a damn towel!' I yelled and someone handed me one that I wrapped around her.

'Jake?' She looked at me in confusion.

'You almost drowned, you idiot!' I held her face roughly. This girl, this dumb girl had almost died right here, and it would have been at least partially my fault for not keeping a better eye on her when I knew she was too drunk to be swimming.

'You saved me.' Her brown eyes went wide. She shivered.

Then her mother was there, pretty bombed herself, and she was crying and rocking Caroline in her arms.

And I knew it was a dickhead thing to be thinking right at that moment, but I was glad as hell I had my boxers on. I went back to shore and gathered the rest of my things, then stalked back to the big, ornate house filled with shit no one really needed and people no one really liked.

The next morning buzzed bright, the way so many mornings had after I'd been drinking. The difference was that all the other mornings I had been drinking because I wanted to. Last night I had done it without really wanting to. I stood in front of a girl I didn't like while she stripped down to nothing, then got herself into stupid trouble that could easily have killed her.

I wanted to call Bren and tell her what had happened, but it was a lot.

Someone knocked at the door. My first thought was that it would be Caroline up early, but she had just gotten over nearly drowning, so that was unlikely. I got up and pulled a T-shirt over my head and my jeans over my boxers, just to be safe, and pulled the door open. It was my dad.

He still looked spookily like me, but now that I'd

81

had some time to process everything, I could see the real differences. For one thing, he was smaller than I was, skinnier. I figured that his would have been more my build if I hadn't busted my ass working for the past few years. He also had perfectly done hair all the time and did that little goatee thing that I've always hated. He dressed like he wanted to be a lot younger than he was, all tight clothes with big, stupid designs all over them, and always one of those surfer shell necklaces on. I'm sure he thought he looked young and hip, and he kind of did, like a rocker getting older but still cool.

Except I knew he was supposed to have been a father, and hadn't bothered. That kind of took the cool quotient out of the whole equation.

'Hey, son,' he said, then put his arms around me. I didn't want it, but I wasn't exactly sure how to push him away, so I let him hug me. Was he *crying*? I could smell alcohol on his breath. Pathetic.

'What's wrong?' I asked.

'Caroline Morgenstern . . .' he blubbered. 'She could have died last night. *You* could have died last night.'

'Probably not. I've been able to swim since before I could walk. She probably passed out and swallowed water. I think she drank twice as much as I did and she's half my size.' I was explaining it all so I could sterilize it. Because it was weird to have this grown man weepy over me.

'Jake. I want you to think about something,' he sobbed, his eyes embarrassingly red-rimmed. 'I want you to think about becoming a Maclean in name. Legally. Is that something you might consider?'

I blinked hard and took a big step back, away from him and his embarrassing drink-enhanced emotions. 'Why now?'

'Because now is when we have you back.' He was too close in my personal space when he said it. 'Now is the time, Jake. And you *are* a Maclean, no matter what your name is.'

'What does that mean?' I wanted to back away, but I was trapped between him and some big, stupid, boat-themed dresser.

'You stand up for yourself. And to my mother, which is no small thing. You're brave. You act fast. All Maclean traits.' He wiped his eyes with the backs of his wrists.

I snorted. 'I think that's a stretch.'

'No it isn't.' His jaw got tight and his nostrils flared a little. I guess there're only so many times any guy will take his surly kid's attitude. But it was a hell of a lot better having him pissed off than having him weepy, as far as I was concerned.

I crossed my arms and leaned back on the edge of

the dresser, as far away from him as I could get. 'What about being snotty to people you think are below you? What about insane alcoholism? Sleeping around? Abandoning your kids? I wouldn't do any of that, and those all seem to be pretty standard Maclean traits to me.'

'You're just picking what's bad about the family.' He started to poke a finger at my chest, but backed up when I stood my full height. Not that I was considering fighting my own father, but if it came down to it, I could take him. 'That's not really fair.'

Unbelievable. 'You're going to pop into my life seventeen years late and tell me what's fair? Fat fucking chance.' I pushed past him and walked to the door, which I opened for him. 'Leave.'

'Son . . .'

'Don't call me that.' I felt so much fury, I was surprised my voice worked well enough for me to get any words out. 'And I'm sorry, *Gerald*, but I can't call you Dad either. Or take the name Maclean. I'm no good at pretending to be what I'm not. I guess that's the Kelly in me.'

'There's a lot this family could offer you.' The snide way it rolled out of his mouth made it sound pretty much like a threat.

I shrugged. 'I made it all right without you all before. I'm sure I could do it again.'

'You get that from your mother. She didn't give a shit what people thought of her, either.' He gave this repulsive, shitty little half-smile.

'She cared,' I countered, my teeth gritting so hard, the ache went up my temples. 'She cried her eyes out whenever your name came up. I never did understand why until I found out the truth.'

'I would have taken care of her.' He twirled a silver ring that he wore on his middle finger. 'She wanted to get married, but I couldn't. There was Lylee.'

'You divorced her anyway.' I stuck my hands in my pockets hard to keep them from his neck.

He shook his head.

'You and Lylee are still together?' I asked, and this one was a real shocker. Lylee definitely didn't think of herself as a married woman, and I was sure Gerald was no damn angel.

'We've been separated for years, but we're technically still married.' He ran a hand over his face with a frustrated swipe.

'What about Saxon?' I demanded. 'Why didn't you come around and see him?'

'Jake, it's hard to explain it.' He shifted from one foot to the other and waved his hands in an attempt to come up with the words to 'explain it' to me. 'I got caught up in my own stuff. I was selfish, all right? I admit it though.' He glared at me a little, and I thought about how my eyes probably looked just like his when I was pissed off.

'Well, congratulations for admitting it. I guess that changes the past decade. I guess that makes Saxon less of a crazed fuckup. And, if you were going to leave, you could have actually done the right thing and not dumped a guilt trip on Saxon's shoulders.' My hands were stuffed so ferociously in my pockets, I was afraid I'd rip through them.

'I never did that.' He narrowed his gray eyes at me.

'Yes, you did.' I could feel my heart shot hard with adrenaline, running off the rails. I pointed my finger in his face. 'You told him to take care of me. He was just a kid. Where the hell do you get off?'

He jerked his face away from my finger, but he didn't back away completely. 'Jake, I'm sorry. I don't even remember saying that.'

'Must be another Maclean trait,' I muttered. 'I don't want to be rude to you, but I don't really want your company right now.'

He gave a jerky nod, turned, and stalked out of the room, and I was left staring at the ceiling again, wishing I were anywhere but here.

Brenna 2

Evan sat on the shiny tabletop in Trinity's echoing library, long legs crossed neatly, and stretched until the laptop that had been balancing precariously on her thighs jostled, slid off and almost clattered to the polished floor below. Devon reached an arm out and caught it, putting it back on her lap.

'The librarian will shit a brick if she catches you sitting on the table,' he said, his voice low and just on the verge of snapping. He waved an arm around the empty, cool quiet of the massive hall, filled with so many books, their gorgeous smell heavy in every breath we took.

'I am so damn sick of this I could cry,' she moaned, and the sound was loud enough to echo around the dust-mote filled air. She grabbed Devon's hand, and, at that point, he was so completely under her spell he didn't even attempt to pull away. 'Devon, you *always* follow every rule that assface Dr Gorman slaps on us. You can't tell me there isn't a teeny, tiny part of you that wants to just . . . just tear your clothes off and run naked over all those fucking cobblestones!'

She jumped up and Devon barely caught her laptop before it almost crashed to the floor again. She shimmied out of her lilac cashmere sweater, tore off her black jersey cap-sleeved top with tiny mother-of-pearl buttons and tossed it so it landed right over Devon's left eye, and was about to slide the zipper on her tight gray pencil skirt down when he jumped up and shoved the shirt back over her head right in the middle of the library. I glanced from side to side, but I didn't see anyone other than us. Though it would be easy enough to find a corner behind a stack of old, leather-bound books and disappear from view.

'Jesus Christ, you are so melodramatic,' he muttered, ripping the shirt back off her when he realized he was attempting to put it on upside down. Strands of her dark hair flew up around her head in a halo of static electricity. 'Do you want to get out of here? Are you hungry? Why don't you just say what you want instead of staging this whole insane striptease?' He crammed the shirt over her head and shoulders, and pulled back when she attempted to kiss his cheek. 'Brenna, control her!'

'Brenna, don't listen to him!' Her eyes glittered. They actually shined, and I would have been only minimally surprised if bursts of sparkly light shot out of them like eruptions of fireworks. 'Remind him how good I've been.' She wiggled her shoulders until one arm, then the other popped out of the armholes. 'Please? Remind Mr Stick-In-The-Mud that I haven't skipped one single class.'

'You went to four wasted. One so wasted you had to leave to puke.' Devon stretched in the uncomfortable wooden chair, his back arched in an attempt to work the kinks out, his laptop open, his fingers poised over the keys with aggressive intent.

'Only very slightly hungover. Usually. Except that one time. But only one time,' Evan objected, balling up the sweater that probably cost more than the plane ticket to get over here and throwing it at him. 'And how did you know I puked?'

He didn't look up from the screen of his computer as the soft lilac fabric puddled half over one of his knees and half on the floor. 'Brenna sent me down the hall to check on you.'

She clapped her hands to her chest and pulled the corners of her mouth down in a frown. 'Y'all are the sweetest friends I ever had.' She braced her hands on either side of Devon's chair, leaned over his laptop screen, and popped loud kisses all over his face while he tried to bat her away.

'Stop! You are so fucking exhausting, Evan. Being with you is like having a pet monkey on speed.' He grabbed her face in his hands. 'Stop. Stop right now. Tell me what you want, OK?'

'I want . . . to *do* something!' She got up and sat next to me, swinging her arms around my shoulders in an easy hug. 'Please help me help him before he has an aneurysm from staring at that damn screen all day.'

'You'd think just sitting in the same place where the Book of Kells is would inspire something,' I mused.

We'd tried that trick. All three of us had walked in, hushed, the first day and stared at the sheets of vellum with their gorgeous swirls of purples and reds, yellows and blacks under the glass. Even Evan didn't talk then, just traced her fingers over the glass you weren't supposed to touch at all, outlining the gold while her lips moved like she was reading the ancient stories to herself.

They were gorgeous. They shook us with their ancient beauty. They did not make it any easier to write our modern essays.

I leaned my head on her shoulder and breathed in the clean, flowery smell of her. The smell of Evan was so different from Evan herself. She smelled light and freshly scrubbed and delicately floral. She should have smelled like cotton candy, liquor, gasoline and fire. 'Did you finish your paper?' I asked her.

She shook me back and forth until my brains felt

blended. 'How can I write a *bildungsroman* if I haven't even fucking *lived* yet?'

'I managed to write mine,' Devon said to his screen as his fingers clicked over the keys.

Evan bounded back across the table and peeked over his shoulder. Her eyebrows knitted and she moved her plush lips around like she was chewing on the flavor of certain words. After a few minutes, she put her hands up to rub her temples. 'Are you kidding me? Are you freaking kidding me? Devon, look up from that damn computer and tell me that this is a joke!'

'This is an assignment,' he muttered stubbornly and turned the screen away from her even though she wasn't looking any more. 'And it's almost done.'

'Almost done?' She grabbed a paperclip, a packet of sticky notes, a pen and tossed them at him in quick succession. 'Almost *done*? You're writing about the fucking *birds*? You're writing about the *ocean*? You don't give a single shit about birds or oceans!'

'So?' He did finally look up, and his hazel eyes were pink on either side from staring at the computer for so long. 'I need to write this. I need to finish. Why go to all these classes for all these hours if you're just going to blow off the final assignment?'

'Blow it off?' Evan sat on the side of the table and gave a long, exaggerated laugh that filled the entire room, right up to the top of the arched ceiling. 'You don't think you're, maybe, blowing it off in your own cowardly way by writing that inane crap?'

'You don't even have one word written yet,' he said in the long-suffering voice he'd honed around Evan.

'And you have nothing but bullshit. That's it. We're going. Right now. Out! We're going out to *live* for a few hours. I promise I'll get you back in time to write a new essay.' She pulled me up by the hand, and I couldn't help the laugh that burst out. She twirled me around and we were both laughing while Devon scowled.

'I don't need to write a new essay. Mine's almost done.' He shut his laptop and placed it carefully on the table.

Evan grabbed me around the waist and dipped me low. I looked at Devon from my upside-down vantage point while Evan shook her head. 'Sorry, sweetie. I know you think I'm a world-class slacker, but retiring to the ladies' to chuck during Gorman's lecture on Yeats is one thing. Turning in a steaming pile of turds like you're about to? That's a sad, sorry waste of intellect.' She righted me, kissed both my cheeks, and reached for Devon's hand.

'That essay is based on what we learned from reading all the greats of Irish literature. Oh, wait, you didn't bother to read half of it, did you?' He curled his lip in her direction, and Evan's happiness dropped like leaves drifting from an oak at the end of the autumn.

It took her a long few seconds to string her words together. 'I could recite Yeats in my sleep all night long, Devon.' Her voice was a mix of fist-hard and kiss-soft. 'I'm telling you that your essay sucks because it sucks. You're smart enough to know that imitating the greats doesn't make you great. It just makes you a decent copycat.' She pressed her lips into a tiny hyphen. 'Maybe you should listen to me some-time. You know how you got waitlisted?' He nodded, a quick jerk of his chin. 'And most people applied?' I nodded, my breath held, waiting to hear what she'd say next. 'Well, they sent me a letter of invitation, and it wasn't because of my family's shitty lace.'

Devon's eyes glinted with new respect, then he crossed his arms over his chest. 'Why did you get an invitation?'

She took a deep breath and pulled her hair over her shoulder, weaving a quick, distracted braid with her fingers. 'You know how I drink?'

He tapped his foot in an edgy, impatient rhythm. 'Yep. Like a fish. You're practically professional.'

She shook her hair back out and her smile was like the first sip of icy lemonade on a dusty hot day. 'I'm at least three times better at writing than I am at drinking.' She tugged at my hand. 'Brenna? What say you?'

'My essay is pure shit. I'm in.'

She pulled me close and everything about her, her clean smell, her quick breathing, the cymbal crash of her heart, the energy that prickled off of her like live-wire electricity, everything made me feel like I had pure adrenaline running through my veins.

'C'mon, Devon. Come with us.' I held my hand out.

'Where?' he demanded, arms still crossed tight.

'To make errors!' Evan's laugh was inflating, and I suddenly knew exactly what it would feel like to be a balloon full of helium. 'They are, after all, the portals of discovery.'

'Joyce,' Devon griped, following us as we tiptoed down the hall, past all the students bent over their laptops with their textbooks wide open in front of them. When we burst through the door and into the dimming late-afternoon sunshine, Evan gave a series of whoops and ran too fast on shoes that were basically begging fate to twist her ankle.

She spun around in wide circles, arms flung out at her sides. 'Devon! Don't believe Joyce! Araby will be amazing when we get there! Mangan's sister was worth the trip! Or, you know, Mangan himself, if you'd prefer.' She stopped spinning and stumbled toward him, grabbing his forearms, and laughed like a maniac. 'We will find the bazaar and spend all our damn florins on gorgeous stuff, and we'll give gifts to our sweethearts that will make them swoon – swoon with eternal love! What say you?'

'I say you'd probably do really well in an insane asylum.' He tried to make the words ring out with clear aggravation, but he couldn't disguise the blur of a smile.

'Oh, holy Jesus.' She smiled. 'You saw it right, Brenna? Be careful, Captain Crabass. Didn't your gramma tell you that your face will get stuck like that if the wind changes?'

Evan tweaked his nose and he let out a long sigh. She pulled us into a dark, seedy pub and bought a round. She was always super-generous with her money, and had insisted on buying us pretty much every meal we ate outside the cafeteria.

We'd only had a few weeks together, but I felt like Evan was the missing piece to a puzzle I'd always thought was complete. She had been my constant confidante, along with Devon, and she'd crept into my room or I'd crept into hers every single night so we could stay up late and whisper about every detail of our lives, every hidden secret. Sometimes I fell asleep with her dark hair curled on my pillow, listening to her snores, and dreaming about fields of violets and pansies and daisies with thorns like barbed wire.

'Let's truth toast,' Evan said as soon as the drinks got plunked on the greasy tabletop.

'What's that?' Devon asked with the careful reluctance he maintained like a shield when he was around her.

'We all tell one deep, dark truth before we take a sip. One that we've never told anyone else, and it never leaves this circle. You in?' She waggled her eyebrows at me, and my stomach churned. My gut feeling was to say no, but I sometimes felt like a cobra in a snake charmer's basket when I was around Evan.

I wrapped my hand around my beer. 'OK,' I said and swallowed hard.

She zoomed in on Devon who shook his head and pushed up the sleeves of his striped pullover like he was preparing to get down to work. 'Fine,' he grumbled.

'Excellent! Me first, since it was my fat idea.' She raised her glass and I watched the beer slosh slightly as her hand shook. 'Rabin cheated on me with my best friend. I walked in on them, but they didn't notice, so I snuck back out. I never told either one of them that I knew, and I've been hating them this whole time, so much I think I burned an ulcer in my guts.' She batted her lashes too fast and clinked her glass to ours so quickly I was afraid she'd smash them.

I wanted to say I was sorry, ask her why she'd

never told me during all our midnight to dawn whisper sessions, but her look thrust at me like a spear point. 'You're up, Bren.'

'All right.' I looked down into my beer, the foam already disappearing from the surface and thought about the thing that was too small to be a big deal and too weird to just forget. The thing that it would feel so good and right to admit to them and lift, like a cinder block, off my own chest. 'Saxon called after Jake and I were back together and, um, asked for phone sex. He was ... he tried really hard to persuade me. Really, really hard.' I squirmed at the memory. All four eyeballs stared at me, waiting. 'He was so high. I mean, really high. I didn't say anything back, of course. I mean, nothing sexy. But we talked for a while. I never told Jake, and I don't think Saxon even remembers he did it.'

'I need a drink now,' Devon declared, and we clinked glasses and took a sip.

The table was quiet for a long, uncomfortable stretch. Evan must have tried poking Devon under the table, because she was staring right at him, but jabbing me in the shin with the toe of her shoe. I poked him instead, and he scowled.

'Fine!' he barked. 'You two have been really aggravating this whole trip, you know that? I thought I was going to get some peace and quiet. I thought I might meet some nice, normal dorks who love Irish literature. But, no, I got stuck with you two freaks.'

'You got stuck in our perfect triangle of freakiness because you belong,' Evan corrected with a gleeful smile, making her fingers into a triangle to better illustrate. 'Now make our truth oath complete. Spill your dirt.'

When he spoke, the words were so rushed, I don't think he took a breath the entire time.

'When I was at my aunt's, just before I got the call to come here, her friend stopped by while she was picking us up lunch. We started talking, and he kissed me. We wound up making out, and I think my aunt would seriously blow a gasket if she knew, because he's older. Not like *old*. He's in college.' Devon blindly pushed his glass to the middle of the table and we clinked and sipped.

'We have now solidified our eternal bond. We're going to be friends for-eva,' Evan said with perfect solemnity.

Devon snorted and rolled his eyes, but he raised his glass and we drained our beers. He took Evan's out-stretched hand and mine when we were done.

'All joking aside, I feel like this is the land of magic and pots of gold and all that gorgeous bullshit.' Evan closed her eyes and took a deep breath of the damp, yeasty pub air. 'We're free here. We don't have to be the people we are at home. We don't have to live with anyone else's expectations. Isn't that amazing?' Her eyes flashed open and she squeezed our hands. 'Doesn't that just . . . put things in perspective? I wish I could be half as honest back home as I am right here with y'all.'

'It's not always that easy.' Devon pulled his hands away and tipped his chair back. 'We act the way we do back home because people aren't safe. I know I complained about you two, and I'm right. You're crazy idiots half the time. But you guys accept who I am, and the people back home don't. I don't think I have the energy to put up with people hating me for a whole bunch of new reasons back home. It's hard enough dealing with what they hate now.'

I ran my fingers over the smooth polish on Evan's nails. 'And I screwed up big time with Jake. I broke his heart, and it was a shitty thing to do. I can't risk doing that again just because I decided to listen to his brother's weird sexy phone call or because I sometimes feel like Saxon and I have this connection. The way Jake loves isn't easy, and if I'm going to learn to love like him, I have to stop letting myself get pulled in a million directions, even if the tradeoff is that I'm not so honest.'

'Y'all, I'm going back to a crazy scenario. I have to dump Rabin, and he's gonna lose his shit big time. My best friend is a lying whore. I doubt my daddy can foot the bill for the private school I've been going to and I'm flunking anyway, so I might get kicked into public. My mama is all but moved in with her boyfriend, some lowlife shitbag who wants to move to Mexico with her or some bullshit. This is the last little bit of happiness I have before I go back, and I just want you to know . . .' Her voice cracked.

Devon and I both scrambled to find a napkin or tissue, anything to blot the eighteen coats of mascara. We'd seen the havoc they created when they ran down her face, and it wasn't pretty.

'C'mon, no crying.' Devon pulled a crumpled tissue of questionable sanitation out of his pocket and mopped under her eyes with clumsy swipes. His voice got fuzzy around the consonants from the emotion he was attempting to strangle. 'We love you, too, OK? You know I just bust on you. And you can call us or text whenever. Dry up, now. It's our last night of freedom. Let's go.' He pulled her up.

'Where?' She hiccupped and looked over at me for a hint, but I had no clue what insane thoughts had temporarily rewired Devon's brain.

'We're young, we're hot, we have all these deviant secrets. We're all a pint down. Let's go dance or something.' He hooked an arm around her waist and bumped her hip with his. 'C'mon. It kills me to see you so upset. Fuck what we have to go back to. Who knows? Maybe it will wind up being the best year of our whole lives, right? But there's no point worrying. OK?'

She nodded with a damp laugh and we all ran out of the pub and into the twilight. It was too early for any dance clubs, but Devon was a man on a mission. He marched us in and out of pubs, looking for a place with a jukebox or a DJ. What he found was a tiny pub that was already starting to crowd while a few men and women tuned instruments that looked like they came straight from a Tolkien book.

'Is a céilidh touristy or true?' he asked, looking at both of us.

Evan turned her head to the side and closed her eyes as the cacophony of tuning up smoothed into the harmony of five people who would explode with music unless they played. 'It's true. It's true as hell, and we need to dance. Now.'

They'd barely started the sweet strains of the first song before Devon led our little group to the center of the tiny dancefloor. Every single bleary eye in the bar was on him, but Devon danced like he was in the middle of the hottest club in Dublin.

Evan, never one to be outdone, shimmied right over to him, and they both pulled me in. We danced and the music seemed to shimmer around us and then through us. So we responded the only way we knew how: by shaking our butts and throwing our arms in the air, until we were sweaty and gasping for breath and the bar was full with its evening crowd.

'Let's roam, kids!' Devon shouted, high on endorphins and the insanity of our last night together.

We followed him like he was our Pied Piper into the cool night air. Evan nuzzled against my arm as we made our way to another, cooler dance place.

'Are you positive you want to stay in New Jersey, sweetie? I've gone to the beach in November in Georgia. Not to swim, of course, but can't you picture it? You and me, tiny bikinis, all that sun?' She purred against my neck.

I felt my eyes prick with tears. 'I can't even tell you how awesome that sounds. I'm going to miss you so much, Evan. I feel like we just met, and it's already all over.'

'Don't get all emotional on me now. Devon barely saved me back there with that gross-ass tissue I don't even wanna think about.' We both laughed and quickened our steps to keep up with Devon's frantic pace. 'What I was saying before? At the pub? I just want you to know that I never had a friend like you. I know that sounds so stupid, 'cos it's like we just met and all—'

I stopped in the street, in the middle of some shady

section in Dublin I didn't know, and hugged her hard. 'Shut up, right now. It's not stupid. I love you, too.'

She crushed me so tight, the air couldn't claw back into my lungs.

'Is that Joyce?' Devon asked.

Evan and I turned and looked where he pointed. And there he was, head tilted back, cane in his hand, looking up like he was expecting something amazing to open from the sky and inspire a crazy tale or two.

'Do you think he's bird watching?' Evan asked with a sly smile, jumping up on the base of the statue, her arm wrapped around his dark metal waist. '*Croi follain agus gob fliuch*, Prick with a Stick,' she said affectionately, pressing her lips to his molded cheek.

'Speaking Gaelic and insulting Joyce? I feel amazed and scandalized all at once,' Devon said, shaking his head.

Evan hopped down and waved at Joyce. 'I only speak Gaelic as far as blessings and beer go, and I'm just using the Dubliners' own pet name for our favorite author. Also, you must realize you just made me fall in love with you?' She slid her arm through his and kissed his shoulder. 'By the way, it translates to "healthy heart, wet mouth", and I think it's awesome advice. Let's go!'

The rest of the night was a crazed explosion of

dancing madness, and Devon led us all with unbridled, insane enthusiasm. He danced like it was our last night of freedom, our last chance at happiness. Evan clung tight to us all night, and we drank in her flowery smell and her honey-thick laugh.

By the time we trudged back to the dorms, it was closer to morning than night.

'Ugh. You two better get some sleep. I have an essay to write.' Her lavender suede stilettos were hanging on her two fingers, slung over her shoulder.

'Sleep,' Devon snorted, leading the way to my door. 'I can't hand in that stupid essay about the fucking birds and ocean. Ladies?'

I yanked Evan into my room and the three of us set up our laptops and got typing. There wasn't a sound except the steady clack of our fingers on the keys. I glanced up now and then to watch Evan, her eyes flying back and forth across the screen, and Devon, his entire face pinched and absolutely serious.

It felt like my heart, every crazy thump, every joyous jump, had a direct line to my fingers, and every single word that splattered out on the page reflected this burning, desperate feeling, this honesty in me that was completely raw and true.

'Evan?' I whispered after the last, final, agonizing reread.

She looked up, so tired her eyes were slightly crossed, a sleepy, dreamy smile on her lips.

'What's up, sweetie?'

'I wrote the truth. It's so true it's scary.' I licked my lips nervously.

'That's the only way to do it, sweets.' She tapped a finger along the top edge of her laptop. 'And this . . . this is so true, it's burning a hole in my gut just imagining it out there. And I can't decide if it's gibberish or Joyce-inspired.'

'I bet it's Joyce-surpassed.' Devon yawned, smiled, and snapped his laptop shut. 'I sent mine to the drop-box, so say a couple Hail Marys for me. I'll leave you girls to finish. The sun is up, and I bet I can find us some coffee.' He stalked out of the room.

Evan pushed her laptop off her legs, and I crawled over and hugged her tight. 'I wish we had more time together, Bren. Maybe you can come down to Georgia?'

'If I can, you know I will. Same to you. I want you to meet Jake. He would love you, and I know you'd be crazy about him.' I laid my head on her shoulder.

She ducked her head and looked into my eyes, and her smile stretched soft and sweet, like taffy. 'I can tell. You know, my sixth sense is strong with you. I can see so much love in your face when you talk about him. I really hope I get to meet your man. And I hope I can find that kind of love for myself. I'm going home to horrible times. I swear to you, I'm no cry-ass, but I'm feeling teary thinking about it.'

I sat up straight, threw my arms around her shoulders, and shook her back and forth gently. 'You don't know that. You have no idea.' I took her hands in mine, ran my thumbs over the delicate ridges of her knuckles. 'I have a feeling about you. This year, when you think you're going to lose everything? This is going to be the most amazing year for you. You're going to meet the right person. The polar opposite of that fucking douchebag Rabin. You're going to have the most incredibly, awesome, blow-all-the-other-years-away year. Ever. I promise. Epic year.' I put every ounce of my confidence behind my words, praying she believed me.

Tears pooled in her eyes, and this time she waved away my attempt to give her a tissue. 'It's OK. Let it all run off. I just wanna good cry with you.' She leaned hard on my shoulder and I could feel warm tears and goopy mascara run down my arm. She cried and I cried and we both laughed at how ridiculous it all was. 'We're seriously gonna look a hot mess.'

'I don't care.' I wiped my tears away with my fingers and grabbed some napkins I'd stuffed in my purse after our last visit to Evan's favorite coffee place. I rubbed as much of the blackish goop off of her face as I could, but her skin wound up having a weird, undead, gray tinge.

'It's not fair.' She gave a tiny smile and sighed. 'The first people I ever meet who really care about me, and I have to give you guys up after a few weeks. I hate it. Are y'all gonna head home and laugh about the crazy Southern girl who was off her damn rocker?'

'Nope.' I tugged at her hair. 'I'm gonna go home and miss you like crazy.'

We sat that way until Devon brought back coffee so hot it scorched the roofs of our mouths and so strong it propped our eyes open for the rest of the long morning of class, most of which I spent texting back and forth with Evan while Devon ricocheted disapproving looks between the two of us.

When class was dismissed, we had almost no time before our bags had to be loaded onto the transport buses. We climbed on and rode to the airport in a shocked, silent huddle. What would we do without each other? Evan got desperate at the last minute.

'I want to give you something.' She started digging through her purse, but I put my hand on her wrist.

'Stop.' She didn't look up at me. 'I don't need anything to remind me of you. Stop worrying.'

'We should have become blood sisters,' she said, choking around a second set of tears that bubbled up in her throat.

I thought about Jake and Saxon's identical scars from their ceremony so many years before. 'We don't need that, sweetie. You and are connected deeper than blood. And we'll swear an oath over the perfect shoes or a really good bagel, which I'm taking you to my favorite bagel place to get. Because we're going to see each other. Soon.'

The bus pulled up at the airport, and the tour leader announced that Southern Air passengers had to hurry because their flight check in was closing in ten minutes. Evan's lips trembled. 'This isn't enough time,' she pleaded.

'It's *not* goodbye. It's not. OK? I'm not saying it. I love you, though.' I would have been a bawling sack of sad if it wasn't for Evan's frantic look. I had to remain calm for her.

Devon was standing by our seats. 'Evan? I need a hug. And it's OK if you want to kiss me.'

Her laugh was too loud for the somber bus full of tired, anxious students, but that was exactly why we loved it. We collided in a flurry of missed kisses and too tight hugs and awkward attempts to avoid using the words 'goodbye', and then she was gone.

I'd held it all together until I looked out the window and saw her, long hair up in a high ponytail, dragging her bag behind her with one pale hand, her other hand over her eyes, her head bent down. She was crying.

It was like I'd been on an emotional power-cut, and now the power surged on all at once. I collapsed into a sobbing, pissed-off mess, soaking the arm of Devon's shirt while he patted my shoulder a little too hard and told me it would be OK.

Devon managed to scoot me on the plane, helped me tuck my carryon in the overhead, and got my blanket out.

'She'll be all right,' he assured me with a confidence so certain, I was positive it was an act.

'I know,' I warbled, trying to remember the sweet floral smell of Evan that was already wearing dim in my memory.

'We should sleep. We'll be home soon . . .'

I think he said that. Or maybe not. The next thing I knew, he was shaking my shoulder because we had landed. We were home.

It all felt so surreal. We were back home. I could see my parents again. Soon I might be able to see Jake!

I was anxious to talk to him without the time difference. I wanted to tell him the details about my time with Evan that I couldn't get into when she was folding all my notebook paper into origami chickens or trying on my shoes, hoping one of the nines would magically turn eight.

I'd been so completely happy with her and Devon that I'd been able to blanket some of my homesickness for Jake, but now that we were back in the States, it came back with a delicious, anticipatory edge.

Plus, even though Jake and I had talked when we could, I had a feeling there was a lot about his stay with his family that he wasn't being open about. I knew he was probably going through a ton of new feelings and experiences all at once, exactly the way I had, so I tried to be patient with him, but I was beyond ready to be close again.

I was ready to see him, but I also forced myself to acknowledge that it might be a while before we were together again.

So, it was a complete, wonderful shock when I got off the plane and there he was! He was standing by my mother, who looked particularly glowing, and though a piece of me was happy about the little portrait, something about it also raised a red flag of suspicion. I gave Devon a quick hug and kiss, and we promised to call soon, then he rushed to his parents and brother, and I ran to Jake and Mom.

'Mom! Jake!' I called.

Mom was the one who rushed to meet me, and I got crushed in her hug and breathed in her good, flowery-sweet, mom smell. While we were hugging and squealing, I looked over her shoulder at Jake. He was definitely smiling, but it was kind of a subdued smile, like he was happy to see me, but weighed down by something else, something that was heavy on his mind.

'Jake and I thought we'd surprise you!' Mom gushed. 'And we have one even bigger surprise for you. Why don't you tell her, Jake?'

Whoa. This was super weird, beyond any explainable general weirdness. Mom looked so happy, Jake looked so contested, and Mom was giving him the chance to explain.

'My grandmother,' Jake said carefully, as if he were reciting a speech, 'really wants to meet your mother. Her house is huge. And she sent me to pick you two up so you could visit for a while. Now.' Jake's eyes were so bright they looked like newly minted nickels, but I couldn't read what was making them that intense. Was he happy about this whole thing? Did he like the idea?

I kind of hoped he did. It sounded great to me. A few weeks at his grandmother's famous mansion on the lake? My mother flushed and happy? Jake and I able to relax: no Zinga's, no Saxon, no Atlantic Ocean between us. It sounded a lot like heaven. So why did Jake look like he was about to be sucked into the fiery pit of his own personal hell?

'Thorsten? Won't he miss us while we're gone?' I

asked, speaking to Mom, but looking at Jake from the corner of my eye.

'Oh, honey! He's gone to work a documentary series on the West Coast for a few weeks. I was sure I told you when we talked. Anyway, he was glad to hear we'd have some place to go while he's away.'

Mom released her iron hold on me, said something about grabbing bottled waters for the ride, and left me and Jake alone.

I bit my lip and held my breath as he stepped closer, then crushed me hard in his arms. I rubbed my face against his chest, wrapped my arms tight around him and took long, deep breaths, filling up on his smell. I felt like I couldn't smell him and hold him and be near him enough.

Then we were kissing, frantic and hungry, one eye opened to check for my mother's return. It was only after I had temporarily sated myself physically – as much as I could with respect to the crowds and my overbearing parent – that I ventured to ask Jake what was bothering him.

'It's just been . . . weird. At my grandmother's house. With my, um, family.' Jake shrugged. 'It's like, you know those pathetic shows about rich teenagers being crazy?'

'Yeah.' I threaded my fingers through his and wrapped our hands together, thrilling at the rough brush of his palm like it was the first time I'd felt his hand in mine all over again.

'It's like they all feel they're on one of those shows. Lots and lots of drama. At first I kept wishing you could be there.' He took his cap off and pulled it back on, extra low over his eyes.

Some of the good, new, happy shine of seeing him again washed away. 'At first? Like now you wish I wasn't coming?' I bristled a little.

'That's pretty much it.' Jake clenched his jaw, and the muscles went tight right down to his neck. 'Remember how I told you that I wouldn't change?'

'Yes.' The word came out on a breath, because I was still reeling from the fact that one of the first things he'd uttered to my face in weeks was the fact that he didn't really want me around.

'Well, I don't really think I kept that promise, and I hate that. I really hate it, Bren.' He pulled his hand away from mine, crossed his arms over his chest, and scowled.

'Can you talk to me about it?' I clenched my hands together, trying hard to keep my cool. Trying really hard.

He opened his mouth, then twisted it into a wry smile. 'Hey, Mrs Blixen. All ready?'

'Brenna, do you need to use the bathroom or anything?' Mom put a hand on my shoulder.

113

'No. I mean, it's only an hour and a half to home, right?'

'Oh, baby, I thought we'd go straight to Mama D's!' my mother said. In response to my blank look she explained. 'Mama D is what Jake's grandmother likes to be called. And I thought that since you were already all packed, we could just go right there. That will cut an entire hour off the drive.'

'My clothes are dirty,' I said lamely. *And my boyfriend doesn't want me around.*

Mom rolled her eyes. 'I'm sure you'll have a chance to do your laundry there, Brenna! Now come on! This is exciting, isn't it?'

'Yes.' Jake's voice was sober, and his gray eyes went completely flat.

I smiled wide for Mom's sake. 'Yes! It is, Mom.' I grinned at her, then I raised my eyebrows slightly at Jake in an attempt to encourage him to fake more happiness than he felt.

It didn't seem to work. Jake just looked kind of defeated. It was hard to see him look so upset, but not be able to really ask him about it. Mom chatted happily the entire way to 'Mama D's' house, and Jake and I sat a few inches from each other on the bench seat of a truck; not his truck, but one I assumed he had borrowed from a relative at his grandmother's place. We were so close to each other I was almost sitting right on his lap, but we couldn't say a single word that meant anything.

Finally we pulled onto a long, twisting driveway. Jake had rolled the windows down, and there was the thick, spicy smell of pine trees on either side of us. The air was cool and pleasant. We drove through this tree tunnel for a long time, then finally popped out in a clearer place.

There was a huge, shimmering lake, and, dotting the surrounding sand, four of the biggest houses I had ever seen.

'Wow.' I craned my neck to try to look at everything as we passed. 'Your dad's family is seriously rich!'

He nodded, eyes on the windshield, hands fisted around the steering wheel. 'Yeah.'

I tried to ignore Jake's dour mood. Mom and I squeezed each other's hands and giggled. If I managed to ignore Jake's crappy attitude, this was like a dream vacation! The lake, the forest, the massive, old houses . . . it all reminded me of Evan's stories about long weeks at her family's colossal beach house, nestled on a private stretch of beach in Georgia. This was a kind of luxury I'd heard about, but had never seen firsthand.

'Look at all of the character in this architecture. And no one in the country has a private early-American folk collection that can hold a candle to Mama D's.'

My mom sighed. I should have realized that her happiness had something to do with paintings. It usually did.

We got out of the truck, and Jake gently tugged my mother's bags from her hands. He led us to the door of the huge brick mansion sullenly, like he was an executioner leading us to the gallows.

I wanted to know what was wrong, why he felt so dejected, why he wanted to keep me away, but there was no time at all to ask.

Jake walked into the huge foyer, and said, 'If you don't mind waiting, I'll ask which rooms you're in.'

Mom was exclaiming about how the chandelier was done by the man who designed all the crystal in the Vanderbilt house and how the rugs were definitely Aubusson, wasn't it obvious? When Jake came back down the stairs, he was followed by a lady with silver hair and his pretty gray eyes.

'Welcome! Suzanne, welcome! Brenna, we've been waiting to meet you. Jake talks about you incessantly.' She had the kind of stiff manners that were also supposed to be fun and cute, and I smiled while Mom gushed in response.

The Jake comment made me a little nervous, and I glanced at my mom to gauge her reaction. I knew my mother tended to think Jake and I were too wrapped up in each other, but apparently, those words from the mouth of Mama D were completely fine. Mom even beamed a little.

It was all weirdly offset by Jake's silence. It was almost sullenness, and it was so unlike him I just couldn't make any sense out of it at all. I knew he was unhappy about things, but Jake was a roll-with-the-punches kind of guy. He didn't usually let things get him so down.

Mama D led Mom away to her room, and Jake took my hand and practically dragged me to mine. When we got to the big, cheerful guest room (with my own bathroom!), Jake closed the door, dropped my bags and wrapped his arms around me and just held me, still and tight. My heart thumped like a puppy's tail, all new, exuberant excitement. Jake, my Jake, was right here, right in front of me, and I just wanted to sink into his embrace and never let go.

Like an eruption, our hands were suddenly everywhere, our faces brushed, and I tilted my head toward his so we could fall into sweet, melting kisses that burst into something harder and faster with every sweep of our lips. He was moving fast, his mouth hard and sweet as a peppermint candy, and he walked me backward to the bed, our mouths still attached.

I knew Mom was somewhere, maybe right next door, and his grandmother or anyone else could walk in at any second, but the intoxication of the weight of his body over mine more than outweighed any fear of getting caught.

There was this whole frantic rush of actions ebbing and fighting for dominance. I sighed into his open mouth, nipped at his bottom lip, tugged at his T-shirt, moaned at the soft suck of my bottom lip into his mouth. His hands pressed up under my hair like he had a direct line to my brain and knew exactly what would turn my body into a warm, swirling whirlpool of drowning need.

Jake's mouth opened and pressured mine to do the same. I parted my lips and tasted him, pressed into him when he ran his hands over me because it felt like all the stress and sadness I'd bottled over the last few weeks got ripped off, like pulling the husks off summer corn. Whatever he couldn't tell me with his words, he was sending a message loud and clear with the frenzied, sweet press of his body: he had missed me just as much as I'd missed him. That was a relief. I could work through whatever was wrong with him as long as I was sure it didn't have to do with us.

Like us ending.

We were lying on the bed, his body nicely heavy on mine, and I squirmed under him so we met at every logical locking place. He was breathing hard, his forehead pressed to mine.

'What's wrong, Jake?' I moved my fingers along the

curve of his ear and the nape of his neck, then back up into his hair.

He shook his head and smiled, his crooked eyetooth deliciously familiar, and I popped a quick kiss on it. 'Nothing. Not now. Not with you here.'

I moved my hand down between his shoulder blades, where his back was bunched with muscles. That was one of my favorite parts of him, one of the parts of his body that made my breath hitch in my throat every time I saw him. I never would have imagined the few inches between someone's shoulder blades would have made me feel so much, but there it was.

I looked at his face, his gray eyes darting to avoid my gaze, his mouth too flat and twisted down. I knew Jake enough to know something was wrong, and I wanted to know how to unravel this knot of a problem. 'You don't seem like yourself,' I said softly, coaxing him to tell me.

'I haven't been.' He blew out a long, labored breath and shrugged, then closed his eyes. I pulled the very tip of my finger along the impossibly smooth line of his eyelashes, back and forth in a touch so light it barely connected. 'There's a lot I want to tell you, but I couldn't while you were away. And now it's really hard to start.'

'Start wherever you want.' I kissed his chin, first in

the exact center, then right and left, and back to the middle. 'Tell me.'

He opened his mouth, and there was a knock at the door. He sprang off me and I jumped completely off the bed and scurried over to the other side of the room, where I tried to look busy by nervously unzipping my suitcase.

Jake growled a little, then moved to open the door. I was expecting my mom or his grandmother or father, but there was a girl there instead. One I knew, though I couldn't place her for a minute.

Then it hit me. Paris.

'Hi, Caroline.' I blushed, feeling the stupid embarrassment of meeting a casual witness of my past idiocy. The last time she and I were in the same room, I was welcoming in the New Year by making out with Saxon and slow dancing with him for hours. My entire face flushed hot just remembering it.

'Oh, hey, Brenda.' She smiled just meanly enough to let me know her slip-up wasn't unintentional.

I felt instantly exhausted, and missed Evan with an ache that swelled and pierced from my guts up into my throat. I wanted to channel my crazy, brave friend. Evan would have jumped inbetween me and this girl and eaten her like an hors d'oeuvre, without one backward glance.

'It's *Brenna*.' Jake leaped to my immediate defense,

his voice already impatiently annoyed. 'What do you want, Caroline?'

She came in and sat on my bed, which was a really aggressive move, but I had no idea how to deal with it. This wasn't technically my house or my room. Was I supposed to throw her out? Make a snide comment? Act cool about it? I had no idea what to do. I closed my eyes and tried to channel Evan, but I could only imagine her picking Caroline up by her glossy, highlighted hair. Thinking about Evan's sometimes-militant insanity made me smile, but it wasn't my style at all.

'I was just coming to ask if you and her—' she began. 'Brenna,' Jake gritted through his teeth.

Her smile was sharp and as dangerously sweet as a jagged piece of rock candy stuck in your throat. 'Sorry . . . if you and Brenna would like to come to the beach for a bonfire tonight. I promise I won't make you get naked this time, and I won't be so stupid like last time. As nice as it was to have you as my hero.' Her giggle was as precise a weapon as a throwing knife, and I could see a light in her pretty eyes when she realized that I was a clueless, punctured target.

She'd hit her bull's-eye.

Jake naked? Jake a hero? What the hell was going on?

Fury shook Jake's shoulders, made his large hands

into knotty fists at his sides, pulled at his lips so his teeth were bared. I had never seen his eyes glow with such pure hate. Never. 'Get the hell out, Caroline.' He tore each word off at the end with a ferocity that gave me goosebumps.

Her shrug rose and fell in a cute bob that barely disguised her total, buoyant happiness. 'Well, the invitation is open, Jake. Oh. And Brenna, of course,' she sang out with sarcastic cheer so mean it stung like a hard slap.

She left and the air in the room crackled and snapped like a summer thunderstorm was rolling in. The fury that had made Jake so rigid and upset melted away, and all I could see were his eyes, unblinking and begging me to forgive . . . what? I backed away, suddenly fresh out of breath and wishing I could rewind back to Ireland where things were simple, my boyfriend couldn't wait to see me, and he didn't have some terrible secret to confess.

He shadowed me footstep for footstep, only stopping when I'd been cornered against a side table. He was so close I could feel his heart whirring hard and fast like an engine about to overheat. His hands, usually so still and calm, shook, and there was a big knot on one side of his jaw because he was clenching his teeth so hard, I was sure he'd crack a few.

'What did she mean?' I lifted my hand to his face

and touched the bulge on the side of his jaw. He unclenched his teeth and let out a shuddery breath, then turned his lips to my palm and pressed them to my skin in a long, sorry kiss.

He hung his head, closed his eyes, and said, 'Sit down. There's some stuff I want to tell you,' while chills crept up and down my spine.

Saxon 2

I woke up and groaned because I felt like an old, crippled man. Work was turning me into a chiseled god, but, damn, my muscles ached every morning. And night. And all the time inbetween. I'd been pretty in-shape before, but now I was completely cut from lifting thousand-pound bus-pans all day at the diner, and that was after I worked myself into a fucking frenzy doing the million things that needed to be done to Aunt Helene's house just to make it liveable.

Fuck my relatives for leaving her in this dump. I had painted her exterior, weeded and planted enough to start a damn hippie commune garden, fixed her steps and porch, painted every room – the kitchen three fucking times because yellow is a little bitch and it never looked a thing like the damn sample once I got it up on the wall – retiled the kitchen and bathroom floors, and was starting in on the basement, which was a dump. And she had to go down there to do her laundry – and mine, since I didn't know how to use a washing machine.

But my aunt Helene was a goddamn saint and could cook like you wouldn't believe. It kept me from my natural inclination, which was to bitch about my shitty lot in life and whine about all of the work I did. There was no need for my usual little hissy fits. Aunt Helene really thought I was a godsend, which was about as ironic as shit can get. I mean, I was sent to her for having such an assload of coke in the house that even my dipshit drug-tolerant mother freaked.

Anyway, we got along perfectly. She was really happy and liked having me there. That was a nice change from the way things usually went when I was living with someone.

Work at the diner was a little less clear-cut. I had to mentally rewind a little bit, to where the real scariness began. The Erikson siblings weren't bullshitting about their mom.

Rosalie Erikson clocked in at maybe five foot two inches and a hundred and ten pounds. She had long black hair and big doe eyes and looked in no way like she could be the mother of a kid old enough to be in high school, with her little curvy, pert figure that absolutely answered the question of where Cadence got that body from. The three Erikson kids I met were actually three of four. The last was baby Sullivan, always on Rosalie's hip. It made her angry to have to come into work and expose Sullie to hot oil and death metal and idiot workers (her words, more or less). So anytime she busted in, this woman, who might usually be just your average scary bitch, was a raging, blood-thirsty creature of the underworld. Accessorized with the world's cutest little kid.

My one and only saving grace was Sullie's decision that I was cool enough to hang with, and I have to thank whatever deity is up there for that little piece of good luck. The first day Rosalie came in there was fire shooting out of her eyes. It was directed at Brian, the half-witted burger flipper. She came in the double doors, her hair flying around from the anti-fly blower at the door. Everything went silent except for the screaming from the stereo.

Waitresses made themselves scarce, cooks were suddenly totally intrigued by the bubbling oils and vats of relish, and big ol' Sir Erikson himself almost came into the kitchen, caught sight of his woman on a mission, and high-tailed it back to the safety of his office.

'I need to speak to you,' Rosalie hissed, pointing a finger at Brian.

Sullie toddled over to the sink. 'Hi.' He looked at me with huge, brown baby eyes.

'Hey, little man.' I smiled at him.

'Water,' he said clearly, and pointed at the sprayer that gets the crusted-on shit off of pans and utensils.

'Yeah.' I crouched down next to him. 'Smart kid. You want to spray it?'

'Yes.' He gave me a long, quiet look.

I didn't know a lot about kids and how to determine how old they might be. Sullie was little enough that his mom carried him on her hip. He drank a bottle sometimes. He could walk and say a few things. He looked like a baby to me. Anyway, he was no dummy.

I got a crate for him, pulled the water thing down, lined up some metal containers for him to squirt, and he went to town, giggling and screeching while his mother made some noise of her own.

I came in late after hooking Sullie up, but what I heard was bad enough.

'. . . then I hear that you call me "*punta*" behind my back, you little prick? You think you're so hot, you say that word to my face! After my family gives you a good job, a good salary, hires your brother, that's what I have to hear my innocent children repeat that they heard? What do you have to say for yourself? Don't cry now, you little shit. I'm the one who should be crying! All the good I do for you, and that's what you think is appropriate?'

It was fascinating. He really was crying. Poor

douchebag. It was probably one of those passing remarks he made when he was pissed. Oh well, that shit did not fly here, and we got warned all the time. You did not talk about the owners or their kids unless you wanted your ass spanked in front of the whole kitchen.

Brian was apologizing, and Rosalie was accepting as if it were beneath her to even consider doing it. Then it was over, and she realized Sullie wasn't at her feet.

The look of terror on her face made me fear for my life a little. I was the one with the kid.

Maybe she didn't want him mucking in the sink. I waved a little, and she saw me and raced over. 'Thank you,' she said stiffly, sweeping Sullie up. He was still laughing and kissed her. 'Water!' he told her.

'I see that, Sullie boy.' She smiled at him. Holy shit, she was gorgeous when she smiled. Was this woman really the demon who had Brian pulling his ball cap low over his eyes so we couldn't see the residual tears?

'Thanks, Saxon.' She pursed her lips and looked me up and down, assessing my worth. 'Listen, we're going to be short a waiter on Saturday. I hate to throw you in on such a busy shift, but the kids say you're smart and hardworking. And you're pretty cute. You'll get plenty of tips. Cadence will set you up with your gear before you leave tonight.'

'Yes, ma'am.'

She smiled at me regally, then gave Brian a final glare before she headed to the back office to see Tony.

So she thought I was cute? I grinned. Moms usually loved me. I was cougar bait, and I knew it. But my smile was gone pretty fast when I thought about meeting up with Cadence. That wasn't exactly something I was looking forward to.

Cadence had presented a semi-unique problem in the few weeks I'd been confined in diner hell. So she was beautiful. Big deal. I'd slept with girls just as pretty, if not prettier, more times than I could count. I'd been with smarter, more athletic, more stylish, sweeter, more dangerous, bitchier – you name the type or subtype and I'd been with her.

So what was it about Cadence that had me all shook up?

At first I thought that my recent infatuation run was just something I was going to get through and get over. Because I had been a little crazy about Brenna. But that was different.

Brenna had been pretty much instantly unattainable, and somewhere in my subconscious, I had always known that she was in love with Jake. That didn't mean she wasn't attracted to me, too. But I knew attraction; it fizzled. Once Brenna'd had some concentrated one-on-one time, she'd realized that I was basically an asshole and had gone running back to Jake. Where she'd always belonged in the first place.

I kind of wish I hadn't screwed things up with Jake, because I had some serious shit to ask him. Like what it felt like when he saw Brenna, when he hung out with her, and when he couldn't be around her. I wanted to ask him what he felt when he thought they might not be together any more.

Because Jake had fallen in love with Brenna.

Not that I was close to love for Cadence! Good Lord, I wasn't a total and complete masochistic moron. This was just more than lust. Less than love. More than like.

I had no fucking idea what it was.

Which was doubly pathetic when you considered the fact that we had never had one real conversation, never exchanged two words that were better than barely civil, never touched, and never hung out. I knew I sounded like a wanker when I explained it, but it was what I felt. Whether I liked it or not. And I really, really didn't like it.

So I felt like a pretty intense fool when I found myself getting excited about the prospect of working with her. And maybe being a waiter wouldn't suck too much.

I could sense her when she finally came to see me, later that night. She walked up to the sink where I was still spraying chunks of chilli sauce off metal spoons.

'Hey, Crackhead.' She popped one hip against the gleaming, damp side of the sink and crossed her arms tight over her chest. 'Mom told me I have to show you the ropes tonight so you don't screw up tomorrow.' Her voice told me with no doubt that the whole idea pissed her off royally. 'You need to come with me. Will can finish your dishes.' She snapped at Will and he ran over all eager, as if she'd just called him over like a dog.

She told him what to do like she owned the place . . . oh, wait, she did. When she was satisfied with the dishwasher stuff, she led me to the basement.

'What do we need down here?' I stuck my hands in my pockets and followed her down the steep staircase.

'You're not going to be a back-dweller any more.' Her black ponytail swished as she took the stairs two at a time. 'You need a uniform. And, obviously, you need your skates.'

I stopped suddenly, knowing damn well what she had said, but willing myself to imagine that her voice was full of humor. Haha. Big joke.

She glared back up at me, her eyes slits. 'What the hell are you waiting for? I still have a shitload of cleaning to do. Stop stalling, Crackhead.' Then she muttered to herself in what sounded like Spanish. And I only know that because I'm fairly multilingual, if you only count obscenities.

'I can't do that.' I popped my hands up and shook my head ready to stand my ass right in front of those shitty, sweltering sinks for another long jump of shifts. 'Be on roller skates,' I clarified, barely able to say the words.

Roller skates! She couldn't be serious. I had put a lot of my pride into the can when I took this piece-of-shit job, but I wasn't about to be a buffoon on skates for the entire world to take shots at. I had some small shred of self-respect left, and I wanted to keep it intact.

'If you need me to, I'll show you how to skate. Jesus, don't they have roller-skating down on the farm? I mean, they have cocaine.' Her green eyes crackled.

What did I like about her so much? It wasn't just that she was pretty or smart or sure of herself. It was like I was fascinated by her. I wanted to know more about her. And it was definitely beyond my control. Because if I could have turned it off, I would have, in a second. Who would want to deal with this constant ridicule and never-ending shitty mood? I could talk myself out of obsessing over her with logic so firm it would have convinced anyone but a total idiot.

Call me a total idiot.

'Yeah, we have hard drugs and skating rinks.' My voice was more pissed off than I wanted to let on. 'I *can* skate. Like if you held a gun to my head and said I had to skate or get my brains blown out, then technically, yes I can skate.' I glared back at her.

She stomped back up the stairs, until she was just one below me, and she jabbed her finger at my chest. 'Well, there is a gun at your head, asshole. It's called "keeping this restaurant from tanking". Every weekend we don't meet our mortgage goal, my mother and father get this much closer to bankruptcy.' She held her finger and thumb and inch apart. 'And if we go down, your family's precious cash cow is gone. Is that a scary enough gun, rich boy?'

And I wanted to shake her up, even though what she just told me made me realize that part of her crappy personality was probably due to the strain of knowing her parents' investment could take a nosedive depending on the whims of its teenage workforce. But sympathy had never been my strong suit, and my lack of caring didn't fail me this time either.

'Did it ever occur to you, Cadence, that my family has more money than Oprah could fucking dream of? This restaurant is so meaningless it took them almost a week to remember that we had it so they could send me here to rot. If this place goes down, *your* family is the only one on a sinking ship.' I kept my voice even and cold, not letting her see how riled I was.

She kept her chin jutted up and out, but I saw her

bottom lip wobble and she blinked fast. Then she was down the stairs, lost in the maze of shelves and boxes that clogged the basement floor.

I'd made her cry.

And I immediately felt like a huge, gaping asshole.

I ran down the rest of the stairs calling her name, hoping that she would punch me in the face or kick me in the balls when I found her. Otherwise, I wasn't really sure how to handle the situation.

I weaved in and out of boxes listening to the wet, choking sounds that were spilling out of her throat. When I found her, she was sitting on the floor, her knees drawn up, her arms resting on them, her forehead against her arms. She was a tight little ball of misery, and even though I knew I hadn't made the misery, I had unleashed it just by being myself.

Typical.

'Do you want to take a swing?' I asked the little huddled ball of Cadence. 'I deserve it. C'mon. Hit me.'

'You're not worth it, Crackhead,' she croaked, not looking up. Then she hiccupped.

I knelt down in front of her, my hands reaching out but not actually touching her. I was fairly sure she would be pissed off to have me touch her. 'What I said is true. But I was a jerk-off for saying it.'

She looked up then, her eyes red and puffy and said

exactly what I would have predicted she would say. 'Fuck you, Saxon.'

I had thought that when she started using my name instead of just calling me 'Crackhead', it would be a good thing, but I had been overly optimistic.

'What I said . . .' I began, but she didn't even look up at me. 'What I said, I said to get a reaction out of you, OK?'

Now she looked up. Her mascara was ringed under her eyes in black half moons and her lips looked pale and dry. 'But it's true. Don't feel like you told me something I didn't already know. Good God, Saxon, I'm not a moron. This place,' she looked around wearily, 'was my parents' dream. Their stupid, stupid dream. And we're stuck here. Pammy and Jimmy and even Sullie. And me.'

'You're what? A junior? College will be here in no time,' I said, grasping at straws.

Her eyes were so green they looked like sea glass: cold, angry sea glass.

'Have you been listening, half-wit?' she snapped. 'They hardly make the mortgage every month. Where the hell are they going to pull money for college? I'll be lucky if I get enough time away from this shithole to get to community college classes.' Little wispy pieces of her hair were stuck all over her forehead and cheeks. She looked really young, suddenly.

'Don't give up on it yet.' I knelt right next to her. 'Teach me how to skate. I promise you, I'll bring business in.'

She snorted. 'How?'

'Because I'm so fucking fine,' I said, and it felt so good when she smiled a tiny, insignificant smile that it made my chest ache a little. 'And I'm fast as hell. And if I put a fraction of my rotten brain into it, I'll be the best waiter your parents have ever seen.'

'It's a shit job,' she said quietly.

I reached out and made a move to put my hand to her face, but I was watching to see if she was going to flinch or give me that deserved right jab. She bit her bottom lip and closed her eyes. I pushed her hair out of her eyes and cupped my hand under her pointy little chin. Her skin was unbelievably soft and warm. She nestled her face on my palm for a minute.

'I've had shittier.' It broke the spell.

She pulled away from my hand, and I could still feel the residual heat from her cheek on the skin of my palm and up along my thumb.

'All right.' She nodded. 'I guess we should do it, then.'

She got up and pressed her fingers hard under her still-watering eyes, wiping away the leftover mascara. She went through some boxes and fished out a few white T-shirts and black pants, then found three pairs of skates, black with red wheels.

They were the old-fashioned, four-wheeled kind. I had skated on them before, but way back when I was a kid. Even roller blades and hockey skates were about five years in my past.

'You need to try them on,' she said. 'Everyone likes a different fit. And it's not as easy as matching shoe size.'

I put them all on and watched her while I laced up. Some of the enormous wall she had put up was slowly crumbling.

I wanted to see her smile.

I wanted to see her naked.

I looked at her and grinned, and I got my first wish. She obviously had no idea what perverted things I was thinking.

'I think these are the ones.' I moved my ankles back and forth, hoping I chose a good size. I unlaced them and stuffed my feet back in my sneakers. 'Mind if I go around the parking lot a few times before I become your private clown tomorrow?'

She nodded, bit her lip cutely, and tossed me that unbelievably sexy smile. We walked up the stairs, our hands just barely brushing.

By the time we were upstairs, the restaurant was fairly deserted. It was late on a Friday night, and everyone had somewhere to be. Except one juvenile delinquent and the kids of two harried restaurant owners. Pamela and Jimmy leaned against the Jetta, waiting patiently. Pamela on her cell, as usual. When I sat to put my skates on, Jimmy laughed.

'Oh, man, that sucks. Did my mom make you?' He was almost shaky with lanky excitement.

'Kind of.' I tied the laces tight, stood up, and moved forward awkwardly. Pamela ended her phone conversation and hooted.

'Now try it with a tray of food and drinks,' she taunted good-naturedly.

I clomped around the parking lot a little, once in a while glancing down at the unforgiving cement that would be my unquestioned fate if I couldn't keep on my feet.

Or wheels. Whatever.

I started to go faster, and as soon as I got a sense of my balance, I was racing and it felt good. Soccer season seemed like it had been a hundred years ago, and I hadn't been on a dirt bike in months. This was as close to flying as I'd come, at least physically, in a long time.

Jimmy and Pamela cheered and encouraged me to do stupid shit in a way that's probably the copyright of idiot teenagers. I closed in on a cement barricade, put my feet together, and propelled myself over it. Even Cadence cheered at that one.

'More! More!' Jimmy chanted.

The bright white parking-lot lights flooded the cement circle with dizzying blue-white brilliance, and the hot air leftover from the long summer day sizzled off the tarmac and was pushed away by the cool air of the late night. It was just me and the Eriksons and the moths, hanging out in the lonely, nearly empty parking lot of their parents' place.

I skated fast and hard toward a planter that was at least three feet high and jumped it with the worried screams of Pamela and Cadence and the crowing encouragement of Jimmy in my ears. I sailed over, landed fine, but couldn't stop my own momentum, and wound up slamming into the side of the building.

'Stop!' Cadence laughed. 'Stop! You're going to break your leg, and then who will I force to work with me tomorrow?'

I rubbed my shoulder and shook my head. 'You're a cold-hearted snake, Cadence,' I said and unlaced the skates. I put them in the little booth that was no-man's-land, the skaters' hovel, the little piece of random turf between the interior of the restaurant and the screeching cars and chaos of the customers outside. Then I slid inside Pamela's car, stuffing my feet into my shoes as I went.

Cadence didn't plaster herself to her door on this particular night. She didn't curl into my lap like I would have liked either, but it was nice that she was giving me the benefit of some of her company. She put her hand down on the portion of the seat that was technically between us, but if you were a calculating bastard like myself, you would have noticed that her fingertips were just a quarter of an inch closer to my side than to hers.

I tilted my body toward the middle, and she leaned over too. We made a strange double pyramid, inches from touching at the crowns of our heads and growing apart slightly with every inch downward, then closer again at our legs and feet. When she looked up at me, there was something in her eyes that hadn't been there before. Maybe it was friendship. Hell, I would take that happily this time around.

I abandoned any hope of getting her into my bed. I abandoned any hope of seducing her in other ways. For once, I knew that I could do with her what I'd never quite had the guts to do with Brenna.

I could fall for her more than just a little, and pull her into falling for me. And if it all worked without a hitch, we would fall right into each other's arms and mean something.

At that point, in Pamela's backseat, it was just a promise of things that might come and nothing more. But I was willing to bank on that promise. When Pamela pulled up at Aunt Helene's house, I swear I saw a glint of regret in Cadence's eyes. Whether or not we were going to admit it, we were pulling together.

'I'll see you tomorrow.' I slammed my door and looked back in through the open window.

Cadence pulled at her hair, smoothing it over and over in her hands, then nodded. 'Tomorrow, Saxon,' she added.

That was the way I had imagined my name sounding on her lips.

I gave a short wave and walked up the stairs to the food I knew would be warming for me in the oven. God bless my fucking saint of an aunt.

The next morning, I put new shelving in Aunt Helene's linen closet. Whoever had done it the first time must have been on meth. I should know, considering the number of tweakers I'd been around in my short career as a dealer.

It was strangely comforting to go through the motions: cut the shelf, cover it in the smelly flower paper Aunt Helene gave me, measure the brackets, drill the holes, set the shelves up, fold the linens and put them back onto them.

The house was starting to look a hell of a lot better. It had been my idea to paint the mismatched chairs in the dining room one color.

OK, technically it was Cassidy Adams's idea. She

was the dipshit host of some home and garden television show Aunt Helene loved, and I watched it with her. It seemed weird to me to love something like home and garden TV when you lived in a craphole. It was like watching a Food Network show with some fancy-ass chef and eating McDonald's. But when Aunt Helene saw something she liked, I got my shit together and we did it – like the dining-room chairs.

Then we'd got to painting the walls. Then the molding – all set up in fancy rectangles with corners that took me a few hellish hours to get right. Then the chandelier that I almost electrocuted myself putting up. We'd found an old piece-of-shit buffet thing that I stripped down and refinished and put new wallpaper inserts in where the doors were recessed (another Cassidy Adams idea). One day, when I was done hanging up old photos of her parents that I had scanned, enlarged and framed, Aunt Helene had cried.

'What's the matter?' I'd asked, panicked. I'd put the drill on the table and put my arms around her. She was so small, it was like holding a rag doll. Not that I'd held many in my life. 'Do you hate it? The resolution is kind of shitty, but I thought they looked pretty good.'

'No.' She'd shaken her head hard. 'How can you think I hate it? I love . . . I love . . .' She'd flapped her arms up and down, like she had no words for what she loved.

'Well, you just tell me what you like and we'll do it, OK?' I'd kissed her forehead. She'd patted my back, squeezed the skin at my hips, then pulled down my face to her level and kissed my cheeks.

Living with Aunt Helene had changed a lot of what I thought were truths about me and life. For example, I had always thought of myself as a lazy fuck with no motivation. A few weeks ago, if someone had told me that I would tackle a few dozen home improvement projects in addition to having a full-time job this summer, I would have laughed my ass off.

I'd never imagined that it would feel so good to have someone leave me a plate of pork chops and cabbage in the oven. I'd never thought I'd start getting to bed at a normal time and waking up in the morning ready to do something other than snort a line of coke and jerk around.

And, most of all, I'd never imagined that it would all feel so fucking good. That I would actually prefer a life of mundane, blue-collar work in a falling-down house with an ancient aunt and a group of crazy coworkers to my privileged existence as a lonely pampered fucking prince in a cold-ass mansion.

I got ready for work while Aunt Helene fried up some more of her incredible cookies. When I was ready, she handed me a wax paper bag, splotchy with delicious, buttery oil, and I kissed her cheek and headed out to Pamela's car.

'Cookies, compliments of Aunt Helene.' I tossed the bag to Jimmy who cheered, stuffed his face, and passed the cookies around.

Cadence sat stiffly in her seat, pressing down on the pleats of her skirt.

'Hey.' She didn't even glance at me.

'Hey,' I answered. 'So, are you ready for a laugh fest?'

She smiled a tiny, tiny smile. 'You have to try,' she said earnestly. 'Today is going to be crazy. I . . . I tried to talk Mom into getting someone else to do it. I think you're too new. But she said you were here to work. And she said she has a feeling about you.'

'Then listen to her,' Pamela interrupted.

Cadence and I both looked up, surprised. It was a tiny ass car, for God's sake. It wasn't like any of us imagined that anything we said was truly private. We were all always eavesdropping. We just had the good tact not to interfere where we weren't wanted.

'She's smart,' Pamela continued. 'And she knows things. You know what I mean.'

Jimmy, Cadence and Pamela all nodded, and I felt a little creeped out. What exactly had Rosalie said about me? Because, apparently, what she said was pretty much gospel. But before I had too much time to freak myself out, we were at the diner, piling out of the car. For a minute, we stood outside in the hot, promising Jersey sun, willing the work night to be over already. But we couldn't kid ourselves. We had to go through with this, so we might as well not fuck around about it.

Pamela and Jimmy headed inside. She was an indoor waitress and he was a fountain boy, one of the kids who filled drinks for the outside waiters and waitresses. It was too risky to come in and out of the restaurant on skates, so there was this little alcove right by the kitchen and soda fountain with a window. When you worked outside, you stuck your head through the window and sent your order tickets in and got drinks set up for you. Then you took the drinks out to the waiting cars and went back to pick up the food orders. Same as a regular waiting job. Except you were on skates.

'So, um, how do you want to split it?' Cadence asked. Three cars had just pulled up.

'We can do, like assigned spaces or we can alternate.'

'How do you like to do it?' I asked, adding enough sexual suggestion to my voice to give her the assurance that I meant more than I was saying.

She looked alarmed. 'Stop it, Saxon,' she said firmly. 'This is work, OK? I take it seriously. No more bullshit.' Before I could reply, she flicked a gaze at the cars. 'You work all even numbered spots, I'll work the odds. And we'll take turns skating the circuit in case people pull in across the lot.'

'OK.' The diner was designed in a huge circle, so you could potentially have two cars parked on opposite sides of the circle and not notice one at all. And since customers at any eatery are ninety percent tools, it usually worked out exactly that way, according to Cadence.

I skated to my first car. Two older guys.

'Can't we pick our server?' one griped.

They were liver-spot-speckled old fucks who finally had the money to drive the car the guys who used to beat them up in high school drove. And they were leering at Cadence in a way that made me pretty hot. I didn't have one fucking fraction of an ounce of guilt because they were old as fuck. I was ready to beat their ancient grandpa asses.

'Strip club's down the road,' I sneered. 'You want to eat or not?'

They muttered about the shitty service, but gave me the order anyway. I skated back to the booth. Cadence was in there, her orders under the silver bell she was ringing.

'Here.' She handed me a miniature photocopied menu. 'It's for trainees. I forgot to give you one.'

'I already know it,' I tossed it onto the counter, 'but thanks.'

'You know the whole menu? Prices and all?' She leaned against the low red counter. Her legs were so long and tanned, I couldn't help but think about getting wrapped in them. I had to lean over her to put my ticket down, and I could smell the sweet smell of her hair. I put a hand on her waist, as if I were steadying myself.

'You OK?' She grabbed my forearm.

I made my best wussy, worried face. 'Yeah. Just getting my bearings.'

Her green eyes narrowed a little. 'I watched you skate to the booth backwards.'

'Yeah, well, it comes and goes,' I said offhandedly.

She shook her head, then bent over a list of drinks, some scratched out. 'Write your drink orders here for Jimmy,' she murmured. 'He gets ten percent of our tips.'

'The car I just took wanted you.' I flicked my thumb their way. 'Some old geezers.'

She peeked out of the window. Thank God this little booth was air-conditioned. It had to be almost a hundred degrees outside.

'In the blue convertible?' She leaned over to see better, and I saw the edge of her little cheerleader bottoms under her skirt.

I shook obscene thoughts out of my head and tried to focus on work. 'Yeah.'

She sighed. 'Damn it. They tipped me a twenty last week.'

'Doesn't it feel a little whorish?' All right, I was being a prick, but I was kind of hoping she'd ask why I hadn't given her the customers, and then I was hoping she would be thankful that I was protecting her honor.

'I didn't fuck them,' she said, her eyes suddenly that angry-girl bright that's just no good.

'I didn't say that.' I sat on the counter and watched her lean over and add her tickets up, slashing numbers on the paper with neat, precise jabs of fury.

'You implied it,' she growled through her clamped teeth. 'It's money, Saxon. If they like the way I look and the way I smile, and that makes them leave me more, then good. Good for me.'

'Fine,' I snorted. 'I'll pass the next old perverts along.'

'Oh, don't worry, you'll get your share,' she seethed. 'Though I bet when it's some old woman drooling over you, it won't be whorish, right? It will just be making tips.' She tossed her black hair over her shoulder and shook her head. 'Un-fucking-believable.'

'Sorry,' I said, irritated that my intentions wound up being so far off the mark. 'I didn't know that you were so sensitive about it.' Or I could have just said, *'You should throw a super hissy fit and scream at me now.'*

'Sensitive? About being a girl? About being undressed with every pair of eyes out there? About being fantasized over? It creeps me out, but it fills my damn bank account, too. And there's no one else to do it, you asshole!' Her eyes filled with tears that I knew for sure were the product of fury, not sadness. Just then Jimmy stuck his head in and gave us the drinks orders he'd just finished. She took her heavy tray and whirled out of the door, her smile big, fake, and for anyone and everyone but me.

I continued to take orders and bring food out. Cadence was right; the girls and women loved me, and they made it clear with their tips. And, like her, I felt a little cheap, but mostly grateful. Aunt Helene had been eyeing this ridiculously expensive farm sink and faucet, and I wanted to bring enough in to convince her to get it. By the end of a few hours, I had a steadfast argument based on a fat wad of cash.

But I wasn't the only one with good luck in the customer generosity department. Cadence was chatting with a group of guys in a big, shiny pick-up truck. She giggled and tossed her hair, making the most of her generous breasts and touching one of the guys lightly on the hand and arm. The guy looked like one of those Scandinavian giants who hurl logs

149

and drink beer out of animal horns for fun. I'm no small guy, but he made me look like a toothpick. And that was the one Cadence was smiling at and rubbing the bicep of. By the time she finally tore herself away, I felt a lump of anger in my throat.

She skated into our booth breezily, her face relaxed and happy.

'Your customers' drinks are practically warm,' I snapped. 'Jimmy set them out here half an hour ago.'

'Half an hour?' She rolled her eyes at me. 'You're exaggerating.'

She snatched the tray of drinks up and skated away, clearly aggravated by my little outburst. I was also pretty aggravated at myself. I was pissed off both that I gave a shit about her little flirtations and that I was being too much of a pussy to admit that it was normal and human of me to give a shit about it if Cadence was going to mean what I wanted her to mean to me.

I skated outside fast and almost collided with Cadence's goon.

'Watch it!' he snapped, his eyes already on Cadence, a few feet away, taking someone's order.

'You watch it!' I yelled back. 'You shouldn't be out here! This area is for workers!' It was. For workers. That didn't make me sound like any less of a complete dweeb.

'Back off, Skates,' he snickered. His boys hooted. I felt a slow burn work its way down my arm, collecting right in my fist, which I was preparing to slam into Goon's face.

Just then Cadence skated back. 'Hey, Jeff.' She gave Goon one of those little cutesy girly kisses that girls give everyone: friends, babies, puppies, guys they don't want to climb in bed with.

Except Cadence was looking at Goon with a look that I knew well. Because it was fairly often directed my way. It was the look of a girl who was definitely thinking about beds and climbing in.

She skated next to him while he walked back to the huge truck and she wasted another fifteen minutes with him before she skated back.

I hadn't felt like that in . . . forever. I had never felt second best. Except with Brenna, and in that case I was second to Jake, so who the hell could blame her? But this asshole?

There was nothing appealing about him. Though he did drive, which I could, but not now, without a vehicle. And he didn't have to work six days a week, so I guess he could take Cadence out if she wanted to go. I noticed a Rutgers bumper sticker on his truck. He was probably older. A college guy.

I wished I hadn't been such a pussy. I wished I had punched him in the face. Because now I had to live with thoughts that he had one-upped me in so many ways, I couldn't even begin to get a handle on all of them.

When Cadence and I were alone again, I couldn't help myself. 'So you're making the beast with two backs with Monstro?' I sneered.

She looked at me for a long minute. 'That's none of your damn business,' she said evenly. Her green eyes showed how clearly pissed off she was. At me.

'It is my damn business if I'm spending all my time picking up your slack while you flirt.' The rage coursing through me was white-hot and completely blinding.

She just shook her head. 'You're pathetic, Saxon,' she said, and skated away.

I felt like I wanted to scream at someone. I felt like I wanted to break something. I couldn't get a handle on myself. By the end of the night, I had a fat wad of money and a massive headache.

Cadence sat on the counter in the skate booth. She didn't look up when I came in with my last tray.

'Cadence?'

'Mmm?' She was looking down at her phone. It looked like she was texting.

'Can I fucking talk to you?' I asked, my voice louder and meaner than I meant it to be.

She looked up slowly, tilted her head, and stared

at me for a minute. 'What do you want?'

'I want . . . to know if you want to go on a date with me?' I asked, and I felt my traitorous wussy heart hammering in my chest.

'As sweet as that was, I'm going to have to say no,' she said absently, staring at the screen of her phone.

I grabbed her hand, the one holding the phone, and she jumped back a foot.

'Don't touch me!' she hissed.

'Hear me out.' I realized that I was about to throw a match onto a big-ass pile of lighter-fluid-soaked timber. 'I feel like there's something between us. I think you know what I mean. And if you're willing to get busy with a meat-wad like that Jeff guy, I deserve a chance.'

She stared at me with those killer eyes and that perfect pouty mouth and gave me a look of pure disgust that I should have expected, but honestly hadn't.

'Let me set you straight.' Her words frosted out, total ice. She was just as scary as her mother, and I was trapped in a tiny-ass booth with her. 'You are a piece-of-shit, spoiled rotten, arrogant, unmotivated jerk-off. Guys like you are a dime a dozen. You're going to compare yourself with Jeff? Jeff's been working since middle school. Jeff has respect for the girls he dates. Jeff is enrolled in college and paying for it on his own. He's interesting, he's good-looking, and I like him.

So back off, Saxon. You don't stand a chance.'

'So you're telling me that you don't feel anything. Between us,' I demanded, forcing myself into her line of sight.

She kept her eyes down. One hand reached up and twirled a piece of silky black hair around her fingers. She looked straight at me. 'That's right, Saxon. I. Feel. Nothing. For. You.'

But her chest was heaving up and down from how hard she was breathing and her cheeks were red and her eyes were bright.

She was full of shit.

And I, Saxon Maclean, resident piece-of-shit, spoiled rotten, arrogant, unmotivated jerk-off was about to woo Cadence Erikson like a motherfucking romantic.

Jake 2

For the second time in my life, I had to sit Brenna down and tell her what an asshole fuckup I had been, and this time I told her face-to-face, so I had to actually watch all of her happiness crumble away and see her eyes get teary and blink hard.

I had to tell her about how I drank even though I didn't want to, and how one drink turned into more than I could count faster than I could control. I had to figure out how to tell her about Caroline and skinny-dipping and my idiotic rescue, and I tried to make it sound less damning than it was, but also tell it fast, like ripping a tooth out by its root instead of wiggling it slowly when you were a kid. When even the painful things were pretty simple.

When she finally opened her mouth to say something back to me, her voice was cracked and scratchy, the way I hated to hear it. Because I really did love her more than I could say, more than I could get a handle on. And that meant that seeing her sad or upset for any reason tore into me, and I hated it.

And when I was the cause of her pain, I hated myself.

'So, are you and Caroline a thing? Were you a thing?' She was holding her eyes open too wide, a trick she used to keep from crying. My heart seized and stuttered.

'Never. Not for one second.' I tried to make her hear the truth of it in my voice. 'Listen to me, Brenna. I saw her totally naked, and I didn't feel a thing. Not one fucking thing, OK?' I looked at her eyes. They shone kind of blue, kind of green, clear and pretty. Usually all I could focus on was how gorgeous they were. Now they just shifted and darted away from my gaze, frantic with all that hurt.

'She's pretty. I mean, it's stupid to lie and say that you didn't feel anything. Any guy would have been turned on by her.' Brenna gripped her hands in her lap and twisted them.

I knelt in front of her, laid my head on her lap and took her hands in mine. 'I'm not any guy, Brenna. I'm your boyfriend. I'd be crazy to want another girl. It was a mistake. A big mistake.'

'Do you think you have a drinking problem?' she said slowly. 'Like maybe you have, I don't know, like, some kind of alcoholism and that's why you drink so much when you don't want to?' She rushed the words, like she wanted to push them out of her mouth before they left a permanently bad taste in it.

'Bren, I was just stupid. Once. I don't want to drink any more, and I won't. OK?' I was trying like hell to reassure her. I'd worried about telling her this for weeks, and now here I was, doing it and hating it, but at least it was getting done.

'OK.' She swallowed hard, then looked at the door. I turned and looked too, but there was no one there.

'What is it, Bren?' I rubbed my thumbs over the soft skin on her knuckles. This girl even had great knuckles.

'I just haven't seen my mom since your grandmother took her. It's weird.' She pulled in a long, shaky breath, and I realized she needed comfort, needed to get away from what had made her so sad. From me.

Brenna's mother was kind of a constant worrier. She hovered over Brenna all the time. Not that I was complaining; if I had a daughter like Brenna, I'd guard her with a shotgun.

But I'd witnessed first-hand how the rules changed at Mama D's house. Everyone lived in this responsibility-free, plastic happy bubble, and anything bad that happened, like a girl almost drowning, just got resolved as quickly as it could and was appreciated for all the drama it created.

'This place is like a casino.' I smiled at her, slow and cautious to let her know I wasn't trying to cop out for being a dick earlier. 'You can get sucked in and lose track of time. You want to go find her?'

'Do you think everyone's being nice to her?' Brenna's voice coasted out, small and muted.

I rubbed her hands again, loving how soft they were. 'Yeah, Bren, as nice as they're capable of being. They've been waiting for three weeks for your mom to show up, so they're all going to be bugging her. You know she's probably giving a lecture in front of some old oil painting of ugly kids somewhere.' This time when I put a smile out there, Brenna returned it. Then a laugh tripped out before she could hold it back, and my heart felt fuller than it had since I had said goodbye to her before she went to Ireland.

She pulled me on the bed with a gentle tug and we snuggled close in the block of afternoon sun on the bedspread. Her shiny, good-smelling hair was tumbled all over the pillows. It looked like dark honey.

There was something powerful about Brenna. When I was around her, it was like life suddenly got smoother, cleaner, more focused and generally better. I've never been good with words, and talking about Brenna was basically impossible for me. It was always tricky for me to describe the way I felt about her.

All of that was going through my head, and the fact

that her skin looked so soft, and her mouth was so pink, and she was smiling this smile that walked between the lines of being innocently sweet and dangerously sexy. Her eyes were wide open and looking right at me, and she blinked slowly, letting her lashes flutter a little. I have no clue why her lashes turned me on so much, but they were like a hot button that she knew just how to push.

So I rolled over and kissed her, letting my body press down on hers. She was all soft curves, dips, and creamy skin. I kissed her as slowly as I could, because if I didn't wrap my head around being slow and precise, I sometimes got scared that I would just bust out and maul her. Even now, my hands were everywhere on her, unsnapping her bra, rubbing her neck and holding her head, moving down her back, and then down her stomach. The pace was based partially on pure giddiness at seeing her again after weeks apart, and partially on total relief that she was willing to let me hold her and kiss her after my colossal screwup with Caroline.

'Jake.' The whisper of her voice made my brain crash. I had never felt like I wanted anything as badly as I wanted her. But, of course, I couldn't give in to that.

Brenna's virginity was really important to me.

It sounded ridiculous when I thought about it, but

that was the absolute truth. I had been so stupid about sex and girls, and had been with so many it was insane. She wanted to have sex with me, but I didn't know if I could do all the right things for her. If I'd ever been with a virgin before Brenna, I didn't know it. And even if I'd known, I wouldn't have cared too much. Probably wouldn't even have remembered her name. Because then I was doing it for simple animal comfort. It meant nothing.

I didn't want to have any trace of that with Brenna.

That didn't stop me from doing other things. Hey, no one ever called me a saint, and nothing on this earth could make me happier than making Brenna happy.

I let myself kiss her down her body, along the smooth column of her neck, down under her loosened bra. I loved how she sucked her breath in hard. I loved her boobs, soft and full and perfect. My girlfriend has a lot of great qualities, including the physical ones.

I sucked on her skin until she was squirming under me. She had on this great short skirt, so short there was nothing for me to push up when my hand moved along the inside of her thigh. My fingers reached under her panties, and I could feel how wet she was. It was exciting, to the point where I had to close my eyes and take a couple of deep breaths to keep from turning into a horny beast on her.

All of this might seem kind of elementary for a guy with my past, but it was actually pretty much the opposite. There was never any foreplay before. Even my idiot move this winter, sleeping with that dumb girl from my math class, Nikki, hadn't involved any of this.

I didn't know if Brenna realized that, in some ways, I was ten times the virgin she was. I found the little bead of her clit and rubbed at it, my fingers slick from her. I loved seeing how fast and hard she breathed. I loved how she curved her spine up off of the bed and pushed her hips at me so fast. Then her eyes opened and she grabbed at me and moaned and kissed me, and I could feel that she was coming.

She was kissing me hard, and I tried to pull my hand away, but she grabbed at my wrist.

'Let's do it, Jake.' She licked her lips and her eyes shone bright. 'Please.'

Then I realized that *it* was *sex*. 'Not now, Bren.' I kissed her hard. 'Not here. This is such a shitty place.'

'Why does that matter?' Her voice was still eager, but also a little wobbly, like she knew that she probably wouldn't change my mind.

'Because it's your first time, and I want to make sure that it's special.' What was there to argue about with that kind of reason?

'It will be. It will be special if it's with you,' she said, her voice and kissing and touching suddenly all a lot more urgent.

'Brenna, I promise, if you want we can do it soon. But not now. It's almost dinner time,' I said, finally grasping onto the one fact of real life that might snap her out of this almost-sex thing we kept getting too close to.

'Dinner.' The insistent glow went out of her eyes. She looked like a rational, normal girl again, and I felt a breath of relief.

'Dinner. C'mon. Let's go and find Mom before we go to the dining room.' Brenna's mother was not usually the first person I wanted to see, but in this place, she was the next sanest person after Brenna.

'OK.' She kissed the tip of my nose and smiled. 'I'm going to change.'

I shook my head. 'You look great.' I pulled her hand, luring her back toward me. She fell next to me with a smile so big and sweet, it made my heart trip.

'Jake, I've been in this outfit since yesterday! Let me change.'

'Let me watch.' I could feel my voice stick somewhere low and deep in my throat.

She didn't say anything. If I had to make a bet, it would be that she was running through her head the image of a naked Caroline on the beach with me.

She looked up and her eyes radiated pure challenge.

I should have stopped her then, but I couldn't. She took her tank top off over her head, then slipped her skirt down. She was wearing blue, sky-blue underwear and a tiny little bra with lace. Weird that I had felt both pieces, but didn't know their color until the minute she wanted to show me.

She walked to her suitcase and opened it up. I loved the way her shoulders curved. I loved the dip of her bellybutton. I loved the smooth rounding of her thighs. I tried to tell myself that this was exactly how much of her I would see if I saw her in a bikini.

But it wasn't a bikini.

No one else would see this particular version of Brenna. Just me.

And that made all the difference.

She bent and dug through her outfits and found a yellow dress with a pattern of holes and embroidery. I knew the name: eyelet. She put it on, and I guess she assumed the show was over, but as far as I was concerned, it was still going strong. I watched her brush her hair and put it back in a ponytail. I liked being able to see all of her face. She turned to the side to check the dress, then turned around and looked over her shoulder at the back, straightening the straps. I loved the way her body moved. I loved the serious expression that scrunched her nose and lowered her eyebrows when she was trying to decide whether or not she really liked an outfit.

She went into the bathroom and ran the water to wash her face, and I was left lying on the bed, wondering what would happen tonight. Because she looked way beyond good. And the other guys here were hot for something new.

Caroline had been right about the fact that this place was incestuous, and the fact that Brenna was new meat made her vulnerable to them all. I couldn't afford to let her out of my sight, not for a minute. I needed to keep her close.

When she came out of the bathroom, I pulled her back onto the bed, on top of me because I wanted to feel her, solid and real. This house, these people, had freaked me out since the day I walked into their big, over-crystalled dining room, and I had wanted Brenna with me to face them. Now I just wanted Brenna and not them.

She was kissing me lazily when I heard footsteps. We stopped, and her eyes flew wide open. She didn't want me in here if it was her mother, but short of getting under the bed, I didn't know what to do. The door popped open just as we finished straightening our hair and clothes in that way that always looked a hundred per cent guilty.

'Hey. Dinner.' Caroline smiled smugly, like she

knew she was crashing a party where every single person wanted her gone. Why that would make her feel so good was beyond me, but girls like her never made any sense to me anyway.

'Ready, Bren?' I put my hand out and took hers, noticing that her palm was slightly sweaty.

Caroline snickered. 'Let's hope so.'

'Mind your damn business,' I snapped.

Brenna touched my arm, her eyes wide with nervous anticipation. And I wanted again, badly, to leave.

I bit my tongue and we walked downstairs where the exact same set of faces from my first night smiled too wide at us. I knew names now, but the bottom line was there wasn't one of them I cared enough about to actually bother introducing Brenna to. And there wasn't one of them I felt deserved to meet her.

'Hello, Brenna!' Mama D called.

I saw Mrs Blixen sitting next to Mama D, waving happily to Brenna and me. She was definitely into this whole scene, which shouldn't have surprised me as much as it did.

Of course Brenna's mother would want her daughter to spend her summer with some of the richest, most cultured people in the country. Of course, she was seeing them from her position as an adult and a guest.

Not as a potential fortunate son. There was a big difference between our perspectives.

Brenna and I sat down next to each other, and I could see her glancing down the table at her mother uncertainly. Mrs Blixen was chatting away, accepting another glass of wine, and having a fine old time. It looked a little like Brenna's feelings were hurt.

I squeezed her hand under the table. 'Don't feel bad, Bren. They have that effect on people, you know? They make you feel like you're with celebrities or something.'

She gave me a tiny smile and didn't have to reply because the salad course was being set out. We ate through the next few courses without saying anything. This sucked. Brenna was the one person I could be myself with, open up with. I didn't want this awkward, bumbling silence. They were ruining what we had together.

It was the quietest Brenna'd ever been in the whole time I'd known her. She was almost withdrawn. I wanted to put both my arms around her and not let go. I wanted to take her somewhere, just the two of us, and kick this whole fucking fiasco to the curb.

Mama D wasn't going to let anything go that easily.

'Brenna!' she cried. 'Your mother has told us that you studied at Trinity.' Her eyes were the same color and shape as mine, but I don't think mine ever looked like they were actually boring into another human's skull.

'Yes. Under Dr Gorman,' Brenna said clearly.

'That pisser!' Mama D howled. 'He failed poor Gerald two semesters in a row, didn't he, dear?'

My father looked up, his eyes extra red-rimmed. He held up his glass. 'Here's to the old bastard,' he said and took a long drink.

The table full of people laughed like crazy. I thought he was acting like an asshole, but apparently I was in the minority.

'How did you find him, Brenna?' Mama D asked, totally throwing down.

'He expects hard work. But I've never had a problem with that.' Her smile bloomed, innocently sweet.

I chuckled, and after a short pause, the rest of the table burst into laughter.

'You and Jake make a wonderful couple.' Mama D looked Brenna up and down and stamped her approval. I felt my blood go a little cold. Mrs Blixen had been cool so far, but this was taking it to a whole new level. I knew that any minute she was going to jump up and disagree with Mama D in that polite way that made it all seem so civil. I could practically hear the words ringing in my ears; *too young, plenty of time, see other people, keep things casual*.

She didn't do a thing.

'I'm just glad that Brenna agreed to date me,' I said

in the silence. Every single person eyed Brenna, and it was pretty damn clear that most of them thought Mama D's proclamation was overly complimentary. Which made my blood run hot.

'She obviously knows a diamond in the rough when she sees one.' Mama D smiled. Sort of smiled. At least her lips curled. Up.

Caroline stood suddenly. 'Ready, Bryce?' she snapped.

Mr Abercrombie stood up and followed her sashaying behind, and the rest of the high school and college set got up and slowly started toward the door.

Brenna looked at me like she was unsure, and that was really weird. Usually Brenna knew exactly what she was doing. She didn't need to ask me about any-thing. I wasn't sure how to answer this unasked question. Going down to the lake was what they did, and mostly what I had done too, just because there was nothing else to do and no one else to do it with. Now that Brenna was here, I felt like the possibilities were open again. Her mother's voice interrupted my thoughts.

'Brenna, Jake, you should go with the kids. Don't worry about me.' Her smile was warm, bordering on toasted. Brenna smiled back, and I could tell that was what had been bothering her – that she'd been away for weeks and her mom didn't want to spend time with her. She got up, and I followed her.

She stopped to kiss her mother on the cheek, which I thought was nice, but I caught a couple of rolled eyes. The jealousy and judgment here was so thick it could practically choke you. They were all smiles to your face and big-ass daggers in your back.

'Come on, Bren,' I urged, and she took one look at her mother, laughing at some story someone had told, before she followed me.

'It's just weird,' she said once we were out in the cool night air.

'What's that?' I took her hand in mine. I noticed she was wearing the gold posey ring I had given her this past Christmas. Man, I had agonized over that damn ring. I wanted to give her something nice that wasn't clingy. I think I wound up just freaking her out, because she broke up with me a few days later. It had been a fairly shitty few weeks between us after that.

'It's weird how the rules are all different all of a sudden.' She trailed her fingers over the high clumps of grass on either side of the path. 'Like we're allowed to do what we want here.'

I would have expected that kind of freedom to make her happy, but she just looked worried.

'This is like an alternate universe,' I said. She smiled nervously. 'They do what they want. Whatever they want, whenever. It's just a weird way to be.'

'So, you're not feeling it? I mean, being here with your family hasn't been what you expected?' She pulled her hair out of its ponytail and it all swished down her back in a long, shiny rush. I loved when it flowed long like that.

'I don't think I really expected anything.' I tugged her close and kissed her neck, under all that soft hair. 'I don't like them. I think they're mostly full of shit, and there won't be any tears shed at my end when I finally leave here. I'm ready to go back to normal life, you know?' She smiled sadly. 'I'm ready to go back to you and me and work and school. It was hard, but it's who I am. All of this lounging around makes you spoiled, I guess.'

She swung my hand in hers. 'You deserve a break.' A slow, sweet smile unfolded on her lips. 'And maybe this whole thing doesn't have to be a waste.'

'What do you mean?' I asked, and I couldn't help grinning. I loved when her voice got like that, like she was going to tell me to break the rules and not be a baby about it.

'Let's not go to the beach.' Her mouth was suddenly on mine, right there on the path.

I kissed her back and ran my hands down her arms, then pulled her to me. 'I can't do that yet, Brenna.' I pulled away with a lot of effort. A whole lot of effort.

'I didn't say we should do anything in particular.' Her eyes blinked slowly and her voice rasped out, low and coaxing.

'There's a little boat house,' I said after debating for about half a second, and led her by the hand.

The only light was from the nearly full moon. The boat house was just a huge garage, but the boats stored in it were fancy, decked-out boats. The kind that had cabins below deck. My family, and the others, were so rich that these were just the older spare boats. There were still a ton docked on the far side of the lake for everyday use.

Because everyone needs a garage full of emergency luxury boats, right?

Brenna was giggling, and she looked so cute, I was in on the plan without any regrets. I hoisted her up on the deck of one boat and climbed after her. I took her hand and led her down into the stale-smelling cabin. It was a pretty simple set up; a galley kitchen and dining room, a little sitting space and a room with a big bed, all compact.

'It's like a tiny house,' she whispered, though no one could have heard us down there. I took her hands. 'If we stole this boat, we could live on it and go around the world.' She looked about as if she were considering the plan. 'Can you sail?'

'No,' I admitted. 'But I can figure it out.'

'What if we get caught in a hurricane?' She dragged her fingers along my jaw, slowly.

'I'll keep you safe,' I said into her ear. And then I bit down on her earlobe because I knew she would suck her breath in fast, and I loved making her do that.

'What if we get attacked? By pirates?' She ran a trail of quick, light kisses up and down my neck.

I was already backing up and pulling her over to the bed, drawing her into the little secluded space that would only fit the two of us. I wanted to feel claustrophobic with her.

'I'll fight them all. I'll protect you,' I whispered and fell back onto the bed, yanking Brenna on top of me.

She kissed me, a soft rain of her lips on my mouth and skin. I was happy to have her, so happy I got sloppy. In my defense, it was only a tiny dress, one little piece of yellow fabric that came off so easily there almost didn't have to be forethought before it was just gone without any real contemplation.

And the light blue fabric underneath got wiggled out of so easily, I swear it was just because our bodies were rubbing against each other.

And I was so busy appreciating Brenna, her beauty, her nearness, the smell of her, the way her skin tasted, and the feel of her breath on my neck when my hands and mouth made her sigh and gasp, that reason and logic and thought all bled away.

Her hands were fast and sure, so my clothes were strewn around the bed very soon, and every place we touched was hot and good, because it was just my skin on hers and hers on mine.

It wasn't even temptation; that would mean one of us had something like a thought in our heads. That would be a stretch. This was pure feeling, pure instinct, and it was leading us places that were really, deliriously good.

And really fucking scary.

Brenna rolled over and slid against me, her body one long, smooth, soft rub against mine. I felt a little bit like I had been punched square in the face, and when I closed my eyes I could see stars bursting against my eyelids. We were right against each other, perfectly lined up, and with an easy adjustment or two, we'd be at a place we couldn't come back from. Brenna pushed up and then back down, warm and wet and, I knew, ready.

For one insane minute I pulled my hips back and up and we were almost ready. Then I opened my eyes. There was Brenna's face, her eyes bright and wide and completely trusting. Trusting me.

I wasn't ready to be that guy. I wasn't ready to hold all of that in my hands. I slid down along her body, my mouth a little hard and hungry on her, because I did feel regret, and in the back of my head I knew if we just pushed forward and did this, it would be done and we would wind up doing it a lot more and it would probably all be fine. But I wasn't there yet. And she sure as hell didn't need to be.

I could feel her body humming, with what, I didn't know for sure. I could imagine she was disappointed that I hadn't just gone for it. I also hoped that she wanted to do more with me, even if it wasn't sex.

I kept kissing down along where her hips jutted out and down farther along the tops of her thighs. We had never really been like this, completely naked, completely alone together. I kissed down her thighs, moved my hand along the inside and slid my fingers into her. She was really wet, and I couldn't say that I didn't imagine how good it would have been if we had just done it. I thought about being inside of her while I kissed and touched her. Maybe I should have told her that I thought about that all the time. It was just a hard topic to bring up, and I was never great with words anyway.

It wasn't that I didn't want sex with her; it was actually the scary reality of the fact that I wanted sex with her way too much, so much I had no control over it, that stopped me.

Or slowed me down. Because no one could really define what we were doing as 'stopped'.

I kissed her legs and higher, until my mouth was

right on her. I loved it. I loved the smell of her and the way she tasted. I loved being right there when she came. It was a matter of pride for me that I could make her body feel good like that. And I didn't have to feel guilty about it; it was just me giving her a good time. Of course, I enjoyed it, but she didn't have to do a thing to me. It was safe.

So I licked her and buried my face in her and sucked and kissed until I could feel her bucking like crazy, and then she went rigid and cried out in the stale, dark interior of the boat cabin. I laid my cheek on her thigh and watched her ribs expand and contract with the rush of air in and out of her lungs. Finally she sat up on her elbows and looked at me. She smiled a little.

'Thanks.' Her face was all glowy and her smile was big, wide, and all for me.

'No problem. At all.' Sweet goodness flooded through me.

'I want something,' she said quietly. She sat up and patted the bed next to her. I moved over by her, basically willing to do whatever.

Because I was pretty sure she wouldn't ask for sex, which was my only real hang-up. 'You want something else?' I teased, kissing her nose. 'You're never satisfied, are you?'

'Nope.' She pushed me back with one hand flat on my chest. 'Lie back.'

'Why?' I couldn't break from smiling at her. Man, she was so beautiful, and there was something about knowing her so completely and knowing that she was mine that made her even more attractive to me.

She slid down my body, kissing me so softly it was just barely this subtle, ticklish feeling. Those kisses along with her soft hair brushing over my skin made me feel like every nerve in my body was on edge. Then her mouth was below my waist, and I sat up fast.

I had been so relaxed from seeing her satisfied that I never put it together; she was going to give me what I had given her. I was about to get head.

And I didn't want it. I mean, I wanted it, but I couldn't do it.

'Brenna, no.' I pulled back.

'Why?' she demanded, her eyes all fiery and angry.

'Because it's too fast.'

'You've done it to me a few times now.' She moved back toward me.

'But it's not the same.' I reached deep into my brain for a logical argument. Brenna responded to logic. Unfortunately, logic wasn't always my strong suit. Especially when I didn't have my pants on.

'You got tested.' Her voice was like one of the smart girls in debate club. Uh-oh. 'You can't give me an STD.'

'I know that.' I had gotten a full round of testing

about a year after my wild days were over. And I was damn lucky that what I had picked up could be treated with antibiotics. I thought about it a lot; how my stupid, meaningless sex with girls I couldn't even remember could have messed my health and my future sex life up for good.

'I want to,' she said, her voice insistent, her eyes serious. 'I mean, I'll probably suck, no pun intended. But I want to be part of this, too. I don't want to just sit and let you be the only one doing anything. I want to make you happy, Jake.'

'You do.' I grabbed her shoulders. 'You really do. So don't worry about doing more.'

She sighed. 'It also turns me on to do things to you. In a different way, but I love it. You're not being fair to me. I mean, I know you did this before with girls you didn't love, so why am I off limits?' Her eyes looked hurt and a little embarrassed.

I hated that.

'It's not what you think, Bren.' I raked a hand through my hair. Then I made my weird confession. 'I never did. This.'

Her eyes went from squinted with embarrassment to wide open and completely pleased.

'You've never gotten head?'

'No.' I felt my skin go hot around my neck and ears. 'I told you, Bren. Mostly just drunken sex.

Nothing good leading up. Nothing really good about it.'

'Then I guess you might be nervous,' she said, and looked like she was thinking.

Which seemed like an innocent thing, but there was nothing more dangerous than my girlfriend using her brain to get what she wanted. As smoking hot as Brenna was, it was her brain that was so freakishly incredible. I kind of knew I'd lost the fight right then and there.

Not that I had that many complaints. Seriously.

'Yeah, I'm nervous. And it makes me a little uncomfortable, I guess.'

She grinned now, sure of her next couple of moves. 'It feels like you don't have control, right, Jake?' I nodded. 'It feels like the whole thing is focused on you, and that's kind of weird and uncomfortable, right?' I nodded again. She pushed me back with a gleeful shove. 'I don't get to do much with you that you didn't do before.' Now her voice was kind of low and sexy and I was pretty helpless. 'So, do this for me. OK?'

And in the history of the world, I don't think any guy could have taken that brilliant request and said no unless he was a complete idiot. I was about to get the most rewarding sexual experience of my life. What was there to argue?

But Brenna didn't wait to see if I was going to argue anyway. She moved her mouth down along my body with those soft little kisses. And then she made it all the way down.

For a minute, I could feel her warm breath against me. I guess it was a little overwhelming. And I had no advice to give her, which was annoying. She opened her mouth and all I felt was the hot, wet slide of her along me and all around me.

I swallowed hard and grabbed at the sheets. My mind cracked open and every sexy, hot, unimaginable thing I had ever hoped to do with Brenna raced through to torture me. I had to go blank. I couldn't tell if she was moving awkwardly or not; it felt perfect. I didn't know if I had ever had the feeling like I was the sole focus of someone else, like the world was revolving around me alone for a little while. For a few minutes I was suspended in that weirdly excellent nothing, but my curiosity finally got the better of me.

I sat up a little and saw her and that was pretty much the biggest mistake that I could have made. I never imagined it would be possible to get more turned on than I was, but seeing her blew my mind. And then it was all shot to shit. My brain jumped and crashed, and I fell back on the bed hard and just let go of everything. I never imagined anything could feel so good.

She wiggled up next to me and smiled triumphantly. 'Was it OK?'

I couldn't think of what to say. I couldn't think period. 'Holy fucking hell,' I said. I put my arms around Brenna and held her. My girlfriend. My wildly sexy, way-too-good-for-me, incredible girlfriend.

'So it was good?' she pressed.

'It was unbelievable.' I sat up and looked right at her. I had to look at her, because I wanted her to know just by seeing my face how intensely I felt this. 'You are so sexy, I can't even describe it. I've never felt like that before. Ever.'

She grinned. 'I'm glad you liked it.'

And it would have been pretty awesome to just lie like that for a few more minutes, just wrapped around each other. But we heard the door of the garage smash open and voices bounced off of the aluminium walls and down into our little private place.

Brenna scrambled into her clothes and, as preoccupied as I was with getting dressed myself, I still took a minute to just enjoy her, how she looked and how much I loved just being around her.

'Who's in here?' she whispered.

I shrugged. 'It's been a little while. Everyone who went to the beach is probably trashed by now. They won't even notice us.'

She bit at her lips nervously.

'Don't be nervous, Bren. You have nothing to worry about, OK?' I put a hand up to her face and ran my thumb over her cheek.

'Jake!' a girl's voice called. 'Jake Maclean! Come out, come out wherever you are!'

It was slurred but identifiable. Caroline.

'That's Caroline again?' Brenna's brows knit.

'She's been pretty obnoxious since the whole drowning thing,' I grated out.

Brenna had pointed out when girls hit on me dozens of times when we went out, but I'd never paid it any attention. I knew girls thought I was good looking, but I'd had my fill of mindless one-night stands. I knew damn well how amazing Brenna was, and I wasn't about to let it get out of hand with this girl.

'I'll take care of it.' I climbed up on the deck. 'What do you want?' I asked, not keeping any of the aggravation out of my voice.

'Hey there.' She staggered just a little. Bryce was right there to catch her, but she shook his hand off of her arm. 'Come to the beach with us. Now.' She smiled, a clearly drunk smile.

'No thanks.' I worked hard to keep my voice even and controlled.

She laughed. 'Oh, you and *Brenna* are going to be hanging out?' she said snidely. 'It's a little sad, isn't it, Jake? You should have seen her, all over Saxon. You know what? They make sense together, Jake. Because you're . . . stop it, Bryce!' she yelled, slapping at Bryce and making hard, flailing contact with his face and shoulders. 'Because you're just some fun. You're just some good-looking fun. She'll never really be with you. So why not just enjoy a little? Shut up, Bryce!' Bryce had her arm and was tugging at her, but she wasn't about to give up.

I had planned to just take care of the whole Caroline thing, but what she said was pretty much what I lived in fear of all of the time.

That Brenna would wake up and realize that she and I weren't the same.

That she could do better.

Not that I thought Saxon was better, but there was better. Than me. And this girl was a drunk bitch, but that didn't make what she was saying any less true.

She laughed, a mean, high sound. 'And your "relationship"? I mean, if you want to make out and skinny-dip with random people, just be single, right?'

It never failed to amaze me how a moment of complete perfection could get so royally fucked in the matter of a few minutes.

But it wasn't me who wound up taking care of it at all. It was Brenna.

'Get out, now.' She stood, all of a sudden, at my

side. 'I know this is hard for you to hear, Caroline, but no one wants you around. No one. At all.'

Caroline sneered at her and stumbled.

'You know I'm right,' she slurred, but Brenna was intimidating when she wanted to be. She was sober, beautiful, and looked pretty damn fierce.

'You might be right. But I'm also right. About the fact that you're a nasty, mean, asshole. No one wants you around but Bryce. If I were you, I would take what I could get. Bryce, take her out now.' Brenna switched her gaze to Bryce, and it was so focused and in-control, he couldn't say no.

He nodded.

'You're the asshole!' Caroline screeched. 'You think you're so uppity? You and your mother! You're just little sluts who clawed their way up where you don't belong.'

I don't think I've ever seen Brenna move so fast. She looked kind of shaky, but she was off the boat and down to Caroline, who was being pulled out by Bryce so fast he was dragging her. Brenna made it to her, pulled her arm back, and full-on smacked Caroline across the face.

It was a hell of a slap. Caroline's head snapped over and there was the red print of Brenna's hand across her whole face.

'Say what you want about me,' Brenna said,

looking straight into Caroline's face. 'Don't you dare talk about my mother.'

I was right behind Brenna now, and I boxed myself around her, because Caroline's beery mind was putting it all together and she finally, suddenly snapped and went at Brenna all sharp fingernails and flailing arms. Luckily, I moved Brenna back the same time Bryce pulled Caroline away.

We listened to her scream and cry all the way back to the beach.

I looked at Brenna. 'Wow.' I shook my head. 'I didn't see that coming, Bren. You're scary.' I pressed her hair back from her sweaty face and smiled at her.

Brenna burst into tears. She sobbed and shook, and I could only wrap my arms around her and shush her.

'Please don't cry,' I begged. 'Please relax, baby. Don't cry.'

'I hate it here! I hate them!' she sobbed into my shirt.

'I know.' I ran a hand down her hair. 'I hate them, too.'

Hated them. And *was* them.

Brenna 3

'Evan?' I stalked over to the window of my ridiculous sea-shell-themed guest room and waited, lip clamped between my teeth, for the voice that was like sweet syrup on the snow-cone of my loneliness.

'Brenna!' It was just her voice and my name, but it made the whole world shine brighter for a minute. 'I have missed the hell outta you, girl.'

I twisted the blue and ivory embroidered seashell curtains between my fingers and let them go. 'I think your accent got stronger.'

'Well, that makes sense. It's the height of summer in the south of Georgia. You could cook a pot of gumbo by leaving it on the porch with the lid on, as my gramma would say. But we have air con, sweetheart. The best in the world. Come see me, and I'll put the temperature all the way down to sixty-six, just for you.' I could hear the funny bend of her words that came from talking while her mouth was stretched too wide.

'I want to. I will. I promise. Are you going out?' I heard her press and smack her lips, and I tried to imagine what color her lipstick was.

'I am, but don't rush. I'm really in no mood to drive around with Rabin trying to find parking on River Street and worrying that his precious Vette is going to get scratched. Ugh, I hate that damn car. It's such a balding-man-midlife-crisis car.' She sighed. 'Plus that, I've been in withdrawal, and I need you! I love you! I can't live without you!' I could picture her with the back of her hand on her forehead, and it made me giggle.

'I miss you too, lovey. So, dinner with Rabin?' I didn't say another word about it, but my tone communicated every kick-to-the-groin snag of anger I felt when I thought about him and the brutish, arrogant way he bossed Evan around.

'Don't judge,' she pleaded. 'There's too much going on right now, and all of it is just the baby snowball that's hardly started rolling down the mountain of crazy shit my daddy built. No one outside the family knows, but everything is about to crash down around our ears and Rabin . . . he's complicated, but he's something I know. And I need to just keep things the way they are right now. I can't deal with another change.'

'Oh, Evan.' We had talked a few times about her

family's money problems, and the verdict seemed to be that they had only just begun. Evan had no idea how far it would spiral and if any piece of her life would still be intact after it was all over. 'Is your mom still home?'

'Mama is Cabo-bound. She did make up some bullshit excuse about needing a girls' week with her nonexistent frenemies. Of course, her gigolo was all discreet and took a flight two days before hers.' Her breath shook when she pulled it in. 'Look, if I don't shut up about my sad-sack life, I'll wind up hurling myself off my balcony. Tell me all about Jake's family. Are they a nest of vampire vipers from hell, just like I guessed?'

I would have been happy to listen to Evan talk about her problems for hours, but she had already insisted there was way too much to process at the moment and promised she would spill her guts hardcore as soon as she was ready, so I didn't press her for any more details, even though I wanted her to keep talking about what was wrong. I switched topics, as requested. 'They're awful. I've never felt so out of place in my whole life. And I feel like every single one of them looks down their nose at me.'

'They do,' she said, with the blunt honesty I loved so much about her. 'They look down their plastic noses at everyone else in the whole wide world. Don't you dare let them treat you like shit. And stop feeling bad about slapping that drunk tramp across the face. She was asking for it, loud and clear. Do I have to stomp up there in my new stiletto boots? I sent you a pic of them, by the way. Are you in love?'

'So in love!' I gushed. 'You need something short and tight, but kind of girly and soft to wear with them. Do you have anything like that?'

'I know exactly what would work.' I heard the unmistakable clack of her shaking her nail polish bottle. 'But I can't wear it in this damn soupy heat. And I don't think Rabin deserves it. But no more Rabin talk! He's stricken from the record. Other than Jake's insane family, is everything else all right? Did he climb into your window, Romeo style, after your little sexcapade on the boat and seal the deal?' She broke off from blowing on her nails to laugh at my silence. 'Are you blushing, Ms Blixen?'

'The answer is no. No to all your crazy questions.' I dug around in my make-up bag for my own container of polish. 'It was hard enough to get him to go that far. He's nervous.'

'They need to make a movie about the two of you. I swear to God, I bet he had a golden halo around his head. Does he sparkle?' she teased.

I switched the phone to my other ear and put one quick, slightly messy coat of silver polish on my toes.

'He doesn't. He's just got some weird hang-ups about sex, after everything that's happened in his past, you know?'

'I'm sorry did you say "weird" or "extremely enormous"?' She crowed at her own dumb joke, and I could picture her tilting her head back as she laughed.

'Hardy har har.' I wiggled my toes and grabbed the Q-tips and nail polish remover so I could fix all my mistakes. I heard a loud, obnoxious car horn on her end.

'Good Lord almighty, I'm coming already!' Evan screamed, and I almost dropped the phone. 'Sorry, sweets. My knight awaits.' Her voice was too grim to even be appropriately sarcastic.

'It's OK. I promised Jake I'd chill with him down by the docks. Have fun, be careful, love you!' I hopped up and walked on the sides of my feet so I wouldn't smear my still-wet polish.

'I will, Mama Bren. Love you!'

The connection clicked off, and I felt a moment of dread, wondering what her night and, eventually, her whole year would be like. I only knew Rabin based on what Evan told me, but he struck me as egotistical, mean and shady. Not the shoulder to cry on she was going to need when the shit hit the fan.

I kept thinking about her as I got ready to go to the docks with Jake. My first instinct was to tell my mother where I was headed, but her room was eerily empty. I held the doorframe a little too tight as I glanced in at her neat little space, her familiar things draped here and there. I missed her.

My mother had been pulled into this whole warped universe. Mama D had taken a liking to her, and dragged her on antiquing day trips and gallery openings. Those were things Mom and I would have totally done together in New Jersey. It was weird here, though.

Only really young kids hung out with their parents, and it was clear that they were just counting down the years until they were old enough to hang out at the beach and boathouse and pool and game rooms. Once they hit that magic puberty time, they only saw their parents for the big dinner we all had together.

I was shocked by how naturally Jake took to it all. Not that he liked it or wanted it. He was just cool with it. He was polite to the dozens of maids and cooks and gardeners scampering everywhere and polite to his family, but nothing really impressed him at all.

The way he'd grown up, I would have expected him to be a little more awed by it all. We had been able to spend a lot of time together. A lot. The adults ran around and did what they wanted. Jake had told me that this place was like a casino, and he was totally right. Or maybe it was like a big cruise ship, where everyone just did whatever, and as long as everyone was having fun and laughing, no one questioned anything.

But I just couldn't get into it.

It felt wrong and weird, and I felt, for the first time in my life, like I would never fit in. Like there was no way I could prove myself to these people. And it was strangely sucky. More so than I'd ever thought it would be.

I thought about it when I knocked on Jake's door and kept thinking about it on the short walk to the lake. Jake and I were lying on the enormous dock that jutted over the glistening water. Alone. We were more alone than we would have been just by choice, because once I'd slapped Caroline, no one would speak to me any more. She was pretty intimidating, and I had humiliated her.

I'd thought the slap would feel better than it had, too, and even Evan's insistence that I hadn't done a single thing wrong didn't make me feel any better.

'Does it bug you that everyone here has such a superiority complex?' I fanned my fingers over Jake's face.

His eyes were closed, but I could tell that he wasn't sleeping because he was playing with a straw of grass in his mouth, whirling it around and chewing on it. He spat it out and turned to look at me.

'No.' He put his hands under his head.

'That's it?' I popped myself up on an elbow. 'Just, "no"?'

'No, it doesn't bug me.' He kissed me on the palm of my hand. 'It's exactly what I expected from them. 'Cos they're assholes, Bren.'

'Why are you here?' I hugged my legs tight to my chest and rested my chin on my knees.

'Because I get to be with you every single day. I don't have to work for a little bit. That's pretty much my idea of perfection.' He smiled and leaned his head against my legs. 'Were you surprised by them?'

'Yeah.' I felt a little silly even admitting it. 'I just kind of always fit in. I mean, I've had friends who had lots of money and friends who didn't, and it's never been this issue, you know? I always just got along fine. And here, I don't.' OK, so I downplayed it a little. It was way too embarrassing to admit how much it bothered me.

'It really bothers you, doesn't it?' He grinned and chuckled, plucking a fresh piece of grass to gnaw on. 'Why would you care? You're ten times cooler and smarter than any of them.'

'I know!' I felt the sting of defensiveness shoot through my spine. 'I'm just saying it's weird, OK?'

He was quiet for a minute. He took the straw out of his mouth with his long, strong fingers and said, 'Oh.'

Only it wasn't just 'Oh,' like 'Oh, I see.' It was

'*Oh,*' like '*Ooooooohhhh, it's just become really clear to me, and I'm a little shocked by it.*'

'What do you mean, "Oh"?' I asked, and it was pretty clear that I was more than just a little irritated.

'You're in the Kelly Boat.' He took the blade of grass and drew it along my bare leg so slowly I could see the trail of goosebumps startle on my skin.

'What's the Kelly Boat all about?' I leaned over to pop the brim of his cap up high enough so that I could see his gray eyes, dancing with adorably obnoxious self-satisfaction.

'The Kelly Boat is the boat for all of the losers and nobodies.' His handsome face cracked into a smile. 'Everyone thinks they're better than the people in the Kelly Boat.' He shrugged and nestled his head against my legs until it fit right into my lap, then yawned. 'You might not've had the chance to take a ride in the Kelly Boat if you'd been a better ass-kisser.'

'What do you mean?' I pulled his cap off and stroked my fingers through his sun-gold hair. 'Whose ass would I have kissed?'

'My phony grandmother's. My drunk loser father's. Slutty Caroline's. There's a big list of asses that really, truly think they deserve to be kissed.' He turned his face to my belly and kissed it with a warm, suctioned pop of his lips. 'I love that you're happy to be on the Kelly Boat instead of an ass kisser on the

Rich Bitch boat.' When I didn't say anything, his voice dipped, low and nervous. 'You are happy to be on the Kelly Boat, right?'

'Don't you hate it that they think that? That they honestly think they're better?' I demanded, my ears ringing from the pure, molten fury swirling through me.

Jake sat up and took my hands. 'I'm kind of used to it.' He squinted in the sun and pulled his cap back down. 'And it used to hurt. Because I thought everyone looked down on me, I guess. Then I met you. And you liked me for who I am. That's a crazy thing, Brenna. Most people don't bother with that shit, you know?'

I smiled a little. 'Yeah, I do.' But, whoa, I really didn't at all. I thought I got what it felt like to be Jake. But I had no clue. I hated it, and once again, Jake surprised me with his courage and resilience. As usual, he was unexpectedly incredible. 'Hey,' I added, kissing him softly. 'I like the Kelly Boat. I do.'

'Good. Because it's actually kind of a pirate ship, and if you wanted to leave, you'd have to walk the plank.' He shook his head sadly. 'Then I'd have to jump to your rescue, and we'd probably both get eaten.'

'By crocodiles?' I kissed him, my hands right on the soft brown hair that was spilling down his neck, overlong and a little golden in the lazy summer sun.

'If you want.' He kissed my neck. 'I was thinking sharks. You're always more creative.'

And then he was kissing me on the dock, his mouth nipping along my collarbone and down around the fabric of my bikini top. It was black with little red polka dots and bottoms that tied at the sides.

'Do you want to go back to the house?' I asked, my mouth down close to his ear as his lips wandered all over, making me crazy.

He stood and scooped me easily into his arms.

'You're going to drop me,' I said, refusing to get all screechy and girlish. Even if his arms were bulgingly fantastic, and there was definitely a high, excited buzz working through me.

'Never.' He curled me to his chest a few times. 'I'm getting weak from all of this luxury. I need to work out a little or Zinga's will fire me.'

'Are they holding your job?' I tickled my fingers over his ribs until he stopped using me as an exercise device.

'Oh yeah.' He hefted me up closer to his chest as he navigated the tiny, brambly paths that led to his grandmother's monstrous house. 'The owner's son came back from college for the summer, so they were kind of glad I took some time off so he could get my hours. But they'll need me once he goes back.'

My next questions felt obvious, but Jake could be infuriatingly oblivious to the obvious.

'So, you're going to keep working? Even though you found your family?'

'I get an inheritance, but I can't just live like a movie star.' He was at the door of the house. I reached over and twisted the knob. 'I need to go to college someday and get a job and live with you. And, more importantly, I need to never, ever turn into a prick.'

'I won't let you.' I squeezed his face in my hands and he smiled a squished-face smile. 'I'll make sure you stay in the Kelly Boat.'

He walked up the marble stairs, which were so shiny I could practically see my reflection them. He opened my door and plopped me down on the bed.

'Thanks, Bren,' he said, falling next to me.

'For what?' I rolled into him.

'For helping me keep it real.' He grabbed me in his arms and hugged me hard. 'I'm so glad you're here.'

'I'm glad you're here, too,' I said, and then we started kissing and couldn't really stop. Or I couldn't stop. I didn't want to, but Jake had taken a firm stand on sex, and he just said no, no matter how much I whined and pouted.

We got far enough that he grabbed a pillow and put it over his head so he could scream.

'Brenna, why are you doing this?' he asked, shaking his head.

'Because I think we should have sex. I feel ready, and I don't know why you're all reluctant about it.' I narrowed my eyes at his scowl. 'I have condoms.'

'I don't even want to know.' He blew a long, slow breath out. 'I can't. Not here. Not now.'

'But this might be the most free we'll be, Jake. Once we get home, it won't be like this.'

I grabbed his face and gave him a hard kiss.

'This is weird.' He gestured around the room with a flippant toss of his hands.

'What's weird? This room is beautiful.' It was. The furniture was all super-old and gorgeous, the bed was the most comfortable thing I'd ever slept on, the art and knick-knacks were highbrow and a tiny bit ironic, and the light shined in through the huge, high windows in the prettiest golden waves.

He looked around, and I could see that his eyes weren't seeing what I was seeing. 'This is a room that was decorated by someone who doesn't live here. It was all set up just to impress people. It doesn't have any soul, doesn't have anything real in it.' He let the words drop out of his mouth with slow, sad emphasis. 'Doesn't that make you sad? This is like a fucking fancy, phony showroom.' He sat up and yanked his jeans back over his hips. 'I'm not having sex with you for the first time in this shithole.'

I shook my head. 'I guess I see your point. Can't we pretend it's a nice hotel?' I suggested with my sweetest smile.

He shook his head. 'Nope. This isn't a real room. This isn't our real life. I'm not doing it here, and that's the end of it.'

'Fine,' I said and walked to the dresser. I had finally given in and moved my clothes out of my suitcase and into the drawers. Mom didn't seem like she was in any rush to leave. Thorsten had been able to pick up an extra show at work, so he was happy to get the overtime hours without worrying about us. She felt like this was a good experience for me. I didn't completely disagree.

Except I didn't like myself very much here. I wanted to be more like Jake, but I wasn't. I actually admired so much of what they had and what they did and where they went. Not everything, obviously. I hated their phoniness and the fact that the teenagers and probably adults traded sex partners without even thinking and accepted the alcoholism that pretty much ran rampant. I hated that they were catty and jealous and mean.

But I wanted to be trilingual and get in places no one else could, to have access to all the little best things in life that they could afford to just take for granted.

When Evan talked about having to go to mass in Rome for Easter while she visited her free-spirit aunt or how her father got so many tickets to concerts she literally couldn't make it to every show, I wished I could have those experiences. I hated that I had wound up being so admiring of the whole thing, but I was.

I pulled a little white dress over my head. I had as much of a tan as I was ever going to get, and the dress looked really good on me. I knew it wasn't designer. When had I even started worrying about things like that? Whenever we went out in Dublin, Evan pointed out how great my outfits were and honestly loved them. But she kind of had the choice to spend as much or as little as she wanted on her wardrobe, at least for now. It was hard to be that open-minded when you didn't have any other option.

'It's going to be dinner time soon.' Jake wrapped his arms around me and kissed me on my neck. He smelled like pine and sun and Jake. His arms cradled me, strong and dependable. My phone calls to Evan and being with Jake were pretty much the only things keeping me grounded here.

'We should go down.' We always went together. Neither one of us wanted to face that den of jackals alone.

He took my hand, and I made a stop by my mom's room before we went on. She still wasn't in, and I worried for a minute. Where could she be? What was she doing? Was she still out with Mama D? Why didn't she tell me anything any more?

Jake and I wandered down to the dining room. One of his random relatives called him over to ask him about some motor they were all debating. Jake was about to say no, but I pushed him away. I didn't want him to think I was so pathetic that he could never leave my side.

He got dragged out to the yard to look at the car in question. I could see him from the big plate-glass windows in the sun room. I was watching Jake, and enjoying the fact that he was far hotter than any of his fake-tanned, bleached-out cousins, when I felt someone near me, someone unfamiliar.

When I turned to look, it was a little bit spooky, because for a split second, I thought I was looking at Jake. Then I realized it was his dad.

'Oh, Mr Maclean! You scared me.' My laugh felt too bubbly and nervous.

There were a few reasons Mr Maclean put me on edge. He drank too much. He looked a little shifty. I hated how much he resembled Jake.

His eyes were already red-rimmed and glassy. Jake's father drank more than anyone I had ever seen before. The sweet stinging smell of alcohol was wafting off him, burning my eyes.

'It's Gerald, Brenna.' His eyes drank me in, looked me up and down slowly and made my skin actually crawl. 'So you and Jake are pretty serious, huh?' He leaned just a few inches too close to me.

I took two deliberate steps away and tried not to make a face. I hated when adults asked questions like that. I loved Jake with everything in me. But how was I supposed to answer that?

'Yeah, we're getting married someday for sure!' or, 'Golly-gee, he's just my world!'?

Our love was completely real, but I didn't want to blabber about it. Especially to his dad.

'Um, I guess we are,' I said vaguely, examining a pottery piece on the table next to me to avoid eye contact.

'You and me? We've got something in common, you know. I had a thing with a wrong-side-of-the-tracks girl.' His smile bordered on a leer. 'Jake's mom was hot, a real turn-on. But not really from my world, you know?'

He was trying to connect with me. He was putting Jake down, and he was creeping me out. My heart thudded hard, my mouth felt gritty, and the sweat on my palms made my hands slide on the top of the table when I tried to brace myself. I realized with a panicked sweep of my eyes how alone we were.

There were usually maids bustling around, getting

things ready for dinner. I had never been down here when there weren't a few people fixing themselves cocktails or lounging on the couch. Where was everyone?

I could see Jake through the window, but he was way too far away to help me at all if anything happened. 'I don't know much about Jake's mom,' I stalled, looking around desperately for a way to leave. Jake's father closed the space between us, and I felt the crush of panic avalanching down on me fast.

'She was wild.' He smiled, and it looked just like Jake's smile minus all the warmth and sweetness. The air in my lungs felt bogged down, like I couldn't push it out and let fresh air in. I was suffocating. His next words were coiled and slimy, too close to my ear, his breath hot on my neck. 'She was a little bit of a smartass. And really, really hot. I was smart, from a strict family . . . well, you know that whole thing.'

'Mmmhmm,' I murmured. Instinct overrode my panic, and I took a few quick steps to the side. As soon as there was a little distance, my brain stopped clattering around in my head.

'I think I saw in her what you see in him.' He followed me, and his lazy demeanor was nothing but a trick. He was quick and agile, and he had me closed-in in the twisting labyrinth of too much antique furniture. He put one hand at my elbow and slid it up and down along my forearm slowly. 'I get you, Brenna.' My name dripped out of his mouth, and the sound of it made me cringe.

Finally my voice came back. 'You left Jake. You left Saxon. Never mind their mothers. You don't get me *at all*.' I tried to just run out, which went against my ingrained manners. But this had gone so far beyond fake niceties.

He tightened his fingers on my arm just hard enough to hurt. 'You don't really fit into this world, do you? Sweetheart, you should enjoy your time with Jake. He's not hardwired to settle down, and soon he'll have his pick of anyone he wants.' His eyes were hateful, and I felt a lump in my throat that I couldn't swallow around. He chuckled, a soft, mean sound. 'Soon *you'll* be the girl from the wrong side of the tracks. As far as Mama D and these biddies go anyway. But being the good girl all the time can get pretty old anyway, right?'

I wanted Jake. I wanted my mother.

I didn't attempt to engage in any more ludicrous conversation. I yanked my arm away from his grasp and wiggled past a table full of delicate vases, jarring it with my hip and making every priceless trinket dance precariously. I wanted out. Every hair on my entire body stood on end, and a chill slithered up and down my back.

Gerald grabbed my arm again just as I made it around an old embroidered couch. 'C'mon, honey. I was just making conversation. I never thought you'd be the uptight type.' I tried to pull away, but Jake's dad took my other arm, loosened his hold and rubbed up to my shoulders. He made a low noise in his throat and massaged me a little. 'First love.' His laugh puffed against my neck, and I twisted away from it. 'Gotta love that, Brenna.'

Footsteps came down the hall, and my entire body went slack with relief.

Jake entered the living room and took one look at my face. I felt tears stab at my eyes, and I shook my head to let him know that I was *not* all right. He flew across the room, and every inch he came closer made my muscles relax a little more.

'What's going on?' he demanded, his eyes hard on his father's face.

The room was way too quiet. He looked down at Gerald's hands, still on my shoulders, and his eyes flashed with fury. 'What the hell is going on?' he repeated, his voice icy. His dad let go of me, and Jake grabbed my wrist and pulled me to him.

'Just chatting with your pretty lady, Jake.' Gerald walked over to the liquor cart at the side of the couch and poured himself a huge glass of something amber that smelled like paint thinners.

Jake eyed his father and his scowl was deep with disgust. 'Are you OK?' he asked me quietly. I opened my mouth, but he shook his head and rubbed a hand up and down my arm. 'Don't say anything. I can see you're not.' He turned to his father. 'What were you talking about, Gerald?'

'Life. Love. Nothing too important.' He took a long sip of his drink and cocked an eyebrow at Jake, ignoring me completely. His flippant style was so at odds with the idea of someone who was supposed to be an adult, someone who was supposed to be a father. It shook my sense of right.

Jake narrowed his eyes at his father, then looked at me. 'Keep away from him, OK? This family is more than a little screwed up.' He put his arm around my waist and we walked into the dining room.

My lungs felt pinched. The minute we were out of the room, I had to grab onto a table to steady myself, stop my shaking hands, pull my breath in and out slowly. Tears crept down my face even though I felt like I was making a huge deal out of what wound up being nothing.

'Bren? Jesus Christ, what the fuck did he *do* to you?' He pulled my weight into his arms and pressed my head to his chest.

'Nothing. He didn't really do anything. It was just . . . this sounds so dumb, but he talked to me. Like, kind of sexy, I guess? It just felt really weird. And creepy. You know? From an adult. And, um, your dad.' Jake's hand ran wide, slow circles on my back and the gentle rhythm eased me.

'I'll fucking kill him.' Jake's voice wobbled, and I grabbed him hard and squeezed.

'Fuck him. Don't even think about him again, OK? I'm fine, and now I know to stay the hell out of his way.' I put my hands on either side of his face, because he was staring back into the living room, murderous rage like warpaint on his face. Jake's anger always freaked me out because he was usually such a mellow, laid-back guy. 'Forget it.'

'He gets away with shit all the time. He's a fucking soul-sucking life-wrecker. Who the hell does he think he is?' Jake's entire body trembled with fury.

'Don't,' I urged. 'Don't even think about him. Soon we'll be home, and we can forget about him and all his shitty, selfish behavior. OK?'

I led him to the dining room, where there were people suddenly coming out of the woodwork. Where the hell they'd been twenty minutes ago, I'd have loved to know, but I was just happy to be part of a big group where I didn't have to worry about Gerald's lechery. Jake slid his eyes over to me a few times during dinner, then looked at Gerald, but he didn't say anything else about the whole thing.

When Mama D and my mother came in late, Jake stood and walked to my mom without bothering to tell me what was going on. He took her hand and led her away to the open balcony doors. After a couple of minutes, my mother rushed over to me, her eyes shooting daggers at Jake's dad.

They pulled me out, and the other people in the dining room attempted a hush so they could overhear, but Mama D, with her eyes on us the whole time, wouldn't allow it. She talked loudly and must have said something funny, because everyone laughed hard, and I could hear conversation pick up just after we left.

'Brenna.' Mom's eyes, twilight-sky blue and watery with unshed tears, zeroed in on me. 'What happened?' Her voice jerked and wobbled.

'Nothing,' I said, almost automatically. 'He was just being . . . weird, I guess. He told me that he and I were alike because we both liked rebels or whatever. And he grabbed my arm really hard and told me that Jake would be meeting a lot of new people, then he rubbed my shoulders and said something about first love.' I was trying to tone it down for my mother, but my head was spinning a little.

Jake's nostrils flared. The tears that had been a threat in my mom's eyes slid out of the corners and down her cheeks. Like a reflex, I felt my own eyes brim full of prickly tears.

'That fucking bastard,' my mother hissed, and I laughed a little with relief while she crushed her arms around me.

She was busy comforting me. I was busy being comforted.

Jake marched back into the dining room.

I would always kind of regret that I didn't get to see what actually happened. Later on, Saxon would say the exact same thing.

As the story goes, Jake tapped Gerald on the shoulder, stepped back so his father could stand, then punched him so hard he fell into the roasted whatever-that-was in the middle of the table.

Mama D screamed, which was apparently pretty weird for her. Jake's father actually blacked out from a combination of way too much alcohol and the impact of Jake's fist. A few aunts got hysterical. A few uncles stood and screamed at Jake. Mom and I had already rushed to the arched doorway that led to the dining room and stood, completely shocked, as chaos unfolded in front of our eyes.

Jake walked away from the whole thing, kissed me right in front of my mother, and turned to her and said, 'Mrs Blixen, I'm sorry to cut your stay short, but I'd like to go home now. Would you and Brenna mind coming along?'

At this point my mother had the great luck of an

entire audience of snobs for her reply. 'We'd love to join you Jake. I'm getting tired of all the trash around here,' she said. We went upstairs and packed our bags. Jake just wanted to get us out of there so he didn't have any problem using one of their cars to drive us home. It seemed surreal, leaving so fast, the pines whipping by us, the enormous cloistered houses all shacked up on the shore of the gigantic lake like one big, strange dream.

When Jake dropped us home, I only spent a minute on the porch with him. He kissed me and told me that he had to have a long talk with his stepfather, and that he would call me in the morning.

I walked into my house, our house, devoid of any priceless antiques, with average windows and sticky doors, and a slightly musty smell whenever we left it shut up for more than three days. There was no big lake or dock or garage filled with a fleet of boats. But I had never, ever seen anything as beautiful. Mom and I sat quietly at the dining-room table. She made us a pot of coffee, and once we started talking, we just couldn't stop.

I realized that Mom thought that I was having the time of my life, and I thought she was having the time of hers, and really we both felt lost and out of place and too polite to say.

'It was kind of a godsend that Jake punched that

drunk asshole and got us kicked out,' Mom said, then sipped her coffee politely.

I laughed. A little at first, then loud and long. 'Yeah. Jake has issues with punching people over me.'

Mom raised her eyebrows. 'He's done this before?'

'Um, yeah.' I paused, unsure what to do, but since I had gone this far, I figured I could tell her the rest. 'Saxon. He and Jake got in a fight over me months ago, and Jake knocked him out.'

Mom pursed her lips in clear disapproval, then her brow furrowed for a few long minutes. 'You know, Jake Kelly is a good guy. He knows his own mind, and he doesn't get swayed easily. And he obviously cares about you.'

I was holding my breath. This is what I had waited for my mother to say for so long, it felt strange that she would just be saying it now, as if it weren't what I had been dying to hear for almost an entire year.

'He does really care.' I poked at the handle of my coffee mug and watched the creamy brown liquid slosh dangerously near the edge. 'I'm glad he got to see his real family. And I'm glad I got to see him around them. It just shows that he doesn't get hung up on what other people think of him or expect from him.'

'He has a good, strong character. And it doesn't hurt that he's very good-looking.' My mom winked, then yawned, this cute, big-mouthed yawn. 'Oh, Bren, I have to get to bed. Mmm, how nice to sleep in my own bed! Thorsten will be surprised that we're home so early.' She kissed my head and put her coffee cup in the sink. Before she went up the stairs she stopped.

'Bren?'

'Yeah, Mom?' I asked as I copied her, putting my own mug in the sink.

'Are you and Jake having sex?'

The question sat heavy in the room for a few long seconds.

'No, Mom,' I said, without whining or sounding irritated. It was a fair question on her part. Really fair, in fact. 'He wants to wait.'

She shook her head. 'He's a good guy, Bren.'

I went to my bedroom with a light heart. Mom approved of Jake! It didn't matter that his entire snooty family had pretty much ostracized me; my smart mom had figured it all out and seen Jake's innate awesomeness.

And it did feel amazing to be in my own bed. I stretched over the cover and let out a long, girly moan of pure happiness. I felt tired, but not at all sleepy. I planned to call Evan and tell her everything, but first I popped open my computer and saw that I had four emails in my inbox. From Saxon.

I opened the first one.

> *Blix,*
>
> *I'm in deep here. Lots of shit going down. How does your cell get reception in Europe, but not in Buttfuck, NY? Give me a holler when you get this.*
>
> *Sax*

The next three were variations of the first, all vague and whiny and kind of desperate – for Saxon. I picked up my cell. It was almost midnight. Saxon had always been a night owl, but he was a working man now. What if this wasn't a good time?

I figured he probably set his phone to vibrate when he didn't want it to ring, so I took the plunge and called.

His voice coiled in my ears, as sexy and smoky as always. 'Hey, gorgeous,' he practically crooned into the phone. 'Where have you been all my life?'

I sighed, thoughts of his infamous sex-phone debacle still buried deep in my brain.

'Saxon, are you drinking again? God, you get sappy when you're drunk.'

'Shut up and go with it, Blix,' he hissed. Louder he said, 'That sounds sweet. So when are you coming down to this hole to see me?'

'Where are you again?' I searched my memory for the name of the little Jersey town he'd been sent to rot in. 'Oh, Lodi, right?'

'That's it,' he said, his voice so sunny and happy I was a little freaked out. 'Well, I'll call you, OK, babe?'

'Um, all right, Saxon.'

The connection clicked off, and I was left staring at my cell phone wondering what had happened to Saxon in the matter of a few weeks. I had already talked to Evan and was completely ready for bed when the phone rang again, and I dived for it, thinking it had to be Jake.

'Hey, Blix,' Saxon said, and I could hear the smile around the new sound; was it worry?

'Hey, Saxon.' I snuggled under the blankets. 'What's up?'

'How's life with my big-shot grandma and her league of extraordinary assholes?'

I laughed at that. 'It was hell on earth. Then your dad got a little frisky, and Jake punched him in the face. So we kind of got voluntarily booted out.'

'Jake punched Gerald?' Saxon crowed.

'Oh yeah. Knocked him out on the dining-room table.' I couldn't keep the admiration out of my voice. Wow, did Jake Kelly ever find new and awesome ways to turn me on.

'That little fuck,' Saxon grumbled. 'He's punch happy! I wish I could have seen it. Shit, I wish I could have *thrown* it.'

'It was pretty deserved.' I bit my lip, remembering

the creepy scene that led to the whole debacle. 'Sorry I didn't call sooner. Your family's place is like a huge dead zone.'

'In so many ways,' Saxon drawled. 'It's cool, Blix. I've been kind of screwing things up with this really cool girl I met. So, since I've already royally screwed up any chance of romance between us, I thought you might be the girl to help me.'

'How about the fact that there's hardly anyone who will talk to you any more?' I laughed, but Saxon was strangely quiet. Much as he gave off the whole tough persona, it was sometimes depressingly easy to bring Saxon down, and I always hated myself for doing it, no matter how unintentional it might have been.

'That's no joke.' His voice clanked out, heavy and sad for a moment. Then he switched gears. 'So, you know I'm not going to throw that toxic-ass "L" word around. It gives me the fucking heebie-jeebies. But say I might be hedging right around something kind of like it with someone smart and funny and really, really hot. But she likes an older guy who's all those lame things girls go for.'

'What lame things?' I asked, unable to keep the grin off of my face.

'You know, he's nice and has a job and doesn't deal or do drugs and he goes to college,' Saxon rattled off, and I could practically hear him rolling his eyes over the phone.

'He sounds perfect. Tell her to date him and then leave her alone,' I told him. Again, no joking back or laughter from Saxon.

'Blix, I *really* like this girl.'

'Wow.' I sat up in my bed for a minute. 'You don't just want to get in her pants?'

'Probably won't. She's under lock and key by her crazed parents. And she's a Catholic schoolgirl. I can't remember, do they uphold the stereotype or defy it?'

He was trying to be cute and funny, but I could hear the underlying desperation in his voice.

'This is real?' I asked, my voice a little shaky.

'Yep.' He popped his lips around the word. 'As real as anything I've ever felt.'

'Saxon!' I said and stopped because I just wasn't sure what else there was to say. A teeny tiny part of me felt a little jealous that he'd moved on to someone else. Despite my constant gripes about him, I had always had an extra soft place in my heart for Saxon. A bigger part of me felt like this was a really good thing and exactly what I'd been waiting for since our final relationship fracture. 'This is a big deal. This is real!'

'Yeah.' He sighed. 'And, if you can believe it, my natural charms just aren't cutting it with her. I'm going kind of bat-shit over it. What do you think?'

'I don't know.' I was still trying to wrap my brain around the idea of Saxon in love. Saxon. In love. With someone who was not me. Despite the prickle of weirdness, this was ... good. And I was so curious. 'Tell me about her.'

I heard the creak of bedsprings. I wondered what his room at his aunt's looked like. He breathed a long breath out. 'First of all, she works so hard, it's almost sick. She's a roller-skating waitress and she makes it all look figure-skater easy, but it's hot, heavy, thankless work, and she does hours on end, no complaints. She took her skates off yesterday and her socks were bloody. Her feet were blistered and broken open from breaking in new skates. Can you imagine that?' he marveled.

I couldn't. It seemed incredibly painful. But more difficult to imagine was Saxon feeling so much sympathy and admiration for a girl he liked. This was huge, and all the details only excited my curiosity. 'Tell me more.'

He was in the swing now. 'She's smart. I mean, life smart and generally smart. She reads a lot and gets good grades. She wants to go to college, but her parents' place is on its way to tanking, so who knows. She has this great hair. It's so dark brown, it's almost black. And it smells so fucking good, Blix. And her tits—'

'Hardy har,' I interrupted and he laughed.

'Sorry. Listening to myself being all mushy gets old fast. I have to keep it real.' I heard him jangling something in the background.

'What's that sound?'

'Sorry. My keys. I've become a fucking fidgeter.'

'Shouldn't you start chain-smoking right about now?' I leaned back on my pillow and imagined Saxon with his mouth quirked in a half-smile, blowing out a long, steady stream of bluish smoke.

'Are you encouraging me?' His laugh was a happy rumble. 'I think Aunt Helene is a little allergic to smoke, so I won't do it around her or at home. And at work, I don't get a fucking second. Goddamn slave drivers,' he harped cheerily. 'So I've hardly been able to get through a pack this entire week.'

Wow. It was like Saxon had gone into his own little cocoon and was coming out a healthier, happier, less grumpy butterfly.

'What's her name, Saxon?'

'Cadence,' he said. 'Cadence Erikson.'

'Did you try just asking her out?' I suggested, nestling my arm under my head and cradling the phone closer to my ear. He had practically turned my knees to jelly when he asked me out the first time.

'She's kind of with the college guy. They aren't right for each other, though,' he said confidently.

'Is he nasty to her?' My fingertips traced the seams of my pillowcase.

'Nah.' Saxon's admission was flippant, like that didn't matter one way or another. 'I mean, he's perfect as far as meathead assholes go. He's just not it for Cadence, you know?'

'No, I don't.' I laughed softly. 'Maybe you should just let them be.'

'Nope.' Saxon's voice snagged with an edge of determination I'd never heard before. 'This ain't love I'm busting in on, Bren. With you and Jake . . .' He took a deep breath and exhaled slowly. 'With you and Jake,' he started again, 'I was crashing a party I had no business being at. With Cadence, I'm the one she's gonna love. Once she realizes that I'm not a total asshole.'

'What do you need?' This was real, I realized. I didn't know if it was real for Cadence, but it was for Saxon. A little part of me wondered what kind of girl she was if she wasn't attracted to Saxon. I knew it wasn't just me. He was like a wild animal you saw and had the overwhelming urge to tame.

'I need help, Blix. And I don't have a damn soul to turn to. I only have you.' Saxon's voice was worried.

I knew how he felt. Alone. Out of place. Put down. I knew it all. 'I'll figure something out. I promise. Can I call you tomorrow?'

'Yeah. I'm going into work around noon.' I could hear the relief in his voice.

'Sweet dreams, Saxon.'

'You have no idea.' He laughed softly.

We clicked off and I stared up at my ceiling, my thoughts running like crazy. How was I going to get to Saxon? What could I do to help him? Did I even want to?

I did. I would. I had to.

My head was swimming. I wished Jake was with me. I didn't want to call him, but I wanted to know what happened between him and his father.

Jake had been worried that he'd changed this summer, but any changes he'd made were just for the better, as far as I was concerned. He was more confident, more sure of himself. I fell asleep thinking about Jake and woke up to my mom brushing my fringe back.

'Brenna?' I could see her smile through the blur of sleep in my eyes. 'Sweetheart, are you awake?'

'Yes,' I said groggily. 'Is it late?'

'Not very, honey.' She twisted a length of my hair around her finger and let it fall in a long coil. 'They asked if I could do a late summer session. One of the tutors broke her leg. Do you remember Angela with the freckles?'

'Oh, that sucks.' I yawned and rubbed the sleep out

of my eyes. 'Poor Angela. That's great for you, though, Mom.'

'I kind of hate this.' My mom wrung her hands, her voice a little wobbly. 'We just got back and things were so hard for you. I feel like we hardly saw each other, and this will eat the rest of our summer up.'

I rubbed her hand in mine, looked into her great blue-gray eyes and at the lips she was chewing with worry and felt so good. It felt good knowing that she was doing something she loved again. 'You need to do this. I'm fine. Jake isn't going back to Zinga's for a while. Devon wanted to hang out. Kelsie will be around. All good friends. I'll have fun and be careful. I promise. OK?'

'You're growing up so fast.' She bit her lips together. 'I'm really proud of you.'

'Thank you.' I patted her cheek with my hand. 'I'm proud of you, pursuing your doctoral degree. Seriously, I'm so happy for you.'

She kissed me hard and then she was gone, back to her job, and I was alone. Well, not completely alone.

I was just out of the shower when I heard the crunch of tires on the driveway. Jake!

I ran out, barefoot, damp-haired, and jumped into his arms.

'Hey, you.' His smile was slow and warm just

before he kissed me. 'It was weird that I didn't get to wake up and see you first thing.'

'I know. I thought about you last night. Is it all cool? With your stepfather?' I tucked his overlong hair behind his ears.

'Yeah.' He nodded. 'You know, some people are just always there for you. He's one of them, so I'm lucky like that. I was actually wondering if you wanted to take a little road trip?'

'Sure.' Me and Jake, alone in the truck, windows down, sun out, the last of summer ours to enjoy . . . it sounded perfect. 'Where do you want to go?'

'How does Lodi sound?' Jake grinned.

Saxon 3

'Operation Convince Cadence I'm Not An Asshole' wasn't exactly going the way I had hoped when I started my mission.

I guess what I'd envisioned was Cadence spending time with me, my natural charm wearing away her ironclad defenses, and her deciding to dump her lump of a boyfriend and fall into my arms instead.

But the truth was, Cadence wasn't really much of a romantic, and it wound up that I kind of was one. Because all of my jokes and wooing and gifts and gestures didn't change a few solid facts.

1) I was a 'crackhead'. Granted, most people stopped calling me that once I proved my chops as a waiter, then subbed a day or two at the grill – where men were made. But there was no forgetting that I was here because of all the drugs I had been taking.

2) I had no vehicle. In Sussex County, where the roads were impossibly long, windy and still dirt, that would have been a tragedy. Here it might have been

less of one, except for the fact that I knew no one and went nowhere other than Aunt Helene's house, the restaurant, foodstores, home improvement stores, and stores that sold silly old lady shit, like knitting needles and doilies and porcelain cherubs.

3) I wasn't a rotten, hardworking college schmuck. Nope. I was a lazy, entitled, drug-addled semi-genius. Or at least I was before my ass landed in Lodi and started the Saxon Reformation. I wasn't sure what I was now. Except crazy about this bat-shit girl. Who looked at the facts and made decisions.

Like not to date me because I didn't hold up against the facts of Meathead, her like-interest. Because it sure was no love-interest.

I could tell he bored the hell out of her. I could tell he was basically a nice douchebag, and he knew there was a real reason he should like Cadence. He just couldn't riddle what the hell that reason might be.

But I did know every reason why she was beyond amazing. I knew that she was deceptively brilliant. I knew that she was aggressively hard-working. That she had a thick shell and a soft interior that hardly anyone got to see. And I knew that if I was ever lucky enough to get a glimpse, it would be worth all of the hardship and waiting. Because she was good and kind and funny, and probably damn sexy if someone could just unknot the kinks she'd worked herself into.

Luckily, I was always a champion at deceptive mirages. So I knew that Cadence and the Goon weren't as twitterpated as they were pretending. And I made whatever moves I could to take advantage of that fact.

But my real strike of brilliance was mostly an accident. It was one of those weird, rare nights off that I almost never had. Aunt Helene had been picked up by some of her old crone friends to get wild at the local bingo hall. Before she left, she grabbed my arms hard and told me that I should get out and have some fun. I smiled and kissed her hard because she was so fucking cool, then I pushed her out the door and into the arms of late-night bingo. And I went to work putting up shelving until the goddamn drill lost power. I had forgotten to plug the extra battery pack in. I was shit out of luck.

The night was nice, kind of cool, kind of breezy. I sat on Aunt Helene's front porch and found my pack of cigs. I lit up, but it didn't feel the same. I only smoked half, then stubbed it out and decided to go on a little walkabout. I wanted to see the neighborhood. I wanted to move my legs. It was hard to believe I'd spent so much time back home cooped up in a house or a car, lounging. Now that my body had been working, I felt like I needed to keep it going.

I walked up the street, waving to the vaguely familiar neighbors I passed here and there. I walked back down and looked discreetly into a few lit windows, catching tiny glimpses of normal and not-so-normal families eating, arguing, watching television. I was avoiding one house on the block that I could bet was empty anyway. But I was drawn to it. And if I was right, and it was empty, what was the harm?

But fate was my lady.

The lights were on. Pammy's car was gone and so was Tony's. It was a long shot. I could get an earful of a pretty pissed-off Rosalie Erikson. But I just might get an eyeful of sexy Cadence Erikson. I decided to take the chance.

I was going to lean on the doorbell when I remembered that it was late, and if Sullie was home, he'd be sleeping. This might sound very stalker-esque, but in the moment it felt pretty fucking Dark Knight; I climbed the fire escape on the side of their building.

It had been a set of apartments once, but Tony bought them out and finally renovated it into one big house with some weird apartment hang-ons. Like a fire escape. We didn't have apartments in good old Sussex, so I was kind of jacked to jump up on one and scale it like I'd seen in the movies.

It was just as cool as I'd imagined.

I got to the lit window and peeked in quietly. Sullie was crying in the middle of a girl's room. I couldn't tell if it was Cadence's or Pammy's (or both of theirs if they shared), but he was pissed off. I was so focused on him, I hardly noticed Cadence skid in. She was a knockout, even in bumming-around clothes with panic on her face.

'Sullivan, don't cry,' she begged. 'Here, bub, do you want a baba?'

She held a bottle out to him, but he only cried louder. Then Cadence's face crumpled, and she sat on the edge of her bed, put her hands over her face and cried like a baby.

'I'm so sorry, Sullie. I'm so sorry. I just don't know what you want, buddy,' she sobbed.

Seeing her cry turned Sullie's waterworks on full blast. He was practically screaming when I knocked on the window.

In hindsight, it probably would have been smart to go back down the escape since I knew Sullie was up and Cadence was alone, but the whole moment came on me faster than I could think it through. When Cadence heard the knock, her eyes went wild, and she grabbed a field hockey stick that was next to her bed.

'Who is that?' she yelled. Sullie's little mouth made an 'O' of surprise. 'I will fuck your shit up! Get lost!'

She had good volume, and she was pretty damn scary. I held my hands up, surrender style, and let her see me so I didn't get clubbed in the head.

'Saxon?' She finally put the stick down on the bed, still well within reach. 'What are you doing here? You scared the crap out of me!'

'I'm unarmed.' I gave her my most charming smile. 'I saw the light on and—'

'Decided to spy on me?' she snapped. 'Have you done that before?'

'No!' I cursed my ridiculous need to live like I was the Caped Crusader. 'I was actually a little scared to get your mom and have her kick my ass for bugging you.'

Cadence relented a little. 'She is a little scary,' she conceded.

Now that things were calm again, Sullie's moment of silence was over for good and he was sobbing again.

'I heard Sullie-boy. I thought you might need a little help,' I offered.

Cadence's brow knitted and then her face flamed a bright red. She realized that I had seen her sobbing her ass off. 'OK,' she mumbled.

'Hey, Sullie,' I said through the window. He quieted down a little bit. Cadence unhitched the screen, and I climbed in and bumped my head on the window frame. 'Holy fuck!'

Sullie laughed, a bubbly, happy sound.

Cadence looked at me like I was her knight in shining armor. So I spent the next half an hour being a buffoon, making Sullie laugh in any way I could possibly think of.

Nothing was too humiliating.

I barked like a dog and got on all fours like a horse so Sullie could pound on my back and get a ride up and down the stairs, I got bonked on the head and in the balls to the point where I was fairly sure I was going to be brain-dead and impotent before the night was over, and I sang along to seven lullaby songs, mostly making up words as I went along.

Eventually, I was able to lay Sullie down in his little Winnie the Pooh crib. I finished off 'Twinkle, Twinkle Little Star' for him.

'Twinkle, twinkle little star, I like pickles in a jar, Salami's good, don't eat it dry, Yellow mustard you should try, Twinkle, twinkle little star, I like pickles in a jar,' I crooned quietly.

Cadence was standing in the doorway, arms crossed, her face calm and happy.

'Pickles and salami?' she asked in a whisper.

I shrugged. 'I didn't know the words. I don't think Sullie cared.'

We moved away from his room like ninjas, and once we made it to Cadence's, we both flopped on her bed in happy camaraderie.

She turned and looked at me with big, sweet, green eyes full of pure gratitude. 'Thank you. So much, Saxon. I was losing it for a few minutes.'

'I'm glad I decided to climb your fire escape.'

She smiled a little and smoothed her hair. It wasn't something just any guy would notice, but I was a practiced man-whore. She smoothed her hair because she was wishing that she looked a little better. Because she wanted to impress me.

'Tonight just got all screwed up,' she explained. 'Mom and Dad went to a wedding in Maplewood and they got a hotel room. Pammy is staying out till God knows when after work, and Jimmy went to some all-night video game marathon after his shift. I didn't have work, and I thought that I would have the night off. But since I was the only one home, I got kind of stuck with Sullie.'

'That sucks.' Our hands were just a few inches away. I moved my fingers slightly closer – not quite touching her, but almost.

'I don't want to think about it that way.' She sighed, then turned on her side, pulling her hand away from mine to prop her head on it. 'I love him, you know? It's just, sometimes this family can be really, really overwhelming.'

'So where's Jeff tonight?' I didn't want to get caught in that trap where I joined in and bitched about her family. And that family was particularly scary to bitch about. I wasn't doing cartwheels over the fact that Jeff had already come up, but I needed to know where I stood.

'He's in this fraternity house and they had a big party tonight.' Her eyes flicked down and her mouth crumpled into a frown.

'You were going to go?' I tapped her foot with the toe of my shoe and she looked up at me, those big green eyes tired and sad.

She shook her head. 'It's some kind of thing with the fraternities and sororities. Fraternity guys go with girls from their sister sorority. It's not really a date. It's just tradition,' she explained. 'It sounds like it could be a tradition, right?' She looked at me with such a hopeful expression on her pretty face, I realized that I had two options.

I could blast her dipshit boyfriend out of the water and make a case for why he was probably a lying, sack-of-shit cheater.

Or I could go against my every instinct and be at least halfway reasonable.

This girl was doing strange things to me. I rolled onto my side and looked at her. 'Fraternities and sororities have all kinds of weird traditions. That said, if you were my girlfriend, I'd have them make a new tradition right there.' Before she could say anything else, I changed the subject. 'Did you eat? You want to order something?'

She looked at me for a long minute and pursed her lips. 'Yeah, that would be cool. How about Chinese?'

So we went down to the Erikson's small-as-hell falling-down kitchen, found the Chinese food menu, and started ordering our asses off.

'I have to have fried dumplings.' Cadence looked at the menu intently.

I wrote it down on a Dunkin' Donuts napkin. 'All right. I need barbeque spareribs. And General Tso's chicken.'

'And eggdrop soup.' She closed her eyes and crinkled the menu against her chest. My heart dropped to the bottom of my guts. 'Do you like that?'

'The one with the weird white floaty things?' I asked. She nodded. 'Yeah, that's cool.' I fucking hated eggdrop soup, but I really liked her, so in my warped mind eating that slime soup was a way to show her I cared.

We got spring rolls and egg rolls, cream cheese wontons and extra pork fried rice. By the time I got off the phone, Cadence was smiling hard and didn't want me to see. She looked straight down at her lap.

'What's up?' I pushed on her shoulder with two fingers. It wasn't nearly enough touching, but it was going to have to do for now.

'It's going to be a lot of food.' She shrugged. 'I

can afford it,' she rushed, her smile dropping a little.

'Are you kidding? You could have smashed my head in with a field hockey stick. Or called the cops and nailed me for a breaking and entering. I'm paying as thanks for your overall sanity.'

She laughed out loud. It was a loose, happy sound. 'Thanks, Saxon. I kind of thought tonight would suck. I'm . . . I'm glad you came up the fire escape.' She looked a little embarrassed and flustered.

'Don't thank me yet.' I crossed my arms and leaned back on the counter. 'I might have peaked with my idiotic version of "Twinkle Twinkle Little Star". Maybe it's all downhill from here.'

She shook her head and all that dark, shiny hair spilled over her tanned shoulders and sweet, gorgeous boobs. Like she noticed me checking her out, she pulled it into a ponytail so slowly it was pure torment. 'I doubt that.' She looked around her kitchen, swiveled her sexy hips, and raised her eyebrows.

'What do you want to do while we wait?' I asked. So she could throw out an idea that wasn't me leaping across the room and tearing her clothes off in a fit of uncontrolled lust, 'cos this girl was messing with my head in a serious way.

'I don't know.' She linked her hands behind her neck and let her arms open and close like butterfly wings. 'I don't usually have guys over. Actually my parents would probably kill you if they knew you were here.'

'I can keep a secret,' I promised. 'So, doesn't Jeff come and hang?' There he was again, the Goon-in-the-room, but I wanted to know.

'He's really busy with school and stuff. I only see him when I have a night off and he's up here.' She dropped her hands and grabbed the end of her ponytail, and she was twisting it around her fingers. 'It's not that often. And we always go out. Like with his friends. He doesn't like to hang around here much.'

I just nodded. 'So what do you do with your girl-friends? When they're around?'

'Oh!' She laughed nervously. I had never seen Cadence this jittery. I kind of loved it.

'We do stupid stuff. Like paint each other's nails. Or we do karaoke on the Wii. Or we look at old yearbooks.'

'All right.' I put my hand out. She looked at it for a long second, then took it. 'Let's get this party started. Will karaoke wake Sullie?'

'No.' She squeezed my hand, just slightly, and smiled a little. 'Once he's out, he could sleep through a hurricane.'

'Cool. Um, I guess we should paint our nails while we wait for the food, right? So we can rock our hot looks when we're performing?' I felt a little like a tool, but only a little.

I was usually trying to keep up a persona, and it got old after a while. Being jaded and sexed-up and rebellious was fine, but it was also kind of humorless sometimes. As ridiculous as the night's activities sounded, I was kind of looking forward to them.

'You want me to paint your nails?' Cadence pulled my hand over and inspected my nails. 'Really?'

'Hell, yeah.' I wiggled my fingers at her. 'Don't think I'm going to do yours and not get anything in return.' All right, I had to get one kinky shot in the midst of all of the flaming girlieness.

'I'll be right back.' Cadence ran to the staircase, hopped up a few steps, then looked down at me, smiled, and hopped up the rest of the steps. She came back down a minute later with a bag of nail polishes. There were probably about fifty thousand, and a lot looked the same, but I wasn't going to pretend that I knew shit about what a girl needed to keep her nails different colors.

She handed me the bag and we sat across from each other on the couch. 'OK.' She clapped her hands a little. 'You pick a color first.'

'I like this green.' It was kind of an olive metallic color. Not very girly.

'Do you want me to do your toes or your fingers?'

She grabbed the polish and smacked it against her palm a few times.

I laughed. 'You're asking me that because you've never been exposed to my feet. I guarantee you they stink. You're not getting near them.'

She unscrewed the top from the polish with a twisted smile and took my hand. Hers were everything you'd want a girl's hand to be: soft, small, delicate, pretty.

I loved the feel of her holding my hand, and I loved her painting my nails with her ridiculous polish.

'So you think I won't like you if your feet stink?' She dipped the brush and softly, smoothly, coated one of my nails with a thin coat. Her hands were sure and steady.

'I don't think I've ever talked to anyone about my feet before.' I felt like a slightly different version of myself around Cadence. A more honest version. Who didn't mind letting a hot girl know how bad my feet smelled.

'Didn't any of your girlfriends complain about them?' she asked slyly.

She was fishing hardcore, and I was glad for the interest.

'I've never had any complaints from the ladies.' When she rolled her eyes, I amended. 'I've never had any complaints in the physical department.'

'What *did* your girlfriends complain about, then?' she asked, laying rapid, even strokes of green paint on my fingernails. It was weird to watch them transform.

'Basic stuff, you know. That I'm a cold-hearted asshole. That I'm a womanizer. That I'm an egomaniac. Basic girlfriend gripes.' I wrapped it up with my best cocky smile, even though I was sweating fucking bullets. I wasn't into false advertising, but this was pure kamikaze shit.

She laughed, her shoulders shaking slightly. 'So, are you, like, the Casanova of Sussex County?'

'You could say that.'

She leaned her head closer, and I could smell the girl shampoo sweetness of her hair. 'So every girl just falls in love when you snap your fingers?' Her green eyes flicked up and she stared right at me from under all those sexy black eyelashes.

'No.' At the word, the light in her eyes cooled and changed. She was hooked and hungry for more. 'Not every girl.'

'Even the great Saxon Maclean has been burned?' She was giving every nail a second coat. I was trying to pay attention. It looked easy enough, but like most shit, I seriously doubted it was as easy as it seemed. And I was going to have to do her in a minute. I smiled at my own dirty mental innuendo.

'Yeah, I've been burned.' I watched her cap the polish and flexed my green-nailed fingers.

'Tell me,' she suggested casually. 'Unless it hurts too much.' She lifted my hand a little, pursed her lips, and blew gently on the drying paint.

There was something undeniably erotic about watching her blow on that nail polish. Even though I couldn't put my finger on what it was, I definitely had a visceral reaction to it. One that I had to cover quickly with a throw pillow before I drew any attention to it.

'All right.' I swallowed hard and tried not to stare too hard as she blew on my fingertips. 'I had a thing for this girl. Really, really smart; mad talented; gorgeous; funny, the whole package.'

'Sounds good,' Cadence said coolly, but I could tell her back was up just a tiny bit.

'Too good.' All the stupid fucking memories bumped and burned in the corners of my brain, still pretty raw and mostly just humiliating. 'For me, that is. She thought we might work for about three hours. Then she met my brother.'

Cadence's eyes snapped up. 'You have a brother?'

'Yeah.' My mind flipped back to Jake and, for a split second, I dealt with the weird ache I usually managed to keep smashed completely flat. 'And, unfortunately, he's considered very hot by the womenfolk. He's naturally a nice guy, you know, into all that romantic shit. And he's a little bit of a straightedge, a totally hard worker, and madly in love with this girl.'

'Wait.' Cadence looked up from her torturous nail polish blowing. 'Are you the evil twin?'

I laughed outright. 'I might as well be.' I shook my head and immediately wished I could tell Brenna. She'd like that idea. 'Anyway, they met and it was like fucking Romeo and Juliet, you know? No competition. I did manage to get her away from him for, like, three weeks. But she was just desperate to get back to him as soon as she could. She figured me out quick.'

'What's so bad about you, Crackhead?' She put my hands down on my lap, and I felt a little bad about that. I admired the finished product. I'd never had nail polish on my fingers, so it was kind of fascinating.

'I really am cold-hearted.' I tapped the polished surface of my nails with my thumb, surprised by how smooth they were. 'I don't care about other people. I'm kind of a man-whore.' Her eyes popped wide on that one. 'I have no ambition. I have no respect. I'm too smart to ever worry about school. I start fights on purpose. I've done enough drugs to kill a small horse. I think the real question is, What's good about me? That one might take less time to figure out.'

Her whole face went still while she looked right at me for a long, uncomfortable minute.

'I think there's a lot of good in you, Saxon.'

'Thanks.' I pushed the bag her way. 'Pick your color.' I felt . . . something. The sociopath in me was taking a long hibernation, and I was suddenly curious to know what she saw that was good in me.

She handed me a pale pink. Hardly a color.

'Wuss.' I raised my eyebrows.

She grabbed the bottle back and picked up a bright purple.

'All right, you're brave.' I took the bottle and examined the glittery color. 'But maybe also a little reckless.'

'Is this your first time?' She started to smile at her own joke, but the smile got stuck halfway between flirty and something way more serious.

'You have officially popped my nail polish cherry.' The air in the room sizzled, hot and tense.

'I guess there aren't many girls who can say they've popped any of your cherries.' It made us laugh and burst whatever tense, weird-ass thing we were feeling. She held out her hand to me.

I'm a big admirer of the female body, and certain parts get more worship than others. Hands usually aren't in the running. This time, I was going to have to make an exception. Her hands were soft and small, but the nails were short and clean, for work. Even her knuckles were nice, kind of lovely ridges, and I brushed my thumb over them experimentally. It felt good.

239

It didn't exactly do it for me like a handful of tits or a nice ass grab, but it really felt good. Like essentially, elementally good.

I copied Cadence as best I could, setting up the paint and holding her hands out so that I could see all of her fingers.

'I think your hands are nice,' I said, and it sounded awkward. Especially for me. I'm usually a little more glib, just by definition.

'Thank you,' she said a little stiffly, but with the sweet hint of a smile.

I took the brush and blobbed a dot of purple on her fingernail. She tried not to laugh at me outright. 'Not so much,' she warned. 'Thin coats. Here.' She reached over and got out her bag of cotton balls and the nail polish remover. She rubbed it on the nail and it all came off. 'OK, Casanova. Again.'

So I did it again, and it was better. When I had done one coat on the first three fingers, I felt confident enough to multitask. 'So,' I began, 'tell me about your dating life.'

She rolled her eyes. 'It's a pretty lame story.'

'I love lame stories. For example, I've seen *The Notebook* twice.'

'That is a classic,' she gasped, horrified. We laughed again. 'My love story is pretty basic. I meet a reasonably attractive guy, we date a little, he turns out to be a complete loser, I get dumped. Wash, rinse, repeat.'

I halted progress on her ring finger and stared at her fallen-fucking-angel face.

'You get dumped?'

'Yes.' She pinched her lips tight and nodded. 'People think that if you're a good-looking girl, it just doesn't happen. But I guess I'm dense. Because I've been dumped. A lot.'

'Why?' But I was already answering my question in my head, because the answer was obvious – Cadence didn't put out.

'I don't like to rush things.' Bingo. 'I mean, guys want to do a lot when you've only known them for a few weeks. Then, once they dump me, I feel kind of glad that we didn't do anything I wasn't comfortable with.' She looked up at me. 'Did you stay with any of the girls you dated longer because of sex?'

'Nope.' I had to refocus because I was squeezing her fingers tighter than necessary when the memories popped up. 'Actually, the girl I liked the best wouldn't even think of it. And, frankly, I didn't want it if she didn't.'

'That's cool.' Cadence looked intently at my not-half-bad paint job. 'Jeff has been bringing it up a lot. He says I have Puritan ideals about sex.'

'Sounds like the big man took an intro to a psych course,' I said between clenched teeth. 'Look, if a guy likes you for you, he'll wait, OK? Speaking as a walking hard-on, sex doesn't mean faithfulness. If you were my girlfriend and you wanted to wait, I'd wait because I was into you and that's what you wanted.' Then I looked down at her nails and blew gently.

I heard her draw a quick breath in. What was so sexy about blowing on fingernails?

Crazy!

'Did you mean that hypothetically, or were you being literal?' Her voice was a mix of breathy and high-pitched.

I blew again, slowly, before I answered. 'What do you mean?' I knew what she meant. I just didn't want to get duped. I wanted her to say what I wanted to hear.

'I mean, do you think about me as a girlfriend or is it just a general—'

The doorbell rang. It was loud in the hushed house, and Cadence jumped up to get it. I followed right behind her. She reached out to take the food, but I reached over her.

'Your nails are wet,' I reminded her.

'Oh. Yeah. Of course,' she fumbled.

I paid the guy and over-tipped, just in case this became something Cadence and I did once in a while.

I was already plotting time together, thinking about us as something like a unit.

We unpacked the white paper cartons and spread them on the coffee table in the living room. We sat cross-legged in the dim yellow light and ate our food, laughing now and then inbetween. Slowly, we got closer. Before we knew it, we were sitting right next to each other, close enough that my breath moved her hair.

'You need to have a boneless sparerib. They're the best I've ever had.' I was going to scoop it onto her plate when she opened her mouth and closed her eyes.

I didn't even hesitate. I picked up a piece and put it in her mouth, then tried to control my raging wood when she sucked the meat off of my fingers and licked at the sauce with her hot tongue. The entire thing couldn't have lasted more than a few seconds, but I felt on fire, turned-on like I'd never felt before.

I pulled my hand away reluctantly. We ate in silence for a minute.

'You didn't eat any of the dumplings. I think I ate seven. You need the last one.' Cadence snatched it up with her bare fingers and I opened my mouth.

I know I had talked a big game about taking it slow, but I was talking the big game: sex. Once I'd had a taste of her, even if it was a highly polished taste, I wasn't about to let go without at least taking a swing and trying for some kind of anything physical. I ate the dumpling, then grabbed her hand so she couldn't pull it back. There was a second where we both just stared across the couple of inches that separated us. Then I licked the dumpling sauce off of her fingers. Her eyes were big, but eager. She was waiting for me to make the next move.

I kissed her fingers, then down to her palm, then along her wrist. She was wearing an old tank top that was rapidly becoming see-through from too many washings, which was a boon for me. I kissed up to her elbow, along her bicep, nicely shaped from lifting so many trays, and up her shoulder.

That's where my mouth stopped.

I hovered over that smooth skin, breathed in the smell of her that was partially clean girl, partially something sweet and fruit-like, and mostly just Cadence. Her hand moved then, and I watched it, the purple paint I painted on it rising up until she grabbed at my face, then quickly with her other hand, she pulled me up to her mouth.

My mouth found hers, hot and fast. What had started at barely a simmer exploded into a full-blown kitchen fire.

Her mouth opened up and licked at me, nipped and bit, and I gave her lips and mouth similar treatment. Our bodies strained up and toward each other, her hands ripped at my T-shirt, pushing up underneath it and spreading out over my abs and chest. I lifted her onto my lap, facing me and let my hands roam every good, warm place on her. I didn't venture under her clothes. I wanted to. Holy fucking hell, I wanted her. But I had a feeling letting her be in charge would serve me well.

I didn't know if I had ever been kissed the way she kissed me. It was like her entire body threw itself into the kiss. She was wild, her mouth was sweet and hot, her hands were greedy and quick. I was strained against my pants, and she rubbed against my erection, moaning a little into my mouth. I pulled away from her mouth and sucked down along her jaw and onto her neck. She dug her nails into the bare skin of my back and ground down against me.

'Saxon,' she breathed, grabbing at my shoulders under my T-shirt and kissing all over my ears and neck and down to my arms.

I felt like I was being ripped apart. I wanted so much more. In another life, with another girl, I would have had her on the carpet, my hand down her pants, her shirt crumpled on the floor, my pants undone . . . and she would have been happy with it. At least in that moment.

But this was now and it was Cadence, and there wasn't going to be any of that. I couldn't ruin it like that.

'Saxon,' she said again, this time her voice ragged.

It was like she was begging me. I had to use every iota of patience in my body to wrestle with my need for her.

God, I wanted her, wanted to show her how good it could be, wanted to knock any thought of anyone else out of her mind. I knew I had the skills to do it, but I didn't want to risk it being the first and last time we did it.

She pressed her body to mine harder, said my name again, this time right against my ear, like a promise. She rubbed her face against my neck, and all I could think about was making her mine totally. All of my good intentions were about to burn in Hell when there was a knock at the door. Cadence pulled away from me, her eyes wide with panic.

'I'll get it.' I tried to calm my breathing and figure out what the hell I would do if I wound up face-to-face with her parents.

'No!' Her eyes were perfectly round with startled fear, and it occurred to me that Cadence knew who was at the door. And I was willing to bet it wasn't her parents. 'No, Saxon.' She smoothed her hair down, took a deep breath and walked to the door.

I wasn't about to straighten my shirt and make it look nice. Maybe because I had a pretty good idea who it would be.

'Jeff!' Cadence cried, and she returned his hug. Not

in a half-hearted way. Not like she had just been sucking my face and grinding against my dick for the last half hour.

Jeff had already looked over her shoulder and seen me.

'Who's that?' He pointed at me.

I stood, feeling like a grade-A jerk-off.

Cadence looked at me, her face worried, and shook her head.

'I had to drop something off to Cadence. For work,' I ground out. 'I was on my way out.'

I stood and walked to the door, and Cadence ran after me. In the house, I could hear the Goon call out, 'Who the hell was all this food for, Cade?'

'Saxon, please,' she begged once we were on the porch.

'Don't sweat it, Cadence.' I forced myself to believe I didn't give a fucking shit so I could deliver what I was about to say convincingly. 'I know how to have a good time. I'm not going to rat you out to your sad-sack boyfriend.'

'It's not that.' She wrung her hands and blinked hard, her eyes wet. 'What we did . . . I never . . . I don't think it was just—'

I cut her off before I had to hear anything else. I did what I do best. I fucked it up.

'Please, baby,' I sneered. 'Did that seriously even

register on your radar? The dumplings were probably the most memorable part of the whole night. Don't get your panties in a knot over it, OK? Thanks for everything.'

'Saxon, wait!' Her voice was a mangled plea. 'Please wait!'

But I didn't.

I felt a little like my chest was filled with hot oil, crackling and burning me inside, and I didn't want anyone to know that's what I was feeling.

Especially not the girl who made me feel it.

Jake 3

Brenna's mom was going to be gone all day at school, and it was just the two of us, back in my piece-of-crap truck, going to rescue my brother from his own colossal stupidity. I drove fast and loved catching glimpses of Brenna out of the corner of my eye, her big sunglasses covering half her face, hair flying behind her, face turned up and toward the sun.

'So, what did Saxon tell you?' she asked me. She and Saxon had talked, but she didn't get much from it.

'He told me that he'd had a pretty intense night with this girl, Cadence, and then her boyfriend showed up unexpectedly, and he bolted. He said that she'd tried to talk to him, but he didn't let her.' I grabbed her hand across the seat and hauled her as far as her seatbelt belt would let her go.

She unbuckled and switched to the lap belt in the middle, so we were sitting close.

'What do you think he wants?' It was bugging Bren that she didn't have a good handle on what was up with him. Saxon and I could talk for three damn weeks and never wind up saying anything important. He and Bren had always been able to share one look and know what was going on in each other's heads. It definitely irritated me, but I was working on getting over it.

'Do you think he would want us both to come down?'

'Why not?' I ran a hand over her knee and up her smooth leg. She giggled when my calluses hit the smooth skin inside her thighs. 'He called both of us. He probably knows we're going to tell each other. Saxon's dumb, Bren, but he's not that dumb.'

'He really likes her, doesn't he?' Brenna leaned her head on my shoulder, her voice dreamy.

'I guess so. He's never, ever gotten crazy like this over any girl before.' I realized how dumb I was to have said that. I cleared my throat and mumbled, 'Except you.'

Brenna's eyes went wide with a heavy combination of shock, guilt and hurt. I wished I had kept my mouth shut.

'No.' She shook her head and fisted her hands in her lap. 'He was crazy about what we had, Jake. He was crazy about the first version of love he ever wanted. But you know he wanted us to be happy together. Now he wants it with her. With Cadence.'

'That's one theory,' I muttered, well aware that it would piss Brenna off.

'What's that supposed to mean?' she griped. I couldn't help smiling at her when she went into full-on argument mode. 'Seriously? That one *theory* is logical, OK? It makes sense. If you don't think so, then what's a better theory?' She was pursing her lips, getting all antsy and mad, just like her mother did when she was aggravated. I wondered if Brenna realized that.

'A theory based on tons of evidence would be that Saxon wants down this girl's pants. Maybe he just hasn't gotten any in a while, and that's why it seems so different. Remember, he doesn't have his car, he isn't captain of the soccer team, he doesn't have every-thing that makes him who he is right now.'

It was low-down mean, and I wasn't nursing any particularly nice feelings about Saxon at the minute. But if he'd found his it-girl, I would do my best to be genuinely happy for him. Preferably from far away. But if this was all just more drama, I thought he might just deserve a little shitty discomfort.

'So you think this is just like a male pride, man-whore thing? Really?' Brenna's forehead wrinkled, and her mouth pulled into a pouty frown. She was dis-appointed in me.

I glanced over at her and said what I thought, point

blank. 'You're seriously upset that I don't think better of Saxon?' It was a little bit of a sore spot with us. Brenna had dated him for a few weeks. It still made me a little pissed off when I let myself think too much. About the details. Which I was trying hard not to do at that moment.

'No.' Brenna clutched her hands in her lap. 'I'm upset you don't think better of *romance*, Jake. And you of all people should know that you can't judge anyone based on their past.'

Ooh, below the belt. It was true, but that didn't make it sting any less. The first day Brenna walked into my class, I'd wished I could go back in time and erase all of my previous moronic behavior. But I couldn't, so I was doing my best to just live with it.

We drove the rest of the way in relative quiet. I could tell by the way Brenna bit her lip that she felt guilty about what she said, but I didn't offer her any relief. I've always been a nice guy, but even I had my limits. When we were almost there, I pulled over and parked at a rest stop.

'What's wrong, Jake?' Brenna reached out and pulled my face around so I was looking right at her.

I shrugged. 'I just hate that I can't take back my past.' That was true.

Brenna was already unbuckling her seatbelt and

moving onto my lap. 'Jake, I didn't mean it the way it came out,' she said and she kissed me.

I don't know what it is about her, but Brenna's apology kisses are the most incredible. It's like she wants to take all the bad out and replace it with wild, sexy girl.

She was pressing her mouth to mine, rubbing her body against mine. I put my hands on her waist and held on tight. To her. To the love she gave me. To her crazy ideas about romance and her smarts and her confidence and her willingness to give a shit about me when almost no one else in the world bothered.

'Why are you smiling like that?' She was all out of breath and her hair was flying around her face. Her lips were bright pink and her eyes were bright from the excitement of making out.

I shook my head. 'I just really love you. A lot.'

There were more hot, sweet kisses all over. Soon we were lying on the seat, my shirt unbuttoned down to the last two, my belt and the button of my jeans undone and my fly unzipped. She was wearing a short dress, and I had pushed the tiny straps down and the flouncy skirt up. My mouth was on her breasts and my hands were in her, bringing her to the point of absolute happiness that made me feel so good, it was unreal. She shook under me, bit her lip, pulled me down to kiss me, rubbed against me. I felt my head spin, so I sat up fast and buttoned my shirt.

She stretched a slow, long, delicious stretch and asked in a sleepy voice, 'Jake? Don't you want to have sex with me someday?' She was still lying half-naked and so beautiful it made my breath stick.

'I do.' I cracked my knuckles. 'Someday.'

'So why don't we today?' She smiled at me, a sweet, drowsy smile.

I put my hand on her cheek, and she moved her hand over mine and closed her blue-green eyes.

'We don't because I'm still adjusting to what we do now. Which is a lot. And I don't like you rushing me, woman.' They were all real reasons. Chicken-shit reasons, but real ones.

She sighed. 'If it was up to you, we'd still be just making out.'

I ran my fingers through a long, shiny piece of hair. 'What's your big rush, Brenna?'

'I guess it's easy for you to think it's no big thing. You already *know*. Sometimes I hate that.' She pushed my hand away and sat up.

'Hate what?' I had a hard time watching her without laughing.

She was getting worked up, so her dress was straightened and she was putting her seatbelt on, sitting up all stiff-spined to better lecture me. Luckily, I pretty much loved it.

'I hate that you're, like, this *sphinx* of sex. You know all about it, and I know nothing.'

She let out a long, frustrated breath. I rolled my eyes for her benefit.

'You know that's not it, Brenna.'

'Tell me, then,' she demanded, and I knew she was doing that thing where she tossed me some ridiculous pitch to see if I would swing.

'It's that before I met you I'd never even contemplated sex before I had it, all right? It was just this dumb thing I did. It meant nothing, and I felt nothing, and I think that sucked. So now that I'm with you, I want to make it right. What's wrong with that?' I took her hand.

She squeezed mine and smiled, then gave me a few quick kisses all over my face.

'Nothing. This minute. I have plans to wear you down, though.'

I moaned. 'Don't tell me. You'll be successful. I have no doubt at all about it. I just want to make sure you've thought this through.'

She shook her head and laughed. 'Be on your guard. You never know.'

I laughed at her, but I couldn't lie. I was a tiny bit uneasy about the whole thing. I knew it must seem idiotic that I wasn't willing to grab her up and just let her have her way. But I didn't want her to have the kind of regrets I did.

I was really, really hoping that when we finally had sex, she wouldn't have any regrets at all. But I didn't know if it would all work out. I just felt safer taking it slow.

Brenna seemed happy enough to let it drop, though, and once we pulled up to the restaurant there was no chance of going back to that particular conversation for a while. Because what we saw was so mind-boggling, we just couldn't think of anything else at all.

'Is that Saxon?' I finally asked.

Brenna nodded silently, her eyes bugged out and glued on him. Then we both stared for another long, shocked minute.

Saxon flew by. On roller skates. Fast.

'Is he roller skating?' Brenna's voice was just a hushed whisper.

'Looks like it.' I rubbed a hand over my eyes, but when I took another look, there he was. Still on skates. A kind of crazy happiness bubbled through me when I remembered every time he told me what I loser I was for tossing pumpkins and driving a tractor. At least I never worked on fucking roller skates. 'Holy shit, this is priceless! Hungry, Bren?'

'Jake, no way!' She grabbed my arm tight and shook her head. 'It's not right!'

I couldn't have wiped the smile off my face for a million dollars, and it just made her frown more. 'What's not right? I'll leave a good tip!'

'We're here to help him. Not laugh at him,' she insisted, her eyes all wide and sincere.

'This is Saxon's job. Just because we're laughing our asses off doesn't mean that he's embarrassed. Look at him showing off. C'mon, I really am starving.'

I pulled into a space, but it wasn't Saxon who skated over. It was a tall dark-haired girl who looked like a model, all cheekbones and almond-shaped eyes and full lips.

'Whoa,' Brenna breathed. 'That's her. That's Cadence.'

She skated up to the truck and gave us the friendly, professional waitress smile. 'Welcome to Tony's.' She handed us menus. 'Can I get you something to drink?'

'A chocolate shake, please.' Brenna sounded perfectly normal, but she stared at the poor girl like a total lunatic.

'Could you make it two and two Cherry Cokes, please?' I slid my hand over and gave Brenna's hand a shake to snap her out of her weirdness.

'Sure.' She gave Brenna a nervous smile and nodded at me.

'And could you ask Saxon to stop by for us?' I asked.

She looked at me for a minute, turned her head and looked some more. 'Is Saxon your evil twin?' she asked suddenly.

Brenna laughed out loud.

'If I'm the good one, that's just plain sad.' I offered her my best charm-your-pants off smile. She grinned right back, sweet and warm as syrup over waffles.

'I'll get him for you. Wait just a minute.' Cadence moved like the skates were part of her body.

'She's gorgeous,' Brenna remarked, then looked at me from the corner of her eye and half-smiled. 'I can totally tell you agree.'

I put my arm around Brenna's shoulders and pulled her over. 'You're gorgeous.' I kissed her fore-head. 'Why can't you get a job skating around in a cheerleading outfit?'

'Do you realize how much Cadence probably gets hit on and harassed any given day?' Brenna kissed my neck right where she knew I loved it most.

'Well, I guess you could get a cheerleader skirt and skates to wear around town. We could just go out skating, you know, with you in your cheerleader skirt.' I tugged her tighter and she nestled down, her head on my chest.

258

'Do you know how to roller skate?' She craned her neck to look up at me.

I scoffed. 'Seriously? I practically taught Saxon.'

Just then my evil brother skated over, fast, backward, turned, jumped the curb and landed hard right outside Brenna's door.

Brenna clapped, obviously impressed with his daredevil stunts. 'You have serious moves, Saxon.'

He stuck his head in the window, pulled Brenna over and kissed her, just on the side of her mouth. Kind of like he was purposefully trying to irritate the fuck out of me at first sight. 'Jesus Christ, it's good to see you, Blix. I think you got hotter since school ended if that's humanly possible.'

'It's the tan. Stop trying to butter me up.' She pointed at him and he grabbed her finger. I saw her flush and pull her hand back, then look at me with nervous eyes.

'Get your hands off my girl.' I said it cheerfully, but with an edge I'm positive he heard and understood. Saxon was always a little too touchy with Brenna. He could say whatever he wanted; I knew for a fact that he still found Brenna attractive and somewhere, deep inside him, would probably always have a thing for her.

'Hey, *brother*. How was Mama D?' His black eyes flashed.

'A phony bitch.' I cut him a look and shrugged.

'Heard you clocked Dad.' He gave me a nod that was all admiration.

'Yup.' I felt a little swell of pride. I had punched Gerald for Brenna, but I had me and Saxon and my mom in the back of my head when I was taking the swing.

'Did they write you out of the will?' Saxon's mouth smiled, but his eyes flashed with the hungry worry that comes from wanting something someone else has to give you.

'I hope to hell they did. I wouldn't piss on their money if it was on fire.' I raised my eyebrows and he gave me another curt nod, this one tinged with anxiety. 'You would have had a ball there. Loose women, lots of booze.'

'Hey, I'm reforming. Slowly.' He flicked his eyes back and forth, and his mouth twitched with disappointment when he didn't see what he was looking for. Or, more specifically, who.

'So, she's the one, right?' Brenna wriggled closer to me and kept her voice low, so Cadence wouldn't be able to overhear.

'She's the one I like. I haven't convinced her to like me back. And probably won't.' He leaned on the door and turned to check that she wasn't coming up behind us.

'Why not?' Brenna demanded, squeezing my knee right where she knew it tickled me slightly. 'Have you tried asking her?'

'The douchebag boyfriend caught us together the other night, so it's been all fucking love and roses between them. You know how it goes.' His face was all lumped up with jealous rage.

Man, I knew that look all too well. I'd seen it in the mirror every day he and Bren had been together.

Cadence skated back over, our drinks on a tray. She slid up next to my door with an easy grace and handed the cups in. 'Were you ready to order?' she asked politely.

Saxon grinned at her. 'This is my good twin and the girl,' he said to Cadence as if Bren and I weren't sitting there.

'I figured it out.' Cadence smiled a kind of shy smile that was a little out of place on her face just because she was so beautiful. Girls as good-looking as Cadence didn't usually get all flustered and shy. Saxon would be that good. I exchanged a look with Brenna and she raised her eyebrows high at me.

'I'm Cadence.' She tucked her order booklet into her little apron thingy and stuck her hand out. We shook and introduced ourselves.

Saxon turned to her. 'If we can duck out a little early, maybe you want to hang with the golden twin and my girl, Blix? Shift's over in fifteen minutes, and we could give you a ride if you want.' I could tell he was trying to keep his voice nonchalant, and I was surprised at how quickly he was willing to offer her a ride with Bren and me.

'I have to see what Jeff is doing.' There was apology spread all over her words.

'Yeah, you know. Whatever.' He checked over his shoulder again. 'Look, I gotta take that car of wild cougars over there. Big tip time.'

He pulled in and kissed Bren again. She stiffened and pulled back, but Saxon hardly noticed. He was trying to see Cadence's reaction without being too obvious. I saw Cadence glance at him with wide eyes and a set mouth.

We ordered and Cadence skated away, obviously a little pissed off. I knew how she felt. Brenna gave me a nervous look. 'He really likes her, doesn't he?' she asked.

I nodded.

'I think she's into him, too. Did you see how she looked at him? When she said that thing about checking with her boyfriend? It was sort of like she was apologizing to him.'

I nodded.

'What's wrong, Jake?' Her voice was strained with worry.

'Nothing Bren. I just think Saxon's being weirdly touchy. I have a feeling it's to make Cadence jealous, but I hate it.' I heard more anger in my voice than I meant. I knew I had pushed too far. Bren edged away from me and sat stiff and straight.

'I can't help how he is, Jake. I mean, I didn't grab at him or anything.' She flicked at the straw in her soda. 'It's complicated, you know. I mean, he's still a friend, but sometimes he blurs the line, I guess. If it's weird for you, I could talk to him. I understand, just . . . even though I care about him, it's not like I want him to kiss me and stuff.' Her words were running together and slightly panicked.

'That's not what I mean.' I drummed my fingers on the steering wheel in a furious beat that reflected my swirl of shitty feelings. 'I'm not blaming you. It's just hard to wrap my head around sometimes. You two were together. It's hard for me to forget that.'

'Yeah, we were.' She ran her fingers over mine lightly, like she wasn't sure if we should hold hands or not. 'But I couldn't stand to be with him. Not because there was anything wrong with Saxon. He was actually nice and funny and even occasionally romantic.'

'You're not exactly making me feel better, if that was even what you were trying to do.' I flipped my hand up so my palm and hers were pressed together.

'I'm just saying... I guess we've never talked about it all, and, you know. I want to. To explain better. The way I feel about him, I mean, I care about him. And you. At the same time, but not the same way, of course. It's confusing to explain.' Her chin wobbled a little and her voice coasted low. 'The bottom line is that I don't want to be without you. I never did. If I had wanted Saxon, he would be my boyfriend right now. But I wanted you. And I'm sorry it had to be Saxon I was with when I figured it all out, but it was. But there is good to him, and maybe he can be happy now with Cadence. That's all I'm saying.'

She shifted her eyes and flipped the straw around in her fingers, which was weird because Brenna was never a fidgeter. I tugged at the straw in her hands and she raised her eyes to my face.

'Hey, it's all right. Sometimes I forget you're part of the Kelly crew. Lifetime membership.'

She pointed the straw my way. 'Watch it, Cap'n. I might mutiny and take over your whole ship.'

'Can I still be first mate during your reign of terror?' I pulled her over and she threw her legs over my lap and popped a loud kiss on my neck. 'I kinda like this whole Captain Blixen thing. Bossy women do it for me.'

'I know. You have serious issues when it comes to women in authority. All right. First mate it is. But I run a tight ship, Kelly. Mess around and you'll be on all-day deck-swabbing duty.' She blew a raspberry on my neck. 'And you need to toughen this whole look.' She pulled back, raised her eyebrows dismissively, and shook her head. 'I'm thinking an eye-patch and a couple of back-alley tats to start.'

'I'm just relieved you didn't add a peg-leg to the list.' I kissed her ear.

'I need you for hard labor. But if you fall overboard you'll probably wind up with one anyway, so I think it's a moot point.'

Cadence rolled back at that minute, and Brenna and I untangled quickly to take our bacon cheeseburgers.

Cadence smiled and was pleasant, but I didn't know if that meant she felt friendly toward us in any real way. All waitresses were usually pleasant and smiley like that, at least in my experience.

We were almost done eating when a big, shiny pick-up truck pulled up. A solidly built guy with a crew cut got out, and Cadence skated over. Brenna, my always-hungry girlfriend, dropped her burger and flat-out stared.

At first they seemed friendly enough. But all of a sudden, the big guy grabbed Cadence hard and jerked her closer to him. She pushed at him with both hands firmly up, no joking around, and tried to back up, but he grabbed again, harder, and shook her by the arm so her head snapped back and she almost lost balance. Brenna gasped. I had the door of my truck open when something whirred by. I figured it would happen that way. It definitely helped prove that for all Saxon's smooching on Brenna, he really had his eye on Cadence.

'Stay out of this, roller boy,' the big guy said, and swung an arm at Saxon, who ducked fast.

'Fuck off, meathead,' Saxon growled. 'If she doesn't want you around, take a hint, and get the hell away from her.'

I got out of the truck and stood behind Saxon, just to show that I had his back.

This guy was easily twice as big as we were, but that didn't mean that we couldn't wreak a little havoc. Saxon and I were decent fighters, especially when our blood was hot over something.

'It's fine, Saxon.' Cadence put her hands up and moved back to put some space between them. 'Jeff was just leaving.'

'Fuck that,' Jeff sneered. 'Don't be a bitch just because you're pissed off, Cade. I should be able to come here. This is a fucking free country.'

Brenna snorted. 'Is he seriously invoking the Constitution after he called Cadence a bitch?'

'Keep out of this, girly,' Jeff tossed to Brenna.

Now I was feeling that great, heady rush that I

always felt when someone got fresh with Brenna. I could feel my adrenaline racing and my fists were ready.

'Hey, you don't need to say anything to her.' I kept my voice under control, even though my blood hummed. 'You come over and deal with me if you have anything to say.'

'Jake, don't,' Brenna warned, but I was so fired up I couldn't really focus on her words.

'Look, back off.' Jeff put his arms out and puffed his chest up a little, letting us know he was spoiling for trouble. 'This is between me and Cadence.'

'No.' Cadence shook her head. 'There's nothing between us right now. I just want you to leave, Jeff. Now.'

'I don't want to have to kick your punk friends' asses, but I will.' He pointed at Saxon and me. 'Tell them to back off, and we'll just talk.'

'No. Leave before I get my dad out here. I don't want you here right now. I have a job to do.' Cadence stood tall and scowled. 'I'm going to take care of my customers, and I want you gone by the time I check back.'

We were all on edge, waiting. Luckily, Jeff didn't dawdle too long. He gave us a reason pretty quickly.

Cadence tried to skate away, avoid the whole thing (which would have killed me and Saxon; we were practically salivating for some ass-kicking), and Jeff yelled at her, then grabbed at the back of her shirt. She fell backwards a little because her momentum got thrown. Saxon caught her, and I laid one right on Jeff's dirt-bag jaw.

'Fuck, Jake!' Saxon yelled. 'Can you let me get one in? You gonna fight all my fights for me?'

But Jeff was pissed off enough that he came at me fast and Saxon got to get one in. I backed off. Jeff's nose was squirting blood and he was already getting into his big truck screaming about a lawsuit.

'Pussy! Fuck your lawsuit!' Saxon screamed.

We watched the truck pull away. I shook my hand out, my knuckles bruised to hell. Brenna's hand was pressed over her mouth. Saxon skated towards Cadence. Cadence looked at us all for a minute, then burst into tears and skated away before Saxon could reach her. Brenna grimaced at my slightly swollen hand, then looked up at Saxon and nodded to Cadence's retreating form.

'Go after her, Saxon, you halfwit!' She turned on me, her face full of rage. 'What the hell is this all about, Jake? Have you lost your damn mind?' she demanded.

'What?' I wasn't playing dumb. Because I was a little dumb. Fights always left me brain-addled.

She snatched my hand up and looked at the bruised knuckles with frantic eyes, bit her bottom lip hard, and shook her head. 'Do you think it's broken?'

I opened and closed it. It hurt like hell, but not enough to make me think it was actually broken. 'I don't think so. Bruised, but I'll live. It was totally worth it.'

She put her hands over her face and took a few deep breaths before she looked at me, her eyes hot and sparking. 'Why are you always punching people? Are you planning on punching every single person who says anything mean to me? Or bothers me? If so, you're going to wind up seriously hurt!'

I moved to her side quickly, pressed her against the truck door, and put my arms around her, my hands flat on the warm metal. 'I'm not really good at using words yet.'

'It's not funny, Jake.' Brenna blinked hard and opened her mouth to say something, but it got stuck. She had to try twice more before she got anything out. 'That guy was huge! What if it had kept going? He could have . . . he could have maimed you! You don't need to go from zero to fifty just because he ran his mouth.'

'Fuck him if he thinks he can talk to you like that.' I leaned to kiss her, but she turned her head away.

'You're a fucking idiot,' she whispered, and when she blinked, tears dripped out past her eyelashes.

'What would I do if you got beaten to a pulp, Jake? I swear, I hate you sometimes.'

'Fine.' I nuzzled her neck, and when she turned her face to me, I kissed her hard. 'I love you. And I will fight anyone who ever bothers you. Got it?'

She shook her head and sighed a long, tortured sigh. Then she looked up at me and frowned. 'What about Vin Diesel?'

'Brenna, please. I could take him with my hands tied behind my back.'

'Pink?'

'I don't hit girls. She'd have the best chance of taking me, though. We'd have to see what the circumstances were.'

'That's kind of sexist.' Her hands came up around my neck.

'I'll do that gender studies crap you're always talking about when we go to college.' I kissed her nose. 'Stop crying.'

'There's Saxon and Cadence.' She nodded, and I glanced over my shoulder to watch.

They were walking towards us, Saxon tight-lipped and looking royally pissed off, Cadence puffy-faced and furious. Cadence took our trays and shook her head when I asked about the check. She walked everything back, and Saxon stood staring at the cement. We were awkwardly silent until Cadence stomped back over.

'Our shift is over. Can we give Cadence a ride home before we go to Aunt Helene's?' Saxon gritted out.

'Yeah. Of course. Hop in.' I hadn't talked to Saxon about going anywhere, but if he needed me, I was there.

I could see that Brenna was dying to say something to me, but there was nothing really to say until we knew what was up.

So Brenna stayed uncharacteristically quiet. She slid super-close to me and Cadence got in next to her. Saxon got in last, pressed himself all the way up to the passenger-side door, and half hung out the window. It was like he was trying to put as much distance between him and Cadence as he possibly could.

After a few minutes, Cadence broke the excruciating silence. 'My house is right up the road.' She pointed to a brick apartment building. I pulled over, and Saxon jumped out and tried to take her hand. She pulled it away and shook her head. He stuffed his hands in his pockets and walked up to the door with her.

'How does he manage that?' Brenna asked.

'What?' I watched her watch them.

'To look belligerent just by the way he walks?' She twisted in the seat to better see what would happen next.

'It's just the natural asshole DNA in his genes.' I

checked on them and saw Cadence with her hand on the doorknob, Saxon standing off to the side. 'They don't look all that friendly.'

'She might resent the fact that you two beat the crap out of her boyfriend in her parents' parking lot.' Brenna's voice spilled out sour and moody. 'I'm still pissed off with you about that. You're lucky you didn't get seriously hurt.'

'He was being really aggressive with her and you,' I defended.

She sliced me with one shivery look, her eyes narrowed. 'So you solved the problem by jumping in and hammering him? And stop pretending that was your motive anyway.'

'Why does it bother you so much that I want to protect you?'

'How does punching some random rude guy count as protecting me?' she countered, throwing her hands up. 'I'm not asking for you to brawl for me. I think sometimes I'm just your excuse to let bad boy Jake out of his deep, dark little box.' She stared right at me, not even interested in what Saxon and Cadence were talking about now.

'What?' I shook my head and spluttered for a minute, trying to think what I could say to her accusation. 'That makes no sense.'

'It makes total sense.' I could tell she was about to

really bite into this argument. Brenna didn't let things drop easily, especially if I argued that she wasn't being sensible. 'You're pretty reformed, but once in a while I guess your old urges come back, right? And you do things you *know* you shouldn't, dangerous, stupid things.'

'No.' I gripped the steering wheel hard in annoyance.

She raised her eyebrows and crossed her arms. 'Really?' Her mouth had a pinched look. 'So you getting drunk and skinny-dipping with people you hate, or sleeping with Nikki, or punching every guy who gets you mad doesn't seem a little familiar to you?'

'I'm totally over all that shit, Bren.' I felt pissed off because, as usual, she had a good point I hadn't thought of.

Whatever we were going to say next, it didn't get said. Saxon came back to the truck, got in, and slammed the door so hard that the whole frame shook.

'Let's go.' He stuck his hands into his pockets, I assumed looking for his smokes. He must have forgotten them, though, because he pulled his hands out again and slammed back in the seat.

I put the truck into drive, but we hardly had any distance to go before we pulled up at the neat little row house our great-aunt Helene lived in. As soon as we pulled up, I got déjà vu so strong it made my stomach flip. I had been here before. Definitely. When I was just tiny. I had this really strong sense of my mother, like I could remember holding her hand and walking up the steps slowly when I was so small I still needed help.

I got this strong, vivid picture flashing in my mind of my mom's long hair brushing over my head when she leaned down to help me, red high heels on the stone steps, her voice doing that cooing thing moms' voices do when they talk to their kids, the smell of cut grass and the sound of bicycle bells and kids' happy summertime yells. It all sucked and pressed around me for a crazy second, then snapped back off.

'Jake? Are you OK?' Brenna put a hand on my arm.

Her voice shook me out of my weird spell. 'Yeah. I'm cool. I'm fine. I feel like I remember being here with my mom is all.' The memory had been so real, there was no way I could have imagined it. Could I?

She opened her mouth, but Saxon cut in, 'Yeah, this is where your mom dumped you when she and my mom wanted to go get blitzed and whore it up. Mothers of the fucking decade, those two.' He got out of the truck and kicked the tire.

I was going to yell at him for talking shit about my mom and kicking my truck, but Bren had my hand and squeezed tight, grounding me.

'Don't. It was a dick thing for him to say, but he's in a shitty mood. You know your mom was a good person. Let it go, OK? We've had enough fist fights today.' She pressed her forehead to mine. 'You good?'

I rolled my head back and forth against hers and let my rage go cold. 'Now I am.' I kissed her hard. 'Thank you, Cap'n.'

Her smile gave me the same heady rush that my little piece of maybe-memory had. We got out of the car and followed Saxon as he strode up to the house. I expected him to be his usual dickheaded self, but he cut out his pouting and actually had a big smile on his face. Before the shock could totally settle in, I saw a really tiny old lady bursting out of the house.

'Come here, love!' She held her saggy arms wide-open. She didn't come all the way down the steps, so when Saxon walked up to her and she put her arms around him, it kind of looked like a mom comforting her little boy.

Well, a normal mom and her little boy; the description would probably have meant nothing to Saxon.

Aunt Helene ran a gnarled hand over his hair and clucked nice things like, 'That was a good thing, defending Cadence like that. You need to be more careful, love. Those Stanenbacks are giants! You're lucky you're so quick!'

Saxon walked up the steps and kissed her on the head and crushed her in another hug. 'How do you know all this already? You're the most connected woman in the world. Aunt Helene, stop worrying right now, OK? He was a puss . . . a wimp, and Jake had my back.'

'Jake!' Aunt Helene cried, her hand at her mouth. 'Jake Kelly? Look at how handsome you are!' She caught sight of Brenna. 'Hello, dear. Lovely girl.' She smiled. 'Come in! You're all too skinny! I made too much food! Come in and eat!'

We walked in, each of us grabbed and pinched and hugged by Aunt Helene as we filed through her hall. I had been expecting a little bit of a dump, pretty much because of how the outside looked. Not that it was terrible; it was just a little run down. But this place was gorgeous. New moldings, fresh paint, new furniture, shiny hardwood flooring. It looked great. And not very old lady-ish.

'Saxon,' Aunt Helene said, 'please make everyone comfortable. I'm almost done cooking.'

She bustled back in the kitchen, and Saxon looked at us and gave a hard laugh. 'Hey, just because Aunt Helene is a saint doesn't mean I've gotten any better. If you want something, go get it yourself. You guys are lucky Aunt Helene makes a fucking Thanksgiving dinner every night. Leftovers are unreal around here.'

'You do some work in here?' I looked around, still impressed with how awesome it was.

'Hell, yeah.' He took his phone out. 'After a few projects, I did some before pics, just so I could remember how much goddamn work I did.' He held out his phone, and Brenna and I leaned in.

'Wow.' Brenna glanced down at the little screen, then back up at the rooms. She wandered away after a few shots and checked the other rooms. 'Saxon, you know how to lay tiles?'

'No. Not officially. I almost cut my fucking finger off with the tile saw. I wasted half a box of expensive-ass tiles, too.' He walked over the bathroom where she was standing and peeked over her shoulder.

She turned and they were fitted against each other, almost like they were two pieces that could click into one. I saw Brenna glance over her shoulder with panic, then squeeze tighter into the bathroom, putting a slice of space between them.

He put a hand on her waist, and she moved to one side, skittish like a wild animal with its scent up. He pointed at something and while she followed the line of his finger to look where he directed, I saw him smell her hair.

It was barely a thing; I probably wouldn't have noticed except that I do it all the time because Brenna uses fantastic-smelling shampoo. She turned smoothly out of his arms and started to ask about the brass light switches in the hallway.

She didn't seem to notice, but I sure as hell did. It was kind of intimate, and it irritated the hell out of me.

Suddenly, the idea of Saxon and Cadence becoming a couple was the best idea I'd ever heard. And it was about to become a project I was going to give my urgent, focused attention.

Before anything else happened to make me want to take a swing at Saxon, Aunt Helene bustled out of the kitchen to tell us the food was ready.

Brenna ran into the kitchen and away from Saxon and gathered the cutlery and crockery, with Aunt Helene thanking her and pinching her cheeks lovingly. Saxon and I got the hot stuff on the table. We sat, Aunt Helene beaming.

'It's so wonderful to have you all.' She had a strange accent, sort of Polish or Russian or something.

'It's so nice of you to have us.' Brenna always knew how to talk easily with new people. 'This food smells delicious.'

Aunt Helene dismissed Brenna's comment with a wave and a happy look, we dished the food out, and it was incredible. When I was with my stepdad all the time, we pretty much lived on processed stuff: TV dinners, cold cuts, macaroni-and-cheese out of the box. At Mama D's the food was high-class, but the company was so fantastically shitty, I never really enjoyed it. But this was like the perfect meal.

Aunt Helene's spread was the best I'd ever tasted.

It was a feast. Saxon looked happy. He laughed and was really attentive to Aunt Helene. It was a little weird seeing him like that. He was usually pretty disrespectful or really phony. But not now: now he seemed genuine and relaxed.

'Jake, I have such pictures to show you after dinner. And Brenna,' she said and brushed Brenna's hair back with her hand as she leaned over to put more butter on the table, 'you will like to see these! These two big, handsome boys were little tiny things once.'

'I'd love to see them,' Brenna breathed. Under the table, I squeezed her leg. 'Did Jake and Saxon spend a lot of time here?'

'Oh, yes.' Aunt Helene scooped all three of us extra helpings without asking if we wanted any more, and we all dug in. 'When their mothers went out dancing and having fun, they would drop the boys here with me. I loved watching them. Then Jake's poor mama—' Aunt Helene stopped and pressed a hand up by her eyes.

My mother.

Aunt Helene was crying over my mother.

'I'm so sorry, sweetheart.' She looked straight at me, wiping her cheeks off roughly with her gold-ringed fingers. 'Your mother was so sweet. I miss her very much.'

And then I felt a little weirdly choked up. 'Thanks,' I managed. Aunt Helene reached her little paw of a hand across the table and patted my hand.

'Poor baby.' She pressed her other hand hard against her mouth.

She was referring to me. Poor baby.

I didn't know if anyone had ever said anything like that to me.

Once my mom died, life had been pretty adult. No more 'poor baby'. It felt kind of good to be treated a little like a kid here.

We helped Aunt Helene clean up. Brenna put me in charge of drying and putting away, and Aunt Helene clucked that she could do it perfectly well, but we all just ganged up on her and made her go sit with the photo albums while we finished up in the kitchen.

Brenna's laugh echoed off the shiny new tiles.

'What's so funny, Blix?' Saxon called from behind the four feet of tinfoil he was using to cover one plate.

'It's just funny to see you two in the kitchen, all domestic.' She scrubbed at a pot, the hot water from the sink turning her cheeks pink. 'And your Aunt Helene is so adorable. You two are going to get giant heads if you hang out with her too long. It's like she sees you both as adorable little angels and handsome strapping men all at the same time.'

Saxon shrugged. 'She's like a damn genius. She knows a good thing when she sees it, you know?'

Brenna snorted, and Saxon wound a dishrag up and whipped her with it. Brenna yelped and glared, backing up with her hands out in front of her. He stalked her, his smile ear to ear and badass hungry, his eyes locked on hers. His wrist snapped, and he landed another swipe on her ass. She laughed and darted away from him and behind me while I tried to finish putting the dishes away as best I could. I stopped for a second and gave her a quick smile, and could tell from her half-frown that she was uncomfortable, not sure if this was all fucking fun or if I was pissed off.

It was his face that made me want to punch something, preferably him. He looked at Bren like he wanted to get himself wrapped around her and never let go.

'We done?' My voice whipped out sharper than I meant it to.

I realized my tone was probably borderline murderous. The kitchen went quiet, Saxon stepped away from Bren, and she pressed closer to me.

'Done,' she said softly.

I put the dishtowel on the edge of the sink. 'Cool,' I said. Though it was all about as far from cool as I could imagine.

We filed into the living room, and Aunt Helene patted the couch so we could come and sit. She opened a big photo album.

And then it felt like the whole room closed in and got really quiet. I didn't have many things from my childhood.

But here were tons of pictures.

Me, as a baby, wrinkled and pink like any baby. A younger Aunt Helene held me as proudly as if I were her own. Me and Saxon as fat little toddlers, playing with matchbox toys on the floor of Aunt Helene's living room. There were pictures of me and Saxon splashing in a baby pool, taking a bath together, running around in the snow in too big boots, sitting under a little Christmas tree. The same déjà vu feeling that blanketed me before came back full force as she flipped the pages of the album.

It was like someone was showing me evidence of a childhood I had no idea ever existed. I had no memories of this stuff, or if I did, they were dim and really far away.

And there was my mother. Pretty, with long brown hair and light eyes, lots of make-up and small, tight outfits. But really beautiful.

And the red high heels. The long hair draped partially over me. I traced a finger over the picture. I hadn't imagined it. That was a real memory, a solid picture in my mind of the mother who loved me.

She was holding me in most of the pictures, and the look on her face was the same look I saw on Brenna's when she looked at me.

It was love. She loved me.

Because I always wanted to know she had, but sometimes I doubted it, much as that hurt. I just didn't get her for long enough to make memories that were undisputable. And growing up, Lylee was the closest mother figure I came in regular contact with, and she didn't exactly help paint a mental picture of maternal goodness.

I was glad there was no reason to talk, because my throat felt tight, and I didn't know what to say anyway. Aunt Helene watched me closely.

'I have so many.' She traced her fingers over the stiff, shiny pictures. 'I'm going to make you an album. Would you like that?'

I took out a stiff, brittle picture of my mother and held it in my big, clumsy hand, half afraid I'd break it somehow. 'I would really like that.' My voice was embarrassingly croaky.

Brenna had my hand and squeezed it tight. I was surprised by how much it meant to me that there was actual evidence my mom loved me. It was important to me that she was around and loved me, even if she was a little wild and rowdy and made some really dumb mistakes. At least I knew where my wild came from.

Aunt Helene put the books away, and she and Brenna were chatting, and then they wandered away to look at something, and it was just me and Saxon sitting in the room.

I felt a deep, cold well of hatred for him, and just as much hot, fierce love.

'What the fuck, man?' I said harshly.

'What are you talking about?' He narrowed his eyes at me.

'You feel pretty fucking free to talk shit about my mom, and you'd better cut it the fuck out. She made a lot of mistakes, but she's my fucking mom. Talk about yours all you want. If you ever talk about mine again, I'll knock the rest of your teeth out.' My fists were already balled up.

Saxon's eyes went wide with surprise. He opened his mouth, and I half expected him to tell me that we could take it out back. Instead he said, 'Fair enough.'

'And stay the hell away from Brenna,' I warned.

'I don't want anything like that with Brenna.' Saxon held his hands up. 'Look, I know we had a thing, but I told you, she's always wanted you.'

'I see the way you are with her.' I dropped my voice when Brenna and Aunt Helene turned their heads toward us, always checking in. 'Don't feed me your bullshit. I know you care about her, and I don't blame you. But she's not your girlfriend. You can't keep crossing the line with her.'

'All right,' he said moodily. 'Is that it? Can you get off my fucking back now?'

'I'm done.' I leaned back on the couch, suddenly so exhausted I didn't know if I could hold my eyes open much longer.

I could hear the happy sound of Brenna's laugh, and it registered that that sound was one of the few happy things I heard on a regular basis. Saxon heard it, too, and I saw the look on his face. He was just as addicted to Brenna's goodness as I was.

I felt bad for being hard on him; Brenna was an addiction that was impossible to kick.

Brenna 4

'Did you girls get any sleep last night, 'cos you sound all kinds of loopy?' Jake's smile practically glowed through the phone and made my ears warm.

Or maybe my ears were warm because of Evan's very suggestive dance, cued by Jake's specific ringtone on my phone.

Evan's grandmother had stepped in when things between her parents got too awful. Gramma paid her school bills and for all her dance classes, then brought her to live in Savannah at her palatial house, at least until Evan's parents could get back to normal.

Gramma also said Evan needed some 'recovery time' after a summer spent witnessing her parents' constant bickering and dealing with a very nasty public break-up when Rabin wound up at a party where some strippers were harassed. The strippers brought charges against the rich, entitled ass-hats who abused them, and Rabin was looking at time behind bars thanks to all the publicity the whole case got. To get her away from the reporters who were hounding her, Gramma flew Evan up to me for an entire week, and we'd been up all night talking after Thorsten had picked her up from the airport the night before.

'We sleep like bosses. Most mortals need eight hours, but we only need the magic four. And how is your bike coming, Jake the Speedy Snake?' I swatted Evan on the backside with a ruler when it looked like she might be bringing a lap-dance my way.

'Bren, I love you, but if you actually use any of your totally weird nicknames for me at the race, I'm going to pretend I don't know who you are.'

'OK, Jake "the Jaguar" Kelly. C'mon, that one has a certain ring to it, right?' I said as Evan flopped back and rolled on the bed, giggling with sleep-deprived giddiness.

'You're killing me, woman. So, the bike is kind of sucking huge donkey balls. I'm covered in grease, I've been lying on the driveway messing with it all damn morning, and I don't know if I got it all worked out. A couple more months, and I'll have enough to get myself a shiny new bike and save myself the headaches.' The tired sound of his voice made me wish I could transfer all the hours of extra sleep I wound up wasting to him.

'Will you be OK for the race?' I picked up the clothes Evan had stripped off and left inside-out on my bedroom floor the night before and put them in the laundry basket. I straightened her bags and tried not to freak out over the fact that she was sitting in the middle of my unmade bed. It would be psycho rude to ask her to move just so I could make it.

'Yeah.' Jake was lying through his teeth. I could tell because he sounded so confident. If he was really sure, he'd be more reserved. 'This bike is gonna be fine, and it's not a big deal anyway. This run is more so I don't get rusty. I wound up missing a few big races while I was in New York, and if I want to get any contracts, I gotta be consistently in the top few every race.'

'If you need more time to work on it, you don't have to come by later. We understand.' I looked over at Evan and she nodded emphatically, even though I knew she was totally curious to meet Jake.

'Are you kidding? Miss meeting the famous Evan Lennox? Not on your life. I might be a little later than I thought, but I'll be by and we'll go hang. All right?' He quieted his voice, as if he sensed that Evan's ears were pricked for any lovey-dovey talk. 'I love you, Bren. I miss your face.'

I leaned over, pretending to swipe something from behind my desk. 'Love you, and miss you so freaking much. OK, go work on your bike. I need to see you!'

Evan cleared her throat and gave me a little half smile. 'You don't have to be all shy. I'm happy for y'all, and I actually like hearing all that gooey love stuff. It's good to remind me what I should be aiming for when I get over my dejected misery and consider dating again.' She screwed her eyes shut and gave her head a little shake, as if she could clear out all of her memories of Rabin.

'I'm so sorry he turned out to be such a huge asshole, hon.' I sat next to her and twisted her hair back behind her neck.

'I'm sorry for those poor girls they fucked with at the party. How disgusting. I always knew he was a piece of shit, but I didn't realize he could crawl that low.' She dropped her eyes and twisted the hem of her shirt in her fingers. 'You know, I watched this documentary once about this serial rapist guy. He was just this normal-seeming guy, had a wife, the whole nine yards, but here he is creeping into girls' rooms and raping them. And when they caught him, the wife was all shocked. I remember thinking she must have been a total idiot, just the most oblivious dumb-ass in the world. I thought there was no way you could be with someone day in and day out and not know if they were a creepy fucking freak, right? Winds up I was just as big a moron.'

I squeezed her around the waist. 'Don't you dare beat yourself up. Just, next time, if I tell you a guy's a huge, gaping dickhead sociopath, maybe you can listen to me? Because I love you, and it broke my heart to watch you waste your time with that filthy pig.' She nodded and laid her head on my shoulder. 'Maybe those girls will get an awesome lawyer and take those assholes for all they're worth.'

Evan's smile was half sugar, half purely evil spice. 'Granddaddy was pretty riled up when he heard Rabin was involved. He made a few calls and actually raised his voice. I swear, my granddaddy never, ever raises his voice, and people still always jump and listen to every damn thing he says. I'm pretty sure those poor girls will have the best freaking lawyers money can buy, compliments of a whole lotta lace and textiles and Granddaddy's taste for vengeance.'

'Your life is like a Southern gothic novel,' I breathed, imagining Evan's grandfather as a portly but commanding man with a cigar and a hat who made everyone cower under his iron will.

'You did a unit on Faulkner last year, didn't you?' When I gave a sheepish nod, she laughed, her lips stretched so wide I could have counted every perfect tooth. 'Forget my damn melodrama for a minute. Where are we going tonight?'

'Well, Tony's.' I twisted my hands together and crossed the room, grabbed a T-shirt, and handed it to Evan. 'I guess business was bad, so Tony asked if anyone knew any bands, and you know how I do some

T-shirt stuff for this band Folly?' Evan nodded and opened the shirt. It was a Photoshopped design that I was particularly proud of. The band members were all hanging out of Jake's truck, waving and laughing like lunatics and Cadence was next to them, in her skates, serving them food and drinks off a little tray. 'Tony got Folly to do a show, and I worked up this special T-shirt, so I'm going to drop one off for him to see.'

Evan hopped off of my bed and pulled the shirt over her head, turning from side to side to admire her reflection in my full-length mirror. 'Please tell me you'll get one for me?'

'Definitely.' I hesitated, thinking about the last time Jake, Saxon, and I had been together – at Aunt Helene's.

'Mmm. I don't need to use my amazing psychic powers to know that you are completely worried about this little trip.' She tapped a finger on her chin. 'And I'm gonna guess it has everything to do with Saxon?'

'No!' I said too quickly, folding the T-shirt Evan handed back to me neatly. 'I mean, it was just weird last time we were all together, and I think he and Jake kind of had words. He was also sort of touchy with me.' My stomach churned.

'Touchy?' Evan flipped through my iPod. 'Touchy like he wanted to touch your booty?' She put my favorite mix on and danced over to me, eyes narrowed. 'Touchy like he wanted your body?'

'Not exactly. First he was touchy, I think, because he wanted Cadence to get wildly jealous. Then he was touchy because . . . well, because he was happy. I think.' I took a deep breath and shrugged.

'That doesn't sound so crazy, actually.' She leaned on my desk. 'But I'm guessing Jake wasn't happy about it?'

'Exactly. I get it. I do. We've been through a ton together, and he's got to be weirded out. I was weirded out, you know? I'm not totally sure I can trust Saxon. And I thought . . . I have no clue. Honestly, I thought Saxon and I could find this friend-zone place, but it's way trickier than I thought it would be, so I don't know if it's even possible.'

I yanked open my closet door and made a quick grab for the first shirt on top of the pile of clean clothes Mom had put in my room the day before. I started to hang them up in a color-coordinated pattern, light to dark and, within the colors, short-sleeved to long. It tripped my sprinting heart down to a jog.

'Brenna, do you have a touch of OCD?' Evan gazed over my shoulder, her eyes perfect circles.

'I just like my things neat, I swear. Look, I can hang this orange tank top right in the middle of the blue shirts! Right by this three-quarter shirt. That's crazy, right?' We both looked at the tangerine tank top with gorgeous flower embellishments gliding along the bottom, and I finally flipped it to its rightful spot.

Evan chuckled. 'Shut up. I could have left it there, but it makes no sense!'

The Saxon issue remained completely unresolved. We lazed around and talked about a thousand other things, then had lunch with Mom, who found Evan adorable and hilarious in small doses. When we heard the crunch of Jake's tires on the gravel, it was about two hours earlier than we expected him. Evan grabbed my hand and squealed.

'I feel kinda like I'm about to meet a celebrity,' she whispered for dramatic effect.

'You have no idea how much that would make Jake crack up.' I poked my head into the living room. 'Mom! Jake is a little early.'

'OK, sweetie. You guys drive safely, and keep your cell on.' She got up and kissed me and waved to Evan.

Jake got out of the truck and Evan watched him walk over with a look of pure giddiness on her face. She squeezed my arm tight. 'No wonder you're all gaga. It's like watching the Marlboro man in real life, but younger and hotter.' She waved her hand in front of her face. 'He definitely makes me feel all like swooning.'

I felt a strange prick of pride, and realized now

what people meant when they talked about arm-candy. Jake was, of course, so much more than good-looking . . . but he was *so* good-looking.

When he got close, he took his ballcap off his head! Like he was meeting the Queen of England. He stuck his hand out and Evan gave him her fingertips.

'You must be Evan Lennox? Brenna's been chewing my ear off about you since Dublin. Nice to meet you.' He flashed her that smile, all roguish charm and humble adorableness, and Evan tilted her head back and laughed.

'Can I see your cap?' she asked.

Jake gave me a look, but I had no clue. Evan turned his hat inside out and pursed her lips.

'Funny. I seriously thought there'd be a little golden halo stuck in here. Are you for real, boy?'

He blushed right to the tips of his ears. 'I'm no angel. And that's a hell of a cheesy pick-up line, if that's how you've been using it.'

Evan bounced up and down in her Greek sandals. 'I *knew* I was going to love him. Ooh, I gotta grab my purse. I'll be right back and then we can get outta here!'

Jake pulled me in and kissed me hard. 'She's like a ball of fire,' he said when we pulled back.

'I know,' I sighed. 'I'm kinda in love.'

'Should I be worried?'

'Well, you can't take her in a fair fight. If you think Pink is badass, you have no clue. But I think you're safe enough.' I ran my hands up and down his arms, and his smile faded and was replaced with a worried tick. 'What's up?'

'Just, uh, my bike . . .' He shrugged his shoulders and rubbed the back of his neck.

'That bad? I've got some money put away. I'd be happy to lend it to you—'

'Are you insane?' Jake broke in. 'I'm not borrowing money off you. Definitely not for a damn bike. Jesus, Bren. That's your money for . . . I don't know, important stuff you need. It's actually kind of the opposite problem for me right now.'

'What's that?' I tugged at his hand.

'A brand-new bike got delivered this morning. I signed for it . . . honestly, I ordered a new handlebar set, and I just assumed that was it, but it was, like, the most expensive, amazing bike you could imagine. I guess I should have told them to take it back, but it was like my brain went dead when I saw it.'

'Are you insane?' I grabbed him by the shoulders and shook him. 'How is this a problem? Your bike is all messed up, you can't get it working, you have a big race coming, then a new bike lands in your lap. Am I missing the problem?'

'Brenna.' Jake's voice sounded disappointed.

'Where the hell do you think the bike came from?' Duh.

I knew exactly where it came from.

'So, is it like a peace-offering?' I asked carefully.

'I have no idea. I really don't. But there's no way in hell I'm taking it.' His gray eyes went fierce and serious.

I opened my mouth to argue when Evan flew over, purse in hand. 'I'm starved, y'all. I can't wait to see this place. I've never been to a place where they skate like that. At our Sonic, they just walk the burgers out.' She looked back and forth between us. 'Are y'all OK?'

'Yeah.' Jake's smile was polite and distracted. He walked over to the passenger side and opened our door. Evan flitted a kiss on his cheek.

'You are a true gentleman.'

Evan climbed in, then realized she was in the middle, and climbed back over me, so I could sit next to Jake. Jake started the engine and we were off. I wanted to talk more about the gift from the Macleans, but I had no idea if Jake wanted Evan knowing. Since we were both too distracted to make reasonable polite conversation, we sank into dead silence.

For most people, the dead silence would have just been something to put up with. But Evan was on a one-week timeframe, and she wasn't about to have even one second of the fun ruined without at least investigating why. 'Y'all, what's going on?'

Jake put his hands at two and ten on the steering wheel and looked forward with studious concentration, like he was a professional driver running a swerving course along perilous sea cliffs. I nudged his knee with mine, and he flicked his eyes over. I nudged again and he sighed with irritation.

'It's sort of embarrassing. I have this big motocross race coming up, and my bike is shot. I've been doing the repairs myself, but I don't know if it's gonna hold up for the race.' He truncated the entire story right there in its tracks, and Evan wrinkled her forehead.

'That sucks. I'm really sorry. I got my private dance lessons pulled two months before auditions for a state ballet I probably could have danced in because my daddy used all our money laying bets at the track. It wound up being just enough time to throw me off the mark. It was between me and one other girl for understudy to one of the principals, and I lost out.' She twirled a piece of glossy hair around her finger and watched it unravel.

Jake glanced her way with a look of startled empathy. 'My dad's family sent me a brand-new bike today.'

It was obvious from his tone that this was a problem, but he didn't give a single detail.

'I understand.' Evan slid a tight smile in his direction.

I jumped in. 'But Jake needs the bike to have a chance to win. Who cares if it's from them? They have more money than God, so it's not like this is some huge thing they can hold over his head. I think you should use the bike that's safe when you race.'

'No.' Jake put his left arm out the door and pounded the metal. 'I can't. I won't.'

I was slightly shocked at Jake's uncharacteristic outburst. 'But you could get hurt,' I protested.

'I'll have gear on. I'm not an idiot.' He looked at me from under the brim of his cap. 'All right, maybe I'm a tiny little bit of an idiot, but not big time. Trust me on this one.'

'Evan, you took the classes once the payment came back, right?' I realized from Jake's glare that I was pushing, but he worried the crap out of me.

'Sure.' She rubbed her elbow on mine, and there was the bony bump of our arms against each other that was Evan's warning to me. 'But, in my case, Gramma swooped in to pay, and I love that woman back and forward. Also, I have a soft spot for my daddy, even if he's mostly useless. He never perved it up with my girl.'

'Thank you, Evan.' Jake looked around me and grinned like a fool, happy to finally have an ally in an argument. 'It's sweet to have someone who can understand sense.'

'All right? You want sense? If you don't use the bike they sent, I think you should drop out of the race.' The silence that started the trip fell back over us like a heavy, wet blanket. I put a hand on Jake's thigh and squeezed. 'I know you think I'm being a huge pain in the ass, but if you get hurt, I'm going to beat the crap out of you.'

'I'm *not* going to get hurt. I'm not.' We pulled onto the highway and he accelerated. The air whipped through the car, Evan held her hair to the side with her hand, and I let mine fly wild while I gave Jake a long, steady glare. He shook his head. 'Look, if I was still piss-poor, I'd just be riding my old beater, no questions. So let's just pretend I'm still piss-poor, OK?'

'No way. Because you're not, so you have to take advantage of what that means,' I lectured.

Evan pinched my arm, not enough to leave a mark, but enough to shut me down. I wanted to yell at both of them. Tell them why my point made so much more sense. But I felt like I was outnumbered for once.

We pulled in at Tony's and Evan said, 'I have the bladder of a baby squirrel. Brenna, come to the ladies' with me?'

All three of us got out and went inside the diner, complete with shiny black-and-white tiled floors and sparkly red booths with bright red laminate tables.

'You girls want me to get a table inside?' Jake asked.

'Could you?' Evan's drawl was cinnamon sweet and a little smoky. She dragged me to the bathroom. Once the heavy door swung shut, she put her hands on either side of my face and looked me right in the eyes. 'Are. You. Insane?' She squeezed my face.

'Why? Ow! You're squeezing my face!' I cried.

Evan released me, crossed her long, thin arms over her chest, and tapped her foot.

'What?' I demanded. She just stared, so I stomped over to the sink, yanked on the zipper of my purse, and pulled out my lipstick, a new berry pink color that I still hadn't decided if I liked or not. 'Why would you be mad at me? You think he should ride that bike? Have you ever seen a motocross race? It's dangerous. Even when every single thing works perfectly, it's still scary as hell, OK? His bike was barely making it a few months ago, and now he has the chance to be safe. And win. And be happy. So why am I the maniac?'

Evan made it look like she was rubbing her eyes, but I knew for a fact she wouldn't touch all that expertly applied mascara. 'Sweetie, for someone so damn smart, you can be so damn dense.'

I bit my tongue before I told her that was pretty much the biggest example of the pot calling the kettle black ever and, instead, studiously applied way too much lipstick. 'I'm being dense?'

She waltzed into a stall and slid the bolt over, and when she spoke, her voice bounced off of the pink and cream tiles. 'He's got pride. Crazy pride. And he's not going to just get on some blood-money bike his family sent, no matter what. If he's a good rider, he'll be careful. I'm warning you now, if that boy doesn't win the race, he'll probably have this whole moral breakdown, but you have to step back and let him do it.' She flushed the toilet and came out. This time she spoke so low, I had to bend my head close to hear her over the water running out of the faucet. 'Trust me, Jake is rare. I've seen so many guys who have access to more money than some small countries, and it makes them animals. Appreciate what you have because, sweetie, he's amazing. Seriously. Now I get your meltdown in Ireland.' She took the lipstick out of my hand, put some on, and handed me a paper towel so I could blot off some of my dozen layers.

I followed the click of Evan's black heels to the booth where Jake sat. Saxon was across from him, arms over the back of the booth seat. When Saxon saw us, he jumped up and skated onto the floor. Evan slid into the seat he left open and I got in next to Jake.

'Jake, it's criminal the amount of fine women you convince to hang out with you.' His black eyes were running up and down Evan, who gave him a cheery smile.

'Are you Saxon?' she asked while she perused the laminated menu.

'My reputation precedes me.' He put out a hand, and she shook, not the light, finger-grabbing shake that she'd done with Devon and Jake, but a full-on, business handshake. 'Nice grip,' Saxon complimented. 'I'm not officially your waiter, but I hate to see beautiful women in need of anything. What's your poison?'

'A mint chocolate chip shake, extra whipped cream, two cherries.' Evan winked, and every single coat of mascara did its flirty/lovely job. 'And a water, lots of ice, please.'

Jake ordered a root-beer float, I got a chocolate shake and a Coke, and Saxon skated away to get our drinks. Jake studied Evan, who didn't seem remotely Saxon-interested, then looked at me with a face that let me know he was anticipating a fight and didn't like it. The look on his face got my back up and made me want to explain my points again, slowly, so the logic could be absorbed. But Evan's quiet look of warning stopped me cold. We watched Saxon skate back, our drinks on a round black tray.

'Here you are, m'ladies.' He put our shakes in front of us. 'A little birdie told me someone dropped a shiny, expensive gift at your door.' He handed Jake his drink and raised his eyebrows. 'Guess I can put my summer savings on you at the race after all.'

'I'm not taking it.' Jake jabbed the vanilla-pod-flecked ice cream into the soda and watched the brown foam volcano out the top and soak the place-mat. Evan grabbed some napkins and blotted it. He thanked her.

'I get it.' Saxon sat down on the bench next to Evan, forcing her to scoot in. 'I do. Gerald's a fucking prick. It sucks he's our loser excuse for a father. But he's got money, your current bike sucks ass, and who gives a shit? You don't have to even acknowledge you got the thing. You could throw it off a cliff after you win the race if you want. But use it to win.'

'It's safer,' I piped up, earning a defiant glare from Jake, a warning eyebrow from Evan, and a nod of satisfaction from Saxon.

'She's right, man. Listen to her. It's safer, and you're not going to win without it.' Saxon met my eyes across the table, and we made a silent pact to join forces for Jake's benefit.

Jake fidgeted in his seat, and I know he would have stomped away if I hadn't been blocking him in.

'Didn't we come here to deliver that shirt, Bren?' Evan took a long, slow sip of her minty shake and ignored the semi-dirty look Saxon flicked her way for interrupting our effort to talk sense to Jake.

'Tony's meeting with some vendors right now, but I'll get the shirt to him if you want.' Saxon held his hand out, and I took the shirt out and passed it across the table to him. He unfolded it and his smile unfurled in increments until it changed the shape of his lower face. 'Brilliant, Blix. As usual.'

'Thanks.' We shared a glance that was all about mutual respect.

'I need to go check something,' Jake snapped, and hurried me out of the booth so he could stalk away.

I started to follow, but Evan put a hand on my wrist and shook her head. She trailed Jake to the truck, and Saxon fell onto the bench next to me, arm around my shoulders. I shifted uncomfortably, not sure what to do.

'He's having a shit day, right? I shouldn't be worried he's going to come back and hammer on my face for complimenting your fucking art, should I?' I opened my mouth to reassure him, but he'd already switched tracks, and he leaned closer to me. 'I'm dead serious now. You gotta talk him out of racing that piece of shit. I'm gonna tell you, no joke, and you know I'm no fucking gutless mama hen, that bike is a disaster waiting to happen and he's lucky he hasn't crashed and burned the last five races he rode it in. He doesn't listen to dick I say, so it's up to you to talk some sense to him.'

'It's not that easy.' I turned so we were face to face,

and I felt shades of the old excitement, the old challenge, but something new, too. Saxon wasn't looking at me like I was a bet to win or a problem to solve. We were on a team now, united because we both cared about Jake. It gave me hope that there was still room for us to be something, maybe even friends. 'Jake has serious attitude about his dad and all the Macleans. His vacation this summer just made it all worse. I think he thinks he's got something to prove.'

'He's going to prove himself a fucking concussion and lose the damn title if he rides that piece of shit. Sometimes, Jake is like the smartest guy I've ever met, and sometimes, he's just a big frustrating tool.' He snorted, and I looked up at him and laughed.

'You're telling me.'

He took my hand, and I would have pulled back, except that he looked so sincere and worried.

'I wish Jake and I were still close enough that he gave a shit what I said or thought, you know? Once in a while, and it's rare as hell, but every now and then, I can be pretty clear-headed about something he's just being a maniac about.'

'I'll work on him. Not that it will do much good.' I let Saxon pull me into a hug and even kiss my cheek, and when I got up, I saw Jake at the end of the hall watching us, hands in his pockets, the tips of his ears bright red on either side of his cap.

'Uh, you better go, Blix. I'll take care of the tab, all right?' He gave me a stiff-handed pat on the shoulder as I made my way down to Jake.

'Evan said she was craving pizza.' Jake's words were mechanical, and he didn't make any eye contact. 'You ready?'

I put my hand on his arm, and he stared at it like it was a foreign object. 'Jake, it wasn't what you think. He's worried about you and the race. Me too. We were just talking.'

'Cozy talk.' The words clattered around like change dropped on the floor.

'Jake, please, trust me.' My stomach churned with too much icy chocolate syrup and acid. 'I know how it looked, but you have to believe me, it was all about you.'

He nodded. 'Well, I'm OK, so there's no need for you to worry.' He lifted his eyes and squinted at me. 'You really are worried, aren't you?'

'Yes, Jake "Roadrunner" Kelly.' I put a hand up to his cheek.

'That one's the worst.' He gave me a smile so tiny I could barely feel it under my fingers. 'I don't ride on the roads.'

'Jake "Speedy Gonzalez" Kelly?'

'Wouldn't people kind of expect me to be Mexican and Irish then?'

'Jake "Speedracer" Kelly?'

He wound his arms around me, picked me up, and laughed while he shook me back and forth. 'I love you.'

'I love you too. Now come on and take pity on poor Evan. Who knows what terrible excuse for pizza she's had in Georgia? It's our duty to taste-educate this girl.' He put me down and I linked my hands through his and we left together. I didn't look back at Saxon even though I heard the clack and roll of his skates on the floor not too far behind us.

Later that night, Evan sat on my windowsill, smoking her clove cigarette while I nervously checked the door.

'Bren, you're going to have a heart attack. I'll put it out.' She had popped the screen out and her long legs dangled down outside, her heels beating on the side of the house.

'No!' I shook my head. 'My mom and Thorsten went to Our Place tonight. They always give them a comp bottle of wine, and Fa doesn't drink much, so Mom's out like a light.'

'I'm still gonna think you're cool if you don't want me smokin' like a bad girl.' She laughed, and tiny bursts of grey-blue smoke coughed out of her lungs from the force of it.

'It's not good for you.' I lit a berry candle, trying to

look nonchalant about my attempts to cover up the tangy smoke smell.

She leaned back lazily and flipped open her little gold cigarette case. She stubbed the cigarette out and tucked it away. 'You don't have to worry so much, you know. About me. About Jake. You worry a lot.'

'Well, when the people I love stop murdering their lungs with carcinogenic smoke and racing badly operating machines at accelerated speeds, I'll stop worrying.' I opened the window next to Evan's and popped out the screen, then sat on the sill with her, my knees pulled up to my chest. The clear, warm night felt full of anticipation, even though we didn't have plans that got any more exciting than watching old romance movies and whispering our girly secrets till dawn.

'You need to take more risks.' Evan pointed her toes and tapped me on the knee with them. 'You're young. You should be wild. You should stop worrying so much.'

I flicked her toe. 'Last time I was wild, I worried a hundred times more than usual. Oh, and I almost ruined everything I had with Jake. And I nearly died of pneumonia. I'm not Marianne. I'm Elinor.'

'Are you talking Austen?' Evan wiggled her toes, shiny with green and silver polish that perfectly matched her outfit. 'I always think of you as Lizzie Bennett.'

'I think I'm a little more of a romantic than Lizzie. Or maybe I can't get over the fact that she had a billion sisters. And I sort of hated Darcy.' I clamped my hands over my eyes in shame after my confession as Evan tottered on the window ledge.

'Say that again, girl, because I know I must have misheard! You did not just take the name of Darcy in vain.' She clutched her celery-green tank top with silver silk-screened birches to her heart. 'You have depths of insanity I've never imagined, Brenna Blixen.'

'Edward Ferrars is my main Austen man, gloved hands down.' I crooked an eyebrow up high at Evan. 'So you're waiting for your Darcy? Because you were kind of with . . . well, I was going to say Willoughby, but was Willoughby even that bad?'

Evan snapped and unsnapped her cigarette case. 'Rabin? He was just a mess. If there's a character in any book like him, I hope it's a clearance-rack piece of crap no one ever bothers to read.' She pulled a piece of her long, dark hair over her shoulder and flattened it long and smooth between her fingers, over and over as she gazed into the descending dark. 'Maybe I am looking for Darcy. Maybe I'm in the wrong book?'

'How about Rochester?' I pulled at a thread on the bottom of my shorts.

Evan tapped her teeth with her silver nail. 'Too old. And the wife? The crazy Creole? I liked her too damn much. Actually, I loved her. That woman needs a book all her own.'

'How about Lancelot?'

'Too tragic.' She dragged her fingers along the smooth wood of the window frame.

'The Beast?'

She wrinkled her nose. 'I liked him better as a beast though. He's a man now, and I don't think he can compare.'

'Wolverine?'

She rubbed her chin. 'Tempting. But I don't know if I can be with a guy whose claws might rip through me during a moment of passion.'

'I'm all out of romantic options.' I sighed and was about to hop down from the edge when I heard the low rumble of an engine from the woods behind my house. 'Do you hear that?' I asked, my heart in a canter.

Evan's smile was an Easter basket of sweet secrets. 'Maybe.'

'Evan?' I braced my hands on the window and leaned out, searching the jagged horizon for a clue, but the sound had stopped.

'Change into jeans. And a sweatshirt. It's so strange how cold it gets at night here. In Savannah, you could sleep all night on the roof without a blanket if you wanted. These mountains are so damn cold.' She was purposefully dragging the conversation in a different direction and ignoring my glare. I paced around the room, checked the windows again, and leaned out, listening for any clue, but the night was suddenly devoid of mechanical noises. 'Hurry up and get changed,' Evan scolded.

'What's going on?' I hopped out of my shorts and into jeans, then pulled a hoodie on. I was in the middle of lacing up my sneakers when the bushes outside my window moved, and I gave Evan a quick, startled look, wondering if this was all part of the plan.

'Bren?' Jake's voice came from below. I leaned over the sill and the hook of his wide smile caught me and pulled me tight. 'You ready?' He was breathing heavily like he'd just finished running.

I turned back and stared at Evan, who was rubbing the nail polish off her toenails with languid circular swipes of the cotton balls.

'He's coming by to take you on a ride. On his death machine.'

I gave him a quick smile and backed into the room in a fury. 'I can't go on that with him,' I hissed, crossing the room in a few angry strides so I could argue with Evan quietly enough that Jake wouldn't hear.

The stench of the nail polish remover stung my nostrils. She barely looked up from her task. 'I love you. I really do. But you need to stop being so bossy, especially if you don't know all the facts. Jake is not stupid, Brenna. Trust him. Go ride with him, and trust him to do things right. That's what he wants from you, you know.' Her blue eyes glowed summer-sky bright. 'Be a little wild with your wild boy. Go!'

'What will you do?' I asked, suddenly guilty to leave my newly single friend alone in my room while I went out with my boyfriend.

'I will paint my toes and watch romantic movies and eat all your chocolate. And feel all smug and whatnot that I helped plan this wild romance. Now go!' She pushed me with one half-polished hand. 'Live a little, Elinor.'

I went back to the window and peered over at Jake. He lifted his arms up. He had sneaked in and out of my room more than a few times, and I'd watched him do it, but I'd never jumped out myself. I looked back at Evan, who gave me an encouraging smile, then climbed up on the sill, sat on the edge, and jumped into Jake's waiting arms.

The night was crisp and chilly enough that I was glad I had on a hoodie. Jake's arms folded around me completely and he pressed me against the house, his mouth quick and hard on mine. The thrill of his kisses, the night air, and the unexpected adventure made my skin burn with anticipation.

'Did you and Evan plan this together?' I asked, kissing his neck.

'Yep. By the way, I like your friend. She's smart, like you. But she doesn't constantly worry that I'm gonna break my ass or do something stupid. She actually kinda liked my stupid idea.' The moon was huge and shiny gray in the sky, the exact same color as his eyes.

'So what's your plan?' I pushed my chilled hands up and under his sweatshirt, right against the hot skin of his ribs. He tensed and pulled back.

'Holy hell, how do your hands get so cold so quick?' He yanked them from under his shirt and rubbed them between his hands with quick, short strokes. 'We are going on a ride.'

'A ride?' I felt the little clutch of worry hit right at the back of my throat. 'Where?'

'Nowhere dangerous.' Jake put his hands on either side of my face and just looked at me. 'Sometimes I think it's hard for you to get what I do. Or why I do what I do. And Evan pointed out that it might be slightly easier for you to get it all if I showed you. So I'm gonna show you.' He grabbed my hand and then we ran, over the cool, ticklish grass of my lawn, into the taller, catching brush at the edge of the woods that bordered my yard, then into the dark forest.

I couldn't remember if I'd ever run through the woods at night before. The leaves from last fall were still thick on the ground, slick in a thousand collected layers. Reedy branches swatted against me high

313

and low, and gnarled, knotty roots bumped out in unexpectedly treacherous places, custom-made to twist ankles and trip unsuspecting runners.

I ran half-blind, my free arm waving at the snapping, snaring branches that tore past me. I couldn't get lost in tonight because I was nervous about getting caught, nervous about getting hurt, nervous about ending my time as a runner, nervous about finding Jake's death trap of a bike and falling off, and even more nervous about finding it and loving the ride.

But suddenly, I stopped worrying for a second. I found my stride and cleared my mind, my hand tightened around Jake's, and I felt like I could see everything under the brilliant light of the moon. I was free. We were free. This was one night, one moment where nothing else mattered, no worries could eclipse the pure, giddy, awesome, joyful adrenaline that pushed through me and made my feet unexpectedly sure.

Jake's bike leaned against a tree with half the bark missing, and he walked up and caressed the handlebars with loving pride.

'I'd let you ride on your own, but the throttle's been touchy, plus it's dark. But if you want to another time, I'd be happy to teach you.' The metal was all hollowed shadows and oily-dark gears, and the plastic body was shined and buffed over intense, hard-worn scratches.

'I think I'd like to. When you have time to show me.' I imagined, for a minute, the thrill of riding breakneck over some wide open space, the hum of the engine vibrating through the frame and up my hands and arms while the tires collided with the ground propelling the bike up and forward with another explosive burst of speed.

'Anytime. You'll get your license soon. You can drive over and meet me at the track after work if you want.' The excitement in his voice made me bounce on the balls of my feet, and I wondered if running track would keep giving me the same thrill after all this freedom and speed. Jake handed me a helmet out of a backpack on the ground near the front tire. 'I brought an extra one for you. I wouldn't ride without one, you know. Even if I didn't have you looking all sexy, glaring at me like that.'

'I think it's a real problem that you find me sexy when I'm pissed off with you,' I griped, sliding the helmet over my head.

Jake fished under my chin and adjusted the strap. 'Why's that?'

'I think you get off on getting a rise out of me.' I reached into the helmet and brushed my fringe back. The fashion-obsessed part of me was dying to see what I looked like with a helmet on. My bike helmet was an entirely different animal and, dorky as it might be, I had a desire to see myself in this cooler helmet.

'I also think you look hot right now. That helmet suits you.' Jake gave the helmet visor a playful slap and adjusted my goggles. He put his helmet on, and I felt that rush of edgy, crawly, fluttery, breathlessness that sometimes made me see little pinpricks of black at the edges of my eyes when I looked at him. Jake Kelly made my senses reel big-time. He swung one leg over the seat and kick-started the bike, coaxing a roar from the engine. 'Hop on and hold tight,' he ordered over the rumble of the engine.

I jumped on behind him, wrapped my arms around his waist, and clung tight to the bike with my thighs. For a few seconds, the engine roared, then sputtered a little, but Jake pressed on the throttle and it went back to a rhythm more like a deep purr.

'Ready?' he yelled.

I squeezed him tight to let him know I was.

'Keep your feet on the pegs!' he called, and we took off through the well-worn forest paths. At first it was all chokingly scary midnight black, the burning stench of gas fumes, the jarring lurch of the bike over ruts and bumps in the path, and I clung to Jake for dear life, positive I was going to fly off the back and wind up with something important broken.

But he cruised out of the woods and we raced into a wide-open field. The trees had been hiding a perfectly round, bright full moon, but it shone down on us now and illuminated what looked like a rough track. Jake pulled onto it, and I felt his body relax under my fingers, like his muscles were happy and satisfied to be where he belonged.

I had watched, my heart lodged in a choking lump right at the base of my throat, while Jake flew around the track at races before, but I had never been on the bike because it had always been so completely Jake's territory. But as we got closer to each other, the things that were important to each of us tangled until we were wound tight and intertwined.

Jake coasted and looked at me over his shoulder. 'Wanna jump?'

My heart picked up a startlingly quick rhythm, leaping and diving in my chest. Fear of jumping made my mouth dry and my palms sweat. My stomach knotted and my arms tightened around his waist until I was sure I was cutting off his air supply.

'OK.' The word warbled out of my throat and he snapped the throttle. My eardrums expanded against the screaming whine of hot metal preparing to take off.

The bike tripped forward with unsteady, gasping skips, and Jake had to take us one circuit, then two, to smooth the belching pace. When we finally came to the base of the jump, he leaned forward slightly. Because I had my hands clamped around him for dear life, I leaned forward too, and I scanned the situation, working out all the possible outcomes.

This would *never* work. The bike would seize up. Or flip. Or die and leave us in midair, about to crash to the ground in a crunched, broken heap. I attempted to say something, anything to Jake, but my voice was caught in my throat, raspy and stuck. I kneaded and squeezed at this sides, but he only turned around and gave me a swift, confident smile before he looked forward, apparently oblivious to my sheer terror-shrouded panic.

Maybe it was my good fortune that I didn't know what was coming next because all of a sudden we screamed up the dirt ramp, and then it was pure weightless flight.

I clung to Jake so hard I was fairly sure he'd have fingernails embedded in his skin for weeks, but I peeked one eye open over his shoulder. My stomach rose just a tiny bit in my abdomen, just enough that I felt the sickening–thrilling pull of gravity. Under my body, the heavy weight of metal and plastic that had anchored me to earth was pulling away, slowly, and there was this trick couple of seconds where Jake and I were two people clinging to each other in the cool night air, flying high up over the dirt without anything grounding us.

It was like floating. It was like sucking big lungfuls

of breath in until you were so dizzy you could faint. It was like running to an edge and diving over just to enjoy those heart-stopping few seconds where you were suspended in midair.

And then we crashed back to the ground with one huge thump, and every sensation that had been suspended whooshed back tenfold. The bike jarred me and shook my entire body, my helmet rocked back and forth, the scream of the engine battered my ears, the smell of the exhaust choked me, and a small meteor shower of dirt and mud flecked me from head to toe.

Jake cut the engine and got off the bike, holding it steady so he could look at me. 'You like?'

'I love,' I croaked out, my voice spent before I'd even had a chance to shriek or laugh or cry. 'I know everyone says it's like flying, but it's like daring, right? It's like playing too close to the edge, then just hurtling over it.' I wrapped my arms tight around him and breathed the sweaty–clean mesh of his skin coated with mud and sweat. 'Can we do it again?'

Jake hopped back on and we roared through jump after jump. After three I was able to extract my fingers from his skin. After five I gave out a terrified whoop of adrenaline-based joy. After seven I was planning on getting my own bike, and then Jake's sputtered out. It wasn't when we were super high, but we were high enough that I could hear his angry curse as the bike flew forward and bit the dirt with more malice than it had before.

He jumped off and pulled me with him, steadying the bike with one arm. 'You OK?'

'I'm fine. What about your bike?' We both looked down at the unpredictably amazing machine, now spent and maybe done for.

'It's fine. I know what to do to get it working again.' He pulled the helmet off my head, and strands of my hair, activated with static electricity, buzzed around my face. 'Don't worry about the race.'

'It stalled when we were low on the jump. What if you had been higher?' I felt a chill of fear rattle up and down through me. 'Jake, that could have been really shitty. Why don't you just use the bike your family sent? Who cares?'

Jake put his hands on the handlebars and pushed with his full weight, moving the massive bike with slow, steady steps. 'It's not that simple.'

'So explain it to me.' I followed him while he leaned the bike against a tree and marched back to the clearing where we had left the helmet bag.

It was hard to keep pace when Jake anger-walked.

'Don't ignore me. Explain.'

'You're going to poke holes in my explanation,' he grumbled, kneeling next to the bag. He took a flashlight out of his pocket and shined it in, rooting around for the tools he needed.

'So let me poke holes. That's what I do, right? I argue the sensible side, you hopefully listen. Yes? No?' I knelt next to him, and he looked at me and attempted to smile.

'You're going to poke really smart holes in this because my reasons for doing it are stupid, OK? It's a stupid idea. I should ride the new bike and win the race on it, all that shit.' He gripped the tools in his fist so tightly, the metal handles clanked against each other.

'If you know that, why all this stupid drama?' I put a hand on his shoulder, and he tilted his head up to look me in the eyes before he let out a completely exhausted sigh.

'Because they have a strong pull over me already. Even though I hate their fucking guts. And accepting a gift from them . . . especially a gift like the bike, that they know is all tied to something I give a shit about, it's just opening a whole goddamn Pandora's box.' He slapped the tools against his palm with a rhythmic series of thuds.

I opened my mouth to keep debating, because it was scary when the bike gave out in midair and we were falling. It would have been scarier if Jake had been in a race, going faster, jumping higher, being just reckless enough to win. But I got that this wasn't the argument Jake was arguing, and I wasn't going to change his mind. So I figured I would just be on his side.

'OK.' I slid my hand in his and we started the trek back to his bike.

'Just "OK"? Seriously, that's the end of your whole speech?' Jake pulled me closer, his eyebrows knotted in confusion, his mouth twisted half in laughter and half in disbelief.

'I'm learning.' I put a hand up and stroked his stubbly cheek. 'You're not going to back down and agree. And you have a point. A really stupid, pride-based point that will probably get you maimed, but I can't really argue against it. I kind of, sort of, get it.'

'You're kind of, sort of, the sexiest girlfriend ever.' Jake's mouth dipped down onto mine, and the sweet smell of his mint-laced mouth collided with the fresh, cool night air and made an impossibly delicious combination. I moaned against him and he lifted me slightly under my butt, pulling my body close against his.

My hands grabbed him around the neck and pulled his head down, and I suddenly couldn't kiss him fast enough. He smelled so good, the endorphins from our ride were still popping through me, and I felt like he and I were two stars in the same constellation, linked but independent, together in the deep, inky blue sky.

He pulled me back onto the crinkly carpet of leaves. A rock poked the back of my leg, and his tools jabbed under my elbow, but I didn't care. I loved the weight of Jake on me, and I ran my hands up and down his back, greedy for the feel of him.

'I love you.' He ran a hand over my face, pushing my hair back. 'I know it's a lot for you to hear sometimes, but having you in my life has been the best thing that's ever happened to me.'

'I'm a Kelly Boat lifer,' I promised, tracing a finger over his lips. 'I love you too, so much. I know this summer has been crazy—'

'Definitely crazy. But kind of fun, too,' he interrupted.

'Yes. Crazy and fun. Stop interrupting,' I continued and popped a kiss on his mouth before he could interrupt again. 'And I'm glad we talked and got things out there, because I want to be honest with you.'

'Me too.' He bent his head down and kissed my neck.

'This winter was hard, you know? I always wanted to be with you, but I didn't know how to do that and be myself. And I know, sometimes, I don't just let you do your thing, either. Like, this whole bike thing. I worry about you, so of course I want you to do what will keep you safe. But I'm trying to see it from your perspective and trust you.' I folded him in my arms and crushed him tight. 'But I worry your bike will stop and you'll break your legs or . . . stop laughing! Jake, what the hell could be funny about that?'

I yanked away from him and stared while he sat up, clutched his stomach and rocked back and forth. 'It's not funny. It's not. I'm sorry. I'm stopping.' A new wave of laughter took hold of him. 'I just keep picturing myself with two leg casts, hobbling around after you at school.'

'You're an idiot. Seriously, you're deranged. Stop it! That could happen, you jerk!' Watching him laugh while I kept a straight face was hard, because his laugh was disturbingly infectious. 'I'm not nursing you back to health if it happens!'

'You're so damn mean.' He pulled me up and hugged me hard. 'C'mon. I'll give you a piggyback ride to make up for my stupidity.'

I raised an eyebrow at him. 'I do love piggyback rides. But do you really think it's that easy to be forgiven?'

He waved away my objection. 'I guess we won't know till we try. C'mon.'

I climbed on his back and he hooked his elbows behind my knees while I held onto his shoulders. We tramped through the woods.

'You're feeling better already, aren't you?' He bounced me up and down with his arms. I tugged on his hair. 'Look, there's no need to be embarrassed. You aren't the first girl who got all caught up in my bulging muscles.'

I pretended to choke him, then kissed his ears. 'Ass.'

'Girlfriend of an ass.'

When we got to the clearing, he put me down, and I lay flat on the grass, suddenly having a hard time keeping my eyes open.

'You falling asleep?' His voice was gentle and sweet in my ears.

'Maybe,' I murmured. 'I gotta go home. Mom will be so pissed off. I can't sleep here anyway. Spiders might crawl in my mouth . . . and I'll eat them. By accident.' The world was swaying and contracting, and the last thing I remember was Jake saying, 'I'll protect the spiders from your enormous appetite. I promise.'

By the time Jake shook me awake, I was clammy and cold. The sky was still dark, but it was more a deep blue than black, and the gray light of dawn broke through the trees at the horizon.

'Rise and shine, Sleeping Beauty.' Jake picked leaves and sticks and probably spiders out of my hair with nimble fingers.

'Did you get the bike fixed?' I asked around a yawn.

'Barely. Good enough to ride it back home, though.' He yanked me up by the hand and gave me a long, slow kiss. 'Let's get a move on, girlie, before you turn into a pumpkin.'

I climbed on the back of his bike. 'You wouldn't love me if I was a pumpkin?' I snapped the helmet strap tight under my chin.

'Love you? I'd be that little guy who lived in the pumpkin. What was his name? Weren't they all named Jack?' He turned and looked over his shoulder, his smile crisscrossed with early morning light and shadows.

'He was Peter.' I squeezed Jake around his waist and he roared through the clearing.

My breath hung hard in the back of my throat as we kicked up dry leaves and exploded through small branches and prickly brambles. The mud-flecked sleeves of my hoodie got caught on and pulled by every sharp protrusion of bark or thorn we crashed against, but I didn't care. Now that I had a taste for speed on my tongue, my mouth watered for it. I counted down in my head how long it would be until I got my license and how often I could meet with Jake. I wondered if I might want to trade my track shoes for racing boots.

326

I did love any excuse to buy new boots.

Jake stopped near the edge of the woods and cut the engine, thwarting any further thoughts of new boots and speed obsession. He reached out his hand to take mine.

'Can I walk you home?'

I took his hand and netted my fingers between his. The early morning air was just a little foggy and the sky was getting a shade brighter every second, turning from dark purple to the palest lavender.

'Thank you for tonight. It was amazing.' I bumped into him, and he smiled at me.

'You learned your lesson?' he asked.

'Now you're just pushing your luck.' I squeezed his hand hard. 'What lesson did you think I needed?'

'To trust me. To trust that I don't do bonehead things for no reason. That if I'm going to take a stand, it's because something is important.' His jaw went tight. 'I trust you, Bren.'

'I know that.' Thoughts of the winter, our break-up, Saxon all jostled in my brain. 'I know, and I'm really happy you do. But we're talking about you breaking your neck, OK? I can't just stand by and watch you get hurt without saying what I have to say.' I drew him closer until our legs brushed when we walked. 'So don't go lecturing me.'

'Man, you're a pain in the ass sometimes,' Jake

sighed. I slapped his arm, and he looked over with a grin. 'You got bit by the racing bug didn't you?'

'Maybe a little.' I tucked my hair behind my ear and yawned. 'I think I might be a little freaked out to ride alone.'

'That's normal.' Jake's voice was sweet and encouraging, the way it always was with me. 'Remember, I've been at this since I was four years old. You did amazing for your first time.'

'All I did was cling to you for dear life.' I leaned my head on his shoulder, and he threw an arm around me.

'Trust me, there're even crap backseat riders. You're a natural. I can tell.' He pulled me close and laid kisses all over the top of my head.

'What if I got so good, I started beating you?' I turned my face up, and he kissed the tip of my nose.

'If you beat me fair and square, I'd take silver like a man. But I'd expect you to kickback a percentage to your trainer.' He winked, and I tickled his ribs, then we ran back to my house, panting with exhaustion by the time we got there. He slid against the outside wall and closed his eyes for a few seconds too long. I patted his cheek and he opened one eye sleepily.

'Go home. It's . . . early. You're beat. Be careful.' I kissed him, soft and light as dandelion fluff floating on the summer wind.

He picked me up around the waist and let the kiss

seep in and take root. 'Thank you for last night. And tell Evan I said "thank you". I like that friend of yours.' He nuzzled my neck. 'I love you so much, babe.'

'I love you.' I stood with my back to the wall watching until Jake's body was swallowed into the woods.

Evan's voice drifted down from above me. '*It is the lark that sings so out of tune, straining harsh discords and unpleasing sharps.*'

I reached a hand up, and she helped hoist me in. We fell into a heap on the floor and giggled until our sides ached. 'He wants me to thank you.' I swooped my arms around her neck and pulled her onto the bed. 'Thank you, thank you, thank you, thank you . . .'

Her laugh came out through her teeth, like the sound of waves on the beach. 'Cut that all out, or I'll recite Shakespeare to you all day long.'

'You're dreamy. It was such a cool date.' I pulled a long, thick piece of her hair out and braided it loosely. 'It felt so good. I didn't expect it. Jake and I always have fun, but this was like another level.'

She turned to look at me, her plush lips parted in surprise. 'Well, of course. That boy is searching for a reason to shine for you. So let him shine.'

'He does. He shines just by being who he is.' I undid the brain and ran my fingers through Evan's hair.

* * *

That day sped by in a blur, and the next few days tossed and jumbled so fast it was like dipping your hand into a stream of cool water on a hot day. By the time you got your palm to your lips, all that cool water had gone warm and nearly disappeared. Before I knew it, it was my last day with Evan. She was getting ready to leave, and I was in an uncharacteristically mopey mood.

'Sweets, we beat this week to death.' She ticked off our adventures on her fingers. 'We went to the city with your mom. She took us to that fantastic steak place. We had all that cheesecake.' She rolled another dress and threw it sloppily into her bag. 'Then we did that whole museum day, and Fa was so damn cute and gentlemanly. The drive-in with Jake. The diner run with Devon. Going on that godawful hike with Kelsie. I love that girl, but who hikes for fun?'

I took the dress back out of her bag and folded it, then rolled it neatly. 'I know. She's super-sweet, but nuts. And I loved everything, too. But you *just* got here. Can't you spend another week?' I wrinkled my brow, pouted my lips, blinked my eyes. 'Jake would be so excited to have you at his race. Please?'

'You know I would. Stop making that pathetic face at me! But school starts early in Georgia, darling. 'Cos of all the heat.' She tossed a lacy pink bra back and forth in her hands absently. 'Well, I think it does for me, anyway.'

'You haven't asked your father about school yet?' I pressed my lips together as I tucked her beaded flats, soles aligned, into the corner of her bag. 'Evan? Evan, look at me. You need to know for sure where you're starting school. Ask him.'

She shook her head and threw a bunch of earrings in on top of this perfect silk top. I plucked all the hole-making earrings up and asked, 'Why not?'

'Because I'm afraid of what he'll say.' Her voice stretched and grated against the tears she was trying to hold back.

'But you've gone to the same school since kinder-garten. I know your parents are going through a tough time, but they'll get that you need to be there, with your friends. Right?' I slid her earrings into a bag and ran my fingers down her arm. 'Right?'

'It's a really exclusive school. They won't hold a place for me. And I was on academic probation last quarter. The house is gone, and Gramma isn't close enough to count as in-district. Plus, she wants me to go to her alma mater, so I'll probably start there in a few days.' When she punched down at more clothes in her bag, I didn't even make a move to stop her.

The ringing phone broke our silent reverie. 'Hello?'

'Hey, Bren.' It was Devon, and he sounded

distracted. 'I was wondering if you got anything in the mail from Dublin? Did Evan? Is she still around?'

'She is.' Evan shrugged at me and I held up one finger and made my way to the kitchen.

'Did you get it today?'

There was a little pile of mail on the table. I sifted through it, and there was a large airmail envelope postmarked Dublin. 'I got something.'

'Open it and read.' Devon's voice was tight.

'"*Dear Ms Blixen, The paper you wrote for the Language and Literature of the British Isles Seminar this summer was beyond well done; it was remarkable. Your work has been selected for publication in the collection* Wisdom From the Mouths of Youths. *You and two guests of your choice are invited to a reading of selections of the publication at Vorhees Hall, Rutgers University, New Brunswick, August 20th, 12 p.m. Congratulations on a job well done. Sincerely, Dr H. Gorman.*" Holy shit! Devon, holy shit!'

'I know. I knew you'd get it, too. It was that night, that crazy night and the revisions after Evan said our essays were crap. What did we write? What did you write?' he demanded.

And I felt like the blood was draining out of my body. 'Oh shit.'

'Brenna? What did you write? Because I'm freaking the hell out! I wrote about being gay! I deleted the damn essay about the birds and the ocean. What the fuck was I thinking? My mother already saw the letter. What the hell am I going to do?' His voice was cagey with panic.

'You didn't come out to your parents yet?' I couldn't stop looking at the letters on the paper in front of me, leapfrogging and cartwheeling around in dizzying circles.

'No! I guess I can tell them it's fiction. Oh my God, I don't even remember what the hell I wrote! Goddamn Evan and her fucking crazy Araby!' He took a deep breath. 'Are you still on the line?'

I forced the words out of my mouth. 'I wrote . . . I wrote about Jake and Saxon. I wrote about how it's possible to love more than one person. How I expect to love so many people in my life. Oh no. Oh God.' A queasy lurch of my stomach made a wash of acid hit right in the back of my throat. 'Oh shit. This is really not good. This is really, *really* shitty timing. Jake is . . . this is *not* good. He won't understand that I didn't mean I don't love him. It was just *art*. It was just *poetry*! This is not good.' I wandered around the kitchen flapping the paper in my hands like it was on fire and needed to be put out. Though it did occur to me that if the paper was on fire, I'd just be fanning the flames.

'It doesn't mean that we all *have to* read, right? It doesn't mean that every person will be asked to read the entire paper? Brenna, answer me! Am I right?' Devon's old, panicked self cracked out and bubbled to the surface.

'I don't know,' I muttered, my eyes flicking over the words again and again without managing to read anything. 'I really don't know! Maybe they'll send more information. Maybe they told certain people that they're reading. I'll ask Evan and see if she knows anything about it.'

'Right. Good. That all makes sense.' Devon's voice slowed as he calmed down.

'But I bet we all get a copy of the book or pamphlet or whatever it is,' I chattered nervously.

Why had we written such honest, gut-wrenching final papers? Why hadn't I kept mine about true academic integrity?

What was *wrong* with me?

'Oh fucking shit,' he muttered. I giggled a little.

'What could you possibly find funny at a time like this?' he practically screamed.

'You never swear like you've been doing today.' I giggled harder. 'It's kind of cute, your little attempt at being bad-ass.'

Soon we were both laughing with sheer, gut-wrenching nerves. When I finally caught a breath, I got off with Devon and went to cry on Evan's shoulder.

'Who was that on the phone?' she asked, bopping her hips in time to a song blaring through my speakers.

'Um, Evan? Did you get a letter from Dublin?' My question crept out, afraid to hear the answers I was fairly sure I'd hear.

'Just before I left. Some anthology or something? There was a reading in Savannah I was invited to.' She put a hand to her forehead and gave a long, theatrical sigh. 'I guess they decided my essay on shedding the shackles of sexual shame was just risky enough without edging over into obscenity. I'm really good at riding that line.' She pointed to the piece of paper shaking in my hand. 'And you got your letter, Ms Brilliant?'

'Yes,' I choked out, biting my knuckle to keep from screaming with tangled frustration. 'Devon too.'

'Not the fucking bird paper,' she gasped and shook her head slowly, her eyes bright with disdain. 'I refuse to have my essay in a collection with that twaddle.'

'He changed it. He wrote about being gay. And I changed mine. Evan, I changed it from academic integrity!' I made my bed with irritated jerks of the sheets and duvet, just to keep my trembling hands busy.

She plopped down on my desk chair and her laugh twisted past my aggravation. 'I knew Devon had guts under all that stick-in-the-mudness. And you wrote about boys, didn't you? And love? Jesus, you are such a romantic, girl!'

'Well now I'm fucking screwed! Jake is going to see the paper, and he's already been freaking out about Saxon, and we just had this whole talk about honesty and how we trust each other now, and I'm going to dump *this* on him? What am I going to do? Evan, tell me,' I pleaded, shaking the letter in my hand like I could shake the answer out of it.

'Calm down, Brenna. Deep breaths.' She put her hands on my shoulders, and her voice went low and soothing. 'Look, Jake is going to understand. Remember his halo? I swear to you, he'll get it eventually, even if he freaks at first, all right? And it will be all good in the end. It will be. Just show him, don't hide anything. And believe in your words, OK? You're brilliant, girl! Seriously, that brain is big and beautiful. Trust it. He'll understand.' Her voice crooned me into something like a numb calm.

My brain was so choked up with all of those thoughts, I didn't even put together that Jake was coming to say goodbye to Evan. I didn't even hear his truck pull up while I was pacing the room. All of a sudden I turned around and banged into his warm body. 'Jake!'

'Were you expecting someone else?' His smile

started with his lips closed, the corners slightly upturned, but it grew fast, and soon I could see his crooked tooth and the pure happiness that covered his face for me, all me. I tucked that smile in my memory in case I'd need it later.

'No.' I wrapped my arms around the strong, solid, good-smelling realness of him. 'Not at all. I lost track of time. And I didn't even hear you come in.'

'Yeah. You guys should start locking your doors. Hey, Evan.' Jake gave her an awkward hug, and she kissed his cheek and left a little smear of red lipstick.

'Oh, you know what? I have to . . . make a phone call to Gramma, but she can't hear a thing. I'll go on the back deck so my yelling doesn't bother you.' She squeezed my hand hard and waltzed by. Jake watched me watch her leave.

'I know you're sad about Evan heading home.' Jake rounded his hands under my elbows. 'You look like you're going to cry, Bren. She'll come back. Don't be so upset.' He took me into his arms and rocked me back and forth, making me feel better like the cool, understanding person he was.

And I wished my bedroom floor would open and deliver me into the bowels of hell. At least for a little while. Because I deserved a good roasting.

But the stupid essay was looming, bearing down on what was an otherwise excellent moment. I tried to push it out of my mind, to focus instead on Jake's comforting arms and words, but it was there and completely obstinate.

'Jake, I'm not just upset about Evan. I think I fucked something up.'

He looked at me, a little expectant and pretty nervous. I opened my mouth once, then again, wanting to tell him, but not knowing how.

'I wrote something in my class this summer,' I began. He nodded his encouragement. 'And I guess it was pretty good, like well-written good. They sent me a letter saying it was going to be included in this published collection and some of us were going to get to present them at a little ceremony. But I don't know if I'm one of the ones who'll be presenting or anything.' I was rambling a little. Jake looked confused.

I didn't want to get to the point.

'That's awesome, Bren.' He was definitely pressing his encouragement ahead of his nervousness. 'I'm really proud of you. Are they, like, giving you a scholarship to go somewhere? Are you going back to Ireland?' He was taking a stab at figuring this all out.

'Um, no.' I swallowed. Cleared my throat. Stalled. 'The thing is, we had to write about our lives and what was happening in them, and we were supposed to focus on what we were really passionate about.'

'That makes sense.' Jake smiled at me. No! Not that

trusting smile that I was about to kill! I felt my guts clench hard. 'Did you write about Mom? Or school?'

'No, I didn't.' As awful as it was watching him fumble, I somehow couldn't just put him out of his misery and spit it out.

'Why are you upset about it?' he asked after a few seconds; his eyes were on me, gray and clear and seeing what I was too chicken to just tell him. 'What's the big deal?' His face clouded a little, and I had a pretty good idea he guessed why I was being quiet about it. 'Did you write about Saxon?'

'Yes,' I gasped, relieved to have been outed, finally. Jake sat up straight. Every muscle in his whole body looked stiff and angry. 'I did write about Saxon, but I also wrote about you. Trust me, Jake. It was about how complicated things are. Or were! And it was kind of art, you know? So it might be a little more dramatic than real life. And I just want you to see it for yourself, so you don't get . . . the wrong idea. I guess.'

He raised his eyebrows. 'OK,' he bit off. His mouth worked a little, like he was chewing on words that he wanted to say, but didn't.

'You should read it,' I offered.

He shrugged, his face tense, and his voice slid out with the slow, hypothermic cold of a glacier. 'If you want.'

'I do.' I prattled a little, my nerves unhinging my

tongue. 'I know we're at this good point with trust and all that, and I want you to know, I would never hide this. Evan said you'd understand. It's probably going to sound sort of melodramatic, but remember, that's for class. And I was supposed to be artistic. I mean, the point is to make it sound dramatic, so sometimes I might have gone a little bit overboard. Please don't be upset about it.'

Jake said nothing.

I opened my laptop in the weird, uncomfortable, never-before-registered silence of the room. Jake watched as I searched for the file, opened it, and printed it. I took my time evening the pages and putting a staple in one corner. Various words jumped off the pages. Some made me calmer, and some made my mouth go dry. 'Maybe you should go. Maybe you should read it and then decide . . . whatever you decide.'

'What does it say?' His hands shook a little and his eyes jumped all over, not really following the lines.

I knew the words were swimming on the page in front of him. Jake had severe dyslexia and reading was completely taxing for him. He got through with books on tape, and sometimes I even read the books myself and recorded them for him. But not this.

This was my own.

I cringed, just imagining what it would be like to

read it to him. He'd have to do this one on his own.

'I can't really explain.' I stopped and tried to explain, but all I could come up with was that most pathetic excuse of an explanation. 'It's complicated.'

He groaned. 'Don't say that word. Please don't.'

'Why not?' I reached for his hand, but he flinched slightly, and I backed off. 'That's the word that fits.'

'It's like a code word.' He scanned the paper absently. 'It means that you said things that are probably going to break my fucking heart.'

I bit my lip and shook my head, not sure what to say, or if, maybe, I should just shut up and not say anything. 'I don't know what to tell you, Jake. I wrote what I felt. And I can tell you right now that I love you so much. I *love* you. What I feel for you is way beyond what I feel for Saxon.'

'But you do feel *something* for Saxon?' His jaw went hard and stiff.

'Of course,' I answered, my words choked. 'You know that. It doesn't mean I feel the same kind of thing for him that I feel for you.'

He shook his head, the paper in his hands. I really, really didn't think he was going to leave. He'd never stood me up for a date before. Hanging out together was always so important to both of us.

'I better go read this.' He got up stiffly, the paper still in his hands.

'It's not . . . I don't think it's going to be as crazy as you think.' I tried desperately to smooth it out before he left. 'It's just . . . I mean it's not . . . bad. Or I don't think it will be bad when you read it all. Lots of it is about things in the past. Done. Over with.' I put my hands over my face. I was at such a loss for words, I didn't know what to do.

He leaned in and gave me a chaste kiss on the mouth. 'I'll call you, OK?'

It didn't seem real. I had been looking forward to spending the day with him way more than I realized. I wished I had never answered the phone when Devon called this morning. I wished I had just kept my mouth shut.

But if he was pissed off just based on the vague idea of something I wrote, he had to see the whole thing, and I was going to have to deal with what came next. I was a little nervous about what he would think of it, but it was better to have shown him.

Wasn't it?

I heard him say goodbye to Evan. I strained my ears to hear what they talked about, but it was all murmurs. When Evan walked in, her mouth was set in a tight, straight line.

'I fucked up again, right?' My voice was clogged with tears.

Evan grabbed my hand and kissed it. 'It's only

because he worries that you're not going to wind up with him, Bren.'

'I promised I wouldn't make him feel that again. And then I go and do this kind of stupid shit.' I shook my head. 'I felt so smart and awesome when I was writing it.'

'Can I see?' she asked.

I pointed to the laptop where it was still up, and Evan sat and read. Her eyes went wide and she smiled. When she finally looked up at me, she didn't look like she was facing the world's worst girlfriend. 'It's gorgeous, sweetie. And honest. And true. Jake may not like it, but he loves you, and he's going to realize that this essay is all you, right to the last period. It will all be fine.'

I lay down on the bed and let Evan spoon me, and we told funny jokes, talked about what her first day at her probable new school might be like, listened to music, and laughed to pass the time until she had to leave to get on her plane, where she would go home to her wreck of a life while I tried to clean up the mess I'd made here.

Saxon 4

So maybe I was having a little too much fun playing the hero. Don't hate me because I'm smart as hell.

Or at least partially smart as hell.

Because I had pretty much become an honorary member of the Erikson family. Everyone loved me.

Except Cadence.

So, it was a pretty major snag in an otherwise flawless plan to get her to like me. I thought beating the crap out of Jeff the Asshole would have made her feel something good for me. I don't know what she felt about it, because she wouldn't talk to me. She only said what was absolutely required as a polite human being. Nothing more. At all.

Even Rosalie warmed up to me in a big way. She's always liked me, but even her liking someone was always pretty much an arm's length thing. She pulled me aside the day after the whole incident in the parking lot and hugged me. That sounds so normal, for a mom to hug a guy who protected her daughter, but this was scary-ass Rosalie who made grown men cry and radiated intimidating nastiness.

'That Jeff guy is lucky I didn't get my hands on him first. I swear to God I would have stomped his god-damn guts out,' she sneered, her eyes getting that evil, scary glint. 'But I wasn't there, and I'm glad you were. He can shove his lawsuits up his ass. Nobody lays a finger on my baby.' She hugged me again, Sullie squeezed between the two of us. She was warm and soft and sweet-smelling, the physical polar opposite of what I expected based on her prickly demeanor.

'You bring your aunt to our place for dinner tonight. I'll make you chilli that will knock your socks off.'

So began my celebrity status with the Erikson family. Pammy and Jimmy wanted a blow-by-blow account of the whole thing, Tony couldn't wipe the smile off his face when he saw me, and Rosalie pinched and hugged me whenever I was around.

Cadence was the only one who didn't seem to even acknowledge my presence in the room.

We ate dinner together, laughed and joked, and Cadence wasn't sulky or upset. She was just quiet and unresponsive. When I did catch her eye, it looked like she wanted to say something to me. But it felt like it might be a little more 'You're a two-bit asshole, Saxon' than 'I love you for what you did, Saxon.'

Shit.

Not that what I did was so fucking selfless; I loved a good brawl as much as the next brawler, and it felt great to knock Jeff square on his flat nose. Everyone wound up telling me what they really thought about Jeff and how much they appreciated what I'd done.

Cadence was the only one who was silent about the whole thing.

After dinner – and the chilli did knock my damn socks off – Aunt Helene pulled me aside. 'Saxon, lovey,' she sighed, 'that girl don't want your nonsense.'

'What do you mean?' I had a belly full of delicious beans and spice and my head was barely sitting right on my shoulders from all the pro-Saxon talk at the dinner table.

'She wants someone to see *her*. The real her. Not her family. Not just that pretty face. If you don't show her that's what you see, she's not going to be interested. Smarten up, boy.' She tapped me on the temple with a pointy fingernail.

I kissed her on the head because she's so fucking the real deal, it's disgusting. And I thought about what she had to say. I actually spent a really decent amount of time thinking about what Aunt Helene said.

I did see Cadence.

I saw how she could juggle a dozen cars' worth of orders at a time. I saw how she was stressed and wanted more and better, like college and fun nights out, but she loved her family and wouldn't leave them high and dry. I saw that she was careful to let guys see her as pretty and a little funny and basically smart, but deep inside she was way crazier, way sharper and sillier. She didn't want to let that out most of the time, but she'd done it. That infamous Chinese-food-and-nail-polish debacle showed me that she was just waiting to bust out, hopefully, right into my waiting arms.

But things got better and worse for me way too quickly. Better because the entire Erikson clan fell for me hard and basically initiated me into their club. And it was pretty much assumed that Cadence and I would get together.

Which is what made it worse.

Cadence didn't seem to like the idea at all, pretty much because her family was so hopped up on it. When they teased her about it or mentioned it outright, she rolled her eyes or shook her head. I was getting no points at all with her, and I had no idea what to do about it.

I needed to get her in private, to tell her what I was thinking and what I noticed, but she was sly. She wriggled right out of my damn grasp every time I thought I had her cornered. Finally, I had to take it to another level.

One night when I had been invited round there, I said goodbye to her adoring family, and felt a little pissed off at the relief visible in her eyes when I headed out the door, my hands in my pockets, my head down like I was dejected. It didn't take long for the house to settle for the night. I sat on an abandoned crate in her alley, watching the windows like a creepy stalker and wishing like crazy that I had a goddamn cigarette.

Brenna always hated my smoking, and she once told me that it was just a prop, just something cool to do. And I guess it mostly had been; but it was also a shitload of nicotine, and that's not easy to get over. Especially when I was feeling jittery about other things. Like Cadence Erikson blowing me off.

I knew when it was safe to hop up the fire escape. I can't say how I knew. It was just some kind of innate breaking and entering ability. There was definitely something profoundly fucked up about me and my delinquent sixth sense.

I crept up to her window like a cat burglar. She was sitting on her bed, looking down at her phone, probably texting. I rapped my knuckles on the window and she looked up quickly, her eyes big and nervous. She glared, then came over to the window and slid it up.

'What?' she whispered.

'I want to talk to you.' I kept my voice low. 'Do you want to get out of here? Go somewhere?'

She pulled her gorgeous lips down in a frown and, for a split second, I was pretty sure the window was going to get smashed down in my face. But then there was a tiny little hesitation. 'It's past my curfew.'

'I didn't think we'd ask.' I leaned closer to her. 'Haven't you ever broken a rule, Cadence?'

'I'm not on your level yet, but I'm no angel,' she hissed back.

'Come on. It's a nice night. Let's go out. We'll have some fun. I'll have you home way before anyone knows. Come on.' I could see that she wanted it. 'Be bad. Come on.'

She bit her lip, then nodded. She turned around and went to her dresser and put some shiny goop on her lips, ran her hand through her hair a few times, grabbed her purse and shoes and put a finger to her lips. She stepped out on the fire escape and we made our way down, stopping a few times when we were sure we had woken the whole damn house. By the time we hit the ground, we were so keyed up she just grabbed my hand and ran. I didn't even know where we were heading, and I didn't give a fuck. I was with Cadence, and that was all that really mattered.

We finally stopped running a few blocks away and

she slid down next to one of the buildings, laughing so hard she was almost crying.

'Oh shit.' She wiped her eyes with the back of her hand. 'I'm going to be in such deep trouble if my dad finds out about this.'

I sat next to her, the street pretty deserted, nothing but the distant sounds of traffic, the hot summer air, and me and this perfectly insane girl.

'Let's make sure he doesn't find out.' I looked at her for a minute and we inched closer, exactly the way I had every time I'd been about to kiss a girl. She wanted it. I could practically taste it from her. But she pulled away at the last minute, stood up, and yanked at my hand.

'Let's go do something.' She smiled and her teeth looked bright white in the moonlight. She was wearing a tiny blue tank top and a white skirt and little flip-flop thingies. I couldn't help thinking of how easy it would be to get her out of all of those tiny pieces of clothing. They were practically made to pull off.

'What do you want to do?' I asked, trying to keep my eyes off of her cleavage. I didn't have my car, but there was a lot we could walk to in this city.

'Let's go to the park,' she suggested, her eyes bright. 'C'mon!'

I followed her down the dark street, in-between brick buildings, over a chain-link fence, and into an old, almost-hidden park that time forgot. The kind with scary metal slides that get too hot in the summer and dangerous uncovered chain swings and heavy see-saws that could crack skulls and tailbones. But the pièce de resistance was the big, puke-inducing merry-go-round. It would have taken a good six or seven able-bodied elementary school kids to get the thing spinning, and once it started, the momentum would whip your stomach right up through your throat and out your mouth. Cadence jumped on and sat in the middle.

'Spin me,' she demanded.

'Are you sure?' I grabbed the paint-chipped metal bars. I jogged, pulling the heavy metal disc around slowly, just to remind her of how treacherous and awful it felt.

Cadence closed her eyes and dropped her head back, her long black hair picking up and blowing around her face. 'Yes.' Her voice swept up into the night sky. 'I'm sure. Do it, Saxon.'

She held the bars, her back arched out and her head tipped back. I whipped the heavy metal around, and she grabbed on tight and screamed a little. I wouldn't have been able to stay on it for more than a few seconds, but she was impressively able to handle the crazy spinning. It took a while before her head rolled forward and she groaned a little sickly.

'Done?' I asked, and when she nodded, I stopped the torture and helped her down. She was unsteady enough to have to lean on me. I led her to the swings and we sat.

'I used to love that when I was little,' she said, swinging back and forth gently. Her legs were long and tanned, hanging out of her way-too-short white skirt. Her arms, twined around the chains of the swings, held on tight as she kicked out and swayed forward and backward.

'I'm not really all about the puking sensation.' My sneakers slid in the gritty sand under the swings. 'What's the appeal?'

She shrugged and swung a little higher. 'I think it was just about feeling different. A little out of control.' She went even higher. Her hair flew out behind her, then billowed down and around her face. She looked like a kid, but also very much like a woman.

'Like drugs.' I didn't mean for my voice to sound so fucking full of longing, like some old rehabbed rock star. I really needed some nicotine to calm my jitters.

She planted her feet, pebbles and sand flying. 'No.' Her voice lost all the dreamy fun and slashed at me like a switchblade.

'Yeah,' I countered, my clean system itchy for a fight. Fuck this. I wasn't going to not push her a little. She had done her own judging where I was concerned, and if she was going to be my judge, jury and executioner, I could at least give her something to think about. 'It's a fact. People do drugs to feel different. A little out of control.' I purposefully mimicked her words. 'You get fucked up on spinning around.'

'That's not the same!' Those green eyes flickered with little flames of rage. She hopped off of the swing.

'You do that a lot?'

She stopped and turned to look at me. 'Do what?'

'Leave when someone says something you don't want to hear?'

She marched back over to me, so fast and fucking furious I got instant wood just watching the fury bounce off of her. 'Don't you dare try to make screwing around at a playground the same as snorting cocaine.'

'What's so scary about being similar to me?' I asked. She wrapped her arms across her chest like she was trying to protect herself from me and shook her head. 'The world won't end if you admit that you like me, Cadence. What the fuck is worse about me than that shithead Jeff?' I demanded. 'I'm no goddamn angel, but I've never gotten violent with a girl in my life.'

'So that qualifies you for boyfriend of the year?' Her voice stretched tight and vicious, a rubber band pulled to its limit and about to snap against unsuspecting flesh with a skin-bruising smack.

'I didn't say that,' I said. 'It should give me a shot, though.'

'Well, it doesn't.' Her words lost their sharpness and edged around general panicked fury. 'Just because I agree to sneak out with you doesn't mean that I want to date you.'

That might have burned, except I could see that she was completely full of shit. 'Come here.' She shook her head, so I came closer to her. I half expected her to run, but, like I said, she was full of shit so she held still until I was right next to her, the two of us breathing hard and fast.

'I'm worth taking a chance on, Cadence.' I stared right at her pouty lips, dry and in need of chapstick. Or licking.

'You're fucked up.' She spoke to the ground, and I knew it was because she thought looking at me might shake her resolve. 'I'm done with screwing up.'

'I'm not fucked up,' I said, then thought about that statement. 'All right, I'm a little fucked up. But I care about you.'

She shook her head. She was intoxicatingly good-looking. 'Not good enough. It's just words. And I've heard them all before.'

'I've done a lot,' I confessed. 'I'm not ashamed of it.

I did it because I wanted to know what it would feel like. But I'm smart enough to know that it wasn't all worth it. Drugs weren't.'

Her eyes flicked up in surprise, but she didn't say anything, just nodded quickly.

'Sex with so many people wasn't worth it either,' I added.

She looked at me curiously, and I realized that I was probably giving away more than I needed to. She didn't know everything I was infamous for. But what I was saying was unlocking something in her, and I was willing to put it all on the line to see her respond to me.

'There's a lot that I'm aware of when it comes to my own fucked-up life. For instance, I'm not content to sit on my ass and spend my massive inheritance,' I started. And then it poured out. I don't even know where it all came from. If I had given it one damn minute of thought, I would have turned on my heel and walked the fuck away. But it just poured out and I had no control over it at all. 'I don't want to think of Aunt Helene rotting in this piece of shit house she's in, because I love her. I always liked Brenna, and now that I fucked it all up, I'm afraid I don't have the right to ask for her friendship. I'm crazy jealous of Jake, always have been. I can't stand my mother and it breaks my fucking heart a little to admit that she honestly doesn't give a shit about me. School is only boring for me because I'm so busy keeping up my bored act, and it's tiring as hell. This summer has been the best time of my life. And I knew I wanted you the minute I set eyes on you the first day I came to your parents' piece-of-shit restaurant. You and I are both hiding behind a lot of crap, but all that crap got ripped down for me this summer. And it's time someone did it for you.' I felt the adrenaline raging hard and fast through my system.

She was looking at me – her eyes wide and her mouth hanging open. I didn't even know what I was saying, just that I had to say it and it had to be now or the summer would be gone and so would Cadence. The thought of losing her before I'd had a chance to get to know her choked me.

'So,' she said slowly, her face close to mine, 'you're going to rip down everything I'm hiding behind?' Her voice was husky and sweet, just the combination to make me think about peeling her clothes off and touching and licking her until she couldn't push me away. But I had done that before, and I knew it never lasted. It was a pussy way out, and Cadence deserved better.

'I am.' I kept my hands fisted at my sides. Jesus Christ she was hot, all sure of herself and full of attitude in the moonlight. But I had to prove to her that I deserved what she'd never bothered to give any-one else before.

Not that.

I wanted her trust.

'I am the one,' I repeated. 'I know about you. I know that you work like a slave, and you don't bitch about it, even when you pull your skates off and your feet are bloody.' Her head jerked a little. I could read the shock in her eyes. 'I know that you read trash and the great stuff and you always have a novel tucked in your apron. Last week it was *Forever* by Judy Blume. Right now? *East of Eden* by Steinbeck. Which I love, by the way. I know that you love to let loose and sing, and I know that you don't because you don't want anyone to see you doing something that crazy, because you're proud of how in-control you always manage to stay. And I don't know for sure why you date assholes like Jeff, but I'm willing to bet it's because you know right off the bat it's not going to work out, so there's no risk. And if there's no risk, you can let it end without getting hurt, you can stay in control of the whole thing. But that's not the way to do it.'

'It's not?' Cadence pushed her hair behind her ear with shaky fingers. 'How would you know?'

'Because the weeks I had with Brenna showed me that caring for someone makes a difference. Even if it falls apart in your hands, even if it rips your fucking heart out, it's worth it. And I want to take that risk with you.'

I had already said ten times more than I ever meant to, and I had a fairly strong feeling all of this was going to blow up in my face. But at least I had the balls to say what I needed to say. For once.

She put her hands out and grabbed my fists, wiggled her fingers into them and pulled me closer to her, so close there was nothing to do but crash into each other. So we did.

I kissed her, her hot mouth open and full of small, eager sex sounds. My hands roamed over the thread-bare cotton of her tank top and felt the warm promise of her skin under the fabric. I roamed lower, grabbing her ass hard in my hands and pulling her to me possessively. She pulled my shirt over my head and it fell on the soft play sand. I glanced around to see if anyone might stumble by and notice two horny teens getting their freak on, but it was like we were in some weirdly private alcove, a million miles away from the living, breathing city. She ran her hands down along my back, and her nails dug light trails from my shoulder blades to my waist.

I pressed her against the scratchy bark of an over-grown tree that offered an extra dose of privacy, dragged her shirt over her head and pushed the cups of her purple bra down. She had gorgeous tits, even more incredible than I'd imagined. I hiked her up higher, and she pressed her back against the bark and her hair was tumbling down all over her shoulders, getting wild and messy as I kissed down her neck and her delicate collar bones and then sucked her nipple in and listened to her moan.

Her legs were wrapped around my hips, and I moved one hand down to the soft line of her leg and followed it up her thigh and felt the warm heat of her through her underwear. I sucked harder and felt her hands dig into my hair. I pushed a finger up into her damp heat and practically got my hair ripped out at the roots. She squirmed against my hand, hard, her hips pushing against me.

I could hardly get a rhythm going, she was moving so fast and squirming so much. And it was the most turned-on I had ever been in my life. I had opened the dam with all my semi-lame, heartfelt confessions, but she had let loose physically. I had never been with anyone who just threw herself into sex like Cadence did.

I moved my fingers fast against her until her breathing was just a bunch of ragged pants, and she suddenly pulled back and cried out and dug her hands hard into my shoulders. Technically all I had gotten from the whole thing was a soaked hand and a raging boner, but I felt completely satisfied. Making her come made me feel good and, for once, I wasn't concerned with my own horndog needs.

Her face dropped to the crook of my shoulder and she breathed hard for a minute. I felt protective of her, nestled there against me. I righted her bra and put her tank top back on over her head. I smoothed my hand over her hair and smiled at her. I felt a genuine sense of happiness for once. Her face was sweet and looked . . . kind of loving.

She reached a hand up and brushed my hair away from my forehead. 'You're very nice,' she said a little woozily. 'That never happened before.' She moved her hand down my jaw and rubbed along it with her thumb. I pushed my face against her hand, liking the feeling of being rubbed by her.

'You never got fingered?' I asked, surprised. Then again, I didn't know much about her background, sexually. There was a lot I needed to learn about her.

'No. Not that. I never came. I've never come from someone else doing that. I can do it for myself, but not for anyone else. Except you, now,' she said, smiling, then giggling. 'Thank you.'

'Glad I could help.' I kissed her again. She kissed back. I thought about how open and sensual she was and it made no sense to me how she hadn't come before. Even if the guys were tools. But maybe she wasn't wild with everyone. Maybe she was only that way with me. That would be such a turn-on, I didn't know if I could stand it.

We were about to get worked up again, and much as I liked doing it for her, I was still a living, breathing red-blooded guy, and I needed to give my balls a break. I took her by the hand, and we headed to a warm, soft patch of grass and lay down.

It was the city, so there weren't many stars visible, but we looked up at them anyway.

'I never see the stars,' Cadence said. We started out lying side by side, but she moved over so that her head was nestled against my shoulder. I loved the weight of her on my body.

'You need to visit the country.' I ran my hand up and down the smooth skin of her arm. 'I could show you the stars.'

She laughed. 'That's a smooth line, Saxon. Is that how you lure all the girls to your little pokey town?'

'The stars. My natural charisma. Whatever works.' I kissed the top of her head. Her hair was smooth and sweet-smelling.

She took my hand in hers. 'I like the way your hands feel. They're very rough.'

'They weren't always.' I looked at my hand with hers wrapped around it. 'Once they were the soft, manicured hands of a man of leisure. The roughness is only since I became a respectable working man.'

She rolled her eyes. 'I wouldn't go that far. I mean, you're practically on probation.'

'Yeah, you keep reminding me.' I felt the extremely uncool grip of grumpiness take over.

She shrugged. 'You want to make me face the truth? Then you have to do it, too. You're here because you were an idiot. Admit it.' She sat up on one elbow and smiled down at me. The coil of her smile made my heart feel like it was being squeezed by a beautiful anaconda.

'I admit it,' I said, then pulled her down and kissed her. 'You were dating the world's biggest asshole. Admit it.'

'That one's easy to admit.' She blew on my face and laughed when I blinked hard.

'You had a huge-ass crush on me.' I traced her upper lip with one finger. 'Admit it.'

She blushed a little. Very cute. 'I did. But I thought you were different. I thought you were still into drugs and all that. And I thought you were . . .' She laughed and shook her head.

'What?' I asked. 'Tell me.'

'I thought you were cocky. Like you thought that you were God's gift and all that. But I thought . . . that you'd be really good, you know, sex-wise.' She put her hands up over her face.

I rolled onto my side and looked down on her. 'That

was just a tiny sample. If you want, we could try some more.'

'No!' she cried. 'You made me feel all that in like ten minutes. And it was just . . . it wasn't even sex! You're going to make me into a freak!'

I kissed her hard. 'What would be so wrong about that?'

She kissed me back, her mouth open, her hands all over me. 'Maybe nothing?' She sighed.

We kissed for a while, but there was a lot I wanted to know about her, so I broke it off. Yep, hell probably froze over. I chose talking over sex.

'So you had a major crush on me all this time?' I lay back, eyes half shut, while she kissed my forehead.

'Yeah. That night that you rescued me and Sullie, I had been thinking about you. I thought about calling you and asking you to hang out.' She covered her face with her hands again.

'Did you know Jeff was coming over?' I wanted perspective on that night's insanity.

'No.' She looked down and her lashes made long, spiky shadows on her cheeks. 'I mean, I thought he might because he felt guilty, but it was really late. He wound up being pretty drunk. And he wanted to fool around, but I didn't.'

'You didn't?' I swallowed back the acid taste in my mouth that appeared when I imagined Jeff's hands on

363

Cadence. I squinted at her. 'I remember you being a wild cat with me.' She laughed and punched my arm.

'You bring out something crazy in me. I'm not usually like that,' she insisted.

So the wild was for me. I loved that. 'So you weren't just playing me that night?'

'No.' She pulled the word out, long, slow and sweet. 'I wanted you so badly. I wanted you to stay. And working with you the next day was hellish. I'd never felt that way about anyone before. Ever. I couldn't even stand to have Jeff touch me. It just felt gross.' She looked at me from the corner of her eye. 'And then he came to confront me about it. He didn't want to break up, I did. That's what the fight was about.'

'Why were you so pissed off that I punched him? He was being a dick to you.' I let that big-ass bubble of self-righteousness float to the surface and pop.

'Punching Jeff in the face? In my parents' parking lot? While you were clocked in? They'll be lucky if his family doesn't sue. *You'll* be lucky,' she added sharply.

'I like how you look when you're pissed off,' I said and kissed her. She held back for a second, then put her arms around my neck and pulled me back onto the soft damp grass.

'You're an asshole.' She kissed me again.

'You're the girlfriend of an asshole,' I said, and she smiled at me.

364

She ran her fingers over my ribs, feather-light, until I got ticklish chills. 'What makes you think I'm going to agree to be your girlfriend?'

'Because you want my body, and I'm not the kind of guy who screws around with just any girl.' I raised my eyebrows at her and grinned.

She laughed hard at that. Then she stopped and took a long, deep breath. 'I wasn't really pissed off at you because of some lawsuit.'

'So what was it?'

She looked down, but I ducked my head and met her eyes, determined to not let her look away when she confessed to whatever she was going to confess to.

She gathered up all that long, dark hair at the crown of her head, then let it spill back down her back and looked me in the eye. 'I was pissed off with you because I didn't want to be with you, even though I couldn't stop thinking about you. I have *never* felt so out of control with anyone. Not like I feel with you. And I didn't think I wanted it.'

'So you were mad at me for being so perfect for you?' I ran my hand from her shoulder, down her arm, over her hand, to her hip and back up.

'I was scared of you.' She swallowed so hard I saw all the little muscles in her throat move. 'Jeff was so perfect. He was the most perfect of all of my boyfriends. He met every requirement on my list. And

I felt absolutely nothing for him. Not one thing. And you called me on it, so I hated you. Because I managed to trick everyone else. I even tricked myself.' She rolled on top of me, and I put my hands up into her hair and pushed it away from her face so I could kiss her.

'This night feels fucking weird,' I said once she pulled away.

'I know. Like we might wake up, and it won't be real.' She looked a little panicked at that.

'There's an easy fix for that.' I kissed all over her perfectly warm, sweet-smelling, sexy-as-hell neck, and I went right into super-wood when she moaned and writhed around a little.

'Oh yeah?' She ran her fingers along the inside of the waistband of my jeans, and I had to suck air through my teeth to keep from passing out. 'How's that work?'

'I'm not leaving you tonight,' I managed to grind out. I threw in a shrug to try to keep it casual.

'Saxon, you have to leave.' She sat up fast, leaving the air cool with just a subtle hint of her sexy smell. 'My parents will kill me. Kill. Me.'

I took her in my arms and squeezed her body tight against mine. 'I'll be stealth.' I sucked a little trail along her neck and her shoulders, not hard enough to leave any marks, but enough to bring up a moan again. 'Also, everyone is on opening at the restaurant tomorrow except you and me.'

When she finally smiled, it was the most alluring fucking mix of sweet and sexy I'd ever seen. 'OK. But I'm not having sex with you.'

I held a hand up. 'I vow to stay out of your pants unless you ask me to do otherwise.'

'Let's get home, then, before dawn.' She jumped to her feet and swung her hand down, and I grabbed it and let her pull me up.

We walked back to her house with our hands linked, and she kissed me occasionally because I was pretty damn irresistible. And it felt so goddamn good I stopped halfway home and stood in the street and yelled at the top of my lungs.

'Stop!' she laughed, twining her arms around my neck. 'Stop, you idiot! You're going to wake the whole street up!' She kissed me to stop me from yelling any more.

We climbed her fire escape and slipped in her window, her finger pressed to her lips.

Luckily, her bed was a mess of blankets and pillows, and was pretty high. I would have no trouble hiding in it or under it, whatever would work best, if it came to that.

I took off my sneakers and socks and she pointed under her bed, so I put them there. She shimmied out of her skirt and unhooked her bra and pulled it through the armhole in her shirt. She stood uncertainly in her bedroom where I was suddenly, strangely, an inhabitant. She pulled her tank over her head, then crossed her arms over her chest. Then she changed her mind and let her arms fall down at her sides, and she was totally exposed.

I looked at her body, long and curvy and potentially something I would know very well fairly soon. I felt an instant, painful stiffening in my pants. She pulled me to her by my hands and tugged my T-shirt over my head, then unbuckled my pants and pushed them off of my hips, wadded my clothes up and put them under the bed.

Without a word, she pushed me onto the bed and climbed in next to me. Her eyes were wide open in the dim light of the room. We could see each other because of the streetlight blaring outside her window.

She lifted her hand to my face and touched her fingertips to my eyebrows, my cheekbones, my nose, and chin. Her fingers drifted over my lips and brushed my forehead. We were face to face, our knees bent and crooked together, our lips so close they were almost touching.

'I'm happy you're here.' Her voice was so quiet I almost didn't hear what she said.

'I'm happy to be here.' I moved my hand up to her

face and pulled it down along her cheek, to the side of her neck, down her shoulder, along the dip of her waist, down her hip and held it there. 'I feel like I've been waiting a long time for you, Cadence.'

'Was it worth the wait?' She licked her top then her bottom lip, and I had to shift my leg to relieve my aching dick. But, for maybe the first time in my life, my dick took a backseat. I pushed past the fuck-crazy discomfort and realized that I didn't even want to think about it until she was ready. Because she really would be worth the wait.

'Yeah,' I said, my voice tight. 'Well fucking worth it.' I pulled her close to me and crushed her a little in my arms.

I felt an addiction to the promise of this new love, way stronger than anything I'd ever snorted or injected.

Way more addictive, way more exhilarating, and way fucking scarier.

Jake 4

I drove away from Brenna's house the day she gave me her essay, and I pulled over twice and thought about going back to get her. But something told me that I needed to pay attention to whatever it was she wrote. Brenna was always really good at making me forget everything else, and I didn't want to do that. I wanted to know what she felt.

Even if it kind of killed me.

Because I could see it.

When Brenna looked at Saxon, I saw something. And I saw it when he looked at her. Maybe I was making too big a deal out of it, but it seemed pretty damn unfair that I'd finally found a girl who I loved and who loved me, and I had to share her with Saxon.

Of all the fucking idiots that I might have to fight off for her, why my own dipshit brother?

I didn't want to drive to my house. My bedroom had a lot of memories of Brenna, and I liked the memories that were there. So I just drove until I found a pretty deserted stretch of road. That wasn't hard to find in Sussex County. I know I should have started reading right away, because I was slow as hell, so it was going to take a while. But I felt really alone for the first time in a while, and it felt good.

I thought about what Brenna said about me having a secret wild side. In the last few months I'd knocked three people out for her.

Or maybe she was right; maybe it had a lot less to do with her and a lot more to do with my own crap.

I wanted to leave all my bad shit behind. I wanted to be better. For Brenna and for me. But it wasn't easy.

The couple of months when Saxon and I had run really crazy were not good months for me. We did whatever the fuck we wanted. If we wanted to drink, we drank. If we wanted to fight, we fought. If we wanted to screw, we screwed. We were just two idiot smartasses doing whatever dumbshit thing popped into our heads. It seemed like it should have been a teenage guy's wet dream.

It wasn't.

Now that I was with Brenna, I realized how depressing and lonely and phony the whole thing had been. I didn't want that back. But if Brenna wasn't in my life, I didn't know if there was another alternative. She anchored me, and if what I read in the paper she wrote cut me loose, I had no idea where I'd head.

It was fucking terrifying.

Evan, Brenna's friend who seemed crazy, but was actually pretty damn sensible, told me not to worry. She said some hippie-dippie shit about how she could see the truth in people when it came to love, and she believed Brenna and I would see it through. She'd been right about taking Bren out on my bike and showing her instead of explaining. I hoped she was right about this, too.

I picked up the paper, but the words were swimming, floating around, and mixing up, then blurring and pressing together. It was always bad, but it was a lot worse when I had crap pressing on my brain.

I started the truck and drove some more. I loved driving. Especially in the summer, especially in the late morning, when the sun was high in the sky and the wind picked up, when it was a little cool and the air smelled damp and clean.

I didn't have any idea where I was headed until I noticed that the country was gone and the lights of the city were replacing the lightning bugs blinking in the fields. Before I knew it, I was in Aunt Helene's driveway. I held the steering wheel tight, not sure what I was going to do or why I was even there.

I didn't really remember coming here when I was little. But I had. Saxon and I both had. And maybe I just trusted the fact that it was here for me whenever I needed it. It was a place where there was someone who understood that sometimes a guy needed a good cry and a meal. Maybe it was just because I'd been loved here when I was a kid, and the remnant of that love kind of stuck around.

I saw the front door swing open. 'Jake? Is that you, love?' she called.

I opened the truck door and headed to the stairs. She was above me, the way she'd been with Saxon the other day, the step up making her feel taller, and mom-like. I didn't have to say anything or ask anything. She just held her arms out for me and I stepped into them and held onto her for a few minutes.

And like a huge pussy, I started crying. Soon I was blubbering like a baby, but she didn't freak or tell me to stop or get embarrassed. Nothing.

She just let me pour it out.

'Shh, love. That's OK.' Her voice was the kind people only use for babies and little kids. 'You have a little cry if you need to. That's a boy. You're just fine.' Her voice was really calm and soft and good. She ran her hand over my hair over and over and her other hand patted my back while she held tight.

And when my bizarre tirade was done, she led me into the house and made me lie down on the couch. She put a cold washrag on my head and brought me tea and cookies and sat in a chair close to me.

She put her hand on my head, then flipped the washcloth over so the cool side was against my skin again. We were completely quiet for a few minutes.

'I'm really sorry,' I said finally, sniffling like a damn baby.

She clucked her tongue. 'Hush. Sorry for what? I hoped you would come to me when you feel a little down. I'm happy to have you here.' She smiled, her tanned, wrinkled face so kind and sweet, I almost felt like bawling again.

Almost. I got a handle on myself.

'Brenna and I had a fight. Sort of,' I admitted.

She looked right at me and nodded.

And then it all spilled out. All of it. The dumb shit I had done in my past, the way Saxon and I had just stopped, that day that Brenna walked into my class and I just knew she was it for me, our break-up, our summer, my family, my stepdad. By the time I was done, the room was almost dark, and I felt like a huge weight had been lifted off of me. I had never, ever been able just to spill everything like that before.

Aunt Helene patted my arm and clicked on a lamp. The light blinded me for a second. 'You're a smart boy, Jake. A good boy. I know that you'll do what's right. And Brenna is a good girl. But you need to let her grow and feel. And you need to do the same. Even if it hurts. Even if you have to let go of some things. Do you understand?'

I nodded. Even though I didn't really understand. Because when I thought about letting go of Brenna, my mind just closed down. I didn't even want to entertain the thought.

'She wrote this essay. It's going to be put in a collection. She wanted me to read it. She was afraid it would hurt my feelings.' I looked at Aunt Helene, pleading with her to give me an answer I could live with.

'It might hurt. If Brenna thinks it might hurt, it will. You have to be strong.' Her little wrinkled hand pressed on mine.

'I will.' I said it, but I didn't mean it. I didn't even want to read the damn thing.

At that crazy, embarrassing minute Saxon burst in, grabbed Aunt Helene around the waist and swung her up and around.

She laughed a dry, happy laugh, and he put her down gently and kissed her cheek. Then he saw me.

'What the hell's wrong with you?' he demanded.

Aunt Helene tried to shush him. I wished I were anywhere but there.

'Nothing. I was going.' I stood and felt around for my keys, but they'd slid out of my pocket and were buried in the couch cushions.

'No, no, no!' Aunt Helene said, her voice loud and a little angry. We both turned and stared. Aunt Helene never sounded anything but happy and sweet. 'You are brothers. You need to tell him all this, Jake. Saxon will help you with this.'

Saxon? Saxon – my shithead, misfit, asshole brother? He must have seen the look on my face.

'No can do.' He raised his eyebrows and shrugged. 'I'm going out to see Cadence in a little while.'

'She will understand,' Aunt Helene growled. 'Get the paper, Jake. You go figure this out. Now.'

I went out to the truck and seriously contemplated getting in and driving away. But I couldn't stand to think of Aunt Helene disappointed. Or pissed off. So I grabbed the paper and came back into the house and followed Saxon into his room.

It smelled a little like old smoke, but it was neat and clean, surprisingly. He usually kept his room like a sty.

'Aunt Helene wouldn't put up with a mess,' he said, answering the question I didn't bother to ask.

'We don't have to do this.' I sat on his bed. He sat next to me. He pointed to the paper.

'Bren wrote that?'

'Yeah.'

'And whatever it is has you all fucked up?'

'Yeah.' I had no desire to go into the whole thing with him.

'Give me a minute to call Cadence, OK?' I nodded and he pulled out his cell. 'Hey, babe. Jake dropped by and I gotta talk to him about some shit. Is it cool if I'm a little late? . . . Yeah.' He laughed. 'You too. C'mon, you're giving me a hard-on talking like that. All right. Wait up for me. Soon.' He clicked off.

It was his face that was so shocking. He looked totally fucking in love. It was a freaky look for Saxon. It didn't even look like him, somehow.

'So it's working? With Cadence?' I asked, Brenna's paper tight in my fist.

'Yeah, bro.' He grinned. 'Holy shit, she's fucking hot and funny and smart. I just hope she doesn't get sick of me and kick me to the fucking curb, you know?'

'Yeah.' I swallowed hard and took a deep breath. 'I do know.'

Saxon and I looked at each other and nodded our mutual understanding. 'Give me that paper, Kelly. Everyone knows you can't read for shit, and I don't have all night. I've got a girl wearing very sexy under-wear waiting for me.' He glanced over the paper, and his eyes went a little wide.

I was pissed that I hadn't tried harder to read it. What was he seeing?

'Are you going to read it?' I asked, totally impatient and dreading the whole thing at the same time.

He looked at me, his brow furrowed. 'Yeah. OK. I'll read it.' He cleared his throat and started. *'I'm in love. Twice. It's not a love that divides fifty-fifty. It's not a love that's split between good and bad, safe and dangerous, real and imaginary. It's a mixed up, confused, good, bad, and ugly love, times two, and it's all mine.*

'The beginning? The beginning of my first love was just infatuation and impression, and it quickly turned to warning bells in my inexperienced brain and a note to self; "Stay away! Far away!" Just when it felt safe to take a breath and forget the pull of my heart (and other parts), I fell again, head over heels, uncontrollably and without a chance to grab hold before it swallowed me hard and whole. He was everything I imagined was too good to be true. But who wants that anyway? Too good to be true would have been too boring to handle. I found some bad as well. That was a relief and also a big, colossal, system-smashing shock!

'Fast forward through late-night kisses, stolen moments in each others' arms, long rides in old trucks and fast cars, the smell of cigarette smoke and crisp fall air, the roar of dirt bikes, the flat kick of a soccer ball, and over it all, the pounding of my heart as I pedal and run, run and pedal, sometimes toward it all, and sometimes as far away, as fast as I can.

'I'm in love twice, and why not? I have two eyes to look at them with. I have two ears to hear their stories and jokes. I have two arms; I could hold each one if I wanted. But I only

have one mouth. And I only have one heart. I failed division in elementary school. I failed fractions, too. So I don't know how to divide and fracture the way I should.

'I'm in love twice, and each love is different, unique, incomparable. Asking me to choose between the two loves is like asking me to choose between two parents. Even with that example in mind, I know there's one parent I feel closer to, one I share it all with, one who is better for me. But that doesn't mean the other parent doesn't matter. In fact, the other parent fills in things the first couldn't. Sacrificing one would mean the death of my parents as a whole. Just like sacrificing one of them would be the death of my whole love.

'It would be easier to be Juliet, Lizzie Bennett or Penelope, and love for sure once I decided on one love. But I'm not that simple and neither is my love. It's big and full of nooks and crannies. They need to be filled, and it's a big job to fill it. My parents fill some pieces. My friends fill others. Then there's books, music, nature, running, Christmas, new clothes, the windows down in summertime when you're driving nowhere in particular. And two boys. When I think of it that way, it doesn't seem so crazy. It doesn't seem dishonest or slutty or terrible. It seems like two is just enough and my life is only fractionally as long as I'd one day like it to be. More years equals more loves, so that I will love twice, three times, seventeen times, fifty-four times and it will always be a love that I need. And that I need to give back.

'Because love doesn't have a number or an end. It's big enough. Strong enough. Wild enough. To hold every extra ounce we can pour or wriggle or crowbar in. I'm in love twice. And that's just the beginning.'

Then Saxon folded the paper and handed it back to me, and we sat next to each other on the bed in his room at Aunt Helene's, not really sure what the hell to say.

'I better fucking go,' I muttered and stood up.

'Stay here. Aunt Helene has an old cot from like the Second World War in the closet.' Saxon smiled at me, like a truce. 'I'll take the cot.'

'It's cool, man.' I stood, the folded paper smooth in my shaking fingers. 'I gotta get back.'

'For what?' He pointed to the paper. 'You gonna talk to Bren tonight?'

'No.' I was sure about that. There was just too much going through my head, and I really didn't know what to do with it all.

'Then stay.' He fell back on his bed, arms under his head.

'You and Cadence have plans.' There were so many places I didn't want to be, so many places that didn't feel right, that I couldn't even pinpoint which one would be the worst. But staying with Saxon actually wasn't the bottom of the list.

'She'll come over. It'll be cool. C'mon, stay.' He

rolled his neck back and forth and cracked it. 'Or don't. Whatever the fuck. If you don't want to, don't. But it's cool if you do.'

I realized he was asking me because he wanted me to stay. For whatever reason.

'All right.'

Saxon left to walk Cadence over, and Aunt Helene set out a plate of sandwiches and a bowl of pretzels.

'Sit, Jake. Sit and relax for a while.' She squeezed my shoulder and I sat.

Once the sandwiches were in front of me, I realized that I was starving. I grabbed one and bit into it, and focused for a minute on how damn good it was to eat at Aunt Helene's. It was a chicken sandwich with real chicken, like picked off the bird. Good rye bread, tomatoes that I had seen her bring in from her own garden. It was a million miles away from my usual canned soup/TV dinner/cold cut sandwich routine.

Her house was a good house to be in. It felt warm and comfortable and like home. Not that I had a good grasp on 'home'.

Saxon came in with Cadence. He had his arm around her waist and was smiling like he'd won the fucking jackpot. She had her head tilted towards him and was laughing at something he'd said to her. While they were still in the hall, before they thought anyone could see them, she took his face in her hands and kissed him, then rubbed her nose on his. Like a little fucking adorable-ass Eskimo kiss.

And maybe I had turned into a weepy puddle of blubbering sad-sack emotion, but I missed Brenna. I wished I had gone back to get her, even though I knew what a disaster that would have been. Cadence and Saxon came and sat with me.

'Hey, Jake,' she said, smiling a little shyly.

She was one hell of a knockout. It struck me again as a little weird, how shy she was. Girls that good-looking were usually really over-confident. 'Hey, Cadence.' I returned the smile. 'Sorry you've had to spend so much time with that tool.'

She popped a quick kiss on Saxon's neck. 'I'm just glad you're here tonight to give me some relief from this goon.'

He squeezed her to his side. 'Don't believe the Jake hype, Cadence,' he warned. 'He's just as big a douchebag as I am, I promise.'

We all laughed, then Aunt Helene brought out a card deck for us, and Cadence taught us how to play a game called 'Palace', which required just enough thinking to help me keep my mind off of Brenna. It was perfect.

We played a few rounds, then Cadence started asking about Folly. The show at her dad's place was in a few days and she was fairly worried. It was a chance to save the diner from going under, so she wanted everything to be perfect.

'I have some Folly on my iPod.' Saxon jumped up to get it. Cadence and I were alone in the dining room.

'Um, Jake?' She bit her lip.

'Yeah?' She looked worried.

'Can I ask you something? But, just know ahead of time, you don't have to answer if it's too weird or crazy that I asked. OK?' She focused on examining her fingernails, not really looking me in the eye.

'Fair enough. Ask away.' I leaned closer to her.

'Were Brenna and Saxon really serious?' She kept her voice low and darted a quick look down the hall, where Saxon had just gone.

Her eyes were wide and kind of almond-shaped. And green. A really pretty shade of light green with some brown in them.

It was a pretty uncomfortable question. I squirmed a little, searching for an answer that would save both of us from bruised hearts. 'They've always liked each other. But I think Saxon wanted something that he didn't get from Brenna.'

'Sex?' Cadence pulled at the bottom of the shirt so hard in her nervous distraction, it seemed like she might tear the fabric.

I felt a hot flash of fury just thinking about that.

'No. I mean, they didn't have sex. But I think he wanted, like, the romance part of it.'

'Oh.' She dropped her shirt and fisted her hands. 'They didn't have that?' Her eyes flickered up and she shook her head. 'I'm sorry. This is rude. I'm being really out of line.'

'No, it's all right. Trust me, I get why you want to know.' I wondered how the hell I was supposed to explain the weirdness that had happened this past winter. 'We were always still kind of all about each other, so she and Saxon just broke it off after a while.'

'Um. But, Saxon . . . Saxon told me about this paper. Was it just, like, an assignment or something?' Cadence's mouth pressed in a flat, tight line.

I couldn't believe Saxon had already told her about it. I wondered how much he told her. And why. And if he'd regret it.

'Yeah. Kind of.' A wave of irrational anger washed over me. 'She was supposed to write about something she felt passionate about.'

'Oh. Passion? But she and Saxon dated in the past. It's all done now, right? And they're just friends?' Cadence looked at me like I might have the answer, not realizing that was the same damn question drumming through my head.

I dug deep into my gut for the answer, and said

what I honestly believed was true. 'Brenna doesn't make a hell of a lot of sense to me sometimes,' I admitted. 'She likes to think about things. A lot. But she said they were done a while ago, and I don't have any reason to doubt her. She's loyal and honest, and I believe her.' And I did. Relief skipped through me like a stone skimming on a flat lake.

Cadence reached her hand across the table and squeezed mine. 'Cool. I'm glad we got to talk a little. Maybe we could all go out sometime?'

'Sure. Yeah. That would be cool.' God, she was pretty. She had this silky brown-black hair that shone and nice lips, the kind that looked like they would be good for kissing.

She let go of my hand and it was like my head righted itself again. What the hell was I thinking?

This was Saxon's girlfriend. Didn't I have enough trouble with Brenna? Wasn't I just damning Saxon for exactly what I was feeling? I looked at Cadence, who didn't look away from me at all.

I liked the way she looked. I liked her confidence and the fact that she was sweet and smart and honest. If Saxon had met her a year before, before I had known Brenna, would I have wanted to steal her away?

'I can see Brenna's theoretical problem, you know,' she said and smiled. Great smile. Nice teeth, a little dimple on the left side.

'What's that?' I shook the thoughts about her smile out of my head.

'Well, a lot of guys are just losers. And then there's you and your brother. You're kind of overwhelming, you know? Really good-looking, kind of bad-ass, kind of sweet, just really attractive. And there're two of you. I can see how she might have got caught up in . . . you two.' She tucked her hair behind her ear self-consciously.

I opened my mouth to say something, which, honestly, probably would have been pseudo-flirting, when Saxon came back in. Luckily, he was too focused on his iPod to notice that Cadence and I backed up quickly and looked sheepish. Not that there was anything to look sheepish about.

'This is Folly. I think it's their best, but you'll have to listen and see what you think.' He put one earbud in Cadence's ear and offered the other one to me.

I had to move around the table so that I was sitting close to her. She smelled good. Her skin was dark, tanned, and it looked smooth and soft, the way girls' skin always looked to me. We listened a few inches apart, and I was glad that we had a good excuse to keep quiet. Because I didn't know what to say.

Cadence glanced over at me a few times and gave me that tiny smile, like she was hiding the second part of it so she could share it later. I liked her smile. I liked the look on her face. She would have been really easy to fall in love with.

If she wasn't with Saxon. If I wasn't with Brenna.

Just thinking it to myself, it sounded a little man-whorish. But the point wasn't really that I wanted Cadence. It was that I had been kind of wrapped up in Brenna and there wasn't anyone else I could imagine liking. But I knew that didn't mean that I would never be attracted to anyone else. For me, it was easier because I had been with so many girls. Granted, none of them had been nearly as smart or cool or sweet as Brenna was. But I'd had my shot.

It was hard for me to put Brenna into perspective. The fact was, I had been lucky enough to be right there when she was first looking to date. There hadn't been anyone before me, and she and I got serious fast. Brenna was a fairly independent girl. That couldn't have sat very well with her.

By the end of the song, I felt at peace, but also shaken up. Knowing things, or realizing them, didn't necessarily make them easier to deal with. Not for me. I could understand being attracted to someone else, and wanting the freedom to be with other people. But I loved Brenna. And what I really wanted was for her to write an essay about how much I rocked her world. Maybe it was selfish, but it was also honest. I couldn't hate her for what she wrote, but it made me kind of pissed off that she divided her love up like that. All I had was her. And I loved her with my whole heart.

We played a few more hands of Palace, but Cadence had a curfew and Saxon seemed pretty serious about sticking to it. By the time he got back from taking her home, I had dragged the old musty cot out and was almost asleep.

He fell onto the mattress with a noisy squeak of the springs. 'You asleep, Jake?'

'No.'

'I'm sorry about this whole thing,' he said awkwardly.

I was glad that it was dark and we couldn't see each other. 'Why would you be sorry? Brenna wrote it.'

'Because I shouldn't have butted in with her when I did. I just didn't know what the hell I was doing.' The silence stretched out for a long minute. 'Jake?'

'I hear you,' I said into the dark.

'Now that Cadence and I are together, I just . . . uh, I realize what I was doing.' I'd never heard Saxon stammer for words unless he was hard-core hammered. I knew he was stone-cold sober. 'And it's, well, it's fucked up. I was fucked up. I'm glad you knocked my tooth out. I deserved it. I deserved more.'

It was getting unusually sappy between us. Also, I hated being the recipient of any of Saxon's pity, so I smashed back at him with the biggest, nastiest weapon in my arsenal. 'If I wasn't with Bren, I'd steal Cadence out from under you in a fucking hot second.'

I heard Saxon pull in a sharp breath. 'Dude, I'm going to kick your fucking ass.'

'Do it.' I lay still on my uncomfortable-as-all-hell cot.

It was tense and quiet for a minute. Then Saxon laughed. I couldn't help it; I laughed too. Because it was so ridiculous and stupid, it was funny.

'Go to sleep, you fucking asshole,' Saxon said good-naturedly. 'And tomorrow, go see Brenna. Maybe you can get some make-up sex out of this whole clusterfuck.'

Which was probably not the best last thought before I tried to relax and fall asleep, but there were definitely worse endings to a day like the one I'd had. Brenna was tangled in my dreams, and so was make-up sex.

The next morning Saxon was still asleep when I got up. I went out to the kitchen and Aunt Helene was already awake with waffles and bacon for me. She clucked around and made a big deal out of making sure I ate what I was supposed to. She also had the picture album for me.

'You know, Jake,' she said when she handed it to me, 'you're very young. Just enjoy who you are and what you have now. There will be so much coming to you. Don't be so worried all the time.' She patted my arm.

I got up and hugged her. 'Thanks,' I said, and I meant it. And I hoped she understood all I meant when I said it: thanks for food, thanks for memories, thanks for giving a shit.

I got in my truck and roared away, driving a little too fast. The air was still cool since it was still early. Brenna might not even be awake, but I needed to see her.

I parked down the street, the opposite end that her mother used to drive to work. I went to her window, open like it always was since she liked to sleep in the fresh air, and sat under it for a while, not sure what I wanted to say when I saw her. There was probably no worse idea. By the time five minutes had gone by, I was so chicken-shit I could hardly think about going in.

So I turned my brain off, stopped thinking, and just went ahead and did what I needed to do.

I hoisted myself up on the sill and dropped in quietly, expecting to wake her up. But there was no one in her bed. I felt a minute of panic and was ready to leave when I heard someone else climb through the window behind me. A hundred thoughts went through my head at once, but I wasn't quick enough to actually act on any of them. So I was standing like a dummy in the middle of her room when I realized Brenna was sneaking back in.

She put her hand over her mouth when she saw me and we stood looking at each other across her room for a shocked minute.

'Brenna?'

She flew across the room and threw herself into my arms. Somewhere in the back of my head I realized that she must have been out running. She was sweaty and wearing muddy sneakers and her favorite running hoodie. Just like with the paper, I was kind of upset that she hadn't been sitting in her room, waiting for me, sad about our whole fight.

But that wasn't what I loved about Bren.

I loved that she was herself, fiercely, and she didn't pout or mope. She was honest and open and smart. She was mine in a way, but she was mostly just her own. And that was what I loved most about her.

She hugged me so tight, I was having a hard time breathing. 'I love you. So much! I haven't stopped thinking about you. And I'm sorry. The essay . . . it's just random thoughts, you know? I should have thought about you, how you'd feel. I really like what I wrote, and I hope you realize that it wasn't about how I don't love you. It's about how love can be so complicated and huge and beautiful, and how there's enough of it for everyone we ever meet.'

'OK.' I ran a hand down her hair.

'And when I wrote it . . . I was thinking about love in general. I don't know. I guess I just think it's so stupid to apologize about what I think or what you think, you know? But I do love you. I really love you. So much. And I hope you know that if I didn't feel it for you, I'd just tell you. I'd never pretend or anything.' Her face was really serious and worried. She was beyond just beautiful. She was strong and smart and pretty fucking perfect, mind-boggling essays included.

'I believe you.' I meant it. And then I kissed her. Because we had wasted a lot of time not doing that. And that was the worst waste of time I could imagine.

'You did read it?' she asked, pulling her mouth away.

Her hair was all falling out of her ponytail and surrounding her face like a golden-brown cloud.

'Of course I read it.'

She bit her lip. 'Was it hard to read? I mean to get. Not that you couldn't get it—'

'I had Saxon read it to me,' I cut in.

Her face went bone white. 'Saxon read it?'

'Yeah.' And just so we were all clear, I added, 'And I don't know if Cadence read it, but Saxon told her about it.'

Brenna's mouth got small and she shook her head.

'I'm sorry. I mean, I didn't realize that so many people would, um . . .'

'Be affected?' I offered.

'Yeah.' Her eyes were wide with terror.

'Cadence seemed OK with it,' I told her.

'How do you know?' Brenna asked eagerly, grabbing my hands in her still-cold ones.

'Because we hung out last night. Cadence and Saxon and me. And she said that she could see your point.'

Brenna's eyes got narrow and suspicious.

'What point?' She was talking carefully, listening carefully to what I said back.

'That you found me and Saxon attractive. Like that it was overwhelming. To be around both of us. At once.' And each word I said made her look more pissed off and made me wish I hadn't mentioned it. But at the same time I was glad I brought it up. Brenna had a flash of rage.

'That's *not* what I meant, Jake.' She smiled a little and tried to keep cool, but I could see the worry in her eyes. 'So you and Cadence talked about it? Hmm.'

I couldn't stop smiling. 'Sucks, doesn't it?'

'What?' She was having a hard time keeping her voice light.

'Being jealous.' I couldn't tone my grin down.

'I'm not!' she insisted too fast.

'Yeah.' I had to laugh at her. 'You definitely are. But Cadence helped me get it, you know?' I knew I was wading in deep, but I couldn't help myself.

'How?' Brenna asked.

'Because she's really good-looking and nice and smart. And I figured if it had been Cadence and Saxon before I met you, I might have tried to get her to date me. So I get it.'

She shook her head and opened her mouth, then closed it and shook her head again.

'Seriously?' she finally wailed. 'That's it for you? That's what you think?'

She was mad, like self-righteously mad. 'Yep. I think that's it. And I think I'm right, Ms Blixen.'

And, finally, she really calmed down and laughed a little. 'Maybe you're right. Maybe.'

She glared, but it was mostly all an act.

'You're just mad that I've got you figured out, and you aren't all that deep, after all.' I kissed the top of her head. 'Should I go? Is Mom up yet?'

She shook her head. 'Don't go. Will you hide under my bed?'

'Brenna,' I groaned.

'Please!' she cried. 'Please, please! C'mon, we had a pretty crappy day yesterday. Let's just hang around. Just me and you. No more crazy surprises, I promise. Maybe we can ride again?' She smiled coaxingly.

394

'Please? Under my bed. She'll leave for work soon. Pleeeease?'

I laughed again, and it felt damn good. She was a pain in the ass, but she made me laugh like no one else could. 'All right,' I said, lying on her floor and wriggling under her bed. 'I can't believe the things I do for you!'

She hung off the side of her bed, her hair down around her face. 'Thanks, Jake. For lots of cool stuff you do.' She moved her face to mine and kissed me, Spider-Man-style, then grinned and headed out of her room, leaving me shaking my head under the bed.

It figured that when we kissed Spider-Man-style, it was Brenna who got to be the superhero.

Brenna 5

'I wish I could be there tonight.' Evan sighed into the phone. 'Why did you have to meet me right when I turned over a new leaf and decided to stop skipping school? Last summer, I would have been back on a plane to see you already. First class. Are you excited?'

'I am.' I had Evan on speakerphone so I could straighten my hair while we talked. 'And I wish you could be here, too. How is school? It's so weird you're in school already. Seriously, starting in the summer should be illegal.' I gooped shine enhancer on my hair and clamped the paddles high up on my scalp, pulling the hair through until it fell glassy smooth.

'It's been all right. I'm hell-bent on straightening myself out and all. So no more shenanigans. Or, not many shenanigans. I'm trying to organize my school folders. Gramma says I need to stop flying by the seat of my pants and start doing all the work. I need you to help me arrange my files. You're a born organizer. Like a human queen bee or whatever the big ant who hatches all the babies and controls the zombie minion ants is called.'

'Aw. That's the creepiest, sweetest thing anyone's ever said to me. You can mail me your stuff, I'll organize it and mail it back.' I ran the paddles over my hair again.

'Gramma wouldn't approve. I have to learn to be more like you. I promise I will be a hive of product-ivity. Or an ant hill. Or something productive and organized.' The sounds of some sappy love ballad were playing in the background, and I could hear the mix of love words that were so break-up related, like *never again* and *let you go* and *stole my heart*, that I felt a little burst of worry. We hadn't really talked about the whole Rabin thing much, and she sometimes seemed too over it to truly be over it. 'On that note, what's happening with your whole presentation? Is Jake going?'

'Jake is.' I suck my breath into my lungs. 'Mom and Fa are going, and Devon's whole family will be there. It'll be fine. It will.'

'Will it?' Evan's voice is soft and prodding at the same time.

'It will. Now that it's out in the open, I think it actually made things between Jake and I better. And, of course, my mom is thrilled. Any event that means we can go shopping for a new outfit gets her all giggly.' I glance over at the binder that holds my essay and try not to think about how much I wish Saxon could be there for the reading.

'That Jake is a smart one. I knew it would turn out alright.' Evan never was very good at hiding her feelings, and I could tell there was a subtext to what she said: namely, even though everything was ok my end, it was still a disaster at hers.

'So, what's up with you? Is it better starting at a new school with all new people?' I looked at my own reflection in the mirror and tried to sound more cheerful than I looked. I just had this feeling that Evan was going through things she wouldn't tell me about.

Evan turned the music up a notch and clicked her tongue. 'I'm trying. It's not easy. Savannah is so big, but so claustrophobic. Everyone knows everyone else's business, so it's not like I get a clean slate.' She sighed and said, 'But I don't want to talk about my boring, lame-ass school life. The shirt you sent me is freaking amazing, by the way. I love how you did that special thing with the little green stars all over the sleeves. Did Tony get back to you? Did he like it?'

'He did! And Cadence was happy with it, which I was worried about because it was her picture on it and all. It's tonight, and Jake should be here any minute, but I wanted to call you and talk before I went out.'

'Girl, you better hop to. It's late already. And I have

these damn files to go through. My life is a miserable, rotting pile of boredom, isn't it? But I'm being a good girl. You would be so proud. Did I tell you I haven't even been out drinking more than, like, three or four times since Dublin?' Evan relayed the news with confident enthusiasm.

'I *am* proud of you. I'm sending you queen ant zombie transmissions. You are going to kick your binders' asses!'

'Thank you for making me feel less like the loser I truly, truly am. Mwah, darling.'

'Love!'

We disconnected, and I worried about my outfit. I was wearing the T-shirt I designed which I had cut and tailored with Mom's sewing machine so that it was extra fitted and the V-neck was almost scandalously deep, a pair of skinny jeans and my favorite green Converses. I had painstakingly straightened my hair, just to make it extra shiny. And I did my make-up smoky and sexy. I was aiming for hot, but didn't know if I only managed to pull off 'trying hard to be hot'. Because I had a worry that I'd never really had before.

Cadence was gorgeous. Like runway model hot. I had completely beautiful friends, Kelsie and Evan at the forefront. But there was something approachable about Kelsie's kind of beauty, and Evan was so easy about the way she looked, it never bothered me. I barely knew Cadence at all, and she sort of scared me.

And there was the added complication of Jake's comments about her. Not that I thought anything was going on. It was normal for any guy with functioning eyes to drool over Cadence. But Jake had never talked about a girl the way he talked about her.

It sucked because I felt like I was getting a well-deserved dose of my own medicine. Jake had been pretty cool about the whole thing with me and Saxon, and he'd actually had to watch us date; at least I had nothing like that to worry about.

I hoped.

Ugh! I hated that I was thinking that way. Not only did it make me feel like a complete tool, it made it hard to get comfortable around Cadence, which made me feel like a bigger tool.

Before I could get too sucked in, the doorbell rang and I heard Mom get it.

'Hi, Jake,' she said, her voice newly friendly.

It had taken a while, but now that Jake had won her over, Mom was a lot more accepting of him being around.

'Hello, Mrs Blixen. The weather's been great this week.'

I smiled at his good-boy manners. I heard my mom laugh at Jake's attempts at small talk. She felt completely open and free with him after our time together at his family's place in New York; but Jake still felt like he was being judged and measured whenever my mother was around. I raced out to rescue him.

'Bren.' He raised his eyebrows behind Mom's back. 'That shirt is ... um looks ... it's great. It's really good.'

What Jake was trying to say was that the shirt showed a lot of cleavage. Which was helped by a really nice push-up bra I had recently purchased and never worn before tonight. I could see that Jake appreciated the effects.

'Well, we better go. We'll probably be a little late,' I said apologetically to Mom. I was appreciative of the fact that my parents never set a curfew for me, and I tried to be respectful about that.

'It's OK, honey.' Mom adjusted the hem of my shirt. 'Go and have fun! I'm so happy about how your shirts turned out! You can tell me everything in the morning.'

I kissed her, knowing full well I could tell her tonight if I wanted. Mom never went to sleep before I was safely home and tucked in.

Jake and I ran out to the truck, and he opened my door, but pulled me over to him before I could get in. He yanked me so close, our hips bumped.

401

'Hey-a, Good-looking.' He grinned, then leaned in and kissed me softly.

When he pulled away, his gray eyes looked almost silver. I loved how his hair was getting kind of long and wild and all streaked with gold from the summer. He had a great tan, and had actually developed more muscle on his summer off. Jake got bored if he didn't have things to do, so he'd bought himself a weight bench.

I really appreciated his need to keep busy.

'Hey-a yourself, hot stuff.' I smiled back, warm and dizzily happy.

'I just thought I'd take a minute to tell you how damn sexy you look.' He drew one finger along the soft curves of breast popping out of my V-neck. 'You make me a little crazy, Bren.'

'That's the point.' I shook my boobs proudly. 'Don't they look great?'

He chuckled. 'Yeah. I mean they always do. They just look . . . eager.'

I waggled my eyebrows at him. 'It's a new bra. You like?'

'Probably like it more off,' he said in a low voice, and I felt a little rash of shivers along my neck.

I pressed my hands to his chest and kissed him, wanting to do a lot more. But we were in my driveway, and we had already dawdled for a long time. Mom would wonder why we hadn't gone.

'Maybe later?' My words were tinged with all kinds of reluctance as I slid into the truck.

Jake slammed the door shut and winked at me. 'I'm not hiding under your bed.'

'Fine,' I muttered and stuck my tongue out at him. We started to Lodi in a good mood, which helped the massive flock of butterflies kickboxing in my stomach. This was the first time we'd be seeing Saxon and Cadence after my whole essay debacle, and I was all jammed full of nerves.

'What's up?' he asked. I sneaked a look at him, driving with one hand, the other arm resting half out of the open window. There was something incredibly sexy about the way Jake drove.

I blushed, embarrassed to bring the whole thing up again. 'I'm just nervous. New T-shirts, new crowd, big concert.' I took a few slow, deep breaths.

Jake took my hand and squeezed before he had to let go and shift gear. 'It will be awesome. I have a good feeling.'

It didn't necessarily make any practical sense that his gut feeling would make me feel better, but it did somehow. I trusted Jake's gut feelings. He was reliable like that.

He left me in silence, just flipping me a comforting

smile across the seat once in a while when we caught each other's eye. By the time we were really close, I was feeling pretty calm about the night ahead.

When we pulled up to Tony's there was a fairly good number of cars. Tony's was built in an enormous circle, so cars could pull up around the outside. In through the high plate-glass windows, we could see the interior.

All the booths were around the outside of the circle, and the tables that usually filled the inside had been moved out, so there was a huge, open floor space. The booths were filled, but the waitresses were only serving at the counters for the night. You had to go up to the counter to order any food you wanted. And there were tons of people up there.

'Hey, look. They're wearing your shirt.' Jake pointed, and I craned my neck to see a few kids wearing the new Folly design. Jake kissed my temple and grabbed my hand, dragging me inside.

We walked through the doors, and I finally released the huge breath I hadn't even realized I was holding.

The whole place was filling up fast with decked-out kids. You could tell the Sussex County kids; a little punky, a little country and fairly out of place. The local kids all looked a lot older and a little bored and too-cool, but that might have just been my uptight impression because we were out-of-place visitors.

I saw Tony Erikson, who I recognized from his picture on the website I researched for the T-shirts, off to the side, smiling. The band was setting up and sound-checking. I caught Kelsie's eye right away.

'I feel like I haven't seen you in months!' She hugged me hard around the waist. 'You look fantastic! How are you?'

'Good.' I shook my hands out anxiously, checking the crowd for Saxon or Cadence. 'I hope tonight is fun.'

'It's going to be awesome! The band is so excited they're about to ralph!' Kelsie crowed happily. 'Oh, and we sold a million T-shirts.'

I looked around and realized that at least half the room was wearing them, Kelsie included.

'That's awesome.' My eyes were darting around a little frantically, for what, I wasn't sure. Or wasn't admitting.

'So did you know that Devon Conner is gay?' She lowered her voice conspiratorially.

'I actually did,' I confessed. 'He and I were in Ireland together when he told me.'

'He looks so good.' Kelsie searched across the crowded diner to Devon, who was laughing with a cute-looking guy with a lip ring. He saw us and waved, then they ambled over.

'Hey, Brenna,' he said, and I hugged him quickly

because he was still in that way-too-awkward social stage where touching was uncomfortable. 'Hey, Kelsie. Guys, this is Marcus. My, um, my boyfriend.'

Kelsie's eyes widened very slightly, then she stuck her hand out. 'It's so nice to meet you, Marcus.' I smiled at him and eyed Devon, who looked like his bones went soft with relief as Marcus smiled and shook hands.

'You look hot,' Devon said, eyeing my shirt.

'Right back at you.' I pushed him away and surveyed his outfit. 'I like the tie.' He had on a black shirt with one of my older Folly shirts on over it, a lime green tie and a great pair of dark, cuffed jeans.

'Hi, Jake,' he said and we introduced Marcus, who returned Jake's shy smile. Did Devon and I both have shy boyfriends? It was nice to know I'd have someone to talk to about it. Devon looked at me and raised his eyebrows, but I shook my head at him. I knew he wanted to talk about the essays, but I didn't want to bring it up now, in front of Jake, with Saxon around . . .

Somewhere.

It was unusual to walk into a room where I knew Saxon was, but not have him come to find me right away.

'So, did you guys know Folly is set to release a brand new album, probably October?' Jake smiled and put his arm around me.

They were still chatting about Folly when I finally caught sight of Saxon. He was standing with his arm around Cadence's waist, so they mirrored me and Jake across the room.

They looked great together. They looked like they belonged, and I was at the same time happy and a little sad about it.

Cadence looked really pretty. Her long, dark hair was up in a messy bun. She wore one of my Folly T-shirts with a black long sleeved shirt underneath, a short pleated black skirt, and black boots with fur. It was one of those outfits I would have looked like a lunatic in, but she managed to rock it and look totally gorgeous and sexy.

It wasn't just the way she looked, though. She had a nice smile and she laughed a lot – it was a big, easy laugh that made everyone else laugh with her.

And Saxon was looking at her like he was an astronomer and she was a once-in-a-lifetime comet. It was close to worship.

He had on a Folly shirt too, a little tight and beat up in a way that could only be the result of wearing it every day while he did construction projects around Aunt Helene's. The result was a purposefully un-intentional added coolness that was made edgier by his nod-to-the-blue-collar black work pants.

Oh, and he was wearing Converses, all black,

which would have made me feel a hint of camaraderie except that I didn't want to feel anything like that toward him tonight. For too many reasons. His black hair was getting long and it was shiny and messy. He was smiling, and the look of contented, in-love ease made him even more gorgeous than his old bored attitude ever had.

He saw us across the expanse and came over, pulling Cadence by the hand.

'Hey, guys.' I saw something impatient in his eyes. He pulled Cadence forward. 'Cadence, this is Kelsie and Devon. This is my girlfriend, Cadence.'

Devon grabbed Marcus's hand, cleared his throat, and said, 'Nice to meet you, Cadence. Saxon, Cadence, this is Marcus. My boyfriend.'

Saxon met Devon's eyes and a slow smile of respect spread across his face. 'Nice to meet you, Marcus,' Saxon said. 'You go to St Luke's?' Marcus nodded and Saxon said, 'My girl goes to Immaculate.'

Cadence and Marcus immediately started talking about schools and Saxon stood back, arms crossed, looking satisfied.

And in that minute, I knew what the impatience was all about. Saxon couldn't wait to show her off, to announce to the world that she was his girlfriend.

It made me glad. It really did make me happy to see Saxon happy. I had never liked being his girlfriend. We had never fitted together the way he and Cadence did. He never had that easy, relaxed look with me. I smiled at Cadence and she smiled back. Then I saw her eyes go to Jake and they shared a conspirator's smile.

'Hey.' Jake nodded down to her feet. 'I like your boots.'

He liked her boots? He liked big boots with fur on them? I looked at Jake curiously and wondered what kinds of other crazy things he liked and didn't tell me about.

'Thanks.' She turned one long, slim leg so that we could all see her boot from the side. 'I've been waiting for an excuse to wear them.'

Cadence was absolutely cute and sincere and stylish, and I liked her. Though the look of appreciation my boyfriend was giving her boots (and leg) was just a teeny tiny bit irritating.

'The place looks amazing.' I glanced around at the cool 50s-style decorations. 'I've never seen the inside at night. The mirror ball makes it look like a whole different place.'

Cadence looked around with a lot more resignation. 'Yeah, my dad went kind of crazy in here.' She shrugged. 'We've never done anything like this. Thank you for your help, Brenna. The T-shirt design was a really good idea.'

'No problem.' I smiled at her.

'And thanks for putting me on it. That was crazy!' She looked down at her shirt and laughed and everyone joined in, including me, though I felt like I was a poseur laughing along, but I was relieved that everything felt decently normal, and it didn't seem like there was any lasting craziness from my too-much-information essay.

Devon did, however, wind up getting me into a corner while Marcus picked up food from the counter. 'Is everything OK with you?' he asked, half-hiding his mouth behind a cup of soda like we were in some bad spy movie.

'Fine now. It was a little rough for a bit. And it looks like things are pretty damn swell for you. I'm seriously so happy for the two of you.'

'Yeah. I'm lucky, you know? He's amazing. And I figured, what the hell was I hiding him for? I gotta say, I was scared shitless, but it's been OK. It really has been.' He let out a long breath. 'I mean, even Saxon Maclean managed to not be an asshole.'

'Saxon has his moments,' I said, forcing myself not to look for him just because we said his name. 'So, what was the homefront like?'

He rolled his eyes and lowered the cup. 'Mom was pretty supportive once I went to see the shrink she sent me to.'

'She sent you to a shrink?' I knew my jaw was swinging open, but there was nothing I could do about it. I was in way too much shock.

'Yep. You know, because sometimes being gay is just a phase. Didn't you know that?' We both laughed and he shook his head, his laugh a little sadder than mine. 'It's not, like, her fairy-tale dream for me. No pun intended. But she's OK with it. She joined a group. You know, parents of gay kids, they talk and cross-stitch rainbows all over everything.'

'Nice,' I say, and can't help giggling. 'What about your dad?'

'Oh. Dad? He was cool. He was really cool, in fact. And then he told me he'd known since I was in sixth grade, but he didn't want to make me feel uncomfortable.' He shrugged.

'That's so sweet.' I put a hand out and touched his shoulder, just for a second, just to let him know I knew it was hard as hell to be honest about the things you knew other people might not understand.

'It is. I wish he'd been less afraid of making me uncomfortable, though. It would have made things . . . less uncomfortable.' We smiled, and Devon waved to Marcus, who winked.

'My God, he's so damn cute,' I said.

'Trust me. I know,' he sighed.

Then the band started for real and we went to

411

watch and jostle with everyone else. It felt good to be there, in a crush with a bunch of people I didn't know but felt close to because of the music and the fun of the night. Tony and his wife, Rosalie, were on the side looking happy and kind of relieved.

But something felt flat for me. I couldn't put my finger on it, and I couldn't shake it at all. I told Jake that I was going to the bathroom, but I really just needed some air. The parking lot was empty, cool, and quiet: a perfect place to escape for a minute.

'Blix.'

I turned around and there was Saxon, looking all cocky and so wonderfully, totally cool it was as irritating as a splinter under my fingernail.

'Hey.' I didn't try to smile at Saxon, because there was never any point in pretending anything around him.

He walked up to me and put an arm around my shoulders, and I sneaked a look back toward the door to make sure Jake wasn't standing there. Saxon's orange Tic Tac smell was familiar, but incomplete without the usual sting of smoke, and the feel of his arm was too heavy, too close, and too much of a complication.

'So, I read your essay.' His voice rubbed against my ear, half purr, half growl.

I turned under his arm and looked into his black eyes. 'I know it.'

412

'It was a little weird. I mean, I had to read it to Jake.' His voice was barbed with an edge of humor and something that furrowed so much deeper, no matter how I twisted it, I couldn't figure it out.

'Sorry. I mean, I'm sorry you didn't get a chance to just sit and read it and react, I guess.' I meant that. 'I could get you a copy if you need one.' Then I remembered and blushed when the full repercussion hit. 'Oh. I almost forgot your photographic memory. So now my essay is embedded in your brain forever.'

For a few seconds, all I could hear was the electric buzz of the lights, the screech of the bugs, and the subdued din of the music inside. Then Saxon's voice rasped out and broke the hush.

'You sound like you think that would be a bad thing.'

We locked eyes, and I saw those little gold flecks that rightfully belonged to Cadence now.

'You said it was weird.' A sticky, gapped feeling netted over my heart like a wide spiderweb.

'I meant it was weird circumstances.' He dropped his arm from my shoulder and ran both hands through his hair, kicked the cement, and shook his head. 'The essay itself . . . you wrote it a few weeks ago, right?'

'Yeah, at the workshop I went to this summer.' I trapped a huge lungful of breath, slowed my heart, didn't blink, and just waited for whatever he would say next.

He grabbed me by the shoulders so hard his fingers bit into my skin and pressed his forehead to mine, his eyes screwed shut, his mouth ironed into a flat line, then pulled away and looked at me with eyes so intensely focused it was like watching gold fireworks bursting against a midnight sky. I tried to inch back, but his hold was iron-gripped and absolute. 'What you wrote . . . I'm really happy that it's going to be stuck in my head for ever.'

His face moved so close to mine I was half sure he was going to kiss me, and panic made me rear my head back. My mind whirled around, grasping for an escape hatch before we let things spiral out of control, but he never closed the gap.

'You liked it?' My voice was trapped in the space between us, flickering and bumping like a lightning bug trapped in a jar.

When he opened his mouth, there wasn't a hint of sarcasm or snark or mind games, and the raw, clean honesty of what he said left me jelly-limbed and quaking-hearted.

'I think it was one of the bravest fucking things I've ever read in my life. And I know that I'll never mean what Jake means to you. But to know that there's a piece of you that cares about me means a lot. More than I can say. I haven't had many people give a shit. I know you're sacrificing a lot to take a chance on caring about me. And I've been a dickhead sometimes. But I want you to know, it's appreciated.'

He yanked me to him, wrapped his arms around me, and put his face into my hair, and I registered the sharp scent of him and felt his strong arms around me in a kind of distanced shock while he just held on.

I had been so worried about Jake hating it and Saxon thinking it was pathetic, I hadn't left any room in my head for the possibility that maybe what I did was good in some completely unexpected way. That maybe, in some really private, quiet place, it made a difference. And I realized that the private, quiet place was in my heart and Saxon's, and wherever the crossover place between them was, and that gave me a huge sense of peace. Finally.

I pulled back and kissed him on the side of his mouth, in that barely-OK friend place that's intimate but allowed, because I knew we both understood what it took to walk right out onto that shaky, unsettling limb and hop around, too curious about what it would be like to take a minute and fear the possible fall. 'Thanks. Seriously. I was sort of wishing that I never wrote it at all.'

He sucked a breath in through his teeth. 'That would have been a fucking tragedy.' Then he let me go. He watched his own hands let go of me and he took two deliberate steps back.

Anyone else would have felt like there needed to be something else, like something else needed to be said, but Saxon was such a completely lovable sociopath, he just turned on his heel, hands in his pockets, and went back into the crowded, hot room. I felt an easy, happy bubble of a feeling, like it was all going to be all right. Like I could let go of some of the angst and stupidity Saxon and I had fostered for a whole long, bitter year. Like I'd figured out a way to love him that had nothing to do with games or hurt or upsets.

That's when I noticed that I wasn't alone and hadn't been the whole time. Jake was by his truck, across from us. I felt a sinking feeling in my heart. If he had seen it all, he was probably pissed off.

He walked over, and I looked at what Cadence had admired and I had pretended to be dense about the day before; these two were a pretty high concentration of amazingness.

Even while my thoughts were running the gamut from guilt to aggravation, there was something really overwhelming about Jake, and it always clouded my judgment. He had on a light blue shirt, rolled up to his elbows and a pair of relaxed jeans. If he'd had a pair of boots and a Stetson, he'd have that modern cowboy thing going on big time.

I was so busy admiring his confident stride and very nice biceps that I didn't pay attention to his face.

Which was smiling, strangely.

'Was it about the essay?' He stuck both hands deep in his pockets. I nodded.

'I know I was pissed off about it,' he said, then kicked at the loose gravel, as if he could loosen whatever else he needed to say.

'You had every right to be pissed off.' I reached a hand out and he took it. I inched up to him and looked right into his gray eyes. 'I definitely would have been. Every once in a while, I do something weird and it doesn't work at all. Or, it works out, but in a totally different way than I expected. But I get why you're pissed off. I'm actually glad you've been so understanding.'

He shrugged and swung my hand back and forth. 'It's just plain old jealousy. What you wrote was so crazy and real. In a good way. But I wished you'd written just about me. Not that I'm saying I deserved to have some essay you wrote dedicated to me.'

I rushed the tiny space left between us and put my hands up to his face. 'Jake, you do deserve it. You so do. I just haven't figured you out enough to attempt to write anything like that.'

'I should be glad that you're willing just to be honest. You never feel like you have to lie. That's a really good thing.' He rubbed his face against my palms. 'Maybe I don't seem like I appreciate it all the time, but I do. I would hate it if we lied to each other.'

'You want honest? It's scary to love somebody like I love you.' The words came out whisper-quiet. 'And sometimes I feel like I mean so much to you, and you mean so much to me, it's just overwhelming. You know?'

'I know that.' When he smiled at me, his crooked eyetooth glinted in the parking-lot lights. He ran a hand over my hair. 'You don't have to be everything to me, Brenna. I know I've leaned on you hard, but I'm not going to fall apart.'

'I know that. I'm glad you and Saxon made up. I'm glad you reconnected with your Aunt Helene.' I paused and did up a button he'd missed on his shirt. 'I'm sorry it didn't work out with your father and all the rest of them.'

He shrugged. 'Fuck 'em. The Kelly Boat runs better with a tight crew anyway.' Then he pulled me so we were hip to hip and I felt that indefinable rush that always washed over me when my skin touched Jake's. It was huge and real and took my breath away.

I put a fist up. 'Kelly Boat for life.'

He bumped my fist. 'We really need to perfect a secret handshake.'

I raised my eyebrows and kissed the warm

knuckles of his fist, then lifted on my toes and kissed his lips with slow, sweet pressure.

'That's a pretty awesome addition to the hand-shake,' he said. 'But we can't have everyone in the crew doing that. I mean, I'm cool with Saxon, but I can't go that far.'

'Do you want to get out of here?' I asked around my bubbling giggles and his quick, sweet kisses.

'Yep.' He lifted me up and put me over his shoulder and ran across the parking lot to his truck. The bump of his shoulder on my gut actually hurt a little, but there was something freeing about the way I was bouncing around with only his body to hold me steady, and I loved it.

I could think of a fairly appropriate ending to the night, but it was a weird thing to plan. Or maybe it wasn't a weird thing to plan at all?

'Jake? I was thinking that we could . . . um, find someplace to park.'

He was looking over his shoulder as he backed out, but he hit the brakes and switched his gaze to focus right at me. He licked his lips nervously and set his attention straight ahead, out the bug-flecked windshield.

'Tonight?' He jiggled the shift stick nervously.

'Yes.' I took a deep breath. 'If you want! No if you don't. Not a big deal.' I put my fingers over my eyes and talked though the crack in my palms. 'Am I making this weird? Am I ruining the moment? You can tell me. I am, aren't I?'

His Adam's apple hopped up and down. 'No. It's good. We should talk about it. I want to. But in my truck?'

I waved my hands around. 'I happen to find this truck very romantic. We've had many very romantic moments in here.' I waggled my eyebrows and shook my shoulders.

Jake laughed, but it was a nervous, quick sound that ended with a lecture before it ever really got going. 'Bren, it's a big deal. It's important to me that it's nice for you.'

Then I remembered Mom's convention. 'Hey! I have the house to myself next weekend.'

'Oh?' He tapped his fingers on the steering wheel. 'All right,' he said finally. 'Next weekend then.'

'Only if you want to!' The weirdness factor wrestled with the anticipation factor . . . which really just added to the overall weirdness.

'I do!' He jumped the words with too quick a start, and we both went completely quiet, not sure what topic of conversation could follow up planning a date to have sex.

It felt totally, completely weird to actually set aside a date for something that was usually so spontaneous.

Like too spontaneous.

I mean, there was usually a hot-and-bothered, rolling-on-the-sheets, forgot-the-condom scenario when you were young and lusty. Right? Did people plan this stuff?

I felt a little ripple of anticipation course through me when I imagined the night. I knew, without a single doubt, that I wanted to do this and I wanted it to be with Jake. We would be safe and it would be good. I knew it would be.

Jake didn't say anything, just sat kind of stiff and concentrated on the road.

'Jake?' I ventured.

'Yeah?' he asked, his voice way too loud and eager.

'We don't have to. Seriously. We don't. If this freaks you out, if you want to wait, I really get it, and I don't want this to be some weird thing, OK?' I reached over and squeezed the back of his neck right in that place that made him roll his shoulders and smile. He didn't even roll his shoulders and smile. Jake was obviously freaking out about it.

'I know that.' He grabbed the steering wheel like we were sinking on the Titanic and the steering wheel was his lifesaver. 'I really want to. I'm just nervous.'

'You've had lots of practice,' I joked. Whoa, wrong joke. Jake's mouth shriveled to a tight, white line, and he shook his head a little.

'No I haven't.' He gritted the words out.

'Sorry. That was a bad joke.' Although what I had said was mostly true, I never said it with the intention of hurting his feelings.

'You really don't get it, Brenna.' The words weren't snappy or angry. He was just telling me, giving me the facts. 'I've done it so many times and it meant *nothing*. It's hard to have all of your experiences of something be kind of crap. I mean, it makes me nervous.'

'Oh,' I said dumbly. We'd had versions of this conversation before, but we had never been about to actually have sex when we'd talked about it. 'All right. I get that. But you shouldn't be nervous. It will be different because it will be you and me. That's all that matters, right?'

'I think so. I mean, that makes sense. I just want it to be really special for you.' He added, 'And me.'

I realized that the whole experience was probably coming with a lot of pressure for Jake; more than I had really understood.

I went back to my previous mantra of comforting insistence. 'We don't have to. If you're not ready, I'm not ready. No big deal.'

There was a long pause that seemed to be full of things he wanted to say, but wasn't saying. I could feel the nervous tension, like a motor running too fast, just on the verge of blowing. All I had to do was be patient and wait. Before I knew it, he was talking, saying all the things I knew he really didn't want to say. 'This winter,' he said, his words stilted, 'when I did it with Nikki, I was so mad at you—'

'I know.' I cut in to let him know that I did know, but mostly I really didn't want to think about that time or what he had done with her or why, just like he didn't want to think about my brief time dating Saxon. But this was all tangled up in our decision to have sex, so I owed it to him to think about it and talk about it. Much as it sucked.

'When it happened this winter,' he continued, his words marching on with grim determination, 'she and I didn't connect or anything. I mean, she wanted to more than I did, and I just did it, I don't know, like to get back at you I guess. It made no sense. And it felt like shit. Again. So, it still makes me kind of freaked out, Bren.'

A huge sigh flipped out before I could stop it. There was no big, perfect pink eraser to run over all our screw-ups. Even if there was, I knew from years of sketching that even the best erasers leave faint traces of the marks you'd made underneath. Our histories just weren't made to be ignored or run away from. 'I know,' I said. Although, again, I didn't *really* know.

'You have a lot of expectations.' His voice was prayer-in-confessional quiet.

'No I don't.' I shook my head. 'Just you and me. That's all, Jake. I know it might be . . . not perfect. I don't expect or want perfect. I just want you.'

'I know you,' he insisted, giving me a secret side-long smile. 'You've run through this in your head, and I know what you're imagining. I'm kind of nervous about living up to it all.'

'Logically, there is only evidence supporting you being good.' His smile quirked wider, and I leaned close, my voice husky. 'Really, really good.' He laughed a little and blushed. 'Extremely good,' I said, just to rub it in a little.

'Thanks, Bren,' he said and finally, finally his shoulders relaxed a little. 'I take it seriously.'

I rolled my eyes a little. He had this way of talking about the fact that I was a virgin that reminded me of an old lady handling her best china. 'Jake, it's going to happen at some point! This isn't medieval times. I want it to be with you.'

'All right.' He took off his cap and ran a hand through his hair before he put it back on. 'Do you mind if I flip topics? I'm not trying to get out of talking about it with you.'

'Yeah, sure,' I laughed. 'OK, what's up?'

'I talked to my . . . dad. To Ron Kelly.' It was so weird that he was using his stepdad's full name to identify him, but how else was I supposed to know what 'dad' meant after this crazy summer? 'I'm signed up for Share Time.'

'Jake!' Immediately I started playing out the year in my head, loving the idea of me and Jake, classes together every day. I had been pushing him toward it for months, and now it was really going to happen. 'Jake, that's great news! I'm so happy for you!'

'And has Saxon talked to you about what he's doing?' Jake's voice trod around that topic like he was walking over a frozen lake, half sure the ice was about to crack under him.

'Um, no.' I was suddenly sure that I didn't really want to know.

If Saxon didn't mention it to me, there was probably a reason. Like he didn't want to tell me something I didn't want to hear. I realized now why he looked so serious and worried in the parking lot.

There was something he was too chicken to tell me.

'Oh. I thought he might have told you. Before.' Jake looked a little uncomfortable, like he wasn't sure if it was his news to tell. Extra bad.

'What's up, Jake?' As bad as the news could be, it couldn't possibly be worse than this suspense. 'You two are going to be OK at Frankford together, right? There's not going to be any big kick-down fight or anything stupid like that.'

'Nope. And that's a guarantee.' Jake stomped

through the ice of his secret. 'Bren, Saxon isn't doing his senior year at Frankford.'

I felt like I'd plunged into frigid water.

Saxon wouldn't be in school with us this year? I had never considered school minus Saxon. Shock kept me silent for a long minute.

'Why?' I wondered. 'Is he dropping out?'

'No. He's enrolling here. At Aunt Helene's. He's not coming back.' He was trying to remain calm, but his voice dripped with sweet triumph.

'In Lodi?' I repeated a little dumbly.

'Yeah. I don't know if he's enrolling in public. The school system there is shitty. He might go to one of the private schools. Anyway, he's not coming home.'

The initial shock wore away like alcohol on an open wound. The sting was there, then gone, and all that was left was an ache you'd hardly notice.

Considering the fact that Jake was doing Share Time this year, this was a good thing, no question. The two of them were better kept far apart, no matter what kind of peace they'd managed to make. Jake and Saxon were matches and firecrackers together . . . and there was never any telling if the explosion would be celebratory or majorly destructive.

But school without Saxon? That would be like sushi without wasabi. Definitely delicious, but lacking that certain kick.

Jake was and always would be my dependable go-to rock.

Saxon served an entirely different purpose. He added a little competition, a little challenge. Saxon pushed the envelope. I would seriously miss that.

Then I thought about things from Saxon's perspective. And it all made so much sense.

He wouldn't have to deal with Lylee. He wouldn't have to go back to a school population that saw him as some indolent bad boy and hero-worshipped his crappy attitude and refusal to play by the rules.

Saxon would be with Aunt Helene, who loved him, and Cadence, who he cared about. He could recreate himself however he wanted. He could keep a job, take school seriously, be in love, stay away from drugs.

This was only good for him. A Saxon Reformation. A Saxon Renaissance.

'I think it will be good for him,' I said out loud to Jake. I really meant it, and I knew Jake could hear that.

'I thought you might be upset about it.' Jake weaseled a nervous look from the corner of his eye.

'I liked having classes with him and seeing him in school,' I understated. 'But it's better for him to do his thing here.' Definitely better. Even if it left me with a feeling of empty longing.

'All right.' His shoulders lost their tightness and his hands loosened their grip.

'And I'll see you all day now.' I slid my hand across the seat and grabbed his. 'How freaking amazing is this? I used to have to wait all morning to see you, and now, we'll go in together every single day. This is so cool.'

'Um, I took some tests, too. To see if I might be able to place in some honors classes. They gave me this thing called an IEP,' he admitted, his voice all low and tongue-tied around the words.

'When did you do all of this?' The secrets he hid like nesting dolls kept surprising me, one by one.

'This past spring. You were running track a lot, so I had some time.' There was a braggy note of pride in his voice.

I pinched his cheek. 'My little covert operative, all hiding information behind my back! Isn't an IEP for, um, learning disorders?' I asked, hoping that he wouldn't get offended.

'Yeah.' His voice was easy and confident. 'So my dyslexia is workable. They did this oral testing with me. They have this program where I set up a whole computer thing and I can speak into it. It was pretty incredible. I mean, I'd have to do it separate from everyone else, but I actually kind of wrote an essay.'

'Wha ...? Why didn't you tell me about this? Seriously? We were together all summer. How did this never come up?' I was so shocked, I could barely process. This was a big deal! This was important! Why didn't he tell me?

'I didn't want you to get your hopes up. But I got a letter this morning. It said I placed into some honors classes.' Pride glowed on his face.

'What!' I screamed, bouncing up and down. 'Why didn't you tell me?' I repeated.

'Because I didn't want you to get all excited then it wound up I was just a dummy like I'd always thought.'

I ignored his self-dig and resisted the urge to jump across the seat and kiss him like crazy.

'Are you kidding me?' I couldn't get my excitement under control. 'I'm so mad you never told me!'

'Well, I'm not sure if I'm going to do it. I mean, it might be a lot.'

It was like the brakes screeched on the whole exciting run. 'You're not serious.'

'It's a lot,' he repeated, his voice edged with warning.

'No.' I shook my head at him. 'Do *not* do that to yourself. You are so smart. You can ace these classes, Jake!'

'I need to get a computer with the programming that they have. For myself. Like that I didn't have to borrow.'

'So? You have money saved, don't you?'

429

'Yeah,' he said vaguely.

I couldn't put my finger on what he was getting at, but I knew I was missing something, and he wasn't saying something.

'So buy it.' I threw my hands up in frustration. 'What's up? Why are you even considering not doing this?'

'Because what if I'm smart?' His voice dropped.

'You are smart,' I argued, kind of automatically.

'Not just to you, Bren,' he countered. 'What if I'm actually smart? It kind of screws up my long-term life plan.'

'Which is?' I pressed.

'To be who I am and do what I do. To work. Hard. And get money. And provide.' He took a long breath. 'For you. With you. Wherever you need to be.'

'Jake,' I said, and stopped. That was it, I guess. If he deviated from this structured plan of his, he got freaked out. 'That's really sweet, but I'm planning on providing for myself, and I want you to do your thing, too. I thought you wanted to go to college.'

His jaw set and he stared straight ahead. 'I want to go if you go. I want you,' he insisted stubbornly. 'That's it. I just want to be happy with you.'

'Jake, I'm not marrying you right out of high school or anything.' I felt a little shaky in the face of his totally stubborn plans. 'I'm going to college wherever I get in

430

and want to go. I might even go in another country. And I'm going to do internships. And have jobs. And have my own place.'

'So you don't want to be with me?'

I felt like he was purposefully missing the point of what I was saying.

'I didn't say that.' Frustration made my cheeks flush hot. 'I don't want being with you to be my only plan. That's all. And being with me can't be your only plan either. That would be a disaster. There's so much we should both plan on doing, and it might be separately.'

He shook his head.

'What?' I asked.

'You just don't get it,' he muttered.

'What don't I get?' I felt like shaking him or choking him or smacking him upside the head. 'You could be in honors classes and go to college and do things for yourself. And we can be with each other, even if we're not always physically together. So what am I not getting? What's so complicated?'

'You have your home right now.' His voice creaked out, rough with emotions he didn't want me to hear. 'You have your mother and Thorsten, and maybe even a dad somewhere who cares about you. You have that.'

'You have Ron,' I argued. 'Who's stood by you this whole time.'

'He . . . stands by me,' Jake agreed. 'But he's not home. I don't have one. Or the promise of one, except with you.' He took a deep breath. 'If I work hard for us, you can do your thing, and I'll be waiting for you. That's a decent plan.'

He was so serious about it, but I was not going to let him think that I was happy with his plan.

'I don't want that.' I felt my teeth click together, I clenched them so hard. 'I want us to be together, but also doing our own things. If you don't do these classes, and if you don't go to college or at least do something for yourself, I *will* break up with you.' It was extreme, but it was the honest truth.

'What?' Jake blinked hard and his nostrils flared slightly. 'You can't break up with me over classes.'

'Oh yes I can.' I crossed my arms over my chest, trying to hold back every spluttering emotion broiling in me. 'I can and I will. If breaking up with you makes you go after what you need, I'll do it in a second. That's how much I love you.'

Jake's jaw got tight. 'That's stupid.'

'Your plan is stupid,' I countered, my voice ferocious with equal parts hope and terror.

'I knew you wouldn't get it. I don't know why I even brought it up in the first place.' His fists death-gripped the steering wheel and his entire face was hard-lined and tense.

I took a deep breath, ready to smooth some peace over all this, but not prepared to back down either. 'I'll be here for you. I will. But I think you're using your feelings for me as a cop-out. There have to be things you do just for yourself, Jake.' I couldn't believe he was considering anything else.

'Why?' he snapped.

'Because . . . it's obvious why!' I took a deep breath and counted to ten. Then eleven. I made it to twenty-seven before I felt remotely able to talk. 'Look, I know we're in the Kelly Boat together, but I'm staging a mutiny if you start drinking the salt water. That's all I'm saying about this. All right?'

'Aye aye, Cap'n.' His smile was a blurry, faded photocopy of its usual self.

'Just promise me you'll think about all this. I'm telling you, you're going to realize I'm right.'

He took a deep breath and nodded. 'I love you for being so worried about me. I'll think about all this.'

We rode the rest of the way to my house in silence, and even though once Jake pulled into my driveway, we kissed and touched like two out-of-control animals, it all felt a little off.

I watched him pull away, went in and kissed my parents goodnight, and tried calling Evan, but there was no answer. Her Facebook status had been updated two hours before and read, 'Out making mischief . . .'

All of my problems with Jake and Saxon, sex and school paled for a minute and fear gnawed on my nerves.

'Mischief?' I rolled the word around on my tongue as I wriggled into my pajamas. Technically all it meant was mildly troublesome behavior without malice. Well, that was one definition anyway. How far would my friend take it?

One of the scariest things about Evan was she was like that girl in the nursery rhyme with the curl. When Evan made up her mind to play it like a good girl, there was no one better. But when she decided to let the bad girl out . . . I decided I'd better sleep with my phone by my ear, and made up my mind that I would use the number her gramma had sent to my mother in case of emergencies if I hadn't heard from her by early the next morning.

Saxon 5

The Folly concert was a total success. Tony and Rosalie were pumped about the whole thing, and when all was good in the Erikson house, all was good with Cadence.

Which was beyond good for me. She was beyond good for me.

She'd been nervous about the whole concert thing. Especially once she saw Bren's design, which freaked her out a little. I thought it was damn cool, and kind of talked Cadence out of freaking about it.

'It's me!' She held the concept shirt Bren had left at Tony's out in front of her. Her hands were a little shaky.

I grabbed one hand, bright pink paint on the nails compliments of me. 'It's cool.' I squeezed her hand tight. 'Bren's an art genius. If she thinks it's good, it's good.'

Her mouth did this sexy twitchy move that let me know loud and clear she didn't love that I'd said that.

She'd been jumpy about Brenna since the whole essay thing came up.

'Do you still like her, Saxon?'

We were in her room, door open, Sullie running by at a hundred miles an hour, the smells of Rosalie's tortillas wafting up the stairs and making my stomach rumble. It was loud and chaotic and not remotely private, but I loved it.

She was sitting cross-legged on her bed and I was sprawled on the floor. I definitely mostly played the hands-off good boy at her place. No use dredging up trouble with her fucking scary parents.

'Not the way you're asking. Do you still like Jeff?' I poked her leg with my foot.

'No.' She grabbed my foot. I knew what was coming, because my girlfriend is a sex goddess. She pulled my sock off and grabbed a bottle of lotion from her dresser, then gooped it on her hands and rubbed it into my feet. 'But that's different. I never really liked Jeff.'

'Oh my God,' I moaned. Her fingers were sure and relaxing and fucking magic. 'What do you want, woman? Anything! You can have anything!'

'Just you.' Like a damn angel, she smiled over my disgusting lotioned feet.

'Liar,' I accused. 'No one gives something that fantastic and gets something that shitty in return unless she's a moron. And I know for a fact that you're no moron.'

She laughed, her big-smiled belly-laugh that I loved so much it made me a little nervous. She had these great, full lips . . . great at smiling, great at kissing, great at telling me to shove it up my ass, and great at telling me how much she loved me. Perfect lips.

'I want to know about Brenna.' She looked right at my lotion-gooped feet, avoiding any eye contact at all.

The thing with Brenna was, if I could have taken her essay and turned it around on her I would have. Reading that to Jake was pretty much the hardest thing I've ever done in my life. Because I knew exactly what she was saying. And he didn't.

Just like Cadence wouldn't.

Because Brenna and I had something that was deep and real, but it wasn't exactly love. Not the way I felt about Cadence or that Bren felt about Jake. I knew why Brenna was freaked about Jake reading it. I would have burned it and any record of it if I'd had the balls to write something like that and Cadence wanted to see it. No way in hell would I try to explain it all.

But Bren was always more fearless than I was. I needed her in my life.

Not as a girlfriend: I'd thought that would work, but it didn't. And I'm glad that we tried, because if we hadn't given it a shot, I would have sworn to God that dating was the thing for us. But I knew now that Bren and I had to be where we were, and who we were to each other, and just let it go.

It was pretty much impossible to explain. Especially to someone I loved and wanted to make happy.

'Brenna is special to me, Cadence,' I said, and, even though her hands never stopped moving, I could see that her face tensed up. 'C'mon, babe, it's not like that.'

'Like what?' Her words trickled out, deceptively serene.

'Like I want her to be my girlfriend.' Her thumb glided over my arch and I bit my lip hard to keep from moaning.

She shrugged. 'I thought she didn't want you.'

And therein lay my girl's powers of genius. Here she was rubbing my feet like some kind of perfect saint, rendering me defenseless as she barbed me with her dead-on quips.

This was love.

'She didn't want me, but she gave me a fair chance. And much as thought I wanted her to want me, in the end I really didn't. It wouldn't have worked between us. We didn't have the right chemistry.'

'What does that even mean?' Worry lines popped out on her forehead.

I pulled my foot out of her hand and knelt by her bed. I grabbed one of her feet and kissed her toes, made her giggle, and then leaned up and kissed her mouth. 'It means I was waiting for you.'

She rolled her eyes. 'Sussex County Casanova strikes again.'

'Not Sussex County any more, babe.' I kissed her neck. She smelled like some kind of cookies. Vanilla wafers, I thought.

'Why not? Are you extending yourself past Sussex County? Are you going to be the New Jersey Casanova? Or the East Coast Casanova?' She giggled as I kissed her collar bones and down to her breast-bone, all the time keeping one eye on her open bedroom door and the currently empty hallway.

'No.' I ran a hand up under her shirt, all the way up to the bra that I could feel was little more than a tiny bit of lace. God, I loved her underwear. 'I have no plans to expand. In fact, I'm contracting.'

'What?' she asked, her voice a little giggly and off. She bit her lip a little when I got my hand under the lace.

She felt amazing.

'I'm relocating, and downsizing,' I explained. Then I saw Sullie run down the hall pulling a wagon full of toys that would serve equally well as run-of-the-mill playthings and items of torture – for my head and sack. I pulled my hand and mouth away from my very hot girlfriend, sat back to wait for Sullie to administer some pain, and finished explaining. 'I'm an official Essex County resident.'

Sullie came in and pulled out a heavy toy keyboard, dropped it on my bare foot, and clapped along to 'Bingo' while I screamed in agony.

'What do you mean?' Cadence asked, her focus snapped back as mine blurred out in a red cloud of pain.

'Ow, damn, Sullie, that hurts!' Sullie laughed and held his hands up. I swept him off the floor and jostled him on my shoulder. 'I mean that I can't leave Aunt Helene in her rotting hole of a house. What the hell will she do about the ice and snow? What about the heat? That fucking boiler is a hundred years old. I'm surprised you don't have to shovel coal into it.'

'Don't swear in front of the baby,' Cadence said absently, which was a fairly hilarious warning considering their mother's language could melt the ears off a fucking truck driver. 'So you're going to fix Aunt Helene's up more?'

But, like I said before, my girl's no moron. Her eyes were shiny with the promise of what she wanted me to say.

I pulled Sullie's shirt up and blew a loud raspberry on his belly. He screamed with happy laughter. 'Yeah,

I'm fixing it up more.' I paused to give one more tremendous raspberry, then let the news drop. 'And I'm enrolling.'

'Here? At George Washington High?' She leaned towards me.

'Here. At Immaculate Conception,' I corrected. I was down on all fours, Sullie on my back and kicking his little heels into my sides hard. I plodded around the room and fully realized how ridiculous I must look.

'You're going to my school?' Cadence's mouth twitched into a smile.

'Yep,' I said, then picked up the pace in response to Sullie's incessant kicks. When I stopped, I was right in front of her. 'You cool with that?'

She pulled Sullie off my back and swung him onto her hip, mercifully allowing me to stand upright. 'I'm so happy.' She threw her free arm around me tight. 'I'm so glad, Saxon. I . . .' I felt her give a little sob. Sullie patted her head.

'What's up, babe?' I asked, dipping my head to see her face.

There were runny mascara-tinged tears all over her cheeks. 'You . . . I was so nervous . . . I thought this might be . . . a summer thing . . .' She laughed and sobbed a little, and I pulled her close, her face making my shirt wet and gray with smudgy tears.

'Shh. What are you, insane? I'm not going anywhere. Not unless you agree to come with me.' That made her cry a little harder. I laughed, and my whole chest felt loose and free when I did it. 'Stop. Don't cry. You look like a zombie.'

'Oh, shit.' She wiped under her eyes with shaky fingers.

'Don't swear in front of the baby.' I rubbed a thumb over a sooty tear on her chin.

'Shut up!' She looked up at me, so gorgeous it squeezed the breath right out of my lungs.

'Do I still look like a zombie?'

'Yeah.' I leaned toward her ear. 'I'm feeling a strange surge of necrophilia.'

'I bet you say that to all the pretty zombies.' She bounced on her toes and kissed Sullie's head. Just then Rosalie called us down to dinner.

I'd been getting fairly regular invites to Cadence's house for dinner. At least when they had it, which wasn't often with everyone working so much. I always invited Aunt Helene, but she had a pretty rocking social life for an older lady, and it was fairly rare that she didn't have something else on her busy-ass bingo-and-reading-club-filled agenda.

I liked the big, noisy dinners with the Eriksons. Pammy and Jimmy accepted me like I was a real sibling; which meant that they switched between loving me and giving me merciless hell.

Tony had already come over and spent some time in the driveway with me, showing me how to do basic shit like rotate tires and change oil, which I really appreciated. Google can take you so far, but after that you're just shit out of luck if you screw up your car.

And Rosalie was as mean and unforgiving to me as she was to her own brood, which I knew was her form of love, and I ate it up.

So I was pretty glad that I was so crazy about Cadence, because she could have been a hag and I might have kept hanging around anyway just to leech off her family.

But, much as they all liked me, I still felt weird telling them the news about my move. I had talked to Lylee about it; she was pretty fucking thrilled with the idea of having her house to herself and the ability to do whatever the hell she wanted whenever the hell she wanted. She took my word for it when I told her I wasn't hooked on drugs any more.

And Aunt Helene had cried and hugged me and tried to stuff more food down my throat. Damn, I loved that woman.

But those two were predictable variables in my world. The Eriksons were a whole different story. I wasn't sure if they would be happy to see me. Every day. All year.

We sat down at dinner, and while Cadence snapped Sullie into his high chair, she announced, 'Saxon's enrolling at Immaculate.'

There was that terrible choked moment when I thought all shit would hit the fan, and Tony would tell me summer was enough and Rosalie would say that I was invading her family, and I would walk back to Aunt Helene's cold, empty house like a stooge.

'Catholic school, huh?' Tony scooped a huge blob of sour cream onto his plate to combat Rosalie's fiercely spiced tortillas. 'You Catholic, Saxon?'

'No, sir.'

Rosalie handed me a glass of iced tea. 'It's a pretty strict school,' she warned me, pursing her lips. 'They aren't going to put up with any crap.'

'I don't plan on giving any, Mrs Erikson.'

She frowned. 'I don't know if you can help your-self.' She flicked a look at Cadence. Or maybe I imagined she flicked a look at Cadence. 'You're a wild one, Saxon.'

'I think I'm done with all of that.'

Cadence's parents looked at each other and laughed loud and long.

'You'll probably be fine,' Tony said, choking so hard Rosalie had to smack him on the back a few times.

And that was it. It registered with them, and they let it go. I mean, it cracked them up, but they didn't have a shit-fit or kick me out or anything. And as I ate Rosalie's cheesy delicious tortillas and thought about why I was so worried about it all, I couldn't come up with anything that really made sense. I guess it was just my fucked up perception of myself and all the people who had the bad luck of having to deal with me. It made me worry that everyone in my life was just biding time until they could get rid of me.

I left after dinner, but not before Cadence whispered that she would sneak by later. Aunt Helene slept like the dead, and Cadence and I had planned to get together for a while. I felt a little nervous about the whole thing. I had never really orchestrated any kind of actual dating life.

Brenna had been the closest and it wasn't like I was eating dinner with her family and spending hours flipping through her old yearbooks and photo albums. Which I did with Cadence, and it was, astoundingly, a pretty cool thing. I felt like I got to see her grow up a little. She was a damn cute kid, even when most people are going through their ugly, gawky stages.

I'd never been asked into those intimate places with other girls. Or maybe I had never cared to be asked. It didn't matter. The bottom line was that Cadence and I were in uncharted territory.

So I cleaned up my room for her and took a shower and made sure the mood was acceptable to get her out of most or all of her clothes. Which meant candles and a good, emotionally nuanced indie mix playing.

I was waiting in the kitchen when she scratched at the door. I opened up and she smiled at me. A smile like I was the only person in the world she wanted to see. A lot of girls had probably smiled at me like that before, but I had never bothered to give a damn.

With Cadence it was all I was waiting for. I pulled her into the house and let her come at me. She wrapped her legs around my waist, and I navigated to my room, Cadence kissing my face and neck and ripping at my shoulders and bucking against me.

It was fucking hard to keep quiet.

We fell on my bed and she pulled my shirt over my head. I gave her the same treatment. She snuggled down on top of me, all soft, warm girl boobs and hot everywhere kissing. All it took was a flick of my fingers and her bra was gone, one push to get her jeans off, and then . . . nothing. She wasn't wearing anything else.

'Saxon!' she said against my ear, her hands fumbling at my jeans. She yanked them down, and my boxers with them and I kicked them the last of the way off.

I rolled her under me and kissed her harder, my hands on her and my lungs pulling deep breaths of her into my body. She smelled and tasted fantastic. Her arms and hair were tangled around me, trapping me. I was happy to be trapped for once.

I ran my hand up and down the long length of her back. She kissed me softly.

'You look like Juliet.' I rubbed my forehead against her shoulder.

'Like *Romeo and Juliet*?' Her fingers combed through my hair, pushing it back off my face.

My lips traced all along her arms. 'Yeah.'

'How do you know what Juliet looked like?' she asked, kissing my bottom lip.

'From what Romeo said,' I told her. 'Dark haired. So pretty it would stop your heart.'

So I was paraphrasing. I was probably high as a damn kite when we read Shakespeare in school. Every time we read Shakespeare in school. But I did know that Juliet was dark-haired. And stunning. Like stars or jewels or flowers. Or Cadence.

'Do I stop your heart?'

I could hardly see the green in her eyes, her pupils were so huge and black. Her left ear was pierced twice, and there was a beauty mark next to it. The right was pierced three times, but one was closed up. She had told me all about it. And the funny thing was, I had been completely fucking fascinated by her ear-piercing stories.

'No.' I pulled her hand down to my chest, over my heart – my racing, flipping, pounding heart. And my work-hardened pecs. No point in having a developed set of muscles if you didn't get to make a girl sigh over them once in a while. 'You give my heart something to beat for.'

'You're just trying to get into my pants.' She nuzzled my neck.

'You don't have any pants on,' I pointed out.

She wiggled under me. Pantless.

We had talked about a lot of things together: friends and enemies, parents, school, music, movies, food. Almost everything. But we had rattled around sex.

Thanks to her noisy clan of a family, we didn't get a chance to physically get this far often. And when we got here, there was never any time to get anything good started. But tonight, as far as I knew, we had all night.

'Juliet was a virgin,' Cadence said suddenly.

I put my hands on her shoulders and slid them up and down along her body, as far as my arms could reach. I liked the line of her from shoulder to thigh and back again. I was memorizing curves spread along warm, smooth skin.

'Yeah.' I was careful and would keep being that

way. With whatever she wanted to tell me.

'I'm not, Saxon,' she said, reaching a hand up to smooth over my eyebrow.

'Me neither.' I rubbed her gently.

'But no one expects you to be.' She tensed and jerked away a little bit. 'Are you disappointed?'

'That you're in my bed, naked? Yeah, Cadence. I'm heartbroken,' I joked.

'That's not what I mean.' Her eyes were wide and a little worried. Her dark hair was all around her face, some pieces stuck to her cheeks.

'I'm not disappointed. If I was, then I wouldn't deserve to be with you anyway.' I moved a piece of her hair that had fallen in front of her mouth.

'I don't want to talk about the other times.' She set her mouth in a hard, determined line.

'That's OK,' I told her. I meant it. Shit, if we started sharing back and forth, I'd need the whole night just to finish.

'They weren't terrible or anything. They just . . . I kind of wish I could get a do-over with them. You know?' She closed her eyes and kissed my lips softly.

'I kind of wish I could get a do-over, too,' I confessed. 'I regret not being with you first, Cadence.'

'It doesn't matter.' She shook her head back and forth.

'For me neither.' There wasn't a way to touch her

enough. My hands were everywhere and completely unsatisfied. 'We were with who we were with. And who I was with led me to you. Somehow. I'm just glad that's where I wound up.'

'They only liked me because they thought I was pretty.' She pressed her nose to my shoulder. 'I think, for a while, *I* only liked me because I thought I was pretty.'

'Didn't you like you because you were smart?' I asked, kissing the top of her head.

'Not really,' she said, then pulled back and raised her eyebrows at me. 'You think I am?'

'Do you think you are?' I volleyed.

'Yeah.' She smiled, and if sex could be an expression, it would be the one on her face. 'I am.'

'What about the fact that you work hard?' I pointed out.

'Ugh,' she sighed. 'You make me sound like some kind of work horse.'

'You inspire me.' I squeezed her bicep. 'I've never had a girlfriend who could benchpress me.'

Cadence laughed, and I had to put my hand over her mouth to keep her from waking Aunt Helene. She had a fantastic laugh, but no volume control.

She licked my palm.

'There are better uses for that tongue,' I said.

She licked my face.

'Not exactly what I was thinking.'

She licked my nipple.

'That's more like it.'

She licked all the way down until she was where I had jokingly directed her, but I pulled her back up.

'You don't want it?' she asked, and seemed really surprised. Although, I guess that was fair.

'I do.' So badly I was shaking hard. 'I want it. Just not first.'

She gave me a look that I just couldn't read.

'I'll do for you,' I suggested. She bit her lip a little and kissed me slowly.

'Why not you first?' she asked. 'Or at the same time.' The logistics were getting sticky fast. 'Do you have a condom?' Her voice was all business.

'I do,' I said, and I went completely hard at the mention of it.

'Let's have sex.' She said it matter-of-factly.

And then we didn't say too much. I reached into the drawer by my bed and pulled out a condom. Cadence slid it out and put it on me with expertise I wasn't about to dwell on. Then she moved over me and slid down, fitted me in and pressed until I was completely inside of her. And it felt fucking amazing.

I had done this a hundred times before. Probably more. But this time there was something else happening.

I had this person who I gave a shit about, and

451

pleasing her meant something. Correction; pleasing her meant everything.

She moved her hips and rocked up and down on top of me. It felt so good, I was sure I was going to blow it, literally, any second.

I had to put my mind somewhere else and focus on Cadence. She was so beautiful, it obscured anything else I tried to think about, and there was something obviously erotic about the fact that she was naked and willing on top of me, along with the fact that she'd chosen me.

But, she clearly had expectations for this whole thing that were fairly low. She didn't seem to be seeing me, and she was moving pretty mechanically.

I'd had sex with a lot of girls I hadn't given a shit about, but I like to think that most of it was mutually good. Getting girls off isn't something every guy is good at, but I pride myself in at least trying. I'm not really a wham-bam-thank-you-ma'am guy, contrary to what my reputation might be. I've always slept around, but while I was in bed, I was willing to fall in love a little for the duration of the sex. I think that's what gave me such a ladykiller reputation. I was good at faking it, and good at making them believe the fantasy. Which was another huge reason why this was blowing my mind.

I couldn't fake a damn thing with Cadence, and

once it was real, there was huge potential for everything to go wrong fast. So there I was, watching her gyrate kind of half-heartedly, and for once I wasn't positive what to do.

It was a fucking shame that Cadence was so sexy and funny and gorgeous, and all she expected was a boring grind. She had mentioned that her other experiences were just OK, and it almost made me want to choke the losers who hadn't given her what she needed. But I changed my mind about that quick. If they hadn't sucked so badly, I might not be here, able and willing to show her what it could be like. I wanted, more than I'd ever wanted anything else, to rock her world.

I could see it wasn't happening now. She had pulled away since our kissing and now she was on autopilot. I just stopped thinking, let my gut kick in and guide me, and tried to pay attention to what she might need to open up.

I put my hands on her hips to slow her down, and her face snapped up, shocked.

'Do you mind? If we switch it up a little?' I asked.

Her face clouded. 'Don't you like it?' she asked tensely.

'Hell, yeah. But do *you* like it?' I trailed a hand down her body, starting at her neck and stopping at the hot skin right above where her heart was hammering.

She looked down for a minute. 'It's good. I mean, it feels good.'

'You're perfect and what you're doing is amazing,' I said, leaning up to kiss her. 'But I want it to be better than good for you. All right?'

'All right.' She squeezed her eyes shut for a second.

'Trust me,' I said.

'I do.' She closed her eyes and kissed me again.

I sat up, so I could hold her closer. We were suddenly pressed against each other from chest to hips. She wrapped her legs around me and I moved my hands down along her back, inching her closer, pushing in deeper until we were pressed as hard against each other as we could get. She made little noises that made my brain spin, so I knew I was on the right track.

She was right up against me, and I made good use of that fact. I kissed and sucked and licked every piece of sensitized skin I could reach. I ran my hands up and down her body, stopping at all the places that got a reaction from her.

Cadence was definitely responding. She moaned, her eyes fluttered shut, she ground against me harder and changed positions a few times. I realized she was desperately trying to get herself to wherever that place that did it for her was, and I let her do her thing. Once she got close to the spot, it was pretty obvious.

Suddenly her breathing was hard, sharp and fast, almost at that totally satisfied place. I kept up my end of the deal, agonizing as it was.

How could I have her that close to me, that ready, that excited and simultaneously keep from blowing my load? I tried to stay focused on not being a selfish dick; she had obviously been a little screwed over in the sex department, and I was not about to be a notch in her lukewarm experience belt.

Problem was, it had been a while since I'd had sex, and the last time was not with my perfect, gorgeous girlfriend who had inadvertently been giving me blue balls all summer. I wanted to go crazy, pump into her, and lose control a little.

She was still trying to find a spot that did what she needed done again, and I was hanging on for dear life when I dipped my hand between our bodies, because I wanted to help her. I also wanted to not lose my shit. She resisted at first, but I eased up and found a rhythm that worked for her, and she finally let go. Then her body shook a little and a little more and she tensed and clawed her hands at my back.

I flipped her over, happy that she was coming, happy that she was moaning my name, happy that I was finally able to do this with her. With someone who mattered.

I finally couldn't hold back any more, and we

crashed down together, breathing hard. I had to move to take the condom off and throw it away. This was usually the part where I got up for real, pulled my pants on and made some crack about needing a sandwich, but this time I got right back into that bed.

'Saxon?' she said, her voice wobbly.

'Yeah?' I said as I breathed heavily and kissed her hairline, along her ear and on her beauty mark then over her forehead.

'I think I came.'

'Yeah, I think so, too.' I put my arms around her, and it was pretty unreal; to want to lie around with the girl I had just had sex with. If it wasn't Cadence, I would have used more colorful language, but this moment didn't feel particularly suited to my dipshit brand of flippant humor. I knew I was slipping into a dangerously romantic area when I started to think about how good her body felt against mine, how I loved the feel of her hair in my hands and was waiting to talk to her again. Jesus Christ, I was wrapped up in her.

'I've never come during sex. That was really good. Really good,' she repeated and laughed a little. She burrowed against my body harder and kissed me all along my chest.

'I'm glad I was the first for that,' I said and meant it. It was a pretty huge badge of honor for me. Then I remembered that she had said the same thing when I fingered her. 'Have you ever come with anyone else? I mean, with anything? Dry humping? Getting eaten out?'

She shrugged. 'No. I thought I was a cold fish.'

I laughed and shook my head. 'That's the most ridiculous fucking thing I've ever heard.'

'Was the sex good for you?'

'Were you there?' I asked. 'It was fucking incredible. I've never had sex anywhere near that good before. Ever.'

'You've had a lot of sex, right?' she pushed.

'Yeah. Roughly a ton.' I grabbed her closer and she nestled so we spooned as tight as we could.

'Pretty girls?' she wondered.

'Look at me, Cadence.' I turned her around and busted out my best serious model face. 'Do I look like a guy who sleeps with ugly girls?'

'You look like a guy who sleeps with easy girls,' she said and smiled.

'You weren't easy,' I pointed out, kissing the edge of that smile.

'I'm not ugly either. I guess I'm forcing you to bring your standards up a little.' She relaxed into my arms.

We talked that kind of back and forth intimate bullshit that marked two people as really close. It felt like an hour, maybe, had gone by when the light started to turn gray in my room.

'That's the sun, Cadence. We have to get you home.'

'I don't want to leave you,' she murmured, her eyes still closed.

I looked at her, peacefully asleep next to me, and for the first time in my life, I was choked with a weird regret at the thought of being without someone. And it felt good.

Jake 5

I kept my arm around Brenna as we walked away from the sign-in table the morning of my big race, because I wanted to show her that I was going to be supportive of her crisis, no matter how ludicrous it might be. Evan Lennox, her crazy friend from writing camp had managed to get herself arrested. Who would have thought these writing dorks would be such law-breaking deviants?

Brenna took my number out of my hands and pinned it to my jersey with quick fingers. 'I'm sorry. This is your big day, and I know you're super nervous, but Evan's gramma was going nuts.' Brenna pushed her fringe up off her forehead and shook her head.

'No worries, Bren. Look, Evan is fine. Her grandpa got her some high-powered lawyer, right? I bet it will be a slap on the wrist.' I kissed her on her temple and worried about the fact that my bike stalled on a practice run this morning. Was it just a fluke, or could it be a bad air filter?

'I know, but she burned down, like, half a pecan grove! And it belonged to Rabin's grandparents, who are super-important pillars of the damn community. It was an accident, but what if she can't prove it? She'll get arson on top of trespassing, vandalism, underage drinking . . .' She counted off her maniac friend's offenses on her fingers, then wrung her hands. 'Her parents are still being totally insane, she's starting at a new school, and now all this? I'm so worried about her.'

I felt for Bren. I really did. I know she loved Evan, but that girl was going through trouble, and I knew better than anyone that the only person who could get her out of all that crap was Evan Lennox. If she didn't want to change her ways, there wasn't anything anyone could do. But Bren didn't like to hear things like that. She cared too much, wanted to help too much, and it made her crazy when anyone told her that she couldn't change the world.

'Don't worry till the judge lays it on her. She's from a pretty powerful family, too. Trust me. Money talks. She might walk away without any worries at all.' I pulled her into my arms and kissed her, but while she hugged me and thanked me for being all supportive, I eyed my old, battered bike, riddled with problems way beyond my knowledge base, repaired by my inexpert hands, and giving me a skull-cracking headache.

It could have been totally random that my bike had lost speed like crazy. Maybe I was more distracted than I'd thought on my run-through and let off too much on the gas. Maybe not.

I didn't know which option was scarier; the fact that my bike was probably an irreparable flaming piece of shit, or the possibility that I'd made such an embarrassingly novice mistake.

This was a big race for a local. I had a lot riding on it if I wanted to attract the attention of the early sponsors for the season, so I could get some better gear and pick up my game.

I had connections, which I could use if I didn't wind up with any local sponsorships. Connections so good that, like Evan Lennox, I could probably set someone's orchard on fire and get away with it. But, unlike Evan, I'd done my shit and learned my lesson a long time ago. If I wanted to prove myself, I had to do it as Jake Kelly, not riding off the coat-tails of the Macleans.

Just as thoughts of my family started to make me feel like I'd eaten a tray of bad oysters, one of the only Macleans I could tolerate strode over, his arm slung around Cadence. The last time he'd come to see me race, it had been a disaster. I'd just punched him in the face a few days before, and I worried the whole time I was on the bike that he was putting the moves on Bren.

'Hey.' I gave them a wave. Brenna turned in my arms and smiled her greeting.

'Hey, Kelly. Just came to watch you rip this shit up.' His eyes went over my shoulder to where my bike sat a few feet away, leaned against the tailgate of my truck. 'Holy fucking shit. You goddamn stubborn asshole! What the fuck is that?'

Bren's arms tightened around my waist.

'Jake fixed it.' Brenna slid her arms away from me and crossed them over her chest, her legs spread apart in this cute, defiant stance, eyes narrowed, mouth set, all ready to stare Saxon down and fight for my honor. Ever since the whole crazy essay debacle, Bren was making an effort to prove her support, and I knew it was killing her. I knew, deep down, my worrywart girlfriend agreed with Saxon on this one.

Her defense made my heart gallop in my chest. Bren believed in me.

'I guaran-fucking-tee he did *not* fix that thing enough to race it.' Saxon was trying hard to keep it cool, but I knew he wanted to scream his ass off at me.

'It will work fine.' For a split second, I was reassured by how confident my voice sounded. Until I remembered that I was lying through my damn teeth. I had no clue if it would work. Brenna's trusting, relieved expression made me feel even shittier for my lie.

'Work fine? You put a fucking Band-Aid over a slit artery. Work, my ass. This is asking for trouble. Race with a bike that actually works or don't fucking race, Jake. You shouldn't be putting your ass on the line because of your fucking pride.' Saxon's eyes were pure black and evil-looking, exactly like they got before a throw-down.

My hands curled into fists at my sides. I didn't particularly feel like beating his ass into the ground. To tell the truth, I was feeling tired and just about done with this whole day before it really got started, but it wasn't in my nature to go down without a fight. Saxon's eyes jumped to my fists.

'Save it. You think I'd punch you in the head before you get on that death-trap? You don't need to lose any more brain cells. Believe it or not, I don't want to see you break your neck, even if it would serve you fucking right.' Saxon stuck his hands in his pockets and we both glared for a minute. Then he said, 'You need help?'

I looked at Bren and could see from her tight smile and big eyes that she was nervous. I tugged on her hand, and she made her smile even bigger, but she wasn't fooling me. 'You all right here?'

'Sure. Of course. Actually, I think I'll get some food.' She kissed me, a quick, light kiss she used to try to trick me into thinking she wasn't remotely worried, and then turned to Cadence. 'Do you want to go get something to eat? I'm starving.'

Cadence glanced at Saxon and he nodded slightly. 'That would be great,' she said and gave Brenna a quick, nervous smile.

The girls walked away, and Saxon and I stared at their very fine asses for a minute. 'We are disgustingly lucky. How did two fuck-ups like us end up with girls like them?' Saxon asked.

I chuckled. 'I heard a rumor we have these irresistible lady-magnet genes.'

He patted his pockets for his cigs, but didn't take a pack out. 'No smokes?' I started toward my bike and he followed.

'It's part of my good-boy makeover. And, honestly, it's the part I'm fucking shedding as soon as I get my car back permanently this fall. I'll make sure I don't smoke in the house, because it really does screw with Aunt Helene's allergies, but I officially love nicotine and miss it like hell.'

We got to my bike and he squatted down by it, letting out a low, long whistle. 'This bike is hurting for retirement.' He ran a hand over the gouged, pitted plastic of the body. 'I don't remember it being this big a steaming pile of shit.'

'It wasn't. I've been training like crazy, probably when I was overtired, and shouldn't have been on the badass tracks I was riding. Plus I got rusty after those weeks with the crazies in New York. I crashed it a few times when I got back on, and just kinda hammered past the dents. I know I probably did more damage than I figured.'

I straddled the front wheel and closed my fingers over the handlebars, loving the fact that this bike had seen me through some tough times. This bike had helped me impress Bren. This bike showed everyone I was something when most people bet I was nothing.

Saxon jumped back to his feet and shook his head at me. 'You're gonna lose. And that's a fucking crying shame, because there isn't one guy on this damn course who could touch you with a ten-foot pole as a rider. You need to shake all this sentimental crap, Jake. Racing could be your ticket to something bigger, and you need to learn to use whoever, whatever, to grab that chance. No one's going to remember the guy who kept his pride, but placed third.'

Hatred for him burned and stung in my throat. I blinked hard and my entire body tensed, because I knew he was right. On every count. I was going to lose. I could get hurt. I could take myself out of the running. And it was all for what? To prove to a bunch of jackoffs with more money than God that I was better than them somehow?

Saxon's hands closed over my shoulder. 'Never

mind. I'm an asshole. This is only a local. You can place high enough to attract the right attention. You don't have to be first.'

'I'm not used to being anything else,' I muttered.

'Well, stop being a stupid fuck-up and use your limited brain power.'

The announcer crackled over the loudspeaker, and Saxon dropped his hand off my shoulder. 'They're about to start. You need anything?'

I shook my head and swallowed hard past the shrapnel-like ball of blatant fucking fear in my throat.

'Aunt Helene is here. I got her a seat already. I bet the girls are with her now.'

'Aunt Helene is here?' I squeezed my temples and regrets toppled over each other in my head, each one vying for first place. 'Nice to have a big audience for my fuck-up debut.'

'I honestly didn't think you'd have the balls to race that piece of shit.' Saxon grinned and put on these aviator sunglasses that should have looked douchey, but didn't. He always managed to pull off shit like that. 'You've got brass 'nads, man.' He gave me a salute. 'I'll be around if you need anything last minute.'

I'd never started a race with such a ball of lead in my gut. I felt like my entire equilibrium was thrown. The whole damn thing felt completely, nauseatingly off. I saw Bren, Aunt Helene, and Cadence, all down by the gate, jumping, waving and cheering, and I waved, but the lead in my stomach got hotter and heavier fast.

The bike hummed nicely under me when I started the engine at the line-up. I'd checked and rechecked everything I could think of, but I wasn't some top-notch mechanic, and fear about what I might have missed fogged my brain. The roar of the other engines helped drown out the worst of my doubts, and I forced myself to focus.

When the flag went down, I attempted to smash my brain into a non-thinking position, the way I usually did when I raced, but it wasn't that easy this time. The grind of the dirt under my wheels, the air off the jumps, the rush of cheers from the audience all felt like these jagged, disjointed moments leading up to a colossal, inevitable fall.

I'd never even considered a wipeout in any race I'd ever run. Now the image of myself ending up with a mouthful of dirt played through my head in gruesome slow motion. It tore through the mental-math guide-map that I normally used to get me round.

They had been my secret power, these weird sets of formulas that just came over me while I raced and plotted the course with all kinds of precise details I could follow every time. And I followed them to win race after race.

In every other race, I always had such a clear, calculated plan. It had always been about weight and speed and height. It was like my body took all the information in and my brain computed fast and hard, then translated all that stuff into how much I should turn, when I should lift, how far I should lean, and at what point I should just pull back and let myself ride free. It was like an internal geometry that clicked through my brain and measured every single move I made.

But this time was completely different. This time the dirt slammed under me with more force than I anticipated. I leaned and felt the skid of the tires, gripping too hard at the loose dirt of the track. I tensed and primed to jump, and landed with a hard thump just a few feet short of what I expected. The crowd's cheers were a muddy blur in my ears, and my eyes rocked to the sides, tracking the less experienced riders who picked up on my lag and pummeled past my jerky lead.

Bikes zipped by, the screech of their engines un-usually loud and horrible in my ears. My concentration flipped to the guy behind me, the one too far on the outside to matter, and the sudden shudder of my bike, which wound up being nothing, but gave me a few seconds of blood-curdling panic.

When the flag finally fell, I was so tired every muscle and ligament in my body ached. And I realized the flag had fallen for the bike ahead of mine.

I can't lie. I was stunned to see the crowd rush some halfwit unknown kid, who was racing a bike so new the plastic hadn't even lost its gleam.

Before my confidence took a complete nosedive, I realized I had my own tiny crowd to rush me.

Brenna hurled her body into my arms. 'You were amazing! That was such a great race!'

I thought she was just being an awesomely supportive girlfriend willing to tell some hardcore lies to spare my feelings, but her cheeks were all pink with excitement and the smile that stretched across her lips was wide and real.

Saxon was loose-limbed and laid-back with visible relief. 'I'm glad I didn't bet on you to win, but that was fucking impressive, man. You get props for winning against the thoroughbreds with that old-ass nag.'

Aunt Helene enveloped me in her flubbery arms, then pinched my sides hard. 'Are you an idiot? Next time, you use the better bike and win! The money this family has? You need to make use of it.'

Cadence attempted a manly punch at my shoulder with one slender, tanned arm. Her fist gave a surprisingly hard-hitting wallop. 'Congratulations, Kelly. That was a hell of a race.'

'Thanks.' A warm flush made my ears burn, and I was glad it was hot as hell outside, so no one could tell it was a blush. Blushing over second place? Man, I was turning into a sad-sack weenie.

'Boys, I'm going to go to the ladies before I head home. I have a big bingo game tonight, so kiss me for luck.' Saxon gave Aunt Helene a kiss on one cheek, and I kissed the other. She grabbed me close and hugged me hard, her old-lady perfume strong and overwhelmingly comforting. 'I'm so damn proud of you, Jake. Next time, don't scare the shit out of your old aunt, OK?'

The girls hugged her, and Saxon offered to walk her to her car, but she brushed him off and informed him she wasn't an invalid yet. Once she was gone, an awkward silence hung in the air. Saxon offered to help me get my bike in the truck, and once we'd heaved it in, he brushed the dirt off his clothes and brought up plans for later.

'I got my car back on probation, and I was going to show Cadence a good time, take her on the one-horse town tour. I got a text about a semi-decent hook-up during the last lap. There's gonna be a bonfire over at Shambles's tonight. It would be cool if you guys showed up.' Saxon searched his pockets again for his nonexistent cigs and scowled.

'A bonfire?' Cadence looked at Saxon with her eyebrows pressed together.

'It's what country kids do for fun, baby. Burn shit. Drink warm beer. Smoke dope and get high under the stars.' He patted her butt and smiled. 'We don't live all fancy-like, like you city kids. You're about to get an education in fun – Sussex County style.'

'I, uh—' I started to make up some lame excuse when Brenna cut in.

'I've never been to a bonfire.' She and Cadence shared a look of relief, and my chin had to have a dirt rim from my jaw swinging open and hitting the ground so hard. 'Like, I've been to camp. And my family has had fires in the fire pit, but I've never been to a bonfire that was like a party.'

'Never?' I couldn't count how many bonfires I'd been to, gotten drunk at, been stupid around. Bonfires were a pretty constant setting for some of my worst behavior during my worst years, and even though I didn't want to relive any of it, I was always game to do something with Brenna that she'd never done before.

She wrinkled her nose and shook her head. 'Is that weird? I've never been to a big house party either. Are they ridiculous amounts of fun? Am I lame and sheltered, and you're laughing at me?' She laughed at herself, a little embarrassed.

'Blix, you spent the summer pub-hopping in Ireland. You've got us beat,' Saxon reassured her. 'But you gotta come tonight. You need to show her the bonfire ropes, man. Something about all that lighter fluid makes Jake get all romantic. At least that's what the ladies always said.' The glint in his eyes was definitely pure dickhead challenge, and he got my back up right away.

Saxon knew he was walking a dangerous line, bringing up my shady past when Bren was around, but she seemed to sense my deep need to knock his ass out and hooked her arm through mine. 'Lighter fluid as an aphrodisiac, huh? I'll have to keep that in mind. So, I guess we'll see you guys at your-friend-with-the-weird-name's house?'

'Shambles,' Saxon and I said at the same time.

'Jinx, fucker.' Saxon pointed his finger like a gun at me. 'You owe me a beer, bro. See you there.'

Bren watched as he and Cadence walked away, Cadence waving at us as they went.

'OK. We seriously do *not* have to go to this thing tonight. You look beat. Movie night?' Brenna's offer was quick, sweet and punctuated with a few hot kisses.

I had my hands on her hips and could already feel myself getting hopped up for more way too quickly. 'I am pretty beat, but fuck it. Summer's almost over, you've never been to a bonfire, and it's my obligation to introduce you to the badass side of Sussex County.' I didn't want to get dirt on her, but I was having a hard time resisting the urge to pull her closer.

'So you want to corrupt me?' She leaned on me heavily, apparently not caring if she got dirt on the sweet little outfit that hugged every single perfect curve on her body.

'Nope. I like you sweet. I want to escort you into badassary so I can supervise. And kick anyone's ass if they mess with you.' I kissed her slow and deep, drinking in her taste, loving the soft feel of her hair under my fingers. I groaned and yanked my mouth away from hers when my thoughts went to places too sexy for my limited self-control. 'OK, this parking lot isn't really an appropriate place for me to jump your bones. I gotta get you home so you can ask Mom about the bonfire.'

'Jake.' Brenna drew my name out long and sweet, like a soft piece of sugary chewed bubblegum stretched out of her cute little mouth on the tip of her finger. I got stuck on the sound my name made coming out of her mouth. 'This is *the weekend*.'

The sun was high and hot overhead, but it suddenly felt like the temperature spiked, and it had nothing to do with the weather. I actually hadn't forgotten. No chance of that. But I didn't know what

Brenna would feel about the whole thing, so I was going to let her take the lead. 'This weekend?'

'This is it.' She bit her bottom lip and broke out the biggest, brightest, most excited smile I'd ever seen.

That smile grabbed my throat and heart and ... other places all at once. How did Brenna manage to shake up and twine sexy and sweet so perfectly? How did she manage to make me want to protect her from anything and everything and corrupt her at the same time?

'So, you make plans with anyone else? Or are you spending the whole weekend with me.' She nodded softly, and I cleared my throat. 'You gotta check in with Mom?'

She held up her phone. 'We've already texted, and I'll check in again later. She knows I'm going out. I'm supposed to have fun – and be careful. Is that what we're going to do?'

Her grin was contagious. 'Get your ass in the truck, woman! I need a shower before we do this!'

My stepdad was out playing pool, so I settled Brenna in my room and got cleaned up. After my shower, I went into my room and found Brenna on the bed, hair hanging off the side, bare feet propped on my wall, studying my motocross posters.

'Were you upset about today?' She turned her head and looked at me with these soft blue eyes. She wasn't giving me any pity, and I wanted to kiss her like crazy just for that.

'I was.' I toweled off, and laughed at her construction-whistle cat calls while I got my clothes on. 'You're a sexual harasser,' I accused, falling on the bed next to her.

'Only for you.' She grinned and ran her hands over my shoulders and down my arms. 'I thought you did great today.'

'I did all right.' I wanted to say more, but I bit my tongue hard before I started spilling all my regrets. It was stupid to go over them. The bottom line was, I needed to learn from what I did and go forward, not worry about what already happened.

'You would have done better on the better bike,' she said matter-of-factly. She nuzzled under my shoulder, and I cradled her in my arms.

'I know.' I ran my nose over her hair, soft and good-smelling. She smelled like home.

'You'd do better if you took honors classes.' It was just another fact.

'I know that, too.' I watched as she fitted her hand to mine, palm to palm. I could bend my fingers right over hers.

'You seem to know a lot.' She turned her head and narrowed her eyes at me. 'But what will you do with all this vast knowledge?'

475

'Is this another attempt to get me to sign up for honors?' I asked. It wasn't an accusation. In fact, I was happy that she gave enough of a shit to keep after me about it.

'No. It's just . . .' She sighed and pushed my hair back off my forehead. I'd needed a haircut for a while, but this summer brought out a lazy side of me I didn't even know I had before. 'This summer has been so crazy. I feel like it's been longer than three months, but at the same time, it went so damn fast. And we both did crazy stuff. Me and my stupid essay—'

'It wasn't stupid,' I interrupted. 'The more I think about it, the more I like it. I reread it a few times, you know.'

I had. I had sat on the edge of my bed and struggled through it three or four more times, until I had it locked in my head.

Her eyes widened till all the lashes seemed to stand out straight. 'Don't read it too many times! I'm going to write more essays. Different ones. That's what I'm trying to say. This whole summer has been crazy, right? You and Caroline and drinking. You punching your dad and Cadence's idiot boyfriend. Me getting a handle on how to be friends with Saxon without letting him drive me nuts. Meeting Evan and listening to her when she told me I needed to do more, be braver. Learning how to be independent, but also

476

follow the rules. All of this stuff . . .' She pressed her lips together. 'Things change so damn fast, and I never, ever want you to be left behind. Do you understand? I never want to feel like I left you behind.' When she looked at me, her eyes were shiny with tears and her voice was tight like a rubber band stretched as far as it would go.

'You know I plan to follow you wherever. Off the plank, if it comes to it.' I threaded my fingers through hers and held her hand tight. 'I've got something to show you.' I got off my bed and went to my closet, pulled out the stack I'd been keeping at the top.

Brenna sat up, her hair a big sexy mess and her mouth rounded out. 'Jake? Are those the books for . . .'

'Honors English.' I sat on the bed while she touched the spines.

'Were you hiding them?' she asked, inspecting the cover of *Song of Solomon* by Toni Morrison with its robed guy in front of a big sun.

I'd been worried about the book when I saw the weird-looking cover. But I was more than halfway through, and had decided Toni Morrison was probably one of those people who would blow your brains away if you ever got to sit down and talk to her for a while in person.

'No.' I took out my iPod and showed her my

playlist, filled with all the books we needed to read. 'You know I listen. I just need the books . . . well, because you need the books to be in class.'

She clutched the book hard in her hands for a minute, then threw it on the bed and dived at me. 'I love you! I love you.' She kissed me all over my face while I laughed, then she stopped. 'Wait. Did you listen to any of this book?' She picked up the crazy *Song of Solomon* book.

'Yeah.'

'And?'

'And I think the women especially scare the shit out of me, but I kind of love all of them, even if they're bat-shit crazy. Am I just insane?' I asked. Or at least, I tried to ask, but she was kissing me and, suddenly, talking about English class was pretty much the last thing on my mind.

'Why didn't you tell me?' She whispered the question in my ear after she pulled her mouth away from mine.

'At first, I didn't know if I was going to stick with it. Then I was thinking you'd just think I did it because you told me to. But I thought about it for a long time. And today, even though I know you wanted me to use the bike my dad sent, you stood up for me. So I know you'd believe me when I tell you that I'm doing this because I trust you, and I really did listen to what you said. And I won't get left behind, all right? Big plans for both of us. But, I'm still following you wherever the hell you go. That's non-negotiable.'

Honestly, I'd made up my mind when I decided I couldn't accept that damn bike. I knew it wasn't in me to take bribes from my family, but I also knew that I wanted the kind of life they had. I wanted to be able to afford good shit and not work like a dog. If I was going to have it all, I had to change. I couldn't just keep doing the same idiot stuff and expect a different result. So I decided to put my lazy brain to work and see where it got me.

For a few seconds after I explained, it was Brenna and me, sliding together like a key in an ignition. Or almost like that.

But not quite. Because I hadn't forgotten this weekend was *the* weekend. And there was another part to my whole grow-the-fuck-up-and-stop-being-chicken-shit plan. A part that scared me so much more than crashing headfirst into a dirt mound on my bike or flunking every test I attempted to take.

Because nothing scared me more than the way I felt about Brenna.

'I've got a surprise for you.' I liked the way I could see her trying to figure it out, like watching gears click and whir together.

'What is it?'

I took her by the hand and led her outside to the truck. 'You just gotta see it. That's all. C'mon.'

We got in and she hung her head half out the window, letting the wind pick her hair up and whip it back. I kept my eyes equally on her and the road, and at least twice had to remind myself to do things like blink and swallow. She was so gorgeous, it ached to look at her.

We turned down a long, unused road I knew like I knew my truck, like I knew my past, like I knew my feelings for Bren, so sure they gave me courage just when I was about to chicken out.

When we got far enough down the road that it petered into nothing but a gravel path, I cut the engine and took it out of gear. 'Wanna drive the rest of the way?'

'Really?' She bounced a little with excitement.

'Have you been practicing?' I tried to use a good school-teacher voice, but I don't think I really had the hang of it.

'Yes!' She clapped a little and her eyes were wide and shiny. 'Mom's been taking me out every Sunday. And Thorsten made me parallel park for two hours in the parking lot at the mall one morning. I'm ready. Is it legal?'

'Yeah.' I paused. 'Kind of. Not exactly. It's just because we're only a year apart. I need two years of being licensed. Legally. But I don't even know if this is a road. Legally. You worried?'

She shook her head. 'Not even a little bit. Can I just say that I've been waiting for months to drive this truck. I'm so psyched. Seriously!'

I hopped out of the driver's side and she scooted into the driver's seat. I walked around the front of the truck, and it was surreal, seeing Bren behind the steering wheel of my truck. I was feeling a weird pride about being one of the people who would teach her how to drive. For me, there wasn't anything that meant freedom and possibility the way a license to drive did.

I got in the passenger side and tried to get comfortable in a seat I'd never sat in before. 'This is weird.' Everything felt weird. Even the fact that the seatbelt got pulled down over my right shoulder instead of my left struck me as profoundly off. 'OK, you got all the basics, right?' I double-checked.

'I've got the basics,' she assured me. 'But Mom's car is an automatic.'

I grinned wide. I knew that and, cool as it was to help teach her to drive, teaching her how to stick shift was even more awesome. 'The pedal all the way to the left is the clutch pedal, OK? It releases the clutch and lets you pull the stick into gear. Make sense?'

Brenna leaned back and checked the pedals, then

tapped the one far on the left with her foot. 'Got it.'

'Push the clutch all the way, and you gotta use your left foot. You never use your left for anything else, but you have to pull it out of gear for this. Got it?'

'Got it.'

'Turn it on.' I watched while Brenna turned the key and the engine hummed to life. 'All right. To move forward, you gotta move the gear shift toward you . . . yeah, left, and you push it forward as far as it can go. Good. Now you're in first. Don't take your foot off the clutch. Now listen, cause this is tricky. Listen first, OK. You're gonna let off the clutch and, simultaneously, you gotta give a little gas. Ready to try?'

'Ready.' Brenna sat on the edge of her seat and leaned forward, let the clutch out too fast, and grunted in frustration when the truck jerked forward and stalled. 'Shit. I stalled.'

'Congratulations. You're learning to drive stick.' I smiled across the seat at her, overwhelmed with a feeling of camaraderie with my very cool girlfriend. 'Do it again. After a couple tries, you'll get the hang of it. It's something you have to just get the feel of.'

She bit her lip and tried again. And again. And once she got it and we stopped lurching like crazy, we worked on moving into second, where she stalled a few more times. Bren was one of those people who tended to have a knack for things and usually caught on quick. It irritated the hell out of her to stall so many times, but she kept at it, and soon she was cruising. Slowly, but cruising.

Brenna drove with a cool confidence that probably had as much to do with the fact that she'd never driven on an actual road as it did with the way she attacked everything: with head-on enthusiasm. She leaned over the wheel slightly, her eyes fixed on the road, her mouth in a serious, concentrated line. She followed the path until it gave up even attempting to be gravel and just turned to high, soft grass. She glanced at me.

'It's all right. You can pull over right there.' I pointed to a flat spot and she pulled in and parked the way I instructed her with coordinated grace, then looked at me like she'd just won her first race.

I shook my head at her. 'I knew you'd be a natural driver. I'd better get used to sitting on the right. It's still kind of weird for me.'

'You should have come to Ireland with me. Then we could have practiced, and you'd get to stay on the left.' She draped herself on the steering wheel and gave me a lazy smile.

'Maybe I will come next time you go.'

At that minute, it felt real. The whole damn world felt real and raw and attainable in a way it rarely ever had before.

The afternoon was sliding into evening, and the air was a little cool. I grabbed a duffel bag out of the back of the truck and walked around to Brenna.

'What's in the bag?' she asked, turning sideways so she could hook her legs around my waist and pull me close.

'Secrets.' I liked the way she kept one hand hooked on the steering wheel. I never imagined I'd be so turned on by watching someone drive as I was by watching Brenna.

'You're pretty full of them this summer, aren't you?' She squeezed her legs and my head swam.

'Not really. I'm just a dumb-ass, and it takes me a while to figure out the answer, even when it's hitting me upside the head.' The strap of her tank top had slid down the curve of her shoulder, and I hooked one finger through and pulled it back up.

She turned her head and watched my hand on her skin. 'Maybe you should listen to me more. You know, since I'm always right.'

I kissed her shoulder and pulled her out of the truck. 'You know, no one likes a know-it-all, girlie.'

'Really? You can't seem to get enough of me.' I swatted her on the behind and she laughed, that bright, clear sound that made my heart seize up in my chest.

We tripped over the big rocks jutting out of the path

and tramped along the grass, crushing it under our shoes until it let out the smell of summertime; sweet, clean, and full of all kinds of twisting possibilities.

We finally got to the edge of a rocky kind of cliff, and I helped her down until we were by a little hidden grove with a waterfall.

All right, it wasn't Niagara Falls, but it was pretty cool. It was a creek fall, so it was mostly this slide of water over a high rock incline. The areas next to the creek were all smooth stones, like maybe the creek used to be higher and ran over the stones for years until it cut back. All above and around were these huge old trees that seemed to pick up the wind and funnel the moans and rushes of the air through their branches, and straight up was the sky, so far away it felt like being at the bottom of a deep well.

Brenna and I didn't talk much at all as I unzipped the duffel bag and unrolled my old sleeping bag, laying it flat so the soft, worn blue flannel side was up. Brenna slid her sandals off, rolled up her jeans, and waded into the water, walking carefully over the uneven, rounded stones.

When I was done spreading the sleeping bag out, I kicked off my boots and socks and rolled up my jeans so I could wade out next to her. The water was so cold it bit at my skin, and the rocks made it hard to keep balance. Bren tucked her arms around me as soon as I got close.

'What is this place?' she asked in a hushed whisper.

'Saxon and I stumbled on it back when we were kids, back when we both raced. There's an old track about half a mile away. Saxon almost killed himself because we didn't realize there was this drop. His bike was pretty wrecked.' I laughed at the memory of Saxon's screams, the crash of the bike, and then our little-kid excitement when we found this place. We were so excited, Saxon forgot all about the bloody gashes and his mangled bike. We didn't find out until later that he'd fractured his arm, and he never bitched because we were so excited to be down in this little magical place we discovered, the pain just didn't register.

'We planned all kinds of crazy shit. We were gonna build a clubhouse or a fort here, you know? Camp out all the time. We did actually sleep here once in a while, but I haven't been here in five or six years probably. It's still exactly the same.'

Brenna linked her arms so tight around me I could feel the pulse of her heart right through my skin. 'Isn't that weird?'

'What?' I dragged my lips over the impossibly smooth skin on her neck.

'That five years can change so much. It can change

486

anything, everything, for us. And then there are these places that feel like time doesn't even affect them.' She rubbed her head on my chest. 'In five years, I'll be almost twenty-two and you'll be almost twenty-three. We'll be adults. We'll be ready to have jobs and apartments and all that stuff. I wonder if this place will still be here.'

'This place will always be here. And we'll come back. In five years.' For a second everything magnified; the creek roared, the water stung like ice, the wind groaned through the trees, the incredible, intoxicating smell of Brenna's hair, like flowers in the rain, all crashed over me. Then every single thing fell away, and it felt like the entire world was just me and Bren – just the two of us in this forever place.

'Five years from today, we'll come back here.' She ran her hands along my back. 'Right here to this place that never changes.'

'Deal.' I kissed her.

'But, Jake, what if this place—'

I put a finger over her lips and shook my head. 'Don't even think it.'

She talked around my finger. 'But what if we ...' Her voice trailed off and I dropped my finger from her lips. She craned her neck and took in everything.

'Never mind. Come with me.'

We walked back through the creek water, and she

sat on the soft sleeping bag, patting a place next to her.

I sat next to her and she tugged at the bottom of my shirt, pulling it slowly over my head. She pulled a hand over my shoulder and down to the center of my chest, where my heart was drumming so hard, I felt like I might be having a heart attack.

Brenna kept her eyes on my face as she slid her tank top over her head, flipped the button and slid the zipper down on her jeans, and gave me an expectant look.

'This is happening? Now?' My voice grated out, harsh with nerves.

'That's why we're here.' She said it like this whole romantic adventure had been her idea instead of mine. She held her hands out in the air between our bodies, and we looked down at them. 'They're shaking.' Her voice barely registered above a whisper.

'They shouldn't be. You don't have to feel nervous. I'm here.' I pressed her back gently and pulled her jeans down her hips, then off her long, perfect legs. I breathed slowly and consistently to keep from passing out.

She held her arms out to me, and I lay next to her, letting her body and mine rub and meet at all the right places.

I knew why I'd brought her to this place that never changed. I knew exactly why. I wanted us to change, right here, and then I wanted to lock that change up so it could never undo itself. Like black magic. Like stupid hope. Like a wish you'd never unwish, no matter how much people warned you that you'd live to regret it. Like a chance, a risk, a leap, an undivided love too gorgeous to let a little thing like the reality of gravity's hard knocks stop you from just diving, head-first, right in.

Brenna 6

There was no going back. This place might not change in five years or fifty or five hundred, but I would and so would Jake. We had come to this strange, almost-magical place one way, and we would leave completely different. Different because we'd be truly together.

I was ready.

Ready, and so scared I couldn't stop the shivers that ran over my body.

Jake kissed me softly, only the barest brush of his lips on my lips and mouth and neck, over and over until he calmed my skin and it stopped jumping erratically at every slight touch. I pulled my hands up and down over his back, so strong and smooth. Even though Jake was young, his back felt like a man's back, bunchy with muscles from doing too much work for too long a time so many days a year. He was propped on his elbows, and his arms tensed solidly next to me, walling me in and making me feel protected.

490

I tried to squirm out of my bra, but Jake reached around my back and unclasped it calmly. I wriggled out of my underwear, and was completely naked, outside in the cool, sweet summer wind, under Jake Kelly, who I loved so much and so hard, my heart punched with the severity of it.

'I don't think I've ever been naked outside before. I mean, not since I was little.' I ran my hands over his hair as he smiled that sweet, shy smile I couldn't ever see enough of and kissed up and down my arms. 'I wish we could skinny-dip in the creek.'

'We could.' His voice brushed against my ears with a rough slide. 'If you want to die from hypothermia.'

'Can't you think of any way to warm me up before I die?' I pulled my legs up and wrapped them around his waist.

'Yep. But we better swim now if you want to, because I'm just about to get to the warming up part.' His words made me shiver and he chuckled softly. 'See? You need to get warm. It's my duty as your boyfriend to protect you from the elements.' He rubbed his big, calloused hands up and down my arms, his skin scratching against mine. 'You have the world's softest skin.'

'I think it's just because you have the world's roughest hands.' I bit my lip as he rubbed in from my arms, his hands on my breasts and down my stomach, then lower.

And then we stopped talking and joking. His fingers rubbed low until he slid inside me and worked a steady, gentle rhythm that made me grab at his shoulders and bury my face in his neck until I shook against his hand. I hugged his neck tight, my eyes closed against his skin, and felt completely safe and treasured in his hold.

'Bren?'

I took one last deep lungful to savor the smell of him and looked at his face, so handsome, his gray eyes soft and serious in the darkening light. 'You're so beautiful,' I whispered.

His smile was half embarrassed, half completely pleased. 'I'm glad you like what you see.' He kissed me, his mouth sweet and slow over mine, while his arms wrapped me tight. 'I've never loved anyone in my life the way I love you, Brenna. And if you want to stop right now, I'll stop, no problem. But if you want more . . . if you're ready to do this, I'm ready to . . . I'm happy to . . . do this with you.'

'I do. I want to.' My voice shook, but I focused on Jake: the warm, sharp mint-and-autumn-leaves smell of him, the heat of his skin, the love that bloomed out of his eyes and twined my heart in a sure, sweet comfort I knew I would never have to doubt.

And then the pace changed. We didn't glide soft and slow any more. I nipped at his bottom lip and he squeezed my butt hard. His mouth dragged down my neck and he sucked lower, then back up, teasing my skin with his tongue and mouth. I rained kisses all over his ears, his jaw, forehead, his soft, sun-warmed hair. My hands pulled and rubbed down his arms, his back, around to his chest and stomach, then even lower. We rolled over, so I lay on top of him, my hand sliding down between our bodies so I could find the zipper and button of his jeans and somehow yank them down. Our hands twisted together in our excited, nervous grope and his laughter hit my ears in a soft wave.

'You're always so eager to get me out of my pants,' he joked as he got his zipper down and slid his jeans and boxers below his hips and off.

When he lay so close next to me, I felt a whirring wonder at the still-new feel of our bodies – so close and so exposed.

'You can't possibly appreciate how cute your butt is out of your pants.' I smiled at him, but my attempt at keeping it light stuck in my throat, because this was real.

It was happening, and I was both so ready for it and so nervous I could hardly think. My body pressed against his, my skin hot on his skin.

He pinched my butt to make me smile, and then he rolled me back under him carefully. My hair tumbled all over the blanket, and his body pressed down on mine. Our smiles faded and he licked his lips nervously.

'You tell me if you need me to stop. If you need anything, you let me know. Right away,' he said, his voice hushed, his eyes dark with worry.

I nodded, my heart doing a wild, adrenaline-powered tap-dance in my chest.

Jake reached for his jeans and pulled a condom out of the pocket. He ripped the foil packet and slid it on, and my mind was racing too fast to process it all. I looked up, and the leaves danced on the wind between the trees above us. The creek rushed and sang, the sky glimmered with the first few, faint, pale stars. And at the center of all this beauty was the gorgeous, loving face of my boyfriend, eyebrows smashed together with worry, mouth flattened in a serious line, eyes burning with focus.

I put my hands up to his face and held it, looking right at him. 'Don't worry. I love you. I love you so much. This is good. This will be so good.' I made sure my voice didn't even shake.

Jake's face lost all its worried lines, and he kissed me softly and leaned his forehead against mine. 'I love you, Bren. Let me know if anything hurts or you need me to stop. OK?'

I nodded and kissed him hard, holding my breath as Jake drew a few inches back. 'I love you, too,' I said, the words taking a quick tumble out of my mouth.

He gave me a final kiss and then it happened.

For one intense, uncomfortable minute, I was enveloped in a shooting, squirming burn of tight discomfort. Jake's eyes searched my face, his mouth bunched in desperate nervousness, and I managed a big smile and nod through the haze of my pain to let him know he could keep going. He made sure he kept his eyes on mine and read my every look, checking to see that I was OK.

Once I adjusted to the feel of him, I tried moving under him, surprised by how much of this was all awkward positioning and strange, burning discomfort. Jake and I had been together for a while, and so much of what we did was easy and fun. A tiny, panicked part of my brain worried that sex would fall into a different category and would forever be like a nightmare game of Twister.

But once I stretched enough that I got used to the way our bodies joined, the pain eased and then it was gone. The tingle that started out overly tight and possibly never-ending bloomed into something more sweetly filling and then, suddenly, so good I stopped tensing and cautiously moved my body in time to Jake's.

Jake's expression was a mix of loose-cannon worry and intense concentration. I squeezed him around the waist and moved my hands to his hips, wrapped my legs around his, and pulled him closer. I could smell the sweaty-sweet tang of his skin and feel his body actually in mine, so intimate and amazing, I wondered how anyone could ever do this with someone they cared about and not be at least momentarily in complete love. Relief that it felt so good made me relax, and it felt even better.

'It's OK for you?' His voice came out on a ragged breath, and he smoothed my hair back with his hands.

'Better than OK,' I said on a breathless laugh, so happy I wanted to stay here, with him, in this place, doing this thing we were finally doing forever.

He locked my mouth in a long, sweet kiss, then changed positions slightly until I felt the same build up of hard-to-control shakiness that engulfed me like a warm bath, reverberated through me like the hypnotic beat of a perfect song, and whirled in my blood like a thousand carbonated bubbles exploding from the top of a champagne bottle on New Year's Eve.

I wrapped my arms around him hard, pulled against him, wanting to be closer to his skin and his body and him, even though we were locked so hard and tight against each other there was no space between us. Jake moaned my name, kissed me again, and then for a few frantic seconds everything rushed and crashed together in a twisting burst of sweetness.

We both panted, arms and legs locked around each other under the soft purple-gray glow of the sky at twilight, and Jake pulled back slowly, untangling himself from the coil of our overlaid limbs, then rolled over to take the condom off. He tucked it back in the wrapper and took a long second to just breathe before he turned back to me and gave me the longest, slowest, shyest smile that I had ever seen cross that boy's lips.

'You feel all right?' He pulled his boxers and jeans back on and sat next to me.

I could have stayed right where we were all night, but the sun had slid completely behind the horizon, and the air was chilly. 'I feel amazing. Thank you.'

His laugh got tangled up in the cool breeze, and he made himself busy gathering my clothes and offering his clumsy help to dress me. I knew it was so I wouldn't see how pink his ears were.

'Thank you.' His voice crept out in the dark. He didn't meet my eyes as he pulled my tank top over my head, backwards, and opened his mouth like he was going to say more. Then closed it. Opened it again. And closed it.

'You look like a fish.' I fixed my shirt and took his face in my hands. 'Are you OK?'

'I've just never felt like this. You know. After. I feel . . .' His voice sounded so scratchy and rough, I had no idea what to expect when he looked up. 'I feel so fucking amazing.' He crushed me to his chest and held me, his breath hot and unsteady through my hair. 'I love you. I wanted it to be like this, but I wasn't sure it could be. I'm just . . . I love you.'

I rolled him onto the ground and kissed every inch of his face. 'I love you. So much.' The moment could have gotten much more romantic, but I smacked a mosquito that had been quietly sucking at my blood, and Jake helped me to my feet.

'Enough lovey-dovey stuff. Finish getting dressed, and I'll pack up. You're gonna get eaten alive here in a few minutes if we don't go.' I watched Jake get busy putting everything away, and felt like a tiny bit of the fairy dust had been rubbed clean from our trip to this secret Neverland.

I pulled my jeans on and put my feet in my sandals. 'We'll come back here, right, Jake?'

'Of course.' He looked over his shoulder as he packed the duffel bag and his smile was so sweet it seeped through all my bitter worries. 'This is our spot now. We'll come back while we're in Sussex County, and then we have our five-year-plan, when we're big, important hotshots. This will be that place we come back to when we need to get away from everything.'

He reached for my hand, and we went back up the rocky incline, away from our little secret sweet spot full of magic. Jake didn't give it so much as a backward glance.

We jumped back in the truck and he whistled. He grinned. He tapped the steering wheel in a happy beat. When he didn't have to shift gear, he reached his hand over and held mine.

'You're in an awful good mood, Jake "Speed Demon" Kelly.' I pulled his hand up to my lips and kissed it.

'I really hope that's a reference to my racing skills and not my, uh, other skills.' He glanced at me and winked.

'Winking! All this sexy time definitely went to your head.' I leaned back on the seat and let out a long, sweet laugh. 'And I think your skills were above average.'

'Above average? Is that, like, a B plus?' He shook his head.

'Yep. And you know what that means?' I winked back at him. 'Practice. Lots and lots of it.'

'I swear I will practice until I get an A from you, Ms Blixen.' He turned the dial on the radio and sang along with the first song that came on.

I'd never heard it, and I don't really think Jake had either, because his version of the lyrics made no sense and he was totally off key. He stuck his head out the window and sang with the full capacity of his lungs, then screamed with pure pleasure into the wind.

'Jake! What's up with you?' I laughed.

'This is just a great day. Just a really great day, and I'm happy. I don't know if I've ever been this happy.' He leaned his head back out the window and yelled again, and everything in me felt fever warm. I switched to the middle lap belt and snuggled against Jake's shoulder, contented and sleepy after a long day of happy goodness.

I had started the day a different person, and had changed in ways that were too new and raw and wonderful to process. I wondered if Jake would come back to my house tonight and stay over. Or maybe we'd go to his. Would we have sex again? My whole world was suddenly full of intimate possibilities that just weren't there before.

My thoughts wandered back to this time when I was a little kid. Mom and Fa bought me a fish tank. We agonized over rocks for the bottom and the background pictures, made the poor guy at the store net practically every fish in the place until he got the three specific ones I wanted. There was a little treasure chest that opened with a geyser of bubbles and a mermaid statue, which I thought was the most beautiful, most amazing thing in existence. We took our time setting everything up, and then Fa plugged it in, and I snapped the power on. The whole thing lit up in a crazy dance of sinuous fish, buzzing too-bright lights, and streams of bubbles. I stayed awake way too late looking at that tank full of beauty, the tank that had been just so many dull pieces in the store, but, all put together, turned into this underwater paradise.

That was today. So many little pieces, all placed just right, now something more than normal. Something with a tiny bit of magic that I would be able to tuck away and look back at forever.

My eyes were just about to close when Jake pulled down a long, bumpy road I'd never seen before and stopped at a squat ranch house with falling-down siding and dozens of people in the yard. Over to the side was a huge, roaring bonfire, fueled by everything from old branches to chairs, boxes, and even what looked like an entertainment center.

We got out of the truck and Jake's arm snaked around my shoulders in a possessive slide down to my waist. His muscles loosened, but he walked with a wary confidence, like he was sure everyone was watching him. I would have thought it was just his nerves, then I noticed people actually were watching him. We walked through the crowds, and Jake kept his arm around my waist.

Jake held his hand up whenever someone called to him, but he never stopped, and he turned down beers from at least half-a-dozen people, mostly heavy-set older guys with neck tattoos and multiple facial piercings who seemed very happy to see Jake around. It was like the entire party was crushing in, nervously excited to embrace Jake back into the fold.

He looked down at me and smiled. 'Kind of my old group. They're nice, you know.' At that minute a guy wearing a skull hoodie threw a dresser with no drawers into the fire, then followed it with an entire can of lighter fluid. The flames shot high and exploded so hot my cheeks glowed from the heat and the fire was thirty feet away. 'Crazy, but nice,' Jake amended.

I looked around with wonder. So this was the kind of gathering where Jake had spent so many summer nights? It was still comfortable and familiar to him. It was also obviously a place he'd grown away from, like a favorite jacket one size too tight that still fits, but strangles your shoulders and clings too hard around the waist.

'Kelly! Blix! Come forth and revel!' Saxon's voice rang out, loud and slurry, but not completely drunk. He sat near a smaller fire, a beer bottle in his hand, Cadence on his knee. She looked slightly confused, and not very comfortable as she ran her fingers through her shiny black hair and looked at us with a helplessly nervous smile hello.

Jake and I walked up to the roaring, belching fire, kindled partially on things that probably weren't meant to be burned. It loosed a chemically, thick smoke and, every once in a while, sputtered or gave off a loud, crackling pop. Jake's arm tightened with possessive constraint around my waist, and I was happy to lean into the comfort of his overzealous embrace.

'Hey, Saxon. Cadence.' I waved at her, and she gave me a shy smile in return.

Jake glanced around and rocked back and forth on his heels. 'There's a shit-ton of people here.' People were spilling out of the dilapidated house, burying their hands in coolers filled with cans of beer, throwing things into multiple fires, and gathering around a huge roasted pig.

'Shambles's dad slaughtered a pig?'

'Would it be a bonfire without a hog?' Saxon raised his beer and laughed before he took a long, eager pull from the bottle. Cadence touched his wrist and shook her head, and he nodded, then laid a long, dramatic kiss on her lips before he turned his attention back to us. 'So, what have you two fine, upstanding youths been up to?'

'Just hanging out,' Jake said vaguely, shaking his head at yet another beer offered by yet another hulking, tattooed man with a huge smile. He pulled me closer when the man licked his lips openly in my direction.

'Jake took me to see this waterfall.' The words flipped out because of a nervous need to fill the uncomfortable feeling of not belonging that dredged up in me. Jake kissed my temple and avoided looking at Saxon, who was staring right at him.

'A waterfall, huh?' Saxon nodded slowly and took another long sip. 'Hell of a way to celebrate that second-place win, eh, Jake?'

Jake's arm tightened into anaconda territory, and he and Saxon locked eyes in a long, nasty standoff of unspoken, raging tempers. I pulled at Jake's hand and squeezed it until his stance relaxed.

Cadence said something sharp and quiet in Saxon's ear, and he locked his jaw tight.

Just when I was getting nervous about how everything would iron itself out, the man who'd ogled me a second before came back to the fire. 'Saxon, could you pull your car around? Davey parked like a fuckwad and can't get his truck out.'

Saxon stood on unsteady legs, and Cadence reached into his pocket for his keys and pressed him back.

'I'll move it.' She started across the field at a brisk jog before he had a chance to argue or follow. About twenty half-drunk male heads swiveled in her direction. Saxon stood back up, weaving from side to side as he attempted to chase her, but he swayed so badly Jake had to catch him before he careered into the fire.

Jake looked at me, and I nodded. I knew exactly what he was thinking, and we didn't need to say a single word. I felt a warm swell of pride that my boyfriend was the kind of guy you could depend on to pick up the pieces when things fell apart.

'I'll help her out, Saxon,' Jake said, his voice cool and smooth around the electric air between them. To me, in a lower voice, he asked, 'Bren, you wanna sit with him while I go?'

'No problem.' I kissed him softly and he smiled his relief and thanks. Saxon shook his head with a bleary jerk and thudded down heavily.

I sat down next to him, careful to maintain a few necessary centimeters. 'How's the bonfire?'

'I'm ruining it for Cadence.' Saxon stretched his lips up in an attempt to grin, but there was a scowl of self-hatred right underneath his expression.

'On purpose?' I leaned forward, pressed my hands between my knees, and squeezed them together. The fire roared when it caught a bunch of pine branches thrown on top ablaze, and I closed my eyes against the explosion of heat.

'Not . . . exactly.' He twirled the brown beer bottle between his fingertips and looked up at me, his face so full of hurt and worry it singed more than the fire. 'What did it feel like when you fucked it all up with Jake?' He slid closer, so our legs were brushing against each other, and I could smell the yeasty, bitter-sweet stink of beer thick on his breath.

'It was awful, but you know that. So why are you asking me this?' My voice shook all over the words I had to rip from my throat, and a little of the glitter of the day rubbed off under Saxon's questioning.

'I'm a little scared, Blix. Help a guy out.' His next attempt at a smile was so far from the real thing it bordered on farce. He patted around in his pockets and found a pack of cigarettes. He lit one with trembling fingers and took a long drag, his face finally relaxing a little.

'What do you have to be scared about? You did it, Saxon. You did what no one thought you ever would. You got Cadence to date you, and she's amazing. She loves you. Her family loves you. Aunt Helene loves you. You proved how hard you can work, you proved that nothing can beat you. What's the problem?' I leaned forward as the cool night wind picked up and sent a shatter of sparks mixed with smoke from his cigarette whirling through the air. He looked up at me, his dark eyes full of a fear so visceral, it popped and crackled in the inky black pigment of his eyes.

'I've been this hero. This whole summer, I've been the anti-fuckup.' Those wild eyes snapped and snarled like rabid black dogs chasing their own tails. I shook my head. 'Hear me out. Hear me out, Blix.' He held his fingers up, the burning cigarette sparked between them. 'They have no idea what a fuck-up I really am. In here.' He tapped his heart with the solid thud of those two long fingers and the orange cherry danced in the darkening night.

'You're not,' I argued, my voice insistent. 'You're going to be totally fine. You've already proven it, Saxon.'

'Shouldn't it be a little less scary?' He took a long drag, then tilted the beer bottle to his lips. I watched his neck muscles work as he drank too much, way more than he needed unless he was going for full-on obliterated. He stopped and wiped his mouth with the back of his hand. 'I think my pendulum swung, you know.' He held one balled fist to his left. 'Dirtbag.' He moved it to his right. 'To hero.' He shook his head and stared at the fist. 'Which am I?'

'Both,' I whispered, wrapping my fingers around his fist and squeezing. 'And they'll all love you no matter what. Trust me.'

His eyes shone with mocking laughter. 'Why? Because you loved me when I was a dirtbag? You're something else, Blix. You can't get it. Oh, and news-flash! Gerald's giving me the money as soon as summer's over.' He ran his hands through his hair, leaving it sticking up at weird, shiny angles. 'All that fucking money. I could just give Aunt Helene a chunk and blow out of there. Maybe I should. Because I have this awful feeling that things are too good, and I'm going to fuck it all to hell.'

I breathed in and out, deep and calming. 'No. Listen to me. You're drunk and you're over-thinking things. Just slow down. Cadence is the one for you. She's amazing. You have to give this a chance. You have to try for both of you. If you leave, you'll regret it forever. I 'm telling you right now.'

He opened his mouth and crooked his lips in a cocky smile. 'Hey, gorgeous. You didn't crash my car, did you?'

I watched Saxon's face and saw the truth of his pro-found sadness mingled with his intense love when his eyes snared Cadence in their sight. He wrapped his arms around her willowy waist as she sat down next to him and she ran her fingers through his hair. I saw in the clutch of his hands, too tight and shaky at her hips, that he wanted to do what was right, but didn't know how.

'We probably need to get going.' Cadence pointed a finger down at Saxon and rolled her eyes lovingly, throwing us an indulgent smile. 'This one has had a little too much to drink.' She got up and lifted him with her. He swayed, but found balance at her strong shoulder.

'I love you. So much,' he said, overly loud and with a twinge of despair that struck me low in the gut.

Her smile was dazzling, and her eyes were full-on adoring and only for Saxon. 'Shh. I know. I love you, too. Let's get home.'

'You need any help?' Jake asked.

She shook her head as she led him away. 'We'll be all right. Thank you, guys! Sorry we're ditching so early.'

Jake and I watched the two of them stumble back to Saxon's car. Then he led me to the log Saxon had been sitting on, and we watched the fire lick all the way up to the navy sky.

'They seem pretty happy.' Jake's voice settled with a peace that felt the polar opposite of Saxon's struggling, mangled confessions.

I snuggled against him. 'They do. I hope they stay that way.'

I wondered if I should tell Jake what Saxon said to me, but decided against it. He was drunk and over-emotional. He'd come back to Sussex County after making so many changes. It wasn't real. It was just too much alcohol and rambling words. Nothing to worry about. I squeezed closer to Jake anyway, clamping next to his skin for comfort.

'The fire is beautiful.' He held me in his arms and rocked me back and forth in a rhythm.

I never wanted to stop.

'Jake, are you planning on taking your inheritance?' I asked as the flames crackled and licked in front of us.

His gray eyes held steady. 'I don't know, Bren. It's a hell of a lot of money. And I was around a whole lot of it this summer. I kinda think it does more bad than good, but who knows? I've got months to think about it, anyway. They won't release my trust until I graduate high school. You worried I'm gonna get rich and up and leave you?'

I stretched my legs out in front of me, hoping Saxon was wrong about the terms of his money, hoping everything was going to work out just the way it was supposed to.

'Nah. You and I are in this for the long haul.' I laced my fingers through his.

'That's right. I love you for life, Brenna Blixen.'

And then he pulled me close in the aching beauty of the fire-backed night and kissed me in the cool, clean air on this evening at the end of a day that had started one way and ended in a whole other, different, better place. I pulled him close and held tight, because, deep down, I knew that Jake Kelly and I were about to face the biggest changes of our lives, and I wanted to hold the beauty of this moment still and warm and forever unchanged in my heart for as long as I could.

Acknowledgments:

There are a vast array of peeps who get my jump-up and high-five thank you grand-slam. They include my ever-loving, drive-me-nuts fam, both blood and married (and any other way we rope them in) and my colossally cool, supportive, amazing friends, and I love each one of them equally as much as they drive me nuts. And, probably, as I drive them nuts. Hugs, kisses, and squeezy-cheeked love!

My books would merely be soggy cucumbers if not for the brine that is my editing/beta-reading/eye-rolling friends. Most of these are people who adore grammar and debate colons and parentheses and hyphenated adjectives with me until the sun goes down, and all of them love angst, romance, youth in revolt, and, most of the time, me. Big love to Elisa Keller, who manages to lay it out for me in such surgically clinical terms, the scalpel of her criticism doesn't even smart. And, to go along with this whole surgeon analogy, she knows exactly when to tell me that my book is riddled with wisdom teeth, gall-bladders, appendixes, and tonsils . . . useless and potentially irritating stuff. Hugs and sloppy kisses to Courtney Kelsch for holding my hand through the swoony memories of our strangely similar teen love days and being so fiercely in love with my characters, I feel like she definitely has possession. And also like Jake, Bren, Saxon, and Cadence need, to get on writing her love letters and making her soulful mixes pronto. Tamar Goetke will totally turn her head to the side when I deposit my millions of kisses, but she deserves every one, both for powering through the teen angst she pretends to hate and for mocking my every grammatical mistake with such naked glee it actually hurts so good. Something a little more risqué for Angie Stanton, who kicks me to push the envelope even when it's downright chokingly scary and blows me away with her talent and enthusiasm. Last minute thanks to Tammara Webber, who pried this manuscript from my cold, aching hands and made sure I had my Southern slang correct, capitalized my brands, and used the universally recognized spellings for my slang. She's an amazing, soulful, brilliant woman and I'm proud to have her and Angie on my side as we forge into the brave new world of Mature YA together. One, two, three, JUMP!

Intense thanks to Abbi Glines, who always goes out

on a limb for her writing and encourages me to as well, and who is never less than amazing when it comes to being a friend and colleague.

To Steph Campbell, all the thanks in all the worlds for filling every moment of my life with great stories, awesome wine, snort-inducing jokes, and honest, relentless love of what we do and how we do it . . . no matter how unhinged or discouraged we might feel. Much, much love.

To my awesome editors, Julia Bruce and Carmen McCullough, who went above and beyond to question and comb until we'd worked out every tangle, so many thanks! To the amazing Lauren Abramo: how do you do it? I'm in awe of your never-ending good humor and ability to juggle a million and one things at all times. So many thanks! To the lovely Rachel Lawston who seemed to pull Brenna, Jake, and Saxon out of my head and make the covers scream with gorgeous sexiness . . . thank you for your amazing eye and wonderful talent!

An expletive-laced thank you to my lovely FP friends, who know exactly what to say during my darkest and lightest hours, and every one in between. I love every one of you to your bones, and wish so much success heaped on all of your heads you faint from the deliriously amazing weight of it all.

If I could list and love every blogger and reader

who helped by beta reading, interviewing, reviewing, and just morally supporting me and being rad, I would, but this book would be 7,000 pages long. That's how many totally cool amazing readers and bloggers there are out there. Hey, I read a lot. A ton. There's awesome, amazing stuff to be read in this wide world, and if you chose to read my books out of the lot, I'm so in love, even my wordiness can't encompass it. My hat is off to the readers who have so much passion for what they read, they just want to spread the goodness around. Your encouragement, love, and sometimes scary demands about when the next book is coming have warmed me, hair follicle to toenail, and the love in my heart for you is explosive. Or, at least, it's definitely bubbly and frothy . . . explosive sounds dangerous!

Big, huge, incredible, mind-blowing 'thank yous' all around!

DOUBLE CLUTCH

The First Brenna Blixen Novel

Who to choose . . . ?

Thrust back into school life after a year in Denmark,
Brenna Blixen is soon making new friends and
catching the eye of two boys with bad reputations.
There's the dark and mysterious Saxon, and
the gorgeous and sexy Jake.

They're both totally hot and totally into Brenna.

But Saxon and Jake have unresolved history and
Brenna's caught in the middle.

It's time to make some tough choices, fast.

LIZ REINHARDT

JUNK
MILES

A Brenna Blixen Novel

When Brenna Blixen is offered a trip to Paris for the
winter break, she jumps at the chance.

After a tearful goodbye with her gorgeous boyfriend,
Jake Kelly, Brenna is shocked to discover that
Saxon Maclean is also headed to the City of Love.

He's trouble and irritating as hell.
But also seriously hot.

Can Brenna resist her animal urges, or is good girl
Brenna about to turn bad . . . ?

FALL GUY

Don't even try to resist...

Fiery Evan Lennox is dreading community service,
until she meets Winchester Youngblood.

Winch is mysterious and sexy as hell, and Evan
soon finds herself falling for his bad-boy charm. But
Winch has some dark secrets of his own and they
threaten to destroy everything.

Should Evan follow her instincts and give in to
temptation . . . or will Winchester prove too
hot to handle?

GAYLE FORMAN

just one day

A heartbreakingly romantic
story from the bestselling author of *If I Stay*

A whirlwind day in Paris . . .
A chance at true love . . .
Heartbreak is waiting just around the corner.

From the author of the international bestseller,
If I Stay, comes a poignant and beautiful story
of love, loss and learning to live again.